TIDES OF HEALING

SPIES OF THE CIVIL WAR
BOOK SIX

SANDRA MERVILLE HART

The characters and events in this fictional work are the product of the author's imagination. Any resemblance to actual people, living or dead, is coincidental.

Unless otherwise indicated, all Scripture quotations are taken from the Holy Bible, Kings James Version.

Scripture quotations marked (NIV) are taken from the Holy Bible, New International Version®, NIV®. Copyright © 1973, 1978, 1984, 2011 by Biblica, Inc.™ Used by permission of Zondervan. All rights reserved worldwide. www.zondervan.comThe "NIV" and "New International Version" are trademarks registered in the United States Patent and Trademark Office by Biblica, Inc.™

Cover design by: Carpe Librum Book Design

Author is represented by Hartline Literary Agency

ISBN: 978-1-963212-17-4

I am still confident of this; I will see the goodness of the Lord in the land of the living.

\- Psalm 27:13

This book is lovingly dedicated to Megan,
my sweet daughter who fills my life with such joy;
To my supportive husband Chris,
who suffers through every writing deadline with me;
And to my faithful readers,
For whom I labor over my stories.

May God bless you.

CHAPTER 1

SATURDAY, JULY 4, 1863
VICKSBURG, MISSISSIPPI

Standing on the sidewalk of her wrecked city on the stifling morning, Savannah Adair couldn't believe the evidence of her own eyes. Emaciated soldiers clad in gray shuffled into town in a steady stream, a mixture of relief and sorrow lining their sunburned faces. These men might be hungrier than the citizens, who at least had begun with stored food and fresh water during the forty-seven-day siege.

An eerie quiet seemed to settle over her and her neighbors lining the mangled street. Its grip held them spellbound as they all faced the bluffs just beyond the city. How unnatural that the footfalls of thousands of men were unbroken by the deep, gruff tones of male conversation.

These were men who'd taken a beating on the battlefield and needed nourishment. Savannah could do little about feeding the men, for their own supply of canned and dried fruit and vegetables was nearly spent, but she could offer them something to quench their thirst.

"Josie, please fetch two buckets of water." She turned to the pretty sixteen-year-old staring at the approaching army with wide brown eyes from beside the black wrought-iron fence that bordered the Adairs' property. Ellen, Josie's mother, was inside their spacious house tending the wounded soldiers that had been left on their parlor rug without Mama's permission. Thank the Lord for Ellen, for neither Savannah nor her mother were good in the sick room.

Josie lifted the hem of her gray dress and hurried up a flight of stone steps leading to the home.

For now, Ellen and Josie remained loyal to the Adairs— unlike Leland, Robert, and Fred, who had claimed their freedom by leaving the day the Union army set up battle lines around Vicksburg. With the damaged fruit trees in their garden, they needed Ellen's husband Gus's help now more than ever. Some trees likely couldn't be saved from the splintering effects of the nearly unceasing mortar blasts from the Mississippi River. Not to mention the work of filling in the cave dug into the side of their garden that they'd no longer need. How she'd learned to despise the dark, dank shelter during the endless onslaught of cannonballs hissing toward the city. One had pierced her home's roof, then crashed through a guest bedroom and Mama's formal dining room before coming to rest in the cellar.

When murmurs that General Pendleton had actually surrendered not only an army of over thirty thousand strong, brave men—plenty bad enough—but also *her* city had reached their dreary cave shelter last night, Savannah had been fit to be tied. Mama had been even more vocal about her displeasure with the Southern general.

Their beloved Vicksburg had fallen because Grant's army's artillery assault by land and Admiral Porter's mortar launch by river had been combined with a siege on them all.

The faces of the gaunt soldiers wordlessly told the tale. Citizens hadn't been alone in their suffering.

"We can certainly give our thirsty men a dipper of cold water from the well." Beside her in front of their elegant three-story brick home, Mama waved an ivory silk fan over her red face. "I wish your father were here. Not only did we endure the siege alone, but now we must face the indignity of arrogant Yankees in our fair city without him."

Not so beautiful now with craters in the road and sidewalks, some large enough to swallow her broad-shouldered father in their depths. And Ellen, Josie, their driver Ollie, their butler Samuel, and Alvera, who had a flair for styling Savannah's blond looped braids, had sheltered with them, so they hadn't been alone. "Mama, please. Papa couldn't know Grant's army would reach us before his business in Tougaloo concluded." It had been an oft-repeated defense of her dear papa throughout the nightmarish attack. He made a good living as a cotton broker with clients throughout Mississippi. Public opinion had swayed many plantation owners to destroy precious cotton to keep it from the enemy, causing Papa to travel farther afield for cotton bales to sell. He'd left at the end of April, and battles around the state had prevented his return. She had prayed that he hunkered down with a client in safety. "He'll be here soon." At least, she hoped so.

"It's good the shelling has ended." Hands on hips, Mama glared at the Union navy fleet which had inflicted such damage on them. "The quiet feels strange after weeks of incessant attacks."

"Agreed." Silence *was* deafening after the onslaught. Savannah focused on the men dodging holes in the lane. Some had stopped to drink at neighbors' homes. Where was Josie? Savannah turned to the house as the girl stepped through the gate.

"Here's two buckets, Miss Savannah." Water sloshed over

the top as she set them down. Ollie, Samuel, Ellen, and Alvera followed her to the sidewalk. With two dippers. Good.

"Thank you, Josie. Help me offer the men a drink." A grimy soldier slowed beside the bucket. She hid a shudder as she grasped a dipper. Had she expected these men to smell of lye soap and sandalwood? Indeed, she and Mama had bathed for the first time in weeks that morning after Samuel and Ollie carried in their furniture from the cave before they went out seeking news of surrender, and then Alvera had styled their hair while the others bathed. Savannah and Mama had been so grimy that they went straight to their baths, intent on donning the first clean dress in their wardrobes that bore no smudges. "A dipper of cold water, sir?"

He took it from her and drained it. "Thank you, kindly. May I have another?"

"Of course." She plunged it into the water again and complied. His scratchy voice suggested he was parched. "Thank you for fighting for us." They'd surrendered, but that had been the fault of General Pemberton, not these privates.

The whiskered fellow bobbed his head and went on. Another soldier stopped and she gave him a drink.

Josie wordlessly offered a dripping dipper to a bearded man.

At this rate, the little bit of water wouldn't last five minutes. Savannah looked over at Ollie. "We'll need more. Fetch us two more buckets."

"Yes, Miss Savannah." He hurried away. As their driver, Ollie had been mostly idle that spring after the Confederate army asked Mama for the rest of their horses. Papa had been away on business when she made the hard decision. However, Ollie's idleness ended when the family needed a large cave dug in their backyard.

Ollie brought buckets with more dippers, which Ellen and

Alvera used for the men now waiting in short lines. Mama fanned herself by the gate. The next few minutes flew by.

When the last of the Southern soldiers moved on, Savannah rubbed her back. A band played somewhere close. Thousands of male voices sang "Battle Cry of Freedom" while marching toward the city like conquering heroes. Her heart felt harder than the rubble on the sidewalk.

A line of blue-coated soldiers marched toward the city from the east—the direction of the battlefield—in a curved line, like a giant rattlesnake coming to devour everyone and everything she loved.

~

irst Lieutenant Travis Lawson rounded a bend beside the front line of the Eighth Illinois Infantry toward the city he and his comrades had fought so hard to capture. It wasn't as impressive as he'd imagined, not with the first row of buildings that greeted him in ruins. Walls bulged in an arc in a few others. As they continued down Jackson Road toward Vicksburg, his men continued to sing with the band, one song after another. Though singing "The Star-Spangled Banner" amidst the rubble and damaged homes might rub the townspeople the wrong way, he wasn't going to steal this victory that had come at the cost of too many good men.

Words couldn't express his relief that the six-week siege had ended. The gaunt condition of Southern soldiers and citizens stirred his compassion, though part of him wanted to shout at them their hunger pains were their own fault for delaying surrender.

As the song ended, Travis strode over by Enos Keller, a private. "You're singing with gusto there, Enos."

"It's a good day, Lieutenant." He grinned, exposing a gap in his front teeth. The two men were bonded because Enos lived in Charleston, Illinois, while Travis's family farm was just outside it. They were both twenty-four and stood a little under six feet, but whereas Travis possessed a muscular build from heavy farm work, Enos was thin. "We waited a long time for it."

"Too long." Forty-six days too long, in Travis's opinion. Sieges starved out the Rebel soldiers and the citizens, including children. It was a nasty business.

The band started playing "Hail Columbia," and Travis stepped away when Enos's bass tones blasted his ears. His singing might never grace an opera stage, but his contagious joy brought a smile from Travis.

They neared the town behind hundreds of Union troops marching ahead of them. Townspeople as dusty as the road stood outside homes. Deep holes and craters marked ditches and lanes, obliging the marching men with their gleaming bayonets to dodge them. Soldiers had been ordered to wear their best and cleanest uniform, whatever their rank. Travis glanced over at his troops. They'd done themselves proud.

"Go back home, Yankees!"

Travis's back stiffened. He glanced ahead to find the woman who had shouted. Each face wore the same belligerent stare. Best ignore the unwise comment.

It didn't bode well for future dealings between the occupying army and citizens.

Four black men sat on the rubble of a wrecked building as the Eighth Illinois approached. One resembled a man who had been at his uncle's house the last night Travis had seen him. Resentment welled up like bile. The hope of ending slavery was the catalyst that drove him to fight.

"You're free now," Travis called to them. Hundreds of fugitives had sought liberation with the Union army that spring. Many more needed that right. "Our victory is your victory."

Their whoops and shouts almost drowned out enraged gasps from some townspeople. Leaping from the broken bricks, the freedmen raised their arms and did a little dance of exultation. Their joy spread to every corner of Travis's heart. As they ran on ahead shouting of freedom, he whispered, "That's for you, Uncle Dabney."

~

*S*axhorns, drums, fifes, clarinets, and cornets in various numbers made up the bands that had already passed Savannah's home. One had included a banjo, guitar, and fiddle and the nerve to pass them playing "Battle Cry of Freedom." One of the lines, "the Union forever" shook her with fury. That wasn't going to happen. The Southerners would rally from this defeat. Then the Union would experience the loss she and Mama experienced on this national Independence Day. A band approached playing "Hail Columbia" with the Yankees singing along. Outrageous to smear their victory in the face of her fellow Southerners' sorrows.

She couldn't help but compare the gaunt, starving, thirsty Southern soldiers that had passed earlier with the relatively clean, well-fed Yankees. Little wonder they'd claimed the victory.

Shameful. Just shameful.

Her throat tightened in anger. Grant's triumphant men in sky-blue trousers studied the havoc their artillery had wreaked on the city.

A tall Union officer with an eagle badge pinning up the left side of his black Hardee hat marched with purpose toward them. One gold bar on his epaulettes signified his rank, whatever it might be. Savannah hardly cared. She gave him a haughty stare, but he peered beyond her shoulder and halted at the fence where Mama's servants observed the parade—for Savannah couldn't think of a better term for the farce. The troops stared but continued on past.

"You're free." The handsome officer with curly brown hair showing beneath his hat line gave Ollie a crisp nod. "These people have no claim on you."

Mama gasped. "Why, I never…"

Savannah sputtered—something she'd never done in her life—but no words came.

"I ain't never been more thankful to meet a man." Ollie kicked an empty bucket out of his way and sprinted toward the Mississippi River with a loud yell.

Eighteen-year-old Alvera, pretty as always with her thick hair woven into four plaits, ran to Samuel, her father, who watched Ollie skirt through the crowd. "Is it true, Papa? Can we really be free?"

Savannah covered her mouth with her hand to keep from screaming. This couldn't be happening. She'd wake up in that awful cave in a minute and be glad it was a dream.

Only, the nightmare was real.

A smile widened on Samuel's face at his daughter's hopeful expression. "Looks like we can. You ready?"

"I've been waiting my whole life for this very minute." Alvera clutched his arm. "You, too, Josie. Let's go."

Hope glowed from Josie's eyes. "Can we, Mama?"

Savannah couldn't breathe. It was as if Alvera had pulled her corset too tightly. Losing their calm, steady housekeeper would be the cruelest blow of all.

"I ain't never been free. Reckon we'll go too." Ellen didn't look at either of the Adairs.

It was as if her decision released them all. Samuel whooped with joy. Grabbing his daughter's hand, he held it high as the two of them ran after Ollie, weaving through the throngs of civilians devastated by war.

"Please. Wait."

Ellen halted at Savannah's request.

"Please stay. Both of you." Savannah reached out her hand

to the slightly plump, petite woman who had been the one she turned to for comfort as a child when Papa was away on business too long. "If you won't remain out of loyalty, will you stay for the sake of the wounded in our home?"

"I don't wish any bad on them, but they fought against the North." Conviction filled the housekeeper's dark brown eyes. "That's not a reason to stay. Freedom is a reason to go." She walked away with Josie at a dignified pace.

"This can't be happening." Mama's voice was faint.

After weeks of terror inside the cave, Savannah feared her mother neared a breaking point. "We'll pay you both salaries."

Ellen halted. Half turned back. "I'll think about it." Then she and Josie seemed to melt into the crowd, so quickly were they gone from sight.

At least Savannah had been able to offer them paying positions before they left. She prayed they'd return.

She cast a haughty glare at the overbearing officer who had no regard for her feelings or the difficult predicament in which his actions placed her and Mama.

Watching Ellen and Josie leave, the officer who had released them puffed out his chest. The corners of his mouth tilted upward.

His happiness over their leaving lashed through Savannah. This was all his fault.

Why, who was going to tend the wounded soldiers lying in their front parlor? Certainly not Mama, who fainted at the sight of blood. Savannah avoided the sick room because she lacked the skills to care for the wounded, unlike her friend Felicity, who volunteered at the City Hospital.

The shocked crowd of civilians turned their attention toward Savannah and Mama. To the Adairs, who enjoyed a high position in Vicksburg's social circle. Some might even gloat at their downfall.

Well, this wasn't going to be the day *that* happened.

Anger at the Yankee who'd brought this calamity boiled up inside Savannah. Papa wasn't here to fight for them. The South's soldiers might have surrendered—she would not.

"Who do you think you are?" Three steps put Savannah beside the arrogant man.

He turned with a click of his heels. "First Lieutenant Travis Lawson of the Eighth Illinois Infantry." Hazel eyes met hers squarely. "Third Brigade of the Third Division in the Seventeenth Army Corps in the Army of the Tennessee." He touched his hat. "At your service, miss."

~

*T*ravis reeled from the storm brewing in the brown eyes of the golden-haired beauty. The feisty Southern belle with her peaches-and-cream complexion was the most beautiful woman he'd ever seen. She'd also taken the time to bathe and change, because he'd learned that during the siege, nearly everyone had stayed in cave shelters. Her pale green day dress, worn with obvious pride on this particular occasion, was of fine quality but without a hoop skirt. Most women in the South had stopped wearing them as they required much often-scarce fabric. Those dresses took up too much space on the sidewalk, anyway.

"My name is Savannah Adair, and this is my mother, Mrs. Lila Adair. Business outside the city regrettably detained my father, or you might not be standing right now." She tilted her head.

"I see." Her regret, no doubt, centered on the fact her father couldn't give him a bloody nose.

"I care little for your rank, sir. You've no right to waltz into our town and say what you said to Ollie." She glanced in the direction he'd taken.

Travis didn't bother to look. Everyone he'd just freed was

long gone—and who could blame them? "President Lincoln's Emancipation Proclamation freeing slaves in seceded states passed in January. I have every right." Travis had little sympathy for whatever small inconvenience her family suffered as a result of the law. "You should have told them yourself."

"Abraham Lincoln is not my president, Lieutenant Lawson." She rested her fists on her hips. "I'm not bound by his laws."

She was outspoken, this one...too much for her own good. She was lucky he wasn't one of his hotheaded comrades. "The Union army will occupy this city, Miss Adair. The sooner you accept that truth, the better."

"I'll never accept Yankees in my city." Every word was clipped.

Cheers from the civilians behind him squelched when he looked around. "It would bode well for you to do just that." That sounded harsher than he'd intended. It wasn't his aim to make enemies on the first day. Even as the rest of his division silently marched past, other citizens showed a keen interest in his conversation with the Southern belle. That made it even more important to soothe Miss Adair's ire. "That is to say, it's best we all learn to respect one another." He nearly gagged on the words. Slavery was not something he could tolerate. He hoped Miss Adair would someday adopt that thinking as her own.

"Respect? How can we Southerners respect men who shelled women and children?" Brown eyes blazed. "There are wounded soldiers in my mama's parlor. Who will care for them now?"

As if it was his problem to care for enemy soldiers. Loud cheers from farther to his left claimed his attention before he could reply.

"Yankees are outside the courthouse." A man pointed.

Travis looked in that direction. The United States flag now waved over the government building in the hot breeze. The sight stirred his patriotic spirit and his comrades still entering the streets, judging by the loud cheers.

Cries of outrage mixed with jeers from citizens. It showed him—as much as his conversation with the beautiful, feisty Mississippi woman had done—that his job wasn't going to be easy.

When he turned back, the blond beauty stood erect, tormented gaze on what she must consider an enemy flag.

She was as impossible to ignore as a golden coneflower or a tender reed that refused to bend under the storm's force.

Something about her called him to stay even as he moved to follow his men, who'd likely soon scatter to explore Vicksburg.

No, she was a Southerner whose family had owned slaves. The two of them couldn't be more different.

CHAPTER 2

*S*avannah stared at the red, white, and blue flag waving over Vicksburg's courthouse, mute testimony more powerful than the presence of Grant's army marching on every street in the city that the enemy had seized control.

"The Union has taken charge of their prize."

Mama's bitter tone at her side startled Savannah from her contemplations of the despised symbol of Yankee victory. "Indeed." They'd attacked her beloved city on the bluffs last summer yet couldn't overcome it. Southern men had fought just as bravely this year, but how could starving soldiers continue to fight?

"Appalling. Simply appalling." Extracting a handkerchief from the sleeve of her gray day dress, Mama dabbed at her eyes. "Our mighty city has fallen. The Yankees' jubilation in the face of our grief is…" Words seemed to fail her.

"Heartless." The brutes. Thankfully, the lieutenant had disappeared, likely to join the blue-coated soldiers surging toward the courthouse, waving their hats. Their shouts increased in volume as more Yankees poured into the city.

"You have the right of it, my daughter."

If only she didn't. Her heart might break as it had when Willie died, but not her spirit. The Yankees claimed the victory on this day, but something must be done to get them out.

"Let's get out of this heat." Mama nudged open their gate.

Mama often avoided the sun when the summer's heat grew oppressive—and certainly, the atmosphere had never been more so. Or she might want to escape gloating gazes from neighbors happy to see them struggle. "I'll see if our wounded soldiers require anything." Though what Savannah could do for them was a mystery.

As she followed her mother up the stone steps leading to the wide portico, Savannah wished she hadn't left the men completely in Ellen's care in the week the privates had been there. Had she helped, she'd know what to do.

"Watch your step." Mama lifted her skirts as they reached the stone portico with its half-dozen columns. "Your father will be glad that our home's exterior escaped with only a few knicks."

"Yes, but what about the interior?" Savannah stepped over shards of broken glass from the eight-foot front parlor window on the left side and two windows half that size in the dining room opposite. She'd been too fearful of what she'd find to search the home earlier and had instead concentrated on the joy of her first bath in weeks. Inside, slivers of glass speckled their spacious marble-floored hall that led to a curved staircase. The banisters no longer gleamed in the sunrays from broken windows. What a catastrophe. "Did any of our windows survive the battle?"

"Doubtful." Mama patted her face with her lacy handkerchief. "I can't bear to look in our parlor—and not only because of the wounded."

"I know." Savannah braced herself and crept near the open double doors to the room that had hosted countless parties. A thick layer of dust lay like a shroud over the entire room. Flying shards had ripped the blue rug that had often been rolled up for dances, liberally marked with rusty stains despite the fact that the wounded men lay on blanket pallets. Who could tell if it was even possible to repair the expensive rug? Cherry wood sofas and chairs with cushions that matched the rug seemed to have mostly escaped damage but required a thorough cleaning. How did one clean such a mess? Not even the cream-colored wallpaper had been spared, for a layer of grime nearly hid the blue forget-me-nots pattern. It seemed a different room in a different house. She shuddered.

"I warned you not to look. Every room I've seen is the same. At least Josie swept the broken glass from our bedrooms before abandoning us." Closing her eyes, Mama touched her forehead. "Savannah, do you suppose this is merely a nightmare? When I open my eyes, will order be restored and everything be as it was before our country divided?" She opened them and looked all around. Unutterable sadness settled across her countenance.

"I'm sorry, Mama." Her heart broke at the sorrow on Mama's face, one she shared.

"Miss Adair, is that you?" A soldier called out from inside the parlor. "Will you send Ellen?"

Mama stiffened and darted a panicked glance at Savannah. "Perhaps you can offer a drink of water. I'll inspect the damage in the back of the house." She dodged broken glass on her way down the hall to the right of the staircase.

Taking care of the wounded was up to Savannah. Mama had fainted many times in the past over the sight of blood. It had made Savannah skittish of the sick room as a child. Yet there was no help for it. After meeting one of the men as he arrived, she'd left their care in her housekeeper's capable hands when they arrived last week. That was no longer an option. Savannah forced herself to enter the room where six men convalesced, four lying on Mama's expensive rug.

The only man she recognized, propped against a cherry cabinet that now displayed broken porcelain figurines, waved her over. "I regret bothering you, Miss Adair. Tex Logue is my name. We met once." He straightened, jarring a shelf of angels. A bright red ridge showed within thick brown hair on top of his head. A bullet had blown his hat off in the battle, grazing his scalp. Ellen had said that other than the terrible headaches he suffered, he'd survive just fine. "Ellen left an hour ago to prepare broth for us. Is it ready?"

Ellen and Alvera had been cooking since Mabel ran off in April—along with some of the maids. Relief washed over Savannah that food had already been prepared because she was as useless in the kitchen as she was as a nurse. "I will fetch it. Ellen...is no longer with us." Anticipating Tex's next question, she lifted her chin. "In fact, my mother and I are quite alone...since the Yankees have taken over our city."

"We surrendered?" Creases in Tex's sunburned forehead relaxed. He exchanged a look with a soldier with bloody bandages around his leg. "Begging your pardon, miss, but I ain't sorry. Our comrades are hungry."

This was surely an understatement. Yet his acceptance surprised her. "You are also. Let me check on your soup."

"No need to trouble yourself, miss. I can get it." Wincing, Tex pushed himself to his feet. Once standing, he supported himself on the cabinet, causing the angels to rattle.

"Please. Save your strength, Private Logue." She gestured for him to sit back down. After she served the soup, she'd have to start cleaning up the broken porcelain. And the glass off the floor and furniture. The only path cleared of glass was from the patients to the hall.

"Calling me Tex would be a sight easier for you." He lowered himself to the floor. "Thank you, kindly, miss."

"You must also call me Savannah, please." He was right. She

had too much to contend with to worry over the formality Mama had once insisted upon.

"Thank you." An angel rocked and then settled when he slumped back against the cabinet. "I'll introduce the rest of the fellows when you return."

"Good." She picked her way from the room. Forget the figurines. Sweeping up the glass was paramount. Where was Josie's broom? No matter. That job must wait. Best feed the men first and then get back outside to monitor what the Yankees planned to do next. Grant's army couldn't be trusted.

A pleasant beef aroma wafted down the hall as she neared the kitchen. The spacious room with cupboards, three long tables lining the walls, two large stoves, a sink with a pump for water, and not a single glass splinter felt welcoming after the chaotic mess in the parlor. Both windows on either corner had been blown out, but either Alvera or Ellen had cleaned the glass before cooking.

Nearby, a regimental band played "Battle Cry of Freedom." Savannah might have enjoyed the music if the words didn't celebrate the Union. Their current struggles could be laid at the army's feet.

"Did they want water?" Mama carried a broom into the kitchen from across the hall and rested the handle against a table by the door.

"Ellen made soup for them. One of the men was asking about it." Steam rose from a pot on one of the two stoves, the source of the delicious aroma. Savannah approached to find that tiny bubbles lined the perimeter of the broth. "It seems to be simmering. Does that mean it's ready?"

"I would guess so, though I'm not sure how we are to manage this, as neither of us has ever cooked." Mama joined her and peered at the brown broth. "No vegetables or meat. Are we out of food?"

"Perhaps." Savannah touched suddenly throbbing temples.

She'd best save a portion for her and Mama. "Or maybe Ellen made the broth thin on purpose for the injured men…"

"Let's pray for the latter. Let me help you dish up the broth. I'll check the pantry once you're ready to serve."

Ready to serve. Other than teatime hostess duties, that phrase had never applied to her. No time to think about that now. Everything had changed. "Should it be served in bowls or cups?"

"Cups will be easier for the wounded."

Where were the dishes? Savannah opened the first cupboard. "Here are a few sacks of dried food. No cans."

"I hope that's not all of it. At least we didn't resort to buying mule meat." Mama grimaced.

Savannah's stomach leaped at the thought. Yankees had blocked entry to the city so no supplies had been delivered. Grocers who had opened their shops during the siege had been limited to what could be found. It was difficult to forgive the overall Union commander, General Grant, for subjecting both soldiers and citizens to the atrocities they'd endured.

"I found the dishes." From the second cupboard, Savannah picked up a chipped cup with the familiar pink river scene design. Then another. There hadn't been the slightest mar on any dish when they began sheltering in the cave. Mortar shells that had relentlessly shaken the entire city must have rattled the dishes together. She stepped closer to examine the plates. "Mama, this plate is cracked." The one below was the same.

"Stacked dishes suffered the brunt of the shelling." Taking the plate, Mama traced a hairline crack with her finger.

Had any of them escaped damage? "These aren't all our dishes, though." They'd had enough of this everyday pattern alone to serve fifty guests.

"No, the rest are packed in sawdust. Those barrels are in the pantry." Mama sighed.

"These will do for now." Savannah began dipping broth into cups.

"I'll sweep the hall and main entrance while you feed the men."

Savannah raised an eyebrow. "Do you know how?" Mama had lived in her father's Charleston hotel as a child until it became profitable and they'd moved into a mansion. To her knowledge, her mother had never performed menial tasks—and likely had never swept up broken glass.

"I've seen it done." She retrieved the broom. "How hard can it be?"

"I'm going to see what's happening on the streets after feeding the men." The worst had already come—surrender. Her beloved Vicksburg was now occupied by the enemy, but she had no idea what to expect. It would be wise to discover the new rules so she could watch over Mama.

"Yes, things will likely change quickly. I'll see about setting the house to rights after I check on the food." Straightening her back, Mama disappeared toward the pantry with her broom.

Shouts drew Savannah's gaze to lacy curtains flapping in front of empty panes. What was happening? Her hands shook as she ladled broth into cups. She must get back outside.

Savannah turned at footsteps by the door.

Mama sagged against the wall. "There isn't any food left in storage."

A few sacks of dried fruit and vegetables were all they had from the stores of food always at hand? Papa had left money for them, but grocers had nothing except mule meat. Savannah pressed her hand against her forehead to stave off a wave of dizziness.

"I wish your father were here." Mama's voice quaked.

"Don't worry." Savannah straightened her shoulders. Someone must see to the needs of her family. Papa wasn't here to do it. She and Mama needed him desperately, but he couldn't help them now. The lot fell on her. "I'll think of something."

~

"That's a welcome sight." Struggling to ignore the stench of death that hung over the city, Travis stared at the river from the courthouse yard, where his comrades milled around in groups on the steep, grassy hillside. The highest point in Vicksburg offered a spectacular view of the city and the mighty Mississippi. It wasn't Admiral Porter's now-silent gunboats in the river that commanded Travis's attention but the dozen ships proudly displaying the Stars and Stripes that were bringing food and supplies toward the wharf from both directions. General Grant had ordered the provisions to feed the citizens and the soldiers.

"Giving provisions may soothe the Southerners' anger." Captain Brian Eaton, Travis's superior in the Eighth Illinois by one rank, clasped his gloved hands as he followed Travis's gaze. His Hardee hat nearly covered his blond hair.

"True. It's the right thing to do, regardless." Travis tugged at his own white gloves, longing to remove them in the sweltering sun. He'd obey Grant's command that they wear their best today. A sudden yearning struck him to be once again working the soil on his family's farm, clad simply in a plaid shirt and comfortable trousers. What he wouldn't give to close this dark chapter of his country's history...and his own life.

Yet he couldn't leave until the job was finished. Capturing Vicksburg catapulted them toward the war's ending...or so he hoped. Travis's personal goal was to end slavery, something he fought for to honor his uncle's memory.

Brian folded his arms across his chest, which his full beard nearly touched. "You'll want to know about Special Orders No. 180 that Grant issued."

Pushing his thoughts aside, Travis turned to him. "What are they?"

"It's what you'd expect about organizing the initial surrender and cleanup."

Plenty to do. Cleaning up the rubble, filling in the caves, and burying the dead would require weeks. "What else?"

"The Forty-Fifth and Eighty-First Illinois Infantry regiments will serve as provost guards under Major General John Logan, who has been named temporary commander of Vicksburg. He's a good choice until General Grant decides who will command the city. No surprises there."

Travis braced himself at the serious look in Brian's eyes. "What's got you worried?"

"Hundreds—no, thousands—of able-bodied black men from this vicinity claimed their freedom today, in addition to those who came to us before the battle ever started. That's a good thing. But they need jobs." The captain sighed and let his arms hang at his sides. "Officers have been ordered to organize them into squads. The colored men will be tasked with policing the town and the surrounding area within the siege lines in support of the Forty-Fifth and Eighty-First."

Travis gave a low whistle. "That will antagonize the Southerners." Freedmen policing their former owners? What was Grant thinking? Could such an arrangement even work?

"Potentially. We'll be camped outside town for the foreseeable future."

Good. Travis would look for ways to aid the freedmen. He prayed that the opportunity for jobs led toward a path of healing.

"First, let's spread the word to townspeople to receive food from the ships." The captain's face relaxed into a grin.

Travis's thoughts flew back to Miss Adair. "That's one task I'll enjoy." Maybe the offer of aid would soothe her anger against the Union. Although...why should it matter so much to him?

~

Savannah could barely move in the crush on the sidewalks and streets. She tucked her skirt close to her legs to keep her hem from soldiers' trampling feet. There must be tens of thousands of military men from both sides mingling together in a city with a prewar population of forty-five hundred. Overwhelming, indeed.

Soldiers from opposing sides swapped battle stories as she crept toward the courthouse, walking against the majority heading toward the river. While it was some comfort that Yankees gave rations from their haversacks to their hungry enemies, there wouldn't have been a need to share if Grant hadn't starved them first.

Regimental bands continued to play. Conversations from every direction made it difficult to focus on any of them.

Tears splotched the cheeks of a solitary woman on her mangled porch, two little boys clutching her skirt. Savannah knew her only by sight as one of the fifteen hundred or so women and children who had remained through the siege. Many of them likely had not possessed the means to flee from battle.

That hadn't been the reason Savannah and Mama stayed. They'd sheltered at the Sandersons' plantation two miles from the city for last year's attack. Mrs. Sanderson had been kind, but no one could forget that Willie, her son who had planned to marry Savannah, had died of typhoid fever in 1861. As for Savannah, she'd looked around for Willie at every turn when at the plantation. She hadn't wanted to put herself through that again and Mama agreed. Besides, they hadn't seen the Sandersons since Mama's annual Christmas ball.

Savannah turned her thoughts from Willie to focus on her top priority—obtaining food. She scanned the crowd for Union officers, especially Lieutenant Lawson, and spotted some outside the courthouse. Her skin tingled at the damage to the once-impressive building. Holes and curved indents in the roof and walls testified the number of times it had been struck. A splintered balcony post was half torn off. Yet the courthouse had fared better than a former house up the hill, now a pile of rubbish. Walls bulged in other buildings. Some businesses and homes lay in ruins. Would the owners rebuild or try to repair? Savannah didn't know which was easier.

Either way, there were no windows intact. She passed a boarded-up store. Anger at the destruction seared a deeper hole in her soul.

A soldier in blue lounged against a damaged building, staring at her with bold eyes.

Insolent. The very reason she must deal directly with officers. Was a woman unsafe in public without an escort? She skirted the slow-moving group of men directly ahead and quickened her pace to the courthouse yard.

"Miss Adair?"

She searched the crowd milling about the building until spotting the approach of the very man she sought. "Lieutenant Lawson." The relief surging through her couldn't be attributed to this man, though his was a familiar face—one that provided some strange sense of comfort amid the unprecedented turmoil swirling in her heart over the condition of her beloved South. Then she recalled Mama's sorrow and worry. How were they to feed themselves and the soldiers recuperating in their home? Out came her next statement with more anger than she'd intended. "I demand your assistance."

~

*T*ravis stiffened. How dare this proud Southern belle speak to him as if she had authority over him? He'd actually been headed toward her home to inform her of the food available for citizens at the wharf. The sympathy he'd felt for her plight cooled.

Yet he wanted good relations between his army and the townspeople. "What may I do for you?" Travis folded his arms.

"Your siege depleted our provisions." She raised an elegant eyebrow. "What do you propose to do about it?"

"Plenty. Food ordered by General Grant awaits you at the river." He gestured toward the sailors already serving lines of citizens.

Her head jerked toward the ships where hundreds of soldiers and families waited. "Ah, that's why it was like swimming against the tide to reach the courthouse."

"Indeed." Did that description fit her life's circumstances right now? "It's always a struggle to go in a different direction as the crowd...yet sometimes it's the right thing to do."

"I'm often the one leading, as I suspect you are." Her head tilted as she studied him. "Be that as it may, I'm grateful for the food. My mother was worried. I'll need enough to provide for our wounded."

"Inform those handing out supplies about them. It will be no problem."

Tension eased from her face. "So much will be difficult to tote up the hill."

True. Her slender frame had likely never borne over five pounds of weight for any distance, and she'd have sacks of food. "It will. Do you have a wheelbarrow?"

She shook her head.

"Take a basket to the ships." That would at least consolidate the load.

"Will you accompany me?"

A question. Not a demand this time, though her request for him to carry her supplies was clear, all the same. He shook his head. "My apologies, Miss Adair. I've other orders."

Her brow furrowed.

Travis wavered at her duress. He truly couldn't see her making it up the hill with an overloaded basket. "It's a long line." He softened his tone. "I will confine my duties to that area in an hour's time. If you have a large basket, I can manage it for you." Doubtful she'd have collected her supplies before that, enabling him to assist her. Her relieved smile lightened her brown eyes, making him feel more gallant than his soldierly duties generally allowed.

As she thanked him and hurried away, he almost regretted his offer. With so many soldiers from opposing sides, maintaining order was of paramount importance. He couldn't afford to be distracted by one citizen, no matter how lovely. Were these not the first hours his men had free in weeks, he could have requested one of them help her. He could still do so. Any of the bachelors would be happy to escort the beauty.

No, better to shield her from unwanted attention. He'd perform the task. When she wasn't issuing demands, he liked her better.

For now, he'd gather freedmen near the river who wanted a job with the army. Even though the Union troops had been victorious, they'd lost too many good men. They needed soldiers, and men pouring into the city from surrounding plantations needed jobs.

His uncle, who had been driving fugitives on the Underground Railroad on the night he went missing, would be pleased.

Uncle Dabney, what happened to you? Even after twelve years, Travis still longed to solve the mystery.

CHAPTER 3

$\mathcal{H}$alf an hour later, Savannah set a wide, round basket on the grass near the wharf. Any refreshing river breeze was stifled by the crowds, and her delicate fan was woefully inadequate in this heat. Out of dozens waiting in line for food, surprisingly, she knew only a few women by sight and not name. She'd decided it was best not to wear the many silk or taffeta dresses in her armoire for a while, but even her finely rouched and pleated cotton day dress was too elegant among the linen and homespun.

Southern soldiers far outnumbered the townspeople in the supply lines, but Luke Shea, her friend Felicity Sanderson's beau and a buddy of Willie's from the old days when life was easier, wasn't among the dear soldiers in gray. He had apparently recovered enough from his recent head injury to protect their city during the battle.

She scanned the crowd for Felicity. How she needed a friend. No sign of her.

Nor of Lieutenant Lawson, who'd promised to carry her basket.

She sighed and allowed her thoughts to wander a well-worn path to her father and his whereabouts. She and Mama had muddled along without him, as they had so often through the years. This situation was different. Surely, he'd arrive at the first possible moment. No one knew how he'd fared through the conflict, nor did he know about them. Mama's resentment over having to endure living in their cave shelter without his protection had escalated during the battle.

Savannah often had to be the peacemaker between them, which was as laughable to her as it was at odds with her take-charge personality—something demanded by her father's frequent absences.

Yet the reason for her being the peacemaker wasn't laughable, for the rift between them was her fault. What began as an innocent request after visiting with a new friend, Mary Grace, had cast a long shadow over Savannah's whole family.

"Next."

Savannah was shaken from her sad thoughts by a booming voice, surprising from a thin man in spectacles not much taller than she. "I'm Savannah Adair, and I've come to collect my food."

"Are you a resident of Vicksburg?" He scribbled on a page of names. Sacks, barrels, and open crates were scattered to either side of him.

"Yes, with my mother, Mrs. Lila Adair." Clutching her basket, she peered at the array of dried vegetables. Mama would be pleased.

"Any others living in your household?" He raised an eyebrow.

"Yes, we have six wounded with us." And Papa would return soon, no doubt. Unless torn railroad tracks delayed him.

"Confederates?"

"Of course." Silly question. Most of their wounded remained in field hospitals during the battle, but the overflow had ended up in Vicksburg hospitals and homes.

"We're providing for everyone. Just keeping an account." The man began gathering sacks that went into her basket.

"Thank you." Amazing that the army was giving three days' rations to over thirty thousand starving people. As she turned away with her considerable load, her fingers stroked sacks of dried corn, rice, cornmeal, sugar, and salt. The faint aroma of coffee beans emanating from a burlap bag brought a burst of gratitude. It had been months since she drank coffee. Bacon was the only meat in her bulging basket, though.

Her stomach rumbled. Weeks of scanty meals that satisfied no one had taken a toll on everyone. Ollie and Samuel had picked apples and peaches during lulls in the mortar blasts. That had been the only fresh food they'd eaten during the siege. The fruit had supplemented the corncakes and peas those final two weeks. At least there were no peas in the rations. She *never* wanted to eat another one.

Lieutenant Lawson was still missing, but the boisterous, loud throng of men near the river prompted her to begin climbing the hill.

Freedmen whooped and shouted in the street. A score of them sauntered along the sidewalk, armed with muskets.

Her heart thrashed against her ribs. Her feet stopped of their own volition as they approached her. She blinked. Leland, Robert, and Fred, who had left the Adairs the day the Union army reached the outskirts of Vicksburg, were among the armed men. In the past, any of them would have stopped what they were doing to carry her heavy basket. Today they simply stared at her.

Leland, who had worked in the stable with his son, Robert, halted ten paces from her. "Get along now." He spoke with authority and something else. Satisfaction?

Blood rushed to her face. Anger, fear, astonishment, and indignation warred within her at his bold stare. Anger won. "How dare you speak to me in such a fashion?"

~

*T*ravis jerked his head around at the unmistakable anger in Miss Adair's raised voice. He'd just returned from leaving his first group of newly recruited soldiers with his captain and had been searching the food lines for her. A freedman from one of their new squads lowered his eyebrows at her. Townspeople and soldiers from both sides had stopped to look. What had the new policeman said to her?

He sprinted up to her, skirting gawkers. "Miss Adair? What seems to be the problem?"

Turning to him, she pressed a palm over a throbbing pulse in her throat. "This man dares to give me orders."

Travis glanced at the tall man who studied him with narrowed eyes. "It's his job."

"His job?" Bright red spots splotched her face. "Leland and his son once worked in my father's stable. Fred was our gardener after Gus left."

"These men are free. They've accepted a job to police the city." Travis's gaze darted at men in gray on every side, his heightened senses attuned to the fact that amidst the noisy celebration throughout the city, the people in their vicinity had grown quiet. This was an unfortunate way for Miss Adair, her neighbors, and the Rebels to learn of Grant's orders to hire the newly freed men to police the city.

Savannah gave him an incredulous stare.

The crowd erupted in gasps and the low hum of asides to one another.

"Have you Yankees lost your senses?" A man shouted from the right.

Travis swung around, searching for the speaker. "Not at all." Impassive faces stared at him. A woman with two little boys clutching her skirt raised a trembling hand to her lips. "These men require the means to support themselves and their families. The United States Army needs soldiers, some of whom will be given the task of policing the city...like these men. Surely, none of you would imagine the few men necessary to accomplish those tasks for a prewar population as adequate for the tens of thousands here today."

No one spoke. Good. Better to de-escalate the situation now that he'd explained.

Travis turned back to Savannah and the freedmen standing closest to her. "Go about your business, men. More will join you in the coming hours and days."

With one more look at Miss Adair, they moved toward the river. The way the squad strode past with heads held high gave Travis a moment's satisfaction for his small part in the change. Uncle Dabney would have been happy to witness the freedmen accepting the responsibilities of paid positions.

Savannah's attention seemed to be focused on the three men closest to her as they passed. Likely, these were the former servants in her home she'd just mentioned.

A desire to protect her from their possible disdain surprised him in its intensity. "Miss Adair, may I assist you with your basket?" Travis stepped forward, arms outstretched.

"Thank you, Lieutenant Lawson." She offered her burden, which he accepted.

"My pleasure." As he walked beside her, he determined to inquire what the freedman had said to upset her. Perhaps a private word with the newly hired policeman was warranted.

~

Shaken to her core, Savannah opened the gate to her house. She'd been silent on the walk to her home, but clearly, the Yankee army needed some guidance. "First Lieutenant Lawson, I've never been more shocked in my life." She studied his profile as he kept pace with her on the stone steps leading to the portico. The man wasn't even winded from Vicksburg's incline, though he carried the heavy basket on his shoulder.

"Call me Travis. Please. 'First Lieutenant' is a mouthful."

"Fine." Relaxing such standards hardly mattered when the world had gone mad. "My name is Savannah." She turned to him as they reached the door. "Had your general been better informed, he'd understand that families will return to the city after the battle ends. There are plenty of townsfolk in need of jobs."

He gave her an incredulous look and then set down the basket. "General Grant stays well-informed through spies and other means." He put his hands on his hips. "Even by your own newspapers."

The city's newspapers had provided fuel for spies? Intolerable. Yet she should have considered that anything printed could reach the enemy. "Then he knows that thousands left in fear for their lives."

"Certainly."

"They require jobs upon their return, as I've said." Such as her father, for where was he to find cotton bales to sell? Though she could not imagine that guarding the city would interest him.

"The recently freed will struggle to find a place to live. There will be challenges for them. General Grant's plan offers them employment. But I have one question for you before I go. Did Fred, Leland, or his son insult you?" Hazel eyes held her gaze.

She opened her mouth to agree and then stopped. Leland's demand couldn't be labeled as such. "It was his manner, his tone, that I objected to more than being told to 'get along.'"

"That's fair." Relief mingled with something else in his expression. Determination? "I'd ask that you grant leniency as these men learn their new tasks."

It had hurt when the men had walked away from a job, a home right here. But the worst pain had been inflicted by Ellen, Josie, and Alvera's leaving. She'd trusted them. Relied on them. Cared for them. Could Travis not understand? "Thank you for your aid, Travis." She lifted her chin.

"It was my pleasure, Savannah." His eyes crinkled when he smiled. "I must attend other tasks. Let me know if I can be of any assistance in the future."

Savannah folded her arms as he ran down the steps. He might regret that offer.

Yet she was glad he'd made it.

Picking up the basket, she carried it into the spacious hall now cleared of glass but plenty dusty. Where was Mama?

"Miss Adair?" Tex called to her from the parlor. "Might I trouble you for some food?"

She'd toted six cups of broth to them three hours ago, and Tex had made the introductions then. Setting the heavy basket on the hall table, she crossed into the parlor. "Yes, Tex. Are you all hungry?" She picked her way to them.

"Caleb hasn't woken up to drink his broth yet." Tex sat with his back to the wall this time, thank goodness, for she had yet to rescue the remaining figurines. "It will taste a sight better if it's warmed again."

"I can manage that." If the stove was still hot. Studying the dark-haired Louisiana soldier near thirty with a shoulder wound, Savannah felt a twinge of worry. The bullet was likely still inside because Ellen hadn't mentioned removing it.

"Peter's fever is higher than this morning." Tex peered at the twenty-year-old lying a blanket pallet over the rug. "Broth's best for him, if we can get him to take it."

"All right." She averted her eyes from bright red stains on the bandages about his waist. There was plenty of broth left.

"Micah's still feverish, too, but he says he could eat something."

The Tennessee soldier nodded, the youngest of the bunch at nineteen. He lay stretched out with shrapnel wounds in his leg beside James, another Tennesseean with bloody bandages below his knee. The last soldier, Nick, hadn't moved his bandaged arm in Savannah's sight. His sweaty face and feverish stare scared her.

"I think the rest of us are ready to eat something substantial, if it's not too much trouble." Tex's stomach rumbled. "Begging your pardon."

"The Yankee army did one thing right today." Only one, in her view. "They're giving everyone provisions. I've just returned with food from the ships."

"Thank the Lord." Eyebrows raised, James looked up at her. "Any coffee?"

"Yes." She had no idea how to prepare it. "Let me see what I can do."

But as Savannah set the basket on a kitchen table, she was at a loss how to prepare not only coffee but also corn muffins or bacon. "Mama? Where are you?"

Her mother stepped out of the laundry room, broom in hand. "Oh, Savannah, you're back." Mama propped the broom in a corner. "Your father may return today, and we can't have the house in shambles. You'll have to sweep the parlor. I've tended to the hall and steps."

"Thanks. I will."

Mama's determination to have everything as organized as possible for Papa's return gave her something to focus on besides the surrender. She'd relied on her staff for such tasks. Savannah was pleasantly surprised at the change.

Savannah gestured toward sacks in the basket. "These are our provisions from the army." Since Travis had carried them, they almost seemed like a gift from him. "Our patients are asking for a meal."

"Which neither of us know how to cook." Mama reached

into the sack on top. "What are these?" She studied the round objects rolling around her palm with a perplexed frown.

"Coffee beans." The aroma gave Savannah the hint, but she understood her mother's confusion. The beans weren't the color of coffee. "Why are they green?"

Mama frowned. "They likely turn brown as the water boils."

Seemed plausible. "Coffee shouldn't be too difficult. We'll put some beans in the bottom of the coffeepot with water. How many?"

Mama tapped her chin. "Four beans for this first batch to make it stretch. Your father left plenty of money, but who knows when our stores will replenish their empty shelves?"

"Good point. I'll make it now." Beans bounced into the bottom of the blue tin coffeepot as she dropped them in with a sense of anticipation. The men would surely want at least two cups of the beverage, so she filled the pot with water to the handle at the top and set it on the stove. Then Savannah opened the door to find embers smoldering on the grate. Oh no. "Mama, the stove's cold. Do you know how to build up the fire?"

"I've no notion what's to be done."

Savannah didn't either. Her own inadequacy sparked a sense of desperation for the first time in her life. Everyone with such knowledge had abandoned them. Well, she wasn't about to desert her mother.

"I'll figure it out." Savannah straightened her shoulders. "Mama, you can keep readying the house for Papa's return."

~

*A*fter returning from his errand with Miss Adair, Travis found his captain on Washington Street, which was lined with businesses and soldiers from opposing sides swapping food, alcohol, and battle experiences. It was comforting to see them mingle after facing each other across no-man's land. "Do you want me to gather another new squad?" Travis removed his hat to swipe a handkerchief across his sweaty brow. "I'm just back from rounding up the second one."

The joy of the freedmen refreshed his spirit more than any celebration. This was what he had worked to accomplish for two long years.

"Hold back." Arms folded, Brian faced the street where a large group of Federal soldiers scuttled past on the opposite sidewalk, occasionally bending to pick something up and stuff it into their knapsacks. "They're looking for souvenirs on the streets and among the rubble. I suppose there's no harm in that."

"Wouldn't be if the folks who own the property have already been through it. Doubt they've had an opportunity." Travis rested his gloved hands on his hips. "Shall I go after those soldiers?"

"Leave them be. Hundreds are doing the same. I'm more concerned with the drinking."

Travis followed his gaze to a score of privates from both sides. A Confederate soldier upended a bottle of whiskey to drink the last swallow. That bothered Travis too. Federal officers were allowing the troops a day of celebration. Moving freely about the city after weeks of confinement behind the protection of earthworks was what they all needed. Yet they couldn't afford to give the celebration a free rein among the thousands, else chaos would ensue.

At the sound of pounding hooves, the crowds scurried from the road, shoving Travis and Brian against a wood building. Four horseback riders cantered past, one of them a Union officer holding a half-empty whiskey bottle.

"Someone will get hurt. Did you see who they were?" Straightening, Brian craned his neck toward the rider's back.

"No. Two of our officers with two Confederate officers."

Travis worried more for the women and children still waiting in food lines at two in the afternoon. "Were they drunk?" Would a sober man risk the lives of so many?

"Maybe. Freed people are selling homemade beer too."

Shouts to the right drew Travis's attention.

"Yankees are breaking into our stores and looting them," a man cried.

Travis's empty stomach soured. This was a nightmare.

"We can't allow that." Brian's mouth tightened. "Let's go."

Travis, his jaw set, strode beside him toward the trouble. Their own men gave citizens searching for grievances against the Union a valid one. Unfortunately, the smell of dead animals wasn't the only stench in the conquered city.

~

"This is private property. Remove yourselves from our land." Savannah paused on a cracked stone embedded in her backyard's hillside path, afraid to approach the two Yankees filling their knapsacks with apples from their orchard. She had grabbed a basket before stepping outside, as if her intent had been to pick fruit and not that she'd spotted them looting her trees from the kitchen window.

"Pardon me, miss." One paused to apologize, but the other man merely sped up picking the fruit. "We thought the house was empty."

"That doesn't excuse stealing. Leave at once, both of you." Savannah gave them her haughtiest stare.

The one who apologized leaped over the wrought-iron fence. His pal picked one more apple before following suit.

Savannah maintained her stance until the men were out of sight, then sagged against a tree. How dare they? Travis would hear about this treachery.

She hadn't been successful in lighting a fire in the stove yet, so there was still no coffee. If only Savannah had recalled the ripe apples and peaches in their orchard earlier. She might have prevented the theft.

Artillery had damaged some of their trees and destroyed a handful. Gus, Ellen's husband, had been their gardener when Savannah was a child. Wishing he were still here to work his magic on the mangled trees, she stepped over fruit rotting on the ground to fill her empty basket with what hung within her reach. Her soldiers were starving. This would hold them off until she got the stove fire lit. The only provision they'd received that Mama knew how to cook was bacon...and that had been an observation of Alvera frying it one day.

Savannah toted the basket half filled with apples to a peach tree. The likelihood that others might come after more fruit when she left nudged her to heap peaches on top.

Something heavy hit the sidewalk across the street. She whirled around. Six Yankees were tearing the boards off Mrs. Bradley's door. The widow had the doors and windows boarded up before fleeing to her daughter's Tennessee home that spring, unwilling to face another attack.

Anger shot through Savannah as she placed her heaping basket on the ground. Gathering her skirt, she hastened to her fence. "Halt, thieves!"

They ignored her as they pushed against the door. It opened under their weight. They sprinted inside.

Desperate to help her neighbor, she ran behind the fence that bordered her land until she was opposite the broken door. "Stop!"

There were soldiers from both sides striding past. Why did no one stop the theft?

A thief carried a tea set outside. Another deposited a calico dress and ribbons on the sidewalk. What need had they for these items?

"Stop them! They're robbing a poor widow."

Several heads swiveled toward the home. No one interfered.

Horrified, she covered her mouth. A table, two chairs, and a blue ceramic clock that Mrs. Bradley cherished were piled outside the home.

"This is outrageous. Stop!"

With barely a glance in her direction, the men toted the widow's belongings up the hill and out of sight.

The soldiers who'd taken charge of her city now looted it. How long would this carnage last before the Union army put a stop to it? Her thoughts flew to Travis. He seemed trustworthy, but maybe it was silly to believe any Union officer would act honorably toward the defeated.

For the first time, Savannah was grateful for the wounded soldiers in her home. If someone tried to break in, she and Mama wouldn't face the danger alone.

CHAPTER 4

*F*ireworks lit the night sky to the cheers of their army back at their camp in the battle lines. Although it was a welcome celebration, for Travis it was eerily reminiscent of the constant artillery they'd poured into the Confederate ranks for weeks. He turned at footsteps rustling against dried grass. Benjamin Woodrum, who had married Travis's sister, Mary, at the beginning of the war, was a private in the Eighth Illinois.

"Long day." Light flashed on Ben's face as he stared at the night sky.

"Agreed." It was good to be back at camp. The day's looting by their own men had finally stopped when the Forty-Fifth Illinois Infantry stepped up to patrol the city in their role as provost guards. Travis and other officers had ordered all Union troops back to their camps. Then, in case anyone tried to sneak back into the city, additional guards had been posted at every camp. "Did you get a letter from Mary?" His sister was raising one-year-old Benny on their parents' farm until Ben mustered out. Then they'd move into the living quarters over Ben's family grocery store.

"I did. Benny is now saying 'Pa' in addition to 'Mama.'" Ben's black hair and beard might blend in with the night, but his blue eyes glowed with pride. "Did you hear from your ma?"

Travis nodded. He'd read the letter from both his parents after supper. "Eliza is about the same." His twenty-year-old sister had been betrothed to Giles Benedict, whose family farmed the adjacent property to the Lawsons'. Eliza's heart had broken when Giles was killed at Shiloh.

"I'd not recover from losing Mary in a year either." Ben's tone was subdued.

"On the other hand, Nancy is convinced she's in love again." He shook his head. This was the third time he knew of that his youngest sister had stated those words about a different boy. "This time with one of our farmhands."

Ben chuckled. "What is she now...seventeen?"

"Last month." As he laughed with Ben, some of the day's tension eased from his chest. He'd been happy to spread the news that those in bondage were now free. That had been tempered by his concern over Savannah's turmoil and the dozens of Union soldiers he'd caught looting. He'd ordered them to return the items and then get to camp.

"She might marry before our term is up."

Cheers erupted when another flash lit the sky.

"Perhaps. We've got another year." While Ben desired to get home and raise his son, Travis planned to serve until the war ended and then go back to his father's farm. Tending the plants had brought him satisfaction before the war.

Another flash of fireworks reminded him of Savannah's feisty spirit. Where might her pa be? Why had he left them with a battle looming?

Had Savannah's home been looted? Duties would take him into the city daily for the foreseeable future. He'd stop at her place to see how she fared.

~

*S*ounds of horses, wagons, and conversations coming through paneless windows awoke Savannah before seven the next morning, her stomach so empty that she'd be happy to eat the bacon Mama had fried last night after Tex started the stove fire. Unfortunately, the meat had been charred on one side and nearly raw on the other. Three years ago, neither Savannah nor her mother would have eaten burnt meat.

That was before the war. Much had changed.

Alvera wasn't here to help her dress or style her hair. It was good that her corset hooked in front. She chose a delaine dress as more suited to cooking and working around the house than her usual finery.

A knock on her bedroom door was quickly followed by Mama entering in her robe before Savannah could respond. "Good morning."

"Please button my dress." Laying her robe across Savannah's unmade bed, Mama turned around. "I'll fry another batch of bacon this morning. I'll flip it over halfway through and not leave it go so long."

Savannah fumbled with the tiny buttons on her mother's green mousseline dress. "And I'll make corn muffins." Though she had no notion of a recipe, she must try. Tex had offered to light the stove's fire upon rising. In fact, the man had been surprisingly resourceful.

Yesterday had been a disaster. From the devastating surrender to Ellen, Josie, and Alvera leaving, to chasing thieves from her property, to ruining the coffee that they'd all craved, Savannah had endured all she could. Who knew one must first roast coffee beans?

Tex.

He'd taken one swallow of the watery beverage and then

pushed himself to his feet. While James spooned broth for Caleb in between bites on a juicy peach, Tex had accompanied her back to the kitchen.

Tex had washed two handfuls of coffee beans and then roasted them in the oven. He plopped onto a chair to stir them often until the beans were dark brown. The cracking sound during roasting was evidently a good sign. A heavenly aroma filled the kitchen when he took the skillet from the oven. After the cracking stopped, he poured the roasted beans into a bowl and shook it to loosen the chaff and then leaned close to blow it away. He'd then shown her how to use the grinder mounted to one of the tables and demonstrated how much coffee to put into a sack lowered into a coffeepot of water.

They must go through all that trouble for a cup of coffee? Savannah's respect for her former kitchen staff deepened.

Drinking that coffee had been like imbibing pure nectar. Mama, who had labored with Savannah to get a fire to stay lit in the stove, enjoyed a second cup while Savannah and Tex served the others. Their gratitude made providing the beverage worth the trouble.

As Savannah finished buttoning Mama's dress, she recalled Tex's matter-of-fact explanation that he'd helped those requiring a strong arm to the water closet and had taken care of those who couldn't walk, so she need not concern herself. It was something she'd never considered. Her face burned like fire again just remembering the conversation. She truly was no good in the sick room.

Last night, she'd been grateful to fall into her comfortable bed in her own room, not in a dark cave. Unfortunately, she'd barely fallen asleep when she'd been awoken by the sound of artillery. She'd shot out of bed and stared at the moonlit river. The gunboats remained silent. One full minute had passed in which terror gripped her before she realized Grant's army had set off fireworks to celebrate their victory. Ill-bred of them, in her opinion, with so many suffering in Vicksburg. She'd tumbled into bed again, thankful the surrender meant no mortar was to be launched at them from her beloved Mississippi River.

"Will you style my hair?" Mama patted her askew bun at her nape. "I kept it up overnight hoping it would still be intact this morning—with disastrous results, as you see. I'm at a loss as to how Alvera fashions it."

"I will." Savannah gulped. She'd inherited her blond hair and brown eyes from her mother. Practicing braiding her own hair last night hadn't borne much fruit. "It's Sunday. Shall we attend services?" How would she ever get herself and her mother ready in time?

"I feel overwhelmed with all that is to be done." Hands fluttering, Mama sat before the mirror and vanity. "Feeding our patients will require a good bit of our morning. We'll attend next week."

"Fine by me." Surely, the churches had suffered the same dust and glass their home had. Savannah tried to refashion her mother's hair from memory.

Mama looked toward the window where sounds of horses pulling wagons up the hill could be clearly heard through the broken glass. "Your father may arrive today. I'm angry with him...nevertheless, I want to look my best."

"I'll try." A fleeting thought that Tex might know how to style hair almost made her laugh.

Truth be told, she wanted Papa to come almost as much as her mother. Yesterday's thievery in empty Vicksburg homes and in her own backyard worried her. Those soldiers wouldn't have stolen their food had Papa been here.

Still, the theft should be reported. The Union army must exercise more discipline over their own soldiers...and she'd remind Travis of his duty as soon as she saw him again.

Why did the thought of that encounter make her stomach flutter? Surely, just the nervousness of confronting the enemy.

~

Soon after breakfast, Travis was overseeing the distribution of food at the City Landing while his men hunted for dead and wounded on the battlefield that stretched for miles. Without a doubt, they'd find and bring back wounded who had been too weak to cry out for help, and then begin a massive burial detail for those who hadn't made it.

Major General John Logan, temporary commander of Vicksburg, didn't want a repeat of yesterday's looting. Union troops had been given tasks that would keep them too busy to cause trouble. Over thirty thousand captured Confederate troops roamed free while waiting to be paroled. Travis was one of the officers assigned to monitor for trouble in the city.

He was also to invite freedmen roaming the city to join the Union army. They'd be sent to camps of instruction to learn soldiers' skills.

Travis swiped his sticky forehead with his handkerchief. Mississippi sun got hot early and stayed that way. Maybe he'd eventually grow accustomed to the heat.

Not much going on at the ships. Citizens waited in orderly fashion for food that must be welcome, indeed. Squads of freedmen new to policing patrolled the streets. He'd stroll about the city searching for men who wanted jobs and later stop by Savannah's home. He headed away from the ships and crossed the wharf.

Rebel soldiers crowded the sidewalks leading to the river. Travis, who wore his field uniform rather than his finery, exchanged cordial greetings with them.

"Pardon me, sir." A six-foot, auburn-haired Confederate soldier with an Irish brogue halted in front of him. "I've been watching ye. You seem a fair and reasonable man, one who will listen to me unusual request. Can ye spare me a moment?"

Travis eyed the man's open, honest face. No harm in obliging the stranger. "Of course."

His gaze darted to the score of men within five paces. "Will ye mind crossing the street?"

Travis followed his gaze toward a weeded lot empty of buildings and people. Perhaps the Confederate knew something about his comrades the Union should know. With a nod, Travis crossed the cobblestone lane and then turned to the soldier. Not many men were tall enough to look him straight in the eye. This man was even an inch or two taller. "Allow me to introduce myself. I'm First Lieutenant Travis Lawson of the Eighth Illinois."

"Private Luke Shea, formerly of the Twenty-First Mississippi." He stood at attention. "I was honorably discharged after flying shrapnel at the Battle of Fredericksburg left me with amnesia." He removed his kepi and touched a red mark on his hairline that would make a dandy scar. "To me shame, I didn't recognize Felicity Danielson, me own girl."

"I'm sorry." A sad tale, but how did this affect Travis? "Perhaps it's best you don't remember the battles. There are sights I'd prefer to forget." Too many to recount. "I'm certain that was difficult for your girl."

"Yes, especially considering what I remembered when the amnesia lifted." His direct gaze faltered to a foot-wide hole in the ground, a remnant of the recent battle.

Travis's interest was arrested. "What was that?"

"I had shot Jack Danielson, Felicity's brother." He lifted tormented brown eyes. "He immediately fell into the river. I saved him from drowning in frigid waters, but he was likely moved to Libby Prison after his wounds were attended."

"That didn't sit well with his sister, I'd wager." He'd heard of brothers facing off in battle. This blasted war. He must trust that victories like the one here sped the end of hostilities.

"Nay. Fair broke her heart." And Luke's, too, from the pinched look on his face. "But she forgave me during the siege. We're betrothed." His expression brightened and then dimmed.

"Congratulations." The situation had ended well for everyone except the brother, but again, why was the man telling him all this? Rebel soldiers were to be paroled and then must await an exchange with a Union soldier before reentering the Confederate army. They'd be fed. They were allowed to roam free until formally paroled. Then they'd leave with three days of rations. What more could the man want? "What's your request?"

"I want to muster into the Union army after the exchange is final. Me loyalties were always with the Union."

He'd heard this after other battles—a sly way for spies to enlist. Yet the man seemed sincere.

"Me request is that I be exchanged for Union Private Jack Danielson. He served with a Michigan regiment. That's all I know." He straightened his shoulders. "Is that possible?"

Flabbergasted, Travis stared at Luke's tormented face. That exchange would release Jack from prison by the man who'd put him there. *Was* it possible?

~

Savannah held her breath while Tex, Micah, and James took gingerly bites of the blackened corn muffins she'd prepared. A pure guess of equal parts cornmeal and water was the best she could do. Was it enough?

Micah coughed hard and grabbed his stomach.

"Not bad." Tex took a long swallow of coffee. "Fellas, coffee takes care of the dryness. Thanks, Miss Savannah."

"My pleasure." Too dry. She forced a smile. No mention of

the charred exterior. They'd likely eaten worse in camp. Perhaps she could do something with the sack of dried corn. A vague memory of her cook soaking dried corn and beans warned that some preparations was necessary before cooking.

Who was she fooling? She and Mama were woefully ill-equipped to cook. They needed help.

Worse, Peter, her soldier who'd been shot in the waist, writhed on his pallet, twisting the blanket underneath. Nick's arm wound made him feverish. Sweat poured down his face. He talked in his sleep, yet his words made no sense.

These men needed a doctor. Savannah's friend Felicity Danielson was a nurse. Perhaps she'd also be interested in a job as cook or maid.

Savannah would walk to the Beltzer home where Felicity resided with her aunt and uncle this morning.

Heavy footsteps thudded up the walk.

Savannah caught her breath. More thieves?

The door opened without a pretense of a knock. Glancing at Tex, she steeled herself.

Tex put down his cup.

"Lila? Savannah? Are you unharmed?"

She sagged against the back of a sofa. At last. "In here, Papa."

∼

*F*ascinated by Luke Shea's request, Travis spent another half hour with him, long enough to take the measure of the man. He'd taken on the responsibility of Ashburn Mitchell's saddle shop and home when Ash and his bride moved to Texas. Luke presented himself as honest and loyal to the Union. To prove it, he and Felicity planned to sign the oath of allegiance that very day.

He advised Luke to sign the document and then find him

later in the afternoon. Travis wanted to discuss the matter with Brian, who was back at camp. It was doubtful his captain had encountered such a request from a Rebel private.

Verifying that Luke and Felicity took the oath would be an easy matter. Some citizens must have been silent Unionists because others had already signed. As time went on, that loyalty would reap benefits not offered to everyone—such as the ability to operate a business.

Travis trudged up the hill with a swipe at his brow. Farming relatively level fields throughout his childhood hadn't trained him to climb this bluff several times daily. He'd best get accustomed to it. This city needed a lot of aid. He'd wager that healing was a long way off.

A score or more of black men with families sat on a wide porch outside a two-story brick building with boarded windows as Travis approached a corner. "I'm First Lieutenant Travis Lawson. Any of you men want a job?"

Several men stood, eyeing him curiously.

"A paying job?" One man with a smattering of gray in his black hair descended brick steps.

"That's right. You'd be trained as soldiers in the Union army." His heart lightened at the hope in the man's eyes.

"What will we do?"

"You'll do tasks of a soldier—drilling, cleaning the town, building fortifications, picket duty, and police duty. Oh, and you'll have some schooling."

The spokesman who might be about ten years Travis's senior turned back to his friends.

"You'll be trained in a camp outside the city. General Grant can use all of you." He'd learned that most folks recognized his general's name. Unfortunately, Travis was talking to the man's back.

After a whispered conversation, the man faced Travis.

"What about my son, George?" He placed an arm around a boy not fully grown.

Travis studied him. He might be malnourished or small for his age. "How old are you, George?"

"Sixteen, suh." The boy didn't meet his eyes.

Even if George hadn't reached that age, his family surely needed his pay. And he had his father's consent. "George can come as well. Follow me, men."

CHAPTER 5

$\mathcal{A}$fter hugging her father, Savannah acquiesced to his insistence to be introduced to his guests. The gracious Southern hospitality with which he greeted each soldier in turn went a long way to restoring her sense of normalcy. Not *everything* had changed.

But Mama didn't know that Papa was here. After he had welcomed the men to his home, she tugged on his hand. "Mama has been worried for you."

"As I have for both of you." With a final nod at the soldiers, they left the parlor. "Take me to her."

"I believe she's in the kitchen." Savannah followed his long strides down the long hall.

"Lila? Where are you?" His pace quickened.

"Arthur?" Mama poked her head out of the kitchen. Gasping, she hurled herself into his arms. "Where have you been? We were so worried about you." Retaining her hold on his waist, she tipped her head to study his dear face.

He kissed her cheek. "I was in Mississippi Springs at Harold Calhoun's plantation when the Union army attacked Raymond in May. We all fled to his daughter's home in Tougaloo."

"Why didn't you come to us? We had to shelter in that horrid cave." Her arms fell to her sides.

"It wasn't safe to do so. I'm sorry." His brown eyes darkened. "I came as soon as I could."

"What of your search for new clients?" She stepped back.

"Brace yourself. There are no clients, new or old." He shook his head. "All the cotton bales that weren't destroyed by the owners' own hands will be stolen from them. Plantation homes all across the state continue to be looted by Yankees."

Mama's face turned ashen.

Heart thudding at the dreadful news, Savannah rushed to her side. "We will make it somehow, Mama."

"I will take care of you, Lila. Just like always." Papa peered around him at the still-dusty hall. "But first, I must learn the damages we sustained."

Since Mama seemed too shaken by her father's loss of a job to speak, Savannah took charge. "All the windows are broken. You've already seen the front parlor. We may as well get the worst out of the way." She led the way to the front of the mansion.

Papa sucked in his breath as he entered the formal dining room. "This place has seen better days."

An understatement. Savannah followed her father's concerned gaze to the foot-wide holes in the ceiling and floor. The cannonball had fallen in front of the buffet and to the right of a pair of mahogany cabinets empty of the family's fine china that had been packed in barrels of sawdust. Layers of dust hid the rich hues of their mahogany table that comfortably seated twenty-four. Mama had often doubled that number for their annual Christmas ball. The thousands of guests they'd entertained over the years would not find a glimmer of the room's former beauty.

Mama stared up at the ceiling, patting her errant blond wisps of hair with shaking fingers.

Savannah grimaced over the fact that she'd botched Mama's hairstyle on the day that Papa arrived. Mama always strove to look her best for him, just as Savannah had once done for Willie.

"The shell pierced the roof, the attic floor, a second-floor guest bedroom, this dining room, and went through to the cellar?" He turned a chagrined gaze at his wife.

"Yes." Mama wrung her hands. "Ollie and Samuel patched the roof in between mortar attacks."

"I suppose it wasn't safe for Ollie and Samuel to begin repairs in here?" Resting his right elbow on his left hand, he tapped his chin as he surveyed the damage.

"Ships sent a barrage of mortar upon our city," Mama whispered. "We were terrified."

"It wasn't safe to be inside during the attack." Savannah placed a calming hand on Mama's tense arm.

"What about when they ended?"

Savannah dreaded telling him that everyone had deserted them.

"Carrying our furniture in from the shelter kept them busy while the others cleaned up the glass. As it was, Ellen had been back and forth to tend the wounded for a week." Mama glanced at Savannah as if pleading with her to deliver the news.

"We were all out on the street giving dippers of cold water to our soldiers entering the city on Surrender Day. They were even hungrier than the citizens." Savannah shuddered to recall her first sight of the emaciated men. "When the Yankees marched into town, a man named Lieutenant Travis Lawson told Ollie he was free. They all left." Including Ellen, who'd been a shoulder to lean on when her parents weren't getting along.

"One could hardly miss the large numbers of fugitives among the Confederate soldiers milling about our city." He ran his fingers through thick brown hair and graying temples. "I reckon they are no longer fugitives but free."

"What are we to do?" Mama wrung her hands.

"I'll finish inspecting our property." He stared out the broken window. "Then we can all take a stroll. Let's learn the changes the victorious army is making to our beloved Vicksburg."

Savannah would keep the soldiers' thefts to herself for now. Papa had received enough shocks.

She had too. The loss of his job impacted them all. What would he do? Surely, he wouldn't leave them again. They needed not only his financial support but also his emotional support.

～

*T*ravis dropped off his second group of recruits to Colonel Henry Lieb before noon. There was quite a crowd of new soldiers gathered on the yard outside the courthouse.

"How many in this bunch, Lieutenant Lawson?" The clean-shaven thirty-year-old colonel eyed the black men who followed Travis into the courthouse yard.

"Twenty-eight, sir." He felt good about that number and about the willingness of the men who'd soon muster into the army.

"Very good." Colonel Lieb wrote the number on a pad. "Any sign of looting?"

"None at all, sir." Thank heavens. Travis had been humiliated by the poor conduct yesterday.

"Freedmen are coming in from nearby plantations. It will soon be difficult for them to find a place to stay." The man of medium height exuded authority. "Escort these men to the training camp and then keep recruiting. Plenty will want jobs."

"Yes, sir." Travis saluted.

Everyone he had approached so far had seemed happy to become a soldier. After explaining where they were going, he led the way out of town.

He'd make Savannah's house his first destination upon his return. He hoped there hadn't been any looting at her house yesterday.

The possibility she might need his help quickened his step. His protective attitude toward the feisty woman surprised him. Was it due to the absence of her father?

Best not to probe those feelings.

~

Savannah walked the congested sidewalks with her parents. Mama strolled with her hand on Papa's arm, holding an ivory parasol. They nodded greetings to many of the hundreds of captured Confederate soldiers they passed. Savannah was thankful not to recognize any of the guards patrolling today because Papa and Mama had dealt with enough unpleasant surprises of late.

Before they left, they had walked the length of their formerly beautifully terraced yard, studying the fragrant orchard on the left and what remained of the pathetic flower garden on the right. Two craters in the beds had sent dirt splattering over the flowers not directly struck. Red petals from her favorite roses sprinkled along the flower bed. None had survived flying shrapnel and clods of dirt. Nor had the snapdragons.

She ignored the gaping doorway of the shelter she'd come to hate. What had been an oasis during the attacks had become an eyesore. Papa had gone inside alone. His only comment upon exiting was that it should be filled in as soon as may be, a sentiment Savannah shared.

Sorrow had filled her soul to meander along imbedded stones to each successive level of the peach, apple, pear, and plum orchards where most trees had, at the least, splintered limbs that must now be pruned. One of the sets of stone stairs had a gaping hole.

Six trees lay on the ground. Artillery had damaged a score of others. The number of new holes of varying sizes that dotted the landscape brought home to Savannah how blessed they had been. Only one cannonball had struck their mansion. None had hit the cave shelter where they'd hidden for weeks. She hadn't prayed for God's protection—she wasn't in the habit of asking Him for anything of importance—but she was grateful all the same.

Now, strolling about the town, she assessed the destruction through her father's eyes. Some buildings lay in ruins. A few former residences resembled mounds of rubbish. Many showed signs of damage. Could bulging walls be repaired? Savannah couldn't find any unbroken windows.

Papa guided Mama around pits in the sidewalks larger than Savannah's dainty slippers. Surely, it was a matter of public safety that the Union army fill gaping craters in the streets.

"Papa, we're on Locust Street where Felicity lives." The Beltzers' black wrought-iron fence loomed ahead on the left. "I want to hire her to be our housekeeper or our cook."

"Good idea." Papa glanced at her over his shoulder. "I've been thinking of who we could hire for both positions. Felicity is also a nurse."

"Agreed." Mama tilted her parasol so that it shaded her eyes as she looked up at him.

Savannah had expected Papa's support. Mama had told her that as a child, he couldn't refuse Savannah. Yet she'd learned the hard way not to request big things from her father, and that had spilled over to not praying for important matters so long ago that it was entrenched in her soul.

"Their house seems to have weathered the attack better than most." Papa opened the gate to the two-story brick home for them and then led the way to the porch.

Mae Beltzer, Felicity's petite, red-haired aunt, answered Papa's knock. Surprise quickly melted into gracious welcome, and Savannah soon found herself seated in a small parlor with Mae's husband, Charles, daughter Petunia, and their young grandchildren, Wilma and Little Miles.

The only one missing was Felicity.

Savannah's parents, who knew the Beltzers through Savannah's friendship with Felicity, asked how they had fared through the siege.

"We lived in our shelter and came outside for breaths of fresh air when the gunboats rested their overheated cannons." Mrs. Beltzer glanced at her grandchildren, who took turns spinning a top on the rug. "Felicity felt she must help nurse patients during the lulls. We prayed repeatedly for her and for Luke."

"Luke Shea?" Papa asked.

"The same." Mr. Beltzer drummed his fingers against his chair arm. "He'd been pressed into service just before the battle despite being mustered out due to amnesia."

Mrs. Beltzer held up her hand. "His memories returned the very day the army insisted he serve for this one battle. He needed those prayers because the fighting was so fierce."

"Was he harmed?" Fanning herself, Mama leaned forward from the sofa where she sat by Papa.

"No, thank the Lord." Mrs. Beltzer clasped her hands. "And he and Felicity—"

"Dear, we should let them share the news." Mr. Beltzer gave a crisp nod.

What? Were Felicity and Luke betrothed at long last? Savannah scooted to the edge of her seat. "I'd love to talk to Felicity directly. Is she at the hospital?"

"No." The joy receded from Mrs. Beltzer's expression.

"Unfortunately, she and Luke are likely taking an oath of allegiance to the Union as we speak."

Anger shot through Savannah. How dare Felicity betray the South? She was a traitor, and Savannah couldn't hire her now. But what was she to do for the wounded men in her parlor? She'd have to seek out a harried, over-worked doctor and convince one to visit her home without delay.

~

$\mathscr{T}$ravis knocked on Savannah's door. The newest recruits were at camp. He'd come straight here without stopping for his noon meal, secretly hoping she'd invite him to pick an apple or a peach for his lunch.

A thin, lanky Confederate soldier with a ridge of red in his brown hair—a path made by a bullet, he'd wager—opened the door with a glare. "The Adairs aren't home, but me and my buddies are protecting her property. So you'd best move along."

Travis blinked at the verbal attack from a wounded man. "Say, fellow, no need for that tone. Surrender was final yesterday."

"And yesterday is when two Yank—er, Union soldiers filled their haversacks with fruit belonging to two defenseless women." His nostrils flared.

Thieves had been here too? He'd feared as much. "I'm sorry to hear that. Did they steal anything from the house?"

"No, Miss Savannah ran them off." His posture relaxed slightly.

"Good for her." A fellow had to admire such a courageous woman. Defenseless? Nope. Not the way Travis would describe her. "I'm First Lieutenant Travis Lawson of the Eighth Illinois, an acquaintance of Miss Adair's." Dare he call himself her friend? "Just stopping by to check on her."

The man hesitated a moment. "Private Tex Logue, Seventeenth Louisiana. There are five other wounded in this hospital." He clutched his head suddenly as though it pained him. "I'm glad you don't mean her any harm. I couldn't have fought you, anyway."

Compassion stirred for the man's pain along with admiration for his bravery. "Do you know when Miss Adair will return?"

"Her pa came home this morning. He met us soldiers. Gave us a fine welcome."

That was a welcome relief, but now that Mr. Adair was here, was there a reason for Travis to stop by?

"She and her parents took a walk to see the destruction in the city for themselves." The soldier rubbed his temples.

"Is there anything I can do for you?" Why did he offer to help this man? He had other orders. Yet one of them was to build good rapport between the army and city residents.

"Miss Savannah made corn muffins, but they're a bit burnt and dry. We need coffee to get them down. Do you know how to make it? I was going to do it, but my headache is making my stomach queasy."

"I will if I can have a cup too." Travis winked to lighten the atmosphere. He hadn't allowed himself even five minutes for lunch. This respite shouldn't hurt anything.

Tex grinned. "You'll have to build up the fire in the stove first. Kitchen's all the way down the hall." He pointed to the right of a grand staircase and then entered the parlor.

Travis strode back toward the kitchen. Perhaps this would soften Savannah's ire against the army, against him.

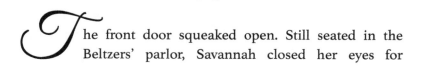

he front door squeaked open. Still seated in the Beltzers' parlor, Savannah closed her eyes for strength. Felicity must be back from her traitorous oath because the rest of the family was here in the parlor.

Felicity entered, followed by Luke. "Savannah, how good it is to see you." The blonde with shoulder-length ringlets rushed forward, hands outstretched. "I planned to visit today and see how your family fared."

"We escaped injury, as you see." Standing, Savannah briefly touched one of her friend's outstretched hands. "You wanted to make certain to declare loyalty to the North before checking on friends. I understand."

"So you know about our errand." Felicity's hands dropped to her side. She exchanged a look with the tall, thin man at her side.

He shook his head slightly.

"I'd only just mentioned it, dear." Mrs. Beltzer drew a deep breath.

Petunia glared at Felicity across the room. "I can't believe my own cousin is a traitor. Why, what will I tell Miles?" Her husband was fighting in Virginia for their beloved South.

"We all must make our own decisions about how we'll go forward." Mrs. Beltzer's lips tightened.

"Thank you, Aunt Mae." Felicity smiled tentatively. "Mr. Adair, I'm glad you made it back to the city unharmed. Mrs. Adair, it's always lovely to see you." Her gaze shifted to Savannah. "As it is you, my friend."

"Friends don't betray friends." Savannah narrowed her eyes at Luke. "Willie would be crushed by your actions. You've disgraced your uniform."

Felicity stiffened.

Mottled red on Luke's face battled against his hair. "Me disgraceful act will be atoned, if God answers me prayers."

"Savannah." Papa's mild tone cooled Savannah's temper. "We had another reason for stopping." He gave her a direct look. "You wanted to offer Felicity a job, remember?"

She blinked at him. He wanted to hire Felicity after her treachery?

"I'm interested." Petunia leaned forward. "Miles hasn't been receiving his pay as scheduled."

"One moment, please. We do have more than one position to fill." Though Petunia was a bit too ingratiating, perhaps she wouldn't mind serving as a maid. Savannah turned to Felicity, pushing back her hurt at her friends' betrayal. "Our front parlor is a makeshift hospital for six wounded Southerners. Ellen, our housekeeper, tended them the last week...before she left. Mama and I are woefully inadequate at cooking and cleaning. Felicity, will you work for us?"

"I need a job." Felicity glanced at Luke, who nodded. "But I still volunteer at the hospital. I can't nurse those men and serve also as cook, housekeeper, and maid." She turned to Mrs. Beltzer. "Since Uncle Charles lost his job at the foundry, do you want to cook for the Adairs, Aunt Mae?"

She laid a hand on her husband's sleeve in unspoken inquiry. At his relieved smile, she leaned forward. "Nothing would please me more."

"I can nurse the men daily and perhaps perform housekeeping duties as time allows." Remnants of the hurtful words shadowed Felicity's blue eyes.

"And I'll serve as maid." Petunia's triumphant tone cut across Savannah's guilt at lashing out at her friend.

"Very well, but if Ellen returns, her job as housekeeper will be restored." She'd already offered it to her. After Petunia nodded her agreement, Savannah looked to her father. "Papa? Can we afford three salaries?" He had lost his job. No telling when he'd find another with all the folks pouring into Vicksburg in need of work.

"Certainly, my dear." His expression clouded.

Was it too great an expense? Mama had said Papa never refused his daughter's requests.

"I'll have to bring my children with me." Petunia's shoulders relaxed.

"That's fine." Not ideal. They would be a distraction for their mother. "Josie may return when her mother does. We'll only require your services three days weekly until then," Savannah told Felicity's cousin.

"I'll come with you to see about the wounded." Felicity turned to Luke. "When is your meeting with First Lieutenant Lawson?"

Travis? Savannah's head reeled.

"Not until later, so I'll escort you to the Adairs'." Sighing, Luke looked around the room. "You all may as well know. Looters broke into Ash's saddle shop yesterday. Thieves stole all me saddles. The skins to make new ones as well—at least, the ones that weren't hidden. The destruction wreaked during the thievery was unnecessary. I'll begin repairs tomorrow while waiting for my parole."

Despite her lingering hurt over Luke's betrayal of the South, the needless ruin stirred Savannah's compassion. It was something he could ill afford.

Still, he could return to saddle-making once he got out of the army. That option wasn't open for her father.

The bigger mystery here was Luke's upcoming meeting with Travis. Did he expect reparation for his losses, or was there more to it?

CHAPTER 6

*L*ate the same afternoon he had visited Savannah's house, Travis was back in the city after escorting another group of new recruits to the training camp. The heat had sapped his energy. If not for his meeting with Luke, he'd have gone straight to his camp for an early supper. Coffee hadn't been an adequate lunch.

He regretted not getting to see Savannah earlier. Too bad he hadn't been the one to catch the thieves on her property. He'd try to see her tomorrow to smooth things over.

He exchanged nods with a Southern gentleman with an expensive watch fob. The overdressed man in gray trousers and coat contrasting with a burgundy vest seemed perfectly at ease, pausing often to speak with Confederate soldiers.

Armed police perused those on the sidewalks as Travis reached the courthouse lawn. The Union officers involved in recruitment were gone—presumably to their suppers. He scanned the abundance of gray-coated men outside the city's most impressive landmark.

"Lieutenant Lawson?"

Travis spun around at Luke's Irish lilt. "Yes, Luke, I was just looking for you. Did you see to the matter we discussed?"

"Yes, sir. Both me and me girl swore our allegiance." His jaw set. "Is it possible for me to be exchanged directly for Private Jack Danielson?"

"That remains to be seen. You've started the process by following through on your promise." But the decision wasn't his to make. He would, however, do all he could. "I will speak with my captain this evening."

"Thank you, sir." He hesitated. "Felicity's friend, Savannah Adair, knows of our meeting but not the reason. Should I keep our discussions private?"

So Luke and his fiancé knew Savannah. He probably should not be surprised because they were all citizens of a city that was much smaller than Travis's hometown. He was pleased to discover another connection with her. "Absolutely. You can tell whomever you choose *after* the exchange. It's likely Jack's Southern friends won't be happy about his Northern loyalties. I'd advise caution."

Luke nodded. "As I thought."

"Nothing can be done until you're paroled, but processing over thirty thousand Confederates won't be a quick matter."

Luke swallowed. "How long do you estimate, sir?"

"A week or more is my guess." General Grant wanted the men paroled and out of the city as quickly as possible to minimize discord.

Even as they spoke, one of the newly armed groups of patrolmen meandered past the courthouse, eying the soldiers. One glared at the Rebels as if daring them to cause trouble.

Yes, Travis agreed with his general on this one. The sooner these soldiers left the city, the better.

∽

*a*n hour after Savannah reluctantly hired her friend to nurse her wounded soldiers, the aroma of freshly roasted coffee beans wafted into the parlor where she sat at a table writing Felicity's notes about the patients. Felicity had requested they all refer to one another by their given names to identify the men more quickly. She'd already noted that Caleb couldn't stand even a gentle touch on his shoulder and his fever was high.

Petunia was cleaning the front half of the long parlor. Savannah had urged her to confine Wilma and Little Miles away from the sick room in the kitchen with Mrs. Beltzer. Dust clouds hung in the parlor where Petunia applied her duster to the furniture with gusto.

Papa had chosen to stay behind with Charles Beltzer, and he'd said not to expect his return until evening. Luke had left for a meeting with Travis, the reason for which Felicity had refused to divulge.

"Peter, no one has tried to remove the bullet in your abdomen." On her knees, Felicity studied the large, blood-stained bandage that his tattered shirt didn't hide.

The emaciated Alabamian shook his head. "There was no room at the field hospitals, so the ambulance brought me here with everyone you see. Ellen was first to bandage my wound. She couldn't feel the metal, so she left it alone."

"That must be removed as soon as possible." Felicity touched his forehead. She looked at Savannah. "Feverish." She moved to James, who'd been shot in the leg.

Savannah sneezed. "Petunia, please work in another room today." Savannah had never realized how much work her servants accomplished daily. Petunia left, and Savannah returned her attention to James.

"Ellen said the bullet went clean through." James, the tall Tennessean, slumped against the wall, his leg stretched on his blanket pallet. "You don't think I'll lose my leg, do you?" His brow furrowed. "My wife, Charlotte, needs my pay. We have a three-year-old."

Felicity shook her head. "I had another patient with a similar wound. Let's be diligent to keep the wound clean and change your bandages often."

Savannah made a note.

Nick began muttering in his sleep.

Felicity hurried to his side. "He's feverish." She probed his arm, and he opened his eyes. "Not good, I'm afraid." She bit her lip.

Nick's eyes widened. He gave his head a tiny shake. "It can be saved, right?"

"I'd say, that arm will have to come off." Tex stared at his buddy from a high-backed, cushioned chair.

"No! I'm keeping my arm." Nick thrashed his good arm against his blanket.

Tex dropped to his knees beside Nick. "Calm yourself. You'll live. That's the important thing."

"No one is doing anything right now." Felicity frowned at Tex and then turned her attention to Nick. "I'm simply a nurse. The doctor will want to evaluate your wound." She clasped his good hand. "We're going to get you the care you need."

"Thank you." Nick's body sagged against his pallet.

Savannah released a breath she hadn't realized she'd been holding. She made a note about obtaining a doctor for Nick immediately. Once Nick calmed, Tex returned to his chair. Clutching his head, he closed his eyes.

"I will fetch you some quinine from the hospital for that headache, Tex." Felicity knelt beside Micah. "Have you been able to eat?"

"Some. I'm hungry now."

Felicity smiled. "My aunt is making you supper." Straightening, she motioned for Savannah to follow her into the hall.

"What's wrong?" Savannah asked once they were out of earshot of the men.

Felicity pressed her hands against her face. "You were right to bring me here. Peter, Caleb, and Nick need a doctor. I think the others will recover nicely under my care. Is there any way to move the three who require a doctor's care to a bedroom?"

"No. My apologies. You know of Mama's fainting spells." It was difficult enough to keep them from Mama's sight as it was.

"Yes, I'd forgotten." Felicity glanced back in the sickroom. "I hate to leave them to fetch Dr. Watkins..."

"Is he at City Hospital?" Long weeks of inactivity in their cave had fueled Savannah with nervous energy.

She nodded. "He's been leaving a note in the nurses' room when he goes to one of the tent hospitals so we can find him."

"I'll go now and fetch him." Guilt gnawed at Savannah's chest, making it difficult to breathe. Had she waited too long to obtain medical care for the men? If anything happened to them, it would be on her.

~

*T*ravis's second day in the city was finally done. Perhaps he could find a battle souvenir that no one else would want. A slight delay in his supper was worth a short search. Instead of walking east toward his camp, he headed toward the middle of town.

A chunk of shrapnel protruded from a brick amongst a building's rubble. He picked it up. Bill, his sixteen-year-old brother, would love this war artifact. Mama had somehow extracted a promise from his brother not to muster in until he turned seventeen next spring. Travis prayed the war would end before then but had his doubts.

"You're not joining in the thievery, are you, Lieutenant?"

He spun around. Savannah stood on a jutted portion of

sidewalk with her hands on her hips. Travis scoffed. "Do you really believe this damaged brick will be used for repairs?"

She studied it. "Keep it. Though I wish I'd had a weapon to scare off two of your soldiers when they stole fruit from our property."

"Tex told me. Sorry about that. The situation got out of hand."

She sighed. "At least we agree on that. I'd like to know who was to blame."

"It's impossible to know who the culprits were." There had been over seventy thousand Union troops in Vicksburg for the victory—well, thousands less because General Sherman had left with his men for Jackson that day to take it back. Still, with tens of thousands in the city, Travis would be unable to find two men who'd sought to satisfy their hunger.

"Tex told me you stopped by and made coffee for them. I'm obliged to you. I took a stroll with my parents. We were gone longer than we anticipated." Her confidence seemed to waver.

"Is there a problem?" He took a step closer.

"I hired my friend, Felicity Danielson, to nurse our soldiers." She averted her eyes. "Three of them need a doctor's care immediately. I'm on my way to the hospital to fetch Dr. Watkins."

"I'll escort you." There were too many strangers about for him to feel good about leaving her. His supper could wait a while longer.

~

*A*s luck would have it, Travis didn't return to camp until eight that evening. Savannah seemed concerned for her wounded, so he lent his support and accompanied her back to her home after fetching the doctor. While waiting for the doctor to examine the patients, he'd briefly met Mr. Adair, the gracious Southern gentleman Travis had spotted on the street earlier, talking with soldiers. Then Mrs. Beltzer, the cook, noticed Travis and offered him a bowl of corn pudding, which Savannah whisked him away from before it was half gone. Dr. Watkins had been so concerned about one of the patients, Nick Farmer, that the physician wanted him transported to the hospital immediately.

Savannah's family owned three vehicles large enough to accommodate the patient, but all of the family's horses had long since been given to the Confederacy. The doctor recruited three idle Confederate soldiers to help Travis carry Nick on a blanket stretcher while Dr. Watkins went on ahead, clearing a path among the hundreds crowding the sidewalks like Moses parting the Red Sea.

As Travis finally returned to the rows of ecru tents lit by lanterns in his camp and the welcoming aroma of bacon sizzling on a myriad of cooking fires, his arms and his back ached and he wanted nothing more than to sleep on his cot. Yet the day's tasks weren't finished.

He found Brian in his tent, penning notes at his camp desk. After explaining Luke's strange dilemma, he sat on his friend's cot and waited.

"Am I to understand that he shot his future brother-in-law and then saved him from drowning while dodging bullets himself?" Brian stared at him incredulously.

"A courageous man, for certain. He gave a few more details in our second conversation." Travis resisted the urge to rub his aching back.

Brian whistled. "Do you trust him?"

"I do. I want him in our regiment."

"Agreed." Brian stroked his bearded chin. "I'll talk to Colonel Haversham in the morning. The colonel has established headquarters in a vacant Vicksburg home."

Travis bit back his disapproval. He was accustomed to the

practice of commandeering homes as headquarters, and it often didn't matter if the owner agreed to the arrangement. The army paid rent to the family—though in this case, the home was empty. Hopefully, no one would try to take over Savannah's home, or there'd be fireworks of a different kind than they'd seen last night.

"We'll make inquiries to discover if Private Danielson is in Libby Prison."

"Luke isn't certain. It's what he was told the night it happened." Travis struggled with his own guilt—only, his was for Uncle Dabney.

"Travis? Did you hear me?"

"What? My apologies." Travis shook his head to clear it. Being in Mississippi had brought his guilt to the forefront. "What did you say?"

"I hope the colonel will want to pursue this. It's common to exchange specific officers—say, a Union captain for a Confederate captain." Frowning, Brian tapped his pencil against his record book. "Less common for privates."

"I'm obliged to you for looking into the matter." Travis stood. "I'll be in bed before 'Taps' is played...unless you need something else?"

"Not me. Get some rest. Tomorrow will be another long one. Same orders as today. The colonel has asked that you continue to be one of the officers on patrol to maintain peace until the Rebels are paroled...unless I need you. I won't tomorrow. Leave for town after you take roll call and set up the day's picket duty."

Back in his tent, thoughts of that last night he'd seen Uncle Dabney alive robbed him of much-needed sleep. He turned on his side as the haunting melody of "Taps" filled the air. Details of that evening swirled in his head.

"I'm sorry, Uncle Dabney. If only I'd gone with you..."

Travis had been twelve on that day that had started out like so many others on the three-hundred-acre farm Pa and his uncle shared equally—except Uncle Dabney was sick. He hadn't shown up to plant beans the whole day but didn't like a fuss made when he was sick. Travis's mama had compromised by sending Travis with a plate of food at dusk...

⁓

*T*ravis strode across the fields to the other side of the farm, where his bachelor uncle's cabin, large barn, and outbuildings nestled in the woods. As usual, he entered the spacious, one-room home without knocking.

And stopped short.

Uncle Dabney wasn't resting in bed. Rather, with no sign of his uncle, two black men stuffed food into a potato sack. One was taller than Travis's six-foot pa. The other wasn't much taller than Travis. Both froze.

Strangers stealing food? "Uncle Dabney!" He must be in the barn. "Thieves!" Travis backed out the door, ready to flee.

Running footsteps approached from the barn. Travis swung around, relieved to spot his uncle closing in on the wooden porch. Alas, he didn't have his musket because why would he need it to milk the cows?

"Travis, be quiet," Uncle Dabney practically hissed, his floppy hat eschew over his shoulder-length brown hair as he leaped on the porch. "I gave them that food for their journey. You can't tell anybody you saw them." His dark brows lowered. "Nobody."

That meant his gossipy ma, most of all. He followed his uncle inside and set the plate on the table. The men continued to fill their sacks while keeping an eye on Travis. "Who are they?" The tall one wore a red-checked shirt that looked an awful lot like one of his uncle's under black suspenders. Both were barefoot.

"Runaways from a cotton plantation down south." His uncle swiped sweat from his grimy brow with the back of his sleeve. He looked more worried than sick. "Not the first to come through here from Mississippi. Many overseers there believe in using the whip."

"Yep, they do." The short fugitive peered out the open front door. "They're on our trail. Don't know how since we stowed away on a ship 'til it stopped in St. Louis."

"They'll not take me alive." The tall one's husky voice crackled as if from lack of use. They resumed putting handfuls of dried beans and corn in their sack.

"No one will find you." Uncle Dabney piled a stack of blankets from a cane chair onto Travis's arms and then grabbed a sack of seed corn. "I'll go finish getting the wagon hitched to take you to the next stop."

Next stop? "Are you running a station on the Underground Railroad?" He'd heard the route for runaway slaves mentioned at school. His teacher, Miss Flanigan, professed a special admiration for heroes who helped the fugitives. One look at his uncle's serious expression made an answer unnecessary. "Where's the next home? Can I come?"

"No. Your pa would skin me alive for putting you in danger." His uncle tossed a pound of coffee onto the table. "Add this to your sack."

He was probably right. Pa was as serious as his brother was fun-loving. Only tonight, Uncle Dabney acted more like Pa.

"Forget you saw anything. Never mention it to anyone." Uncle Dabney dropped the sack. He placed a firm hand on Travis's shoulder. "Because of the new law, not only the runaways are in danger. You hear me?"

"Yep." The men giving chase weren't friendly. He'd witnessed that himself in town once when a sheriff roughed up a fugitive as he hauled him into a wagon for a journey south. Besides that, the Fugitive Slave Act of 1850 passed last year required citizens to turn in runaways. Miss Flanigan had said folks who helped the fugitives could be jailed for six months and fined one thousand dollars—and neither Pa nor Uncle Dabney possessed such a fortune. "I can keep my mouth shut."

"Good."

"Is there anything I can do?" What he really wanted to do was go with his uncle. Someday, he would.

"How about if you hitch Sal and Pete to the wagon for me, but leave it inside the barn." He peered out the window at nearly full darkness. "We'll leave in a quarter hour."

At least it was something. Travis did as he was bid. The first stars were out when the men joined him at the entrance. "How far are you going?"

"Can't tell you." His uncle lifted up a bottom slat that Travis had never noticed in the wagon bed. "This is where you'll ride, men. Keep your bag with you."

They climbed into the hidden compartment without a word. Uncle Dabney replaced the slat, arranged an armful of hay over the top of the wagon bed, and then tossed in the blankets and a sack. The men were well concealed with the hay and supplies over their hiding place.

"How long had this been going on?" Travis asked.

"No details." Uncle Dabney shook his head. "We'll save explanations for another day."

Travis would be hounding him for answers until he learned the truth. "Will you be back for breakfast?"

"Sure will. Feeling a sight better." With a wink, he climbed onto the seat. "I'll tell your ma it was on account of the supper she sent."

Travis returned his cheerful wave and then picked his way over tender plants by the light of the moon with the empty plate.

When his uncle failed to come for breakfast, Pa took him a plate this time—only, his brother wasn't there. The wagon and team were gone. Pa went into town looking for him. No one had seen him. His pa then questioned Travis, who agonized over telling his parents what he knew. After all, he'd made a promise. Yet he was the last person to see Uncle Dabney, and maybe they could help him. He told his pa everything and asked him to keep it from Ma. He cautioned Pa about the terrible law and learned he already knew all about it. Pa continued to search while keeping the details from Ma.

The empty wagon was found with a busted wheel two weeks later beside a creek twenty miles north. The rifle the family kept stored under the seat was gone. Three bullet holes and blood stains marked the seat and bed. For a month, Pa had delayed spring planting scouring the woods near the abandoned wagon. Travis searched with his pa, fear for his uncle turning to dread that they would find him murdered.

They never found him.

~

For the next year, Travis had lived with the fear that the person who had killed his uncle would turn on his pa...maybe his ma, little brother, and three sisters too. It sharpened his senses, strengthened his protective instincts.

It had also fostered a deep hatred for slavery. When the War Between the States started, he was the first among his peers to sign up. This was finally an opportunity to do something significant toward ridding his country of the evil.

He did it for Uncle Dabney.

Yet even now, tossing and turning on his cot outside the biggest prize General Grant and President Lincoln wanted in Mississippi, Travis's deepest regret was that he hadn't gone with his uncle. He could have driven the wagon while Uncle Dabney shot at his pursuers and then reloaded.

Or Travis might have been killed with him.

But they didn't *know* Uncle Dabney had died. His grandparents had held out hope he'd return until their deaths. It had been a dozen years since that terrible night. Uncle Dabney's disappearance had cast a shadow over the family none could shake.

Least of all Travis.

CHAPTER 7

*S*avannah hurried to the hospital to discover Nick's condition after breakfast the next morning. Papa had been quiet throughout the meal they'd shared with Felicity, Mae Beltzer, Petunia and her children in the Adairs' smaller dining room, which was located opposite Papa's study in a hallway behind the stairs. He'd gone out while Felicity spoke to Savannah of her concern for Nick Farmer. Savannah had offered to obtain an update on his condition and report back.

Thousands of Southern soldiers milled about the streets. Some were still sleeping on porches and in abandoned yards at half-past eight.

How was it that she had passed hundreds of folks on this street without spotting one familiar face? Not even Travis, who seemed to be everywhere.

She caught the eye of a huskily built Southern soldier with a close-cropped beard and brown hair that could best be described as a curly mop. Averting her eyes, she quickened her pace, hoping the stranger leaning against a brick building wouldn't try to speak to her.

"Morning, miss." The soldier briefly raised his kepi as he approached.

This man hadn't been introduced to her. She started to go around him, and he sidestepped to prevent it. Outraged, she met his eyes squarely. "Please allow me to pass, sir, or I shall call the guards." Of which there were none around.

"Pardon me, Miss Adair. I'll just take a minute of your time."

He knew her name? She glanced around. Other than a few curious looks, no one seemed concerned. "How do you know me?"

"I saw you giving that Yankee lieutenant what for the day of surrender. I made inquiries." He gestured to a grassy yard beside the building where he'd lounged moments before. "I'm Sergeant Sam Epley. Thought you might want to help us Southerners."

The area he pointed out was a mere five paces off the side-walk, public enough to protect her. She led the way, wrinkling her nose at the smell. Flies swarmed around the carcass of a dead dog at the edge of the building. "What is it you need?"

"You get right to the point, just like I figured you would." He lowered his voice so that she had to lean closer to hear. "I saw that lieutenant was at your house twice yesterday. That's got to gall a fine Southern lady as yourself."

"Lieutenant Lawson has assisted me in various ways. I've been grateful."

"Not grateful enough to turn on our beloved South?" He cocked an eyebrow.

Anger shot through her at his presumption. "Certainly not."

The sergeant widened his stance. "Good, because we figure on taking back the city."

Shock jolted her body, searing like a bolt of lightning. "You're not resigned to losing our beloved Vicksburg?" For the first time since the soldiers took over, hope stirred for her city.

"Not by a long shot." He thrust out his chest. "We'll have to bide our time...wait until we're paroled and out of the city for a time. Long enough most of these Yankees head to battles in other parts. They'll think they've got the upper hand. But we'll be here."

"'We'? How many feel as you do?" She held her breath. Perhaps all was not lost, after all. Not with brave men like this sergeant willing to take the city by force.

"Enough to make it hot for the Yankees who stick around." His jaw set. "You can help."

"How?" Seemed risky. She raised her gaze to the building beyond his shoulders. Part of the wall was missing. The destruction caused by Grant's army would require months—even years—to repair. And then to waltz in as though they owned the town. Heat that had nothing to do with the blazing sun coursed through her.

He shook his head. "No details yet. Just think about whether you want to aid us. We'll talk again soon. I'll find you once things are in place." He stepped around her and blended into the crowd within moments.

Savannah stepped back onto the sidewalk, her thoughts chaotic. What were these *details* on which he refused to elaborate?

~

*T*arnished memories had kept Travis awake long after "Taps" was played. Bleary eyes and body aches hadn't stopped him from performing his duties in the past, and they wouldn't stop him today. His regiment—along with many others—was again scouring the battlefield for the dead, and Travis was back in town on the lookout for trouble from Confederate prisoners.

His senses sharpened as he strode toward the river. An uneasy atmosphere prevailed between a group of enemy soldiers and Union soldiers who seemed to be squaring off with one another. Something was said that Travis couldn't hear. A taunt, judging from the expression on the Rebel soldier's face to whom the comment was directed. He swung his fist, knocking the Union private into his buddies, who prevented his fall.

When the husky, red-bearded Northerner lunged at his attacker, Travis broke into a run. "Halt!"

Punches continued to fly between the two men. Friends shouted encouragement to both aggressors. This could escalate into a brawl. Where were the provost guards? The new police guards?

Removing his sidearm, Travis shot into the air.

Everyone froze.

"Stop where you are." Travis held the smoking gun pointed to the ground. "Anyone here want to end up in jail?"

Men from both sides backed away.

"Federal soldiers, return to camp." He didn't know the privates or their duties, but *his* orders were to maintain peace. Everyone began to disperse.

Travis turned his head at commotion behind him. One of the new police squads rushed down the hill. The watching crowd scattered, but a few Confederates weren't as lucky. Without seeking explanations, the black guards hauled them at rifle point toward the jail. Those rifles shouldn't be the only thing doing the talking for the guards. An uneasy atmosphere descended on those watching.

Although Travis outranked the guards, he didn't intervene, deeming it best instead to talk to their superior officers. Their duties were too new, the men too green, to know how they'd react. It could make the situation worse.

General Grant wanted the black soldiers to aid the rest of the army's efforts in building fortifications around the city, guarding Union lines, and policing the streets. Travis didn't want to gainsay his general but foresaw problems ahead if the new guards abused their power.

~

Savannah, still shaken by her conversation with Sergeant Epley and the news that Nick had refused Dr. Watkins's counsel for amputation, returned home to find her parents waiting for her on the portico.

"Let's talk in the upstairs parlor, Savannah." Papa held open their front door.

"It's still full of glass, Arthur." Mama led the way inside. "Petunia has two guest bedrooms cleaned. I've asked her to come daily, Savannah, until all rooms have received her attention."

"My study and library have also been ignored." Papa frowned. "We'll talk in the family dining room."

"I will ask her to tend to both of those next." Mama pursed her lips.

Savannah's stomach tensed, as it always did when her parents spoke to one another with veiled displeasure, but there was something else concerning her father. He wanted privacy for this conversation. What had he learned on his jaunts about the city?

They settled around the table in their usual spots with her parents at either end and Savannah in the middle. Two cherry wood cupboards in the room were empty of the dishes still packed away along with the silver. The flowers that normally graced the centerpiece were absent. Savannah missed the rose bouquet's fragrance as much as the beautiful arrangements.

"I'm concerned about what's happening. The Union army is making sweeping changes in our city. Our citizens must apply to do business. Permits are dependent upon Union loyalty." Papa laid his palms flat against the cherry table as if bracing himself. "Everyone must sign the oath of allegiance to the Union to receive a permit. Soon that oath will be required to receive rations and other necessities. Difficulties will increase for anyone they deem disloyal."

Those scalawags. It wasn't enough to shell the city, force surrender on them after laying a siege that nearly starved them, and then arm freedmen to police them. Must they impose themselves on every aspect of life?

"Felicity and Luke showed great wisdom in signing the oath." He hesitated. "This morning, I did the same."

"What?" Mama's eyes flashed. "Arthur, tell me you're joking."

"It's done." He tapped his fingers together. "I did it to smooth the path for my family. And I want you both to sign it as well. I will accompany you for support."

"This enemy has overtaken our city." Mama clutched her arms to her chest. "How can you ask it of us?"

Savannah wanted to add her protest, but the words died in her throat. She'd long ago stopped asking Papa for anything of importance. Her experience with Mary Grace had taught her that lesson.

"I ask because it's the only way." Papa straightened his shoulders. "Brace yourself because there's more."

What more could the Federals steal from them? Savannah steeled herself.

"Tell us all." Mama's back straightened.

"In the past, I've supported this family as cotton broker and done quite well."

"Yes, Arthur. You've always taken care of us." Mama stared at him as if waiting for an anvil to fall.

"You've provided everything we need, Papa." He'd earned his commissions by traveling with the cotton he represented to New Orleans or Mobile to negotiate sales. That meant he was often away from home. Since New Orleans had surrendered last year, Mobile was the only option. But that didn't matter if he switched jobs.

"I visited all my old customers—and new plantations too—in recent months, but they had little to sell. As I told you upon my arrival, many have burned their stored cotton to keep it from Union hands, making it scarce." He sighed. "And expensive. As you surmised, this means I can no longer support our family as a cotton broker."

"What will happen to us?" Mama's brown eyes darkened as if with grief and fear.

"Things aren't going well for the South. I fear Mississippians will suffer greater calamities. Confederate currency has lost significant value.'" He blew out his breath. "I don't expect that to improve."

Savannah froze. Her father believed the North would claim the eventual victory in this war—a betrayal to her beloved South.

"I did plan for this eventuality. Part of our wealth remains in gold coins. Prices are escalating. We have three new employees and must hire a gardener. No need to hire a driver until I can replace our horses. My priority is to find means to support us."

A tap on the door caused Savannah to jump, so tense were her muscles.

"Enter," Papa called.

"My apologies for interrupting." Felicity halted at the entrance. "Mr. Sanderson and Mrs. Sanderson have brought their whole family. It appears they walked all the way from their plantation."

Savannah gasped. Her deceased beau's family was here? She hadn't seen them since December.

"I fear the last few months have been detrimental for them. I didn't like to take them into the parlor with our patients. They're waiting in the hall." Felicity gripped the doorknob.

"Bring them in here." Mama rose from her chair, all signs of her agitation masked. "And please ask Mae to bring refreshments."

~

"You're saying that other soldiers have been arrested by your guards?" Travis raised his voice to be heard over the shouting on nearby streets. He'd found Lieutenant Harv Tuttle, one of the officers in charge of the new freedmen provost guards, outside the jail near the courthouse.

"That's right, mostly for drunkenness and disorderly behavior. I agree that this morning's actions won't improve our relations with citizens." The bald lieutenant heaved a heavy sigh. "I'll speak with them about it. But they'd witnessed the fighting while on Washington Street. They were on their way to arrest the whole bunch when you stopped the fight."

Travis scanned the crowd. Seemed orderly enough, and the shouts weren't vulgar.

"I can't say they're doing everything right. One of them pulled a gun on a Federal officer yesterday. The situation didn't warrant that response, of course. My men need more training." Lieutenant Tuttle's gaze darted in every direction. "While most of the Confederates are happy enough to swap stories and food with our men, make no mistake, resentment over surrender simmers just beneath the surface for others."

"The whole situation will improve once they're sent away on parole." It couldn't happen soon enough for Travis.

"General Grant has requisitioned all printing presses in town because there will be three copies of each parole—one for us, one for Confederate officers, and one for each prisoner."

Travis whistled. "That's bound to be a lengthy process." How long would he be here? Long enough to get to know Savannah? Hopefully.

A provost guard hurried over. "Lieutenant Tuttle, you're needed at the jail."

Travis thanked him and set off to do another patrol of the city, one of several officers assigned the same task. He'd no doubt be with his own troops after the paroles were complete.

No signs of trouble near the downtown shops, some of which were open, and his taut nerves relaxed a little. How did the wounded soldier he'd help carry to the hospital fare? He was closer to Savannah's home than the hospital. Perhaps he'd stop by to inquire. That would give him an excuse to see her again. He couldn't deny that her presence in the city made it a more pleasant place, feisty spirit and all.

The ever-growing population of newly freed slaves from local plantations grew daily. He stopped to speak with families who described the conquered city as a haven.

That testimony satisfied some void in Travis's soul, energizing him to continue his uncle's legacy of helping formerly enslaved people. It seemed poetic justice that he was an officer in the army that freed everyone in Vicksburg's vicinity. Those two men his uncle had been transporting on the Underground Railroad had fled from a Mississippi plantation.

Perhaps his duty here would begin to atone for his past mistake with his uncle.

~

Savannah sat around the overcrowded table with the entire Sanderson family...save one...numb with grief. Part of their plantation had been behind Union lines where they'd dug fortifications that destroyed the cotton crop. She'd known the heartlessness of the Union soldiers ran deeply, but the destruction experienced by the Sandersons brought them to a new low.

"Yankees came to our home countless times the past two

months." Will Sanderson, Senior, gripped the table, his gaze on the coffee grains in his empty cup. Thick stripes of gray were now more prominent than blond in the tall man's hair. "The first group demanded our weapons, rendering us unable to defend ourselves from the groups that followed. When the next soldiers demanded our weapons, I told them we'd already relinquished them. They didn't believe me."

"They searched our home and couldn't find muskets." Bitterness dripped from Adele Sanderson's tone. Willie's slender mother was a shadow of her former beauty. "So they took my gowns, Will's clothing, and our wall mirror."

Mama gasped. "What need did Yankees have for your dresses?"

"None." Mrs. Sanderson raised a dull gaze from contemplating cornbread crumbs on the plate in front of her. "Will found my favorite blue silk trampled in the mud, ruined beyond repair."

Senseless. Savannah released a disgusted breath.

"Each successive group became more brazen than the last." Mr. Sanderson shook his head.

"They stole all our livestock." Sixteen-year-old Bart burst out for the first time. He looked so much like his deceased brother with his blond hair and brown eyes that it gave Savannah a pang just to look at him. At thirteen, Curtis beside him had similar looks. Willie's sisters—Sylvia, seventeen, and Deborah, eleven—had inherited their dark-haired beauty from their mother. "There's not a cow, pig, chicken, or horse left on that property. Why, we had to pull our carriage and wagon ourselves, filled with everything the Yankees didn't take. We'll make them pay for that."

"We'd buried our silver and other valuables." Mr. Sanderson eyed Bart but offered no reprimand, perhaps deeming it best to allow his oldest living son to vent his frustration. "Our former servants showed them where to dig."

"The field hands left the first day. All but two of our house servants helped the Yankees strip our home of our possessions, uncaring of destroying what wasn't stolen. Then they left with the scalawags." Speaking almost in a monotone, Mr. Sanderson rubbed his wrinkled forehead. "Our home and fields lie in ruins. The destruction is complete."

"You said that only two of your servants remain?" Mama stared at them in horror.

"No longer." Mrs. Sanderson tugged the sleeves of her dusty dress. "Those last two left us as soon as we arrived in the city today."

Savannah's head reeled. If Willie had stayed home, they'd have been married by now. Willie, as the oldest son, would have inherited five thousand acres of his father's ruined cotton plantation along with the mansion and outbuildings. It would have been her home.

Seeing Willie's family in such straits on the heels of the city's surrender deepened her yearning for the old days and all that might have been.

Given the ties that bound the two families together, would Mr. Sanderson request that Papa provide for them? Her father who had no job.

CHAPTER 8

*S*avannah left her mother and Mrs. Sanderson to deal with sorting which guest bedrooms were inhabitable and free from glass. Indeed, the family would be staying with them for the foreseeable future. She was through her iron gate and on the rutted sidewalk before she knew it. The need to confirm that Travis had no part in the looting and destruction spurred her pace.

Just when she was starting to feel better about Travis, she learned of his comrades' treachery. Had he been one of them? Surely not. He was a man of strong principles. But what about his men?

Blood rushed to her face just to consider that he might have stood idle while his men acted barbarously. Her pace quickened as she scanned the strangers roaming about for the lieutenant's ruggedly handsome face and brown curly hair.

Not that she'd noticed his looks.

Where might he be? She headed toward the center of town.

There he was, striding up the hill on the opposite sidewalk. She lifted her hand to capture his attention. Pleasure crossed his features when he spotted her before a passing wagon hid him from view.

Long strides brought him to her side. "Savannah, I planned to stop by your house today. What's your destination? Perhaps I can escort you."

"I've just learned some upsetting news." She tilted her chin. "Involving your soldiers."

"*My* soldiers?" Eyebrows raised, he scanned the area. "There's no place to sit." Indeed, every porch, step, and deacon seat was occupied by newly freed families or Southern soldiers. Some even napped on the grass. "Shall we stand under that apple tree's shade?" He pointed to a scraggly tree halfway between a house and the sidewalk.

"Stripped of apples, I see." Her tone was petulant, but she'd already spoken of the theft on her property. What she had to discuss was far weightier. "Fine." She led the way, his footsteps rustling the dry grass behind her. Once under the tree, she faced him.

"What's this about my soldiers?" He folded his arms. "They are out on the battlefield searching for the dead."

A gruesome task, but some of those dead were there because of his men. She made a face. "I'm not speaking about today. The treachery happened before and during the siege."

Another grievance against the Union army and another brick in the wall between her and First Lieutenant Travis Lawson.

~

"*T*reachery, you say?" He was taken aback by the sparks emanating from her brown eyes—and something else. Sorrow battled in the midst of her agitation, enabling him to respond in a reasonable tone. "Please elaborate."

"Gladly." She plunged into a stormy narrative of Yankees robbing a local family so repeatedly that the family was left destitute and eventually turned out by their starving state.

His heart squeezed to learn of all they'd lost—except he couldn't regret that the former servants were now free. The rest was a crime in his eyes. Requisitioning was allowed. Unfortunately, soldiers sometimes took this to extremes. "This family owned a plantation on Union lines?"

"A section of their land was on the battlefield. The rest was trampled upon and cannot be saved." Scarlet mottled her peaches-and-cream complexion. "Their livestock was stolen. All the food they managed to keep will last but two weeks."

Travis sucked in his breath. On his pa's farm, fruit and vegetables were dried and canned for the coming years. Plantations fed multiple families and field workers. He could only guess at the staggering amount of food stolen. It was a tragedy that this family's home had also been destroyed.

"Is this what Northern officers are told to do, Lieutenant Lawson? Attack families and steal from them once you've obtained their weapons?" She snapped open her fan so hard, it nearly ripped.

He gritted his teeth. The feisty woman had gone too far. "No, Miss Adair. Our men were allowed to forage in the forest, but looting is not encouraged."

"Why didn't you stop them?"

"You are assuming these men are from the Eighth Illinois. Do you have cause to believe this?"

"Not directly." She lifting her chin. "But you were there."

"We were fighting a battle." He paused to calm himself. She had every right to her anger. He'd have felt the same. "I had no direct knowledge about the looting, certainly not from my own soldiers, though it is common that requisitioning happens during a war. I was aware that a couple of citizens had complained to our generals."

"It's despicable." Savannah's tormented gaze held his as she took a step closer. "A man who dons a soldier's uniform and musters into the army expects to defend himself. Private citizens should not be placed in that position."

His anger died. She was right. Unfortunately, soldiers who had lost family members and buddies sometimes sought vengeance. "Do you know their names?"

Her eyes snapped. "I don't believe they introduced themselves before robbing my beau's family."

"Your beau?" Heart sinking, he took a step back. He should have known she was spoken for. But she hadn't acted like a woman with a beau. "My apologies. I didn't know."

Her gaze fell to the faded grass. "Willie died two years ago of typhoid fever. He had joined the Jeff Davis Guards but never saw battle." The fight seemed to have gone out of her.

"I'm very sorry, Savannah. I really am." He hated that she'd endured such sorrow. She was free to love again, but that didn't mean she'd want to court a Union officer. "Is there...might there be a chance for you to love someone else?"

Her lips parted in a gasp. She stared up at him, clearly aghast. "I...don't know. It's not something I have considered all this time."

"I understand." He'd best concentrate on his life's mission. "He was a blessed man."

"Thank you." She blushed. "As for the matter of the thefts and destruction..."

"I'll make inquiries." He doubted if much could be done without a name, but he'd discuss the matter with Brian. "On another subject, you should consider taking the oath. We're here to stay. Already the oath is required before business permits are granted. It will soon be required for other things too." Such as rations, but he hadn't learned when that would start. "Proving your loyalty will ease your path."

Her face tightened.

"What happened with your...er...friend's family has been a shock." Compassion stirred for how her world had been turned on its head. "Please allow me to escort you home."

She nodded.

He didn't offer his arm, and she didn't seem to expect it. Their conversation left him shaken and ashamed of his comrades, whoever they were.

He'd pray that she healed from her grief for her former beau. Perhaps his regiment would be stationed in the area long enough for Savannah's heart to soften.

~

The next morning, Savannah fanned herself as she stood behind her parents in a line that stretched onto the steps leading into the courthouse's main entrance. Papa had prevailed upon her and Mama to take the oath, something that went against her very core. Papa was troubled about their future in an occupied city. Declaring loyalty to the Union should protect them if his new profession—whatever that might be—took him away from home.

The very real fear in his eyes had convinced her. She was doing this for Papa, not Travis. The officer's initial anger at her accusations and questions yesterday had turned to compassion, and that had befuddled her.

"Did you notice that the Grishams are about to enter the provost marshal's office?" Peering through the open door, Mama moved ahead with the line.

Savannah's gaze darted toward the gray-haired couple who had sat three rows behind them at church for a decade. "Mr. Grisham has often proclaimed his support for the South," she whispered. This sign of their disloyalty was like a physical blow, yet wasn't she betraying her beloved Mississippi too?

Papa's brows drew together. "Let's speak of something else."

"It's good that Petunia was able to get three guest bedrooms prepared by midafternoon." Mama employed her fan, yet her eyes followed the path of a nearby soldier.

"With Felicity's help. Oh, that reminds me. She asked if we could move the patients to their own bedroom upstairs. We'll require the parlor now that the Sandersons are staying with us."

"Impossible." The closer they got to the open doorway, the more Mama's hand trembled. Yet her reply was firm, and the motion of her fan stayed constant. "You know I can't abide the sight of blood. We can't have them milling about the house."

Papa kept his eyes ahead as he stepped into the building. "The only empty bedroom has a hole in the floor and ceiling."

It was their best room. Well, not now. Before Willie passed, the whole family had stayed with them for special occasions. Willie and his brothers had slept in that room.

"We'd need to patch it first." Papa folded his arms as he took another step forward. "We cannot ask the Sandersons to crowd into fewer rooms than we have already given them."

"Agreed." Savannah held back a sigh. Well, she could tell Felicity she had tried...

They were now in the short hall outside the office, close enough to distinguish voices. Her stomach knotted.

"I, Elias Fernbach, do solemnly swear, in the presence of Almighty God, that I will henceforth faithfully support..."

Savannah clutched the doorjamb as a wave of dizziness struck. She was going to swear the oath in the presence of God? Why must they include that phrase?

Not even for Papa could she do this. It was a lie.

A man with a bloody bandage tied about his hand exited the office.

Mama slumped to the ground in a faint.

All conversation ceased. Folks gaped at Mama.

Papa knelt by his wife's side and began rubbing her face.

Savannah dropped to her knees. "Mama, wake up." She patted her hand. Poor Mama—she hated to make a spectacle of herself.

Inside, Savannah secretly rejoiced she'd been saved from speaking the traitorous words.

~

A knock on the door captured Savannah's attention. She was descending the stairs after checking on her mother, who was lying down with a cool compress on her head. Mrs. Sanderson promised to stay upstairs in case Mama called for something.

Papa and the other guests were relaxing on the veranda until lunch.

Savannah opened the door to an unsmiling officer. "Good morning."

"Miss Adair, my name is Lieutenant Colonel Daniel Shriver." The man in his early thirties with brown hair and a short-cropped beard gave a gracious nod. "I've selected your residence as my headquarters."

Her heart raced at his arrogant presumption, yet she didn't dare call Papa to deal with the officer. The way Papa acted these days, he might offer to vacate the whole house. "I regret to inform you that the house is already full to overflowing."

Petunia's children ran across the floor above them. Hopefully, the officer heard the scuffling noise.

"I and my staff will only require the use of the first floor. It will protect your home from future destruction." His expression remained grave.

Her blood ran cold. Was that a possibility? Did the soldiers intend more damage?

"Without doubt, you will not mind confining your activities to the second floor."

As a matter of fact, she minded very much. This man didn't care. The Yankees had taken over her city. They weren't getting her home. She recalled her mother's tactic for handling difficult people. "Well, upon consideration, it will be so lovely of your staff to finish cleaning the broken glass. We've lost every window, as you can see. The breeze brings in the putrid smell of death hanging over the city, but I'm certain you all won't mind such a minor consequence of your glorious victory. Dust clings to every curtain and rug, but one soon grows accustomed to sneezing all day. We are also a makeshift hospital with wounded Confederates in our front parlor. They are the bravest of the brave—your staff will be a tremendous asset in assisting them to the water closet. Oh, and I failed to mention the cannonball that crashed from our roof to the cellar. You all will have to patch the ceiling and floors in several rooms to make them usable, but we'd be ever so grateful."

"There are holes in your floors?" His eyes bulged. "I wasn't aware. I'll find a more suitable residence." Quick strides took him down the stairs. He didn't even look around when he reached the gate.

Someone snickered behind her. Savannah spun to find Felicity collapsed against the wall, laughing.

"Savannah, that was priceless." Tears rolled down her cheeks. "You protected your family from that arrogant man."

Savannah curtsied and then giggled. "It was great fun." Laughing with Felicity cleansed her heart of some of its hurt.

Everyone needed a humorous story. She'd tell them at lunch.

If she must deal with a Union officer, she much preferred Travis.

~

*T*he stench of rotting carcasses of dogs, cats, mules, and horses killed by gunboat fire was still worsening on Tuesday. Travis spent the day with a company of his men as they drove wagons around town to collect them. It was a gruesome task, though less so than battlefield duty, although he wasn't convinced they wouldn't discover a human body or two.

Not one dog or cat roamed about the city. Undoubtedly, reports that citizens' hunger had driven them to eat their pets were true.

He was beginning to discern what people sheltering within the city had endured. He had a job to do, but that didn't keep his compassion from stirring.

Burying the dead was of paramount importance. City officials agreed, and they were establishing a new cemetery for their soldiers.

Confederate officials worked to identify their dead. Soldiers had come up with various ways to be identified should they die in battle—notes pinned to their coats, their names sewn onto knapsacks, or even scratching the information on belt buckles. Everyone wanted their loved ones back home to know what happened to them.

Confederates, freedmen, and Federal soldiers alike were working to transport the dead for burial. That heartened Travis because if they could work together on this important task, they could find common ground on others.

The bulk of his troops, with the help of freedmen, remained on the battlefield searching for dead soldiers. Ten men had been found alive yesterday. There was still a chance for survivors today if the wounded had water. One needed water to survive, especially in this brutal heat. It got hot in Illinois. This was far worse.

His conversation with Savannah ate at him. What those soldiers did couldn't be condoned. Brian had been away from camp until after "Taps" last evening, and there'd been no opportunity to speak with him this morning.

He'd keep his promise to talk to his captain, yet he feared the perpetrators wouldn't see justice this side of heaven. Yet he had to try...not simply for the sake of justice, but also to show Savannah he was an honorable man.

~

*S*avannah picked at her dessert that evening, finding that apple cobbler made with cornmeal wasn't exactly to her taste. Papa had picked up an expanded number of free rations to include the Sandersons. Grocers were beginning to stock food again. They'd purchase a greater variety tomorrow.

"What are your future plans, Will?" Papa, having finished his dessert, sipped his coffee.

"Yankee marauders left us nothing to return home for." Mr. Sanderson's face lost its luster. "They didn't find all our gold and Confederate dollars, but they took enough to beggar us. We'd like to start again fresh in a new place. Since we pulled our carriage and wagon here, I'll need two teams if we are to travel."

"That's a tall order." Papa leaned back in his chair, surveying his friend. "Horses were scarce before the battle. I'll see what I can do."

"I'm obliged to you, Arthur." Mr. Sanderson pushed away his half-eaten cobbler. "Adele and I have talked about moving to Texas—simply because the wide-open range offers the chance for land. We don't know anyone there."

"Yes, you do." Savannah blinked. "I'm sorry. I meant no disrespect, but you've probably forgotten that Ash and Julia Mitchell moved to his uncle's Texas ranch."

Mama brightened. "Martha Dodd and her son, Eddie, also

moved with them. Of course, you remember Julia's mother. Forgive me. I'm still discombobulated from fainting in public today."

"I appreciate the reminder. With all that's happened, I'd quite forgotten." Mrs. Sanderson exchanged a hopeful glance with her husband.

"Julia invited my family to stay with them in Texas until the war ends if we're afraid." Savannah covered her mouth with her hand as she remembered something else. "She extended the same invitation to Felicity and her family."

"Ash and Willie were the best of friends." Mama leaned forward. "I'm certain they'd welcome you also."

Both Julia and Ash had been supportive of Savannah when Willie died, cementing a place for them in her heart for eternity. "I believe you're right, Mama."

"I didn't have a destination in mind." Mr. Sanderson looked across the table at his wife. "Adele?"

"If they've no room for us, I'm certain they'd know of a plot of land for sale." She gave him a smile that steadily widened.

"Then Texas it is, children." Mr. Sanderson slumped back in his chair with a grin as his children cheered.

"Lila, we should go with them." Papa's eager expression was almost like the old days.

Savannah stilled. Surely, he was suggesting a temporary visit. Did he mean to leave her alone while he and Mama made a long visit?

Mama had blanched. "Don't you recall the officer who wanted to claim our home as his headquarters? You may thank Savannah's quick thinking for saving us from that indignity. We can't leave our house for even a month's visit. Why, it would be taken over by the Union before the carriage's dust settled."

It wasn't only to save their mansion that Savannah wanted to stay. Their city needed them. Her thoughts flew to the Southern sergeant who intended to enlist her help to take back

Vicksburg, something that couldn't happen soon enough. She'd do everything in her power to save her beloved Mississippi.

"True. And selling our property amidst the current turmoil is unwise, for we'd not receive the home's value. Perhaps conditions will change for the better after the hostilities cease." Papa swirled coffee dregs in the bottom of his cup. "I believe I will go, anyway. I must find a job, and there's nothing for me in Vicksburg."

Savannah found it difficult to breathe. This couldn't be happening.

Papa was leaving them to fend for themselves again.

CHAPTER 9

*O*n Wednesday morning immediately after breakfast, Travis discussed orders with Brian in his tent. He had just finished reporting the details for their troops who were to dig graves that day. Other regiments continued to scour the battlefields. Brian had passed on Colonel Haversham's orders for Travis to oversee the start of the digging and then monitor the city's streets for trouble from the Confederate prisoners.

"Do you have a few minutes?" Travis asked after he finished.

Brian consulted his pocket watch. "Five. What is it?"

"I'll be brief. First, have you learned if Union Private Jack Danielson is at Libby Prison for a potential exchange with Luke Shea?"

"Not yet, but the colonel was intrigued by the story enough to speak with Major General McPherson." His expression brightened. "If Danielson is there, I believe we'll request a direct exchange for Luke."

"Thank you." A wave of relief shuddered over Travis. Luke was a good man striving to right a wrong. If it wasn't too much trouble to locate Jack, the matter was done. "My other question is about the looting that occurred at many plantations along our Union line. A certain family, the Sandersons, suffered so much at our hand that they've abandoned their property." Part of the captain's job was to issue punishments and conduct court martials, so Travis explained about the thefts and the destruction.

"Sanderson was the name of the family?" Brian's pen scratched across a page.

Travis frowned. "Yes. Savannah mentioned their house still stands yet is much damaged, and they want the guilty punished."

"Savannah?" Brian studied him. "You're on a given-name basis with the citizen who reported it?"

"I met her the first day when I freed her servants. She confronted me, right there on the street."

"I see." Another probing look. "What is Savannah's last name?"

"Adair."

His brow furrowed. "Any relation to Arthur Adair?"

"That's her father. I met him earlier this week. Why?"

"I saw his name on the list of citizens who signed the oath." Brian stacked his papers neatly on his field desk as he stood.

Surprising. "Was Savannah's name on the list?"

"No other Adairs that I can recall." He opened his tent flap. "Regarding the plantation, there's not much we can do. Looting did happen before and during the battle. Foraging is acceptable, but destruction on this level means the plantation owners can't rebuild anytime soon. Advise them to apply for reparations."

Being added to such a list would mean a long wait at best. Would the families be satisfied with that? He'd talk with Savannah today.

~

Savannah didn't want to linger over breakfast where the discussion centered on finding two horse teams for the Sandersons. Mama had been quiet throughout the meal. Savannah intercepted the frosty looks Mama directed at Papa, but he didn't seem to notice his enthusiasm for the trip wasn't shared by his wife or daughter.

"Mama, pray excuse me." Savannah stood at the first pause in the conversation. "I should look in on our patients." Anything to keep her from witnessing her father's joy to be leaving them again.

"Of course, dear." Mama sighed. "It's good that you didn't inherit my queasiness in the sick room."

Savannah kissed her cheek and then hurried away. Her parents were gracious hosts who would see to their guests' comfort. She was strong enough to see to their patients'. She forced her lips into a smile before entering the parlor. "Good morning."

"Good morning." Felicity looked up from Caleb's side. "I can't rouse Caleb. He needs to see Dr. Watkins."

Savannah leaned closer. A pinched look on the sleeping man's face gave mute testimony to his worsening condition. "He's the one whose shoulder cannot bear even a gentle touch."

"Yes. I'm concerned we've waited too long." Felicity rested her palm on his flushed face. "His fever has escalated. I was thinking of fetching Luke to help take him to the hospital. He's working to fix the shambles left by thieves at the saddle shop."

Destruction that happened on Saturday, the day of surrender. The fact that everyone she knew had suffered had cooled Savannah's anger over her friends signing the oath.

Felicity tapped her chin with her forefinger. "If I fetch Luke, do you think Bart and Curtis are strong enough to help him carry Caleb to the hospital?"

"Curtis might struggle." The thirteen-year-old was small for his age. Savannah was too upset with Papa to approach him and didn't feel she had the right to ask Willie's father for help when he was so broken.

"I will help." Felicity stood. "Peter will have to go today too. That bullet must be removed."

"I will also."

Felicity gave a start.

Savannah's offer surprised herself too. "I want to help. Their welfare means as much to me as it does to you."

"Thank you. I'll fetch Luke." Felicity squeezed her arm and then scurried to the door before turning back. "Everyone but Caleb has eaten breakfast. Will you offer coffee or water to them? And keep an eye on Caleb." She stared at him.

"This is madness. You're needed here." Savannah joined her at the entrance. "I'll fetch Luke."

Felicity's face cleared. "Good. I didn't like to leave him."

Savannah rushed out the door, thankful to contribute something to the care of her brave patients. They were one of the reasons she was determined to remain in the city.

~

$\mathcal{T}$hose puffy white clouds gave Travis no relief from the midmorning heat amongst the milling crowds on the city streets. He had decided to visit Luke's house before finding Savannah. There couldn't be more than one saddle shop on Second North Street. To his surprise, he spotted both of them hurrying down the street and quickened his stride.

"Good morning, Savannah. Luke, well met." Travis gave Savannah a tentative smile. Had her anger simmered down over the destruction of her dead beau's plantation?

"Good morning." Her tone was distracted, not angry. A good sign?

"Good morning, Lieutenant Lawson. I hope ye have an

answer for me." Luke's quick pace didn't slow, forcing Travis to hasten his steps. "'Tis anxious I am to learn news about Felicity's brother, but I must not tarry. Felicity needs me posthaste."

"What's the problem?" Travis fell into step beside Savannah.

"Caleb Huntley, one of our wounded, must be transported to the hospital immediately." Surprisingly, Savannah matched their pace. Travis had only seen her maintain a sedate tempo as befitted a Southern belle. "Also, Peter Ford can wait no longer for a bed to open. He needs surgery, and it can't be performed in Mama's house."

"I'll help." He'd done it for a previous patient. Besides, two of the day's tasks involved talking with both Luke and Savannah—and he could peruse prisoners roaming the streets as he carried the pallets.

"Obliged to you." Luke gave a crisp nod as they climbed steps to the Adair mansion. "Buddies who fought with me in the trenches are staying at me home until parole, but they're out searching for wood to repair the saddle shop. Otherwise, they would surely lend their aid."

"Felicity likely has already enlisted Bart to carry a corner." Savannah lifted the hem of her plain green dress. Worry clouded her eyes. "Both she and I can manage the last corner."

Travis's eyebrows shot up, not only because the petite lady appeared as if a strong wind would blow her off her feet but also....where was her father, and why was he not helping?

~

Felicity, who had indeed spoken with Bart, managed to get everyone out the door with amazing speed. Curtis insisted he was capable of helping carrying Caleb. Savannah and Felicity led the way to the hospital in front of the blanket stretcher.

Swarms of flies surrounded wagons from which putrid smells emanated. She caught a glimpse of decaying animals and raised her fan to her face. Little wonder the smell of death clung to the city. A splash of cologne would be doused on the ivory fan before she next left her home. Drivers shouted as they struggled to navigate crowds that spilled over the sidewalks. Most of the soldiers roaming about wore Confederate gray, yet plenty of Union soldiers strode with purpose among them.

"Kindly allow us to pass." Savannah used her most gracious manner to disperse groups who hadn't noticed their strange procession coming.

After asking Savannah's destination, two gray-coated men went ahead five paces and cleared the path. She and Felicity moved back to walk on either side of Caleb, who was blessedly still in a restless sleep. Her heart swelled with thankfulness at the goodness of so many—Travis, Luke, Felicity, Bart, Curtis, and these two strangers—who banded together for the sake of a brave soldier fighting for his life.

Papa and Mr. Sanderson had left to scour the area for available horses before Savannah returned with Travis and Luke. When Mama, who sat on the veranda with Mrs. Sanderson, mentioned Papa's whereabouts, Savannah made certain to casually mention the fact in Travis's hearing because she didn't want him to think badly of her father.

"The crush of soldiers around us is overwhelming, is it not?" Felicity pulled in her black skirt.

"Indeed." Savannah grimaced. "How can our small city hope to accommodate one hundred thousand soldiers?" That was the estimate Ollie had overheard late in the siege. She couldn't stop herself from glancing back at Travis, her gaze continually seeking him.

"*N*ot so many as that now." From his position at the pallet's foot—and Caleb's—Travis had been admiring how the crowd parted for the Confederate soldiers leading them when he overheard Savannah's estimate. "Most of our troops are busy with tasks outside of the city. Sherman's troops left after surrender. Prisoners will soon leave the city." With the killed and wounded heavy on everyone's mind, they didn't need to be mentioned.

"Aye, that can't come too soon." From the front corner, Luke shifted the weight of the pallet to another hand. Travis had whispered the good news to him before they left Savannah's home.

Travis whispered a silent prayer that Union officials soon located Felicity's brother. One wondered how much time they'd expend on a mere private.

"Not only soldiers, but we seem to have become a destination for the freedmen and women. Why, there must be a couple thousand of them newly arrived." Felicity peered ahead to where two or more black families sat on a porch. The women sewed or knitted. One man whittled. Squatting children rolled marbles. "Say, that's Mrs. Dodd's home. Who are all those people?"

Savannah gasped. "Why, it is the Dodd's home. If I hadn't visited Julia's childhood home hundreds of times, I wouldn't have recognized it."

Travis frowned at her suddenly ashen face and gave the home a closer look. Was it the cannonball embedded in the bricks near a large window, the knicks on the chimney, or the hole in the yard as wide as the well outside his Illinois barn that had so distressed her?

"Who are all those people on Mrs. Dodd's porch?" Savannah covered her mouth with her palm. "I know Mrs. Dodd had allowed her paid staff—Silas and Hester and

Hester's daughter, Daisy—to live there until war's end in exchange for watching over the place and keeping it in repair, but there are nearly a score of people milling about the porch and yard."

"Perhaps Silas and Hester gave them a place to stay," Felicity mused. "I've spotted a number of tents where I believe those who have run from plantations are sheltering."

Did Savannah object to strangers taking up residence without the owner's permission? Understandable. Then his stomach knotted at another possibility.

She didn't want freedmen and women in her town.

He prayed it was the former.

~

*A*nger shot through Savannah for Julia's sake over the chaos surrounding her home. With so many pouring into town, an empty home seemed to issue an invitation...and the absent owner had no voice. Just as she'd had no voice in the chaos that resulted from her innocent request so many years ago. The terrible incident had happened when Savannah was eight. Her feet continued their pace as she was transported back to that awful day.

She had been visiting Papa's friend's cotton plantation outside the city with her parents. Savannah had played with their daughter, Mary Grace, a year younger. Her new friend loved skipping around the gardens as much as Savannah. Later that afternoon, Savannah left in the family's landau with her parents, holding a vase of assorted flowers. Gus, the gardener, had cut the magnolia blossoms the girls couldn't reach. Mary Grace seemed to be a favorite of his, likely because she loved the flowers.

Mary Grace had spoken in hushed tones of the prized roses her mother cultivated from England. Roses were Savannah's favorite, and she'd impulsively picked one for her bouquet. Mary Grace had turned ashen. The gardener's indrawn breath had stayed Savannah's hand from picking another one.

Mama and Papa were talking about the pleasant afternoon they'd spent with his new clients. Papa was now the cotton broker for the Jungs' plantation, and he was pleased. But then the crack of a whip had caught Savannah's attention...

~

Savannah craned her neck to look toward the back of the house from her forward-facing seat in the open carriage. A line of red streaked across Gus's bare back. His hands were tied to a pole. Mr. Jung stood, arms crossed, facing as a husky overseer who raised his arm to deliver another blow.

"Stop!" Savannah screamed. "Papa, make them stop. Gus gave me this beautiful bouquet."

"Perhaps that's why he's being punished." His face settled into a mask that belied his stormy eyes from his seat opposite hers.

Her throat constricted. This was all her fault. Mary Grace had said her mama cherished the red roses and only rarely picked the blooms on special occasions. Savannah had waved her concern away because her own mama loved displaying bouquets in their parlor.

She'd never seen anyone whipped. It seemed that every blow fell on her, so upset did she feel. "Please make them stop. I'll give the flowers back." She held them out.

"That won't help him." Papa looked behind them. Another lash found its mark.

Tears clouded her vision. "Please, Papa."

"Lila?" He gazed at Mama's horrified face.

"You must not interfere, Arthur." She lifted her chin. "It will not be appreciated."

Another lash. Savannah began to sob.

Papa's mouth tightened. He scooted to the edge of his seat. "Ollie, stop the carriage."

It creaked to a stop. "Yes, suh?"

"Head back to the house." Papa turned toward their driver. "Stop beside the front steps."

As they sped up the drive toward the brick mansion, Savannah peered toward the back of the house. More red streaks marred Gus's back. "He's bleeding, Papa. Please save him." Servants weren't treated like this in her home. Nor had she witnessed it anywhere else.

"Don't gawk, Savannah. Sit back in your seat." Mama gave her a handkerchief. "Wipe your face."

Papa jumped from the carriage while the wheels still turned. "Wait for me." He strode to the back of the house, out of sight.

"What will he do?" Savannah craned her neck, but the three-story mansion blocked her view.

"Nothing he should be doing. You beat all, Savannah." Mama's lips pursed. "We're not to interfere into such matters. But of course, your father will do anything for his only daughter."

Only *surviving* daughter. Even at her tender age, Savannah had learned that Mama had miscarried two other babies, one before and one after Savannah's birth. Or perhaps the babies had been boys. No one ever told her. It was another one of those matters folks never spoke of.

There were no more sounds of the whip. Mr. Jung yelled something, but Savannah couldn't decipher the words.

Mary Grace ran outside onto the wide portico with her Mama. "Did you come back to play?"

Savannah rested her fingertips against the glossy black wood of the landau, confident in her father's abilities. "No, we came back to help Gus."

"Such interference is scarcely welcome." Mrs. Jung's smile died. "He's not to pick my roses unless instructed to do so. He knows this."

Tears filled Mary Grace's blue eyes. "I'm sorry—"

"It was my fault, Mrs. Jung." Savannah hated the thought of someone being punished for something *she* did. "I picked it. Not Gus."

"He put them in my grandmother's vase." Her chin lifted.

"I'm sorry. I didn't understand." Tears spilled down Savannah's cheeks. "Please don't punish anyone. Here." She held up the porcelain vase. "I'll give everything back."

Mama opened the door. "Please take them, Jacqueline. We meant no harm." She took the bouquet from Savannah and extended it to Mrs. Jung without leaving the carriage.

"Perhaps it's for the best." Mrs. Jung cradled the blue vase decorated with white painted lilies. "I'd want this returned, anyway."

"But of course." Mama's mouth tightened ever so slightly. "We'd not keep a family heirloom from you."

Papa strode back to them, his face thunderous. "Mrs. Jung, we won't keep you. Your husband and I have come to an understanding. I'll return tomorrow for Gus."

Gratitude warmed Savannah. Her tears stopped. "Thank you, Papa." Her father could fix anything...

❧

"Savannah, we've reached the hospital." Travis touched her arm, jolting her back to the present.

"My apologies." She looked around. They were indeed on the grass in front of the building. Caleb's pallet rested on the ground. Luke flexed his shoulders. Bart and Curtis rubbed their arms. Many soldiers basked in the hospital's shade while smoking cigars or playing cards. "I was lost in thought."

"I noticed." Travis sandwiched her hands between his. "Felicity went inside to find an empty bed. Are you troubled?" He leaned close to whisper, his concerned gaze holding hers. "Can I help?"

"It was...an old memory." Her fingers tightened around his. "Thank you." Curious stares caused her to reluctantly tug on her hands.

Travis released her instantly.

Felicity exited the building, and they soon had Caleb on a bed in her second-story ward.

All the while, Savannah couldn't shake the old memory. She had soon learned that her request of her father hadn't been a simple one. The confrontation lost him a customer. And not only did he have to pay Mr. Jung for Gus, but the gardener had feared Mr. Jung would take his wrath out on his wife and children, so Savannah's father had ended up buying them also. That was how Ellen and Josie came to be with them. Gus and his eleven-year-old son had run away a year later.

Worst of all was the wedge the situation put between Savannah's parents. And ever since then, Mama resented the fact that Papa never refused his daughter's requests. From that, Savannah had learned her lesson. She no longer asked her father for anything of importance. Although she was afraid for him to leave her and Mama to fend for themselves in an occupied city, she'd never ask him to stay.

Travis wouldn't stay either. She'd come to rely on his friendship. But, at some point, his division would march away from Vicksburg.

And Savannah would be alone again.

CHAPTER 10

*T*ravis made his way to Savannah's house after carrying the first man to the hospital, tired but happy about his conversation with Luke, who'd been optimistically hopeful. The only person who'd know in advance of the exchange was Felicity, and Luke would only tell her once the matter was firmly decided. Hopefully, Travis's next communication would be to say that the army had heard back from Libby Prison.

Savannah had seemed distracted on the stroll there and back. Something about an old memory. Had she been thinking about the beau she lost? He found himself praying that wasn't the case, that her heart was healing. Either way, he wanted to tell her of his conversation with Brian.

As soon as they stepped inside Savannah's home, Felicity and Luke excused themselves to see about transporting Peter, something Travis didn't have time to do because it was now noon. The Sanderson boys had run on ahead, professing themselves starved for lunch. Travis's hope for a meal invitation dwindled.

He touched Savannah's arm when they reached the portico.

"May I have a moment?" Hoping his empty stomach wouldn't growl, he informed her that Brian had advised applying for reparations.

She sighed. "Mr. Sanderson has done so. There's nothing to be done beyond that?"

"I'm sorry." That the foragers had gone too far was indisputable. Travis wished it was an isolated incident. In his opinion, only General Grant could end the abuse.

"On another matter, my father is looking for two horse teams. He hasn't found any for sale." Something in her brown eyes hardened. "Do you know where the army obtains them?"

"They're scarce around here." He clucked his tongue. "I'd suggest a team of oxen, but I don't know if you want those for your carriage."

"They're for Mr. Sanderson." Her mouth tightened. "He's moving his family to Texas. My father will go with them to find a job. Not much need for cotton brokers in Mississippi right now."

No doubt that was another thing she held against Travis—or at least his army. Yet her potential leaving jolted him. She was becoming more important to him with every meeting. Each day, he looked forward to the possibility of seeing her, even if she still mourned her dead beau. Her hesitation to consider another courtship caused him to believe her heart still belonged to him. Even so, he longed to get to know her better. "You're going to Texas?"

"Mama and I will stay and protect our home." She tilted her chin. "Someone must."

It was the first indication she'd given that her father had hurt her. "It's wise not to leave an empty house in a city overrun with folks looking for a place to live."

"Exactly." She gave a curt nod. "I don't know why my—er, that is, thank you for your help today, Travis. I won't forget it."

Now he was certain she had something on her mind besides an old memory. Was it her father? Or something else?

What could he do to build her trust?

~

*D*uring lunch, Savannah couldn't shake the memories of that long-ago day at Mary Grace's. Truly, she could think of little else after delivering Travis's suggestion for an oxen team to Papa and Mr. Sanderson. That sparked a quarter-hour conversation about the merits of oxen over horses. Savannah was so angry with him that she excused herself as soon as possible.

Alone in her room, she sat on her chair by the window, her favorite place to think. A stroll at the Sky Parlor would have been her preference, as it had been for many couples and families before the war, if the barren hill two blocks from the river wasn't saturated with strangers.

No, this spot where she had so often watched for Willie to ride up would do.

Her handsome, fun-loving beau had mustered into the Confederate army early in the war. She'd been as certain as everyone else that the war would be of short duration, fought in the East far from Mississippi. She'd grown up knowing she'd marry Willie and live on his plantation as his bride. They'd have sons, heirs who resembled their father.

That was not to be. When typhoid fever sent Willie to a Richmond hospital, she'd been too afraid to ask God to heal Willie. She'd only allowed herself to pray for relatively minor needs. Even when circumstances seemed to prove God had listened to her requests, she had feared her prayers were an imposition...just as her mother had insisted her pleas to her father had been. In her childish mind, the two had become embroiled together in a way that she couldn't emotionally sort through.

Look what a fiasco her request of her father had made out of the situation with Gus. Their family money might have kept Gus and his family from beatings, but it had not bought his happiness. Mama had forbidden her to mention the incident to anyone, and she'd obeyed. But Mama had often reminded her of the mistake as a child.

Willie's death had further proven she was in this battle alone. Her friends had nearly abandoned her. Not *all* of them— Julia, Felicity, and Ash had included her in many gatherings for the first year or so. To be fair, Savannah had pushed them away time and again as she had others. Resentment that her friends still had their beaus had gnawed at her. The men might be away at war, yet they were alive. She had especially resented Julia's beau, Ash, for staying home. Julia never knew the worry of her beau in danger's way. Savannah's resentment led to isolation.

Savannah had fought deep loneliness but doubted anyone knew. She'd come to rely on herself for important things.

No one understood how she suffered. Not even Mama and Papa.

And now he was leaving again.

Papa was a leader. Folks looked up to him. Union officials would have listened to his complaints on citizens' behalf.

Mama wasn't the type to stir up trouble. It was up to Savannah to represent the family's interests.

Sergeant Sam Epley offered a way to right this terrible wrong, but how? Spying?

Did she really want to consider that when Travis had been so supportive? Almost like a friend, the way her relationship with Willie began.

No. She wasn't ready to think of Travis that way.

Yet...she wouldn't mind if he stayed and the rest of the Yankees left.

What was she thinking?

Papa was leaving, and she had a decision to make.

Southern soldiers would be paroled within days. Sergeant Epley would contact her soon. What was her answer?

Spying was something *she* could do to fill the void that her city's surrender had left in her heart...as big as the one left by Willie's death. In fact, she feared she'd crumble from the inside out if she allowed any weakness to seep through her defenses.

So she'd not give in to weakness.

Papa wasn't going to fight for their city. She'd do it. She was ready to give her answer to Sergeant Epley.

The Union army had made many mistakes. Her interactions with Travis provided plenty of opportunities to discover information useful for the Confederates wanting to take back Vicksburg.

Spying was the answer to save her city. That must be her focus now.

❧

"Our paroled prisoners leave the city tomorrow." Travis measured his brother-in-law's reaction to his statement two days later on Friday morning. Ben had come to his tent early, and they'd shared bacon and corn muffins.

"Good news." Ben chomped on a bite of bread. "I don't mind telling you that Enos almost came to blows with one of the Rebels yesterday."

Travis's eyebrows shot up. Enos Keller was one of the most even-tempered men in the whole regiment. "What happened?"

"I didn't hear what was said, and Enos won't say. I was working the wagon behind. I sprinted up when Enos squared off with the fellow. His friends called him Sarge." Ben wolfed down the last of the bacon. "Maybe we're all short-tempered from the heat. And no one liked the job we had to do."

"It was necessary." Scouring through rubble for dead animals wasn't pleasant. Yesterday he'd been with them all day.

"Yep." Ben pulled a face. "Please tell me those aren't our orders again today."

Travis shook his head. "Is digging graves any better?"

He grimaced. "Might be. What are your responsibilities today?"

"I'm working with Sergeant Major Ira Hanks to visit makeshift hospitals in homes." And happily for him, Savannah's street was part of his assignment. "We're to ascertain whether the wounded Confederates are ready to march out on parole with their army tomorrow." Travis stacked his dirty plate and utensils to wash later.

"I'll trade you tasks," Ben offered with a grin as they left Travis's tent.

Travis laughed at his teasing. Ben didn't want the responsibilities of an officer. He strode to the tent Ira shared with another officer. In addition to visiting hospitals, he must find Luke today while he was in town. He had good news for him.

~

Savannah hugged her father goodbye on Friday morning by their stable where their vehicles and the two new oxen teams had been hitched. The Sandersons had already said tearful farewells with many promises to write. Mrs. Sanderson and her daughters had chosen to ride in the carriage with trunks and boxes tied onto the top and her husband driving it. Papa and the boys would take turns driving an overloaded wagon.

"Bye, Papa. We will miss you." Tears stung the back of

Savannah's eyes, but she willed them away. He never liked tearful goodbyes. "You have my letter for Julia, right?"

He tapped his coat pocket. "I'll deliver it. Take care of your mama." He kissed her cheek and then held out his arms to her mother.

Watching her mother cling to him stirred Savannah's resentment. Instead of charging *her* to take care of Mama, why didn't he stay and do it?

"How long will you be gone?" Mama whispered.

"I'll be as quick as I can." He kissed her and then climbed onto the wagon, his brown trousers and coat looking out of place on the humble vehicle. "Remember that I'm doing this for our family." His gaze lingered on Mama's tearful face.

Then Mr. Sanderson guided his team onto the crowded road toward the river. The girls poked their heads out. "Come and visit us, Savannah." They waved.

She smiled and waved to the girls who might have been her sisters-in-law. This was a bitter parting, made worse because Papa left with them.

"Take care of each other. I love you." Papa's smile encompassed them both before he followed the carriage down toward the river where they'd ferry across to Louisiana and be on their way.

"You'd think I'd be accustomed to saying goodbye." Mama dabbed at her eyes with a dainty handkerchief. "But this time, your pa intends to find another job."

"This parting is different." Savannah sighed. "We don't know how long he'll be gone."

"Not just that." Mama blew her nose. "If he's successful, we'll be moving to Texas."

Savannah found it difficult to breathe. Was that part of the plan?

No, Papa wouldn't uproot the family. Would he?

~

*M*ama had gone to bed in tears and asked to be alone until lunch, so Savannah didn't bother her when someone knocked on their door an hour after Papa left. She was still emotional herself.

The sight of Travis lifted her spirits. Then she noticed another Union officer behind him on the portico. This appeared to be an official visit.

"Good morning." Savannah inclined her head.

"Good morning, Savannah." Travis tipped his hat. "This is Sergeant Major Ira Hanks. Ira, this is Miss Savannah Adair."

She nodded at the short, stocky man. He held a pad of paper to his chest.

"A pleasure to meet you, Miss Adair."

"We're here to see the patients in your home. You may not have heard that paroled prisoners will be marching out tomorrow." Travis's brow furrowed as he studied her face.

So soon? She must find Sergeant Epley today.

"We need to know if these men are well enough to march out with their comrades."

"They most certainly are not." Every protective instinct heightened. "They're in a nurse's care."

"May we come in, Savannah?" Travis's gentle tone was nearly her undoing. "We must see them ourselves for the record."

Having little choice, Savannah opened the door wider in mute invitation. She led the way.

Felicity raised her eyebrows when they entered.

"Everyone, Lieutenant Travis Lawson and Sergeant Major Ira Hanks are here to see our patients."

Travis nodded at Felicity and then turned his attention to the three men leaning against the wall while resting their long legs on blanket pallets over the rug. "Gentlemen, our army has completed the paperwork for the parole. Your comrades will march out tomorrow. We're here to discover if you're well enough to go with them or if you'll need a few more days to recover."

Tex exchanged a startled look with James.

"Micah Nixon requires medical care." Felicity moved between Travis and the wounded. "There is infection in his leg from a shrapnel wound."

"Can he walk?" Travis studied the man's feverish face.

Ira's pencil scratched across the page.

"With help." Felicity lifted her chin. "Under no circumstances is he able to march with the army."

Travis gave Ira a nod.

Good. Savannah clasped her hands together. She didn't have to fight Travis on this one.

"James Diller is next to him." Felicity relaxed a bit. "A musket ball entered and exited his leg. I'm keeping his wounds clean and monitoring him for infection daily. He'd not ready to go."

"Agreed on both cases." Travis walked over to the last patient. "Tex, you may remember me from earlier this week. I don't remember your whole name."

"Tex Logue is how I mustered into the army." He pushed himself to his feet.

Ira continued to make notations.

"How about you, Tex? Are you ready to march out?" Travis crossed his arms.

Savannah held her breath. She didn't want to lose Tex. He'd saved her and Mama at the beginning.

"I reckon I can walk a mile or so. Is that enough?"

Travis rubbed his clean-shaven jaw. "He'll have to walk three times that much just to make it out of the city, right, Ira?"

"Yep. Lots of uphill walking too." Ira eyed Tex.

"I believe you'll benefit from a few more days of rest."

"Thank you, Lieutenant Lawson." Tex glanced at his comrades. "I've been taking care of my buddies this long... might as well finish the job."

Tears sprang to Savannah's eyes at the brave man's loyalty.

A tender smile crossed Travis's face at her tears.

She quickly blinked them away. No weakness. "Am I correct that you'll allow all our patients to stay?"

"They won't march out tomorrow, but don't expect them to be here longer than another day or two." Travis's gaze shifted to the floor. "Many injured will be discharged from the hospital by tomorrow. As it empties, wounded from makeshift hospitals like this one will move to City Hospital. The sooner we can move all requiring medical care into one facility, the better."

From the army's viewpoint, Savannah didn't doubt it. But she'd miss them when they left. Her father had abandoned her that morning. Her soldiers would soon leave. How long before Travis left too?

CHAPTER 11

*S*avannah ran up to her bedroom to watch Travis leave. He strolled beside her ruined garden, once so well-manicured with sections for roses, daylilies, and shrubs of aromatic sweet olive near the snapdragons. If Travis hadn't been so tall, it would have been difficult to track his progress through the throngs of Southern soldiers and the ever-growing number of freedmen in the city.

Then he rounded the corner and was gone. Excitement mounted to have a new course of action. This was her opportunity to search for Sergeant Epley. She fetched her hat. It was imperative she speak with him today, or all was lost.

It was barely nine and had already been an eventful day. As she headed down the sidewalk, her favorite hat with red silk roses didn't block the morning sun, but she'd remembered to douse cologne over her fan to mask lingering foul smells.

Where was the sergeant? She hadn't even caught a glimpse of him since they met. Not knowing where to search, she headed toward the building where they'd talked. He wasn't there.

She continued on, gaze darting in every direction. How was she to find him?

"Miss Adair, well met."

Her head swiveled to the right at the remembered Southern drawl. There was the very man she sought, looking even scruffier than she remembered. Many of the captured soldiers slept under the stars. Perhaps he hadn't been fortunate enough to find shelter. "Sergeant Epley. I didn't know how to find you."

"Oh, I've been close. I wasn't about to leave without talking to you. Call me Sam." He gestured to a small copse of trees. "Let's stand in the shade."

And away from the crowded sidewalk. Savannah understood and welcomed the suggestion. She followed him up a grassy path.

He stopped when they were under the first tree, well within sight of those passing by. He was taller than her by several inches. Clothed in butternut jacket and trousers, his husky frame testified to physical strength. He'd likely recently bathed in the river, for he smelled of lye soap. "Your pa knows lots of folks."

"Indeed." Papa was a natural born leader, able to influence others. It was one of the reasons he had been able to repeatedly negotiate higher sales prices for his clients.

"He's been all around the city this week, talking with Yankee officers and Confederate officers alike. He even talked with one of them new patrol groups." He crossed his arms. "Don't know if he's for us or against us since he signed the oath."

Savannah blinked. How could he know so much? Unless— "Did you follow my father?"

"Reckon I did. Or had others do it." He spat. "What's important is Mr. Adair is a man who knows how to find out things. He'd make a good detective for that Pinkerton Agency."

"Undoubtedly." How did Sam discover so much about her father so quickly? "Why is that important to you?"

"Because you can ask him questions. Find out what he's discovered and write to me."

Another person interested in her father or his wealth. It didn't matter which. Disappointment numbed her to lose her opportunity to directly aid the South herself. "Then I'm sorry to waste your time. My father left for Texas this morning." She spun around to leave.

"Wait."

She turned back.

"You spend a lot of time with a Yankee lieutenant. Did you know him before?" He scanned the crowd.

"I met First Lieutenant Travis Lawson the day of surrender. We've already discussed him." Why was he interested in Travis?

"He might be useful to us." His gaze darted all around.

"You mean...he's a spy for you?" Her senses reeled.

"Not him."

She took a step back. "Someone close to him in the Union army?"

"Don't you worry none about that." He picked a blade of grass and chewed on it. "You can also help by listening to folks talk—especially soldiers—as you stroll about town. It'd amaze you what I heard this week by being in the right place at the right time and keeping my mouth shut."

That was something she could do. "That requires a bit of luck."

"Your pa knows how to do it. The apple didn't fall far from the tree." He eyed her. "Did you decide to help us?"

Papa had discovered important changes this week that he'd explained to her and Mama before the Sandersons' arrival. She could do it too. "I have. I'll need instructions. Travis told me you're being paroled tomorrow."

"Now, see..." He pointed at her. "That's what I'm talking

about. You get information from him in normal conversations. Just pass it along to us."

From Travis? Second thoughts weakened her resolve. She didn't want to hurt him. "I don't know. We're starting to be friends. It would feel like a betrayal."

"He ain't your friend." He plucked another blade of grass. "He's the enemy, remember? The one who told your slaves they were free."

He'd also shown compassion to the wounded men in her home.

"A lot of townsfolk have left. Your city needs you to be strong." He studied her.

"You're right. I won't fail."

"That a girl." He grinned. "You'll listen real close to the Yankees' plans. Even if it doesn't seem important, I want to know about it. Write about what's happening in Vicksburg. Other spies will discover other information. When we put it together, we see the plan."

That made sense. She'd be acting as a spoke in a wheel, making the whole wheel stronger.

"I'm marching out tomorrow, but a lot of us ain't going far."

A chill of fear mixed with excitement rushed through her. "How shall I get the information to you?"

"Write it in cipher. Here's the code." He extracted a square of paper from his pocket and pressed it into her hand. "Hide it away now."

Her shaking fingers slid it up her sleeve.

"Good. Memorize the code. Practice writing sentences in code. Once you have it memorized, burn the cipher. Don't keep anything in your house. Burn all evidence in case you are questioned."

She swallowed. In a city overrun with the enemy, possessing a cipher was dangerous.

"You'll get your messages to Mrs. Wanda Lakin. Do you know her?"

She shook her head, her thoughts in turmoil.

"Mrs. Lakin is the widow of Oliver Lakin, a saloon owner. Their saloon near the wharves was sold a couple of years ago." He stared at something beyond her shoulder. After a pause, he continued. "What's important to us is that she's a letter carrier. She delivers messages that folks don't want crossing the mail. Secrets we don't want the enemy to read. It's not something she advertises, but folks like us can find her." He grinned. "I met her the day of surrender."

Was Savannah like this uneducated sergeant just because she agreed to spy on the Union? What would Mama think? She wouldn't find out from Savannah.

"Make certain the letters are sealed."

"I will."

"Anyway, I'll introduce you if you have time now. She charges one-and-a-half dollars for each letter you send me."

"That's no problem." Papa had left them money. "And yes, I can go today."

"Very good." The sergeant took a step back. "I don't want folks to see us walking together, especially your lieutenant."

"Agreed." Savannah didn't want Travis to learn she knew Sam either.

"Make your way down to Mulberry Street. I'll find you there." He strode away before she could protest the location near the river where there were saloons and men who might not respect a woman alone.

He was gone. There was no help for it. Avoiding curious stares, she headed down the hill. A quarter hour later, she was on Mulberry Street. Sam was nowhere in sight.

She slowed her pace, looking in every direction, her gaze sliding away from bold stares. Where was Sam?

"Miss Adair." Sam approached with a plump woman in her

mid-thirties from a two-story saloon across the street. Her auburn hair set her apart as much as her sassy grin. "Let's step behind this shed."

Savannah followed them to a wooden building with no walls fully intact from the recent battle.

"I told Wanda you wouldn't meet inside the saloon."

"Certainly not." Savannah lifted her chin.

Sam gestured toward his companion. "I'd like you to meet Mrs. Wanda Lakin."

"How do you do?" Savannah studied the woman's intelligent expression. Here was a woman who would be hard to fool.

Mrs. Lakin extracted a red silk fan from her pocket. "Very well, thank you. I'm glad to meet you, Miss Adair." Curious eyes swept over Savannah's attire, a blue cotton dress as befitted the hot day. "Sam tells me you require my services."

"Yes—er, not today, but soon. Where shall I find you?"

"It's unlikely to be the same place twice. I can be on Monroe Street on this next Thursday morning. Outside the apothecary."

"That's good." Outside the apothecary was an acceptable destination for a woman. Thursday morning was too broad. "Ten o'clock."

"No earlier, please. Hide your letter and money in your fan or a basket." Her green eyes narrowed. "Don't give me the letter. Glance at it and I'll take it from you. We'll set the next meeting place at that time."

"Agreed." The spy was careful. Savannah appreciated that quality, if not her less-than-friendly manner. She turned to Sam. "Do you plan to write to me?"

"It's safer for you not to receive letters. If I do write, burn the message after you read it."

"And I'll require a dollar and fifty cents from you before I deliver mail to you." A stray wisp of Mrs. Lakin's hair stirred when she waved her fan. "Until Thursday." With a nod, she turned on her heel and left.

"What you're doing is important, Miss Adair." Sam's face turned grave. "Staying informed about what's going on in the city will let us know when best to strike. In the meantime..."— his cocky grin flashed— "we plan to make things hot for Yankees and Unionists."

"How?" She didn't want anything to happen to Travis, although she suspected he could take care of himself.

"That's nothing for you to worry about." He gestured toward Clay Street. "I'll walk on one side of the street while you take the other. You won't see me again after we reach Washington Street. I'm certain you can find your way home from there." He lifted his kepi.

"Godspeed, Sam."

"Good luck."

He crossed the street without giving her another glance, but of course, the anonymity protected both of them.

She touched her sleeve where the folded paper was hidden. There was a lot to consider on her solitary walk home.

And Travis would be a source of information, whether she wanted it or not. Her growing friendship and attraction for him was less important than aiding the cause.

～

Travis was up by three on Saturday morning and in position with several armed soldiers from his regiment along the road the paroled Confederate prisoners were marching out on within a half hour. The Eighth Illinois were posted as guards along Jackson Road at Fort Hill for the prisoners leaving. Travis's orders, along with those of several other officers from his regiment, were to search their knapsacks and possessions. Other Federal soldiers closer to Vicksburg verified that each soldier had signed the parole, a necessary step for being exchanged later.

The march out of the city began before the sun peaked over the eastern treetops. Travis started out merely checking knapsacks. All muskets had been stacked by Confederates before leaving the battlefield one week before at surrender.

His searches focused on gunpowder. He found it in toes of socks and in pockets, which his guards emptied into repositories behind them. He found nothing in one private's knapsack yet caught a whiff of gunpowder and searched again. There was none in his haversack either. Travis was about to release him when, on a whim, he asked the nervous soldier for his canteen. There he found the source of the odor. He tipped the canteen to empty not water but gunpowder into the repository.

After that, the line slowed considerably. A dozen other officers joined them to quicken the search.

A butternut-clad sergeant halted in front of Travis with a cocky grin. "Morning, Lieutenant."

Travis gave a nod at the huskily built enlisted noncommissioned officer with a headful of brown curls that resembled his grandmother's mop after she'd just cleaned off the porch. Not many Confederates chose to talk. "Knapsack."

"What ya looking for?" The sergeant handed it over.

"Gunpowder." The fellow no doubt knew that. It was an impertinence Travis could ignore.

"Won't find none there."

Travis frowned. This fellow's arrogance was too much to overlook. He'd seen the man earlier that week, but nothing about him stood out in his memory. They hadn't met. He scanned the man's parole. *Sergeant Sam Epley* wasn't a name he recognized.

Travis returned the knapsack. "The haversack, please."

"Just my skillet and rations in there." Sam obliged. "A fellow would have to be crazy to put gunpowder in his food."

"Agreed." He gave it back after examining the contents. "Now for your canteen."

His smile disappeared as he took it off his shoulder. He unscrewed it and starting dumping black powder on the grass at his feet.

Travis glared at him and extended his hand in a silent command.

Sneering, Sam handed it over.

Travis shook the contents of the canteen into the repository until no more black powder fell. He gave it back. "I suggest you rinse it out well."

Sam's eyes flashed before he marched on.

Watching him go, Travis rubbed his jaw. He'd mention the man's name to Brian. Under penalty of death, paroled soldiers couldn't resume their former role as combatants until exchanged.

But Sergeant Sam Epley might be one who ignored that order.

~

Savannah hurried up the stone steps to her home at the sight of three Union soldiers on her portico at noon on Sunday. She and Mama had attended church services for the first time in weeks. It had rankled to see a United States flag waving in the breeze over her church, making the soldiers who had come calling even less welcome.

"Gentlemen, to what do we owe this pleasure?" Savannah lifted her chin at the open front door. Tex had likely answered their knock because their staff had the day off. She'd deal with the matter by the time Mama, who was climbing the steps at a sedate pace, reached the house.

The three privates looked at one another. One stepped forward. "Miss Adair, we're here to take your patients to the hospital." His Adam's apple bobbed at the expression of displeasure she did not attempt to conceal. "There are beds open for them now, what with recent discharges who marched out with their comrades."

Savannah sighed. Travis had warned her. "We've only just returned from church, sir. I suppose there's no objection to us taking a few moments to bid them farewell?"

"None at all." Tension ebbed from his expression. "Our comrades are in there getting two of them on stretchers. One wants to walk over."

Tex. Yes, he'd be too proud to accept help. "I'm not surprised. He's very proud, as I'm certain you are."

"Yes, miss." He looked over at Savannah's mother, who had just reached them. "Good afternoon, Mrs. Adair."

"Mama, they've come to transport our patients to the hospital. I'm going in to say goodbye to our men."

Mama frowned. "Tell them our prayers go with them." She followed Savannah inside.

"Mrs. Beltzer left us some biscuits and bacon for our meals today." Savannah knew Mama wouldn't want to entertain the soldiers while her daughter was in the parlor. "I'll meet you back in the kitchen after they're gone."

"Thank you, Savannah." Mama inclined her head. "Thank you, men, for taking care of our patients."

"Our pleasure." Their spokesman raised his kepi.

Four men carried Micah into the hall on a stretcher, followed by four others carrying James.

Tex came of his own accord. "We thank you for your hospitality, Mrs. Adair."

Gasping, Mama slumped to the marble floor in a faint.

The soldiers all took a step back, exchanging horrified looks.

Kneeling beside her, Savannah glanced at Tex's scalp, still marked with an unfortunate shade of red. "My mother faints at the sight of blood. Might I prevail upon some of you gentlemen to carry her upstairs?"

⌇

*R*egretful that Mama's fainting spell had overshadowed the parting, Savannah followed the stretchers outside. Mama was awake and resting in her bedroom, a fact which had seemed to relieve everyone. "Tex, will you go home while you await exchange?"

"Yes, I'll finish my recovery at my home outside of Baton Rouge. Becky will be glad to see me." His gaze turned toward the river. "My sons are now five and three. I can't wait to see how they've grown. I'll tell them all about your kindness. Thank you, Miss Adair."

"It was our pleasure."

"And I sure am sorry to cause your mama to faint like that." He paused on the top step, the three Union soldiers who were to accompany him standing just behind him. The others were almost to the gate.

"It was my fault." She'd remembered about the stains on the rug but forgot about his scalp. "Godspeed to all of you."

With a nod, he turned to the soldiers waiting for him. "I'm ready, men." He headed down the steps. Two soldiers went on either side, and one stayed back.

"Sorry about the trouble, Miss Adair." The private who had been the sole spokesman hung his head.

His regret tamped back her sorrow that he was taking away her patients. "My mother will soon be fine." Savannah hesitated. Sam had told her to get the soldiers talking. Did this one have any news? "The streets are far less crowded today—I supposed because the Confederates are gone. It seemed that all went smoothly from what I observed from my window..."

"There were no altercations, true, although we caught some of them trying to sneak out gunpowder."

"How clever of you all to discover it." Hopefully, they hadn't found all of it. "It's good things are going so well for our Union men." The traitorous praise tasted like bile. "Any news of more victories for them?"

The private rubbed his bristled chin. "Well, as you probably heard, our army took Jackson before we attacked Vicksburg. A good bit of the capital was burned. We destroyed factories and warehouses. Left it in sorry shape, but Confederates took it back. Sherman's troops are back there again with a whole corps and divisions from other corps, fighting and building earthworks." He straightened his shoulders. "Don't you worry none, miss. We'll recapture the capital."

Savannah forced a smile. "How brave of you." To attack Mississippi's capital twice was a travesty, especially after they'd nearly destroyed it the first time.

"Yes, miss. We've got more wounded to move. I'll bid you good day."

"Yes, a good day." She'd practice writing this information in cipher and deliver the message to Mrs. Lakin on Thursday. Perhaps Sam's troops could get there in time to help.

CHAPTER 12

On Monday morning, Travis entered the military headquarters on Monroe Street. Colonel Haversham had ordered him to come at eight o'clock. Brian, who passed on the orders, was as mystified as Travis was about the unusual request.

"Come in, Lieutenant." Colonel Wilbur Haversham, a broad-shouldered man in his late thirties with more brown than gray in his receding hair line, didn't stand from behind the oak table in the library he'd claimed as his office. "Please, sit."

"Thank you, sir." It didn't seem that he was in trouble for some infraction of which he wasn't aware. Relaxing slightly, he sat on the brown-cushioned chair indicated.

"Your captain knows of our meeting, which has two purposes. Only one of which you are permitted to speak about to Captain Eaton."

Travis's eyebrows shot up. Had he heard right? Most of his orders since becoming a lieutenant over a year before had come directly from Brian. "Yes, sir."

"The first news is that Union Private Jack Danielson has been exchanged for Confederate Private Luke Shea."

"That's wonderful news." Relief swept over him like a tide. He had no idea how much he'd wanted this until it was accomplished. "Luke's betrothed, Felicity Danielson, knows how to get in touch with Luke. He didn't go far when paroled."

"Pass on the news to her today." He gave Travis an envelope addressed to Luke. "See that she contacts him. I'm glad the Eighth Illinois will receive young Shea as a recruit." The colonel leaned back in his chair. "I don't mind telling you, I had my doubts about his story. We looked into the matter. Enough facts have been substantiated that we're satisfied."

"He confessed to me that he wants to wed Felicity before mustering into our army. Under these extraordinary circumstances, it's possible Jack will come to Vicksburg before going to his home or returning to his regiment. If so, Felicity will surely want her brother to give her away."

Colonel Haversham pressed his fingertips together. "After all they've both endured, I agree."

His heart swelled to imagine Luke's and Felicity's happiness at learning the news. "I don't mind saying that Luke has become a friend. I trust him."

"And that leads me to the second matter that you can't discuss with your captain or anyone else."

Travis stilled. "A secret?"

"A secret mission." He nodded. "Ostensibly, you'll have tasks with supervising your troops cleaning up the city, of which there are many. Those responsibilities will keep you here for your real mission. I've set aside a small room you'll share with Lieutenant Christopher Dunn should you require an office here."

Mystified, Travis stared at him.

"I've had my eye on you for a while. That's why you've had daily responsibilities inside the city. When Brian told me of your suspicions about Confederate Sergeant Sam Epley, I knew you were the man I needed for the job. Epley has been over-heard stirring up resentment in his comrades."

"He was a tad arrogant. Looking back, I wouldn't be surprised if he wasn't successful in smuggling out gunpowder another way."

"Agreed. He's not the only one we're interested in monitor-ing. That's where you come in."

Travis frowned. "I'm baffled, sir. What is the task?"

"Locating Confederate spies in Vicksburg. We'll bring them to justice."

The room seemed to spin and then righted itself. These were the people who'd risk personal danger to recapture their city, where Travis's comrades had sacrificed so much to liberate the slaves. He wasn't about to risk that.

"It will be an honor, Colonel Haversham. When do I start?"

~

*M*idmorning on Monday, Savannah surveyed several rust marks on the blue rug. "Can you remove these stains?" she asked Felicity.

"I truly don't know." Felicity bent to study the stains of varying sizes and shapes. The largest was two feet long and about half as wide. "I can try diluted vinegar, but that may fade the color. Or go through to the beautiful floor. Is it white oak?"

"Yes, and I don't want to ruin Mama's floors." She tapped her chin. "I can't consult her."

"You think these blood stains will cause her to faint again?" Felicity straightened.

"Perhaps. After her most recent episode, I don't want to leave anything to chance. Best work on them outside. This is Mama's favorite room."

"And she can't come in until it's done. I volunteer at the

hospital tomorrow. Let's see how far I can get on it today while Petunia does your laundry. Will you help me drag it outside?"

"Of course."

Felicity turned back a corner and gasped. "Oh, no."

"What?" Savannah was afraid to look.

"It seeped through the rug to the floor."

Savannah peered at the dark stains marring the light-brown wood. "Mama won't be happy about this."

A knock on the front door was a welcome distraction. Savannah hurried to answer it. "Travis, how nice to see you." She peered up at the sky beyond his shoulder. Those gray clouds would bring rain soon. Best leave the rug where it was until Wednesday. "Please come in." She closed the door behind him.

"Is Felicity working today?"

Savannah blinked at his eager expression. "She is. May I ask why?" A flash of jealousy shot through her that Travis might be infatuated with Felicity. Her friend was betrothed to Luke.

"I have good news for her. All of your patients were moved to the hospital this weekend, right?" He peered toward the parlor.

"Yesterday. We're trying to clean." That should hurry him along. She stepped into the room where Felicity stood, hands on hips, surveying the wood. "Felicity? Lieutenant Lawson is here to speak with you."

Her eyes lit up. "This must be about Luke." She sped into the hall. "Good morning."

Travis's gaze darted toward Savannah. "May we speak outside?"

"Of course." If anything, Felicity looked more excited. She stepped onto the portico with him.

Savannah tilted her chin. Whatever Travis had to discuss, he could say it in front of her. Felicity had no secrets from her.

At least, not now that Savannah knew she'd signed the oath with Luke. She joined them by one of the tall columns.

Felicity clutched a letter in her hand. "Truly? Luke was exchanged for Jack?" Tears glistened in her eyes.

"Your brother Jack?" Savannah's jaw slackened. Perhaps she didn't know all of Felicity's secrets. "How can that be, when Jack is a chaplain in a Louisiana regiment?"

Felicity had moved to Vicksburg from nearby Bovina after her parents' deaths. Her only unmarried sibling had married soon after, so Felicity had since lived with her aunt. Her oldest brother, Jack, hadn't allowed the miles between them to keep him from being a rock for Felicity. Luke, whose family had immigrated from Ireland when he was little more than a baby, had met Felicity at church.

"This is a private matter, Savannah." Travis tapped his foot.

A tear spilled over the corner of Felicity's right eye. "Savannah, I must tell someone. Can I trust you to keep my secret?"

It was doubtful that whatever it was affected Sam's cause in any way. "Of course."

"Good. But first, I must add the address and get this to Luke's friend. He'll take it to Luke." She ran into the house.

"Felicity." Travis followed her into the hall with Savannah on his heels. "Jack may come to Vicksburg in a few days. Think about what you'll say to your family."

"Yes." Her face glowed. "Thank you, Travis. I appreciate this more than I can say."

"It wasn't only my doing." He smiled at her. "I merely began the process."

Savannah touched her arm to halt her. "Felicity, if you're going out, may Travis explain?"

She glanced at the officer and then back at Savannah. "If he has the time."

"I will." Travis turned to Savannah. "It's quite a story."

That intrigued her even more than the fact that Travis

already knew secrets Felicity had kept from a friend. "Shall we sit on the veranda?"

~

*A*round table nestled between Travis's and Savannah's white metal chairs on her veranda. A cave shelter with a five-foot opening in the hillside near the veranda began the eyesore that moved up the hill into a terraced orchard in which he counted a dozen dying trees from his chair. Not a single flower had survived in what once must have been a magnificent garden.

All this he noticed within seconds and then focused on telling Luke's experience of accidentally shooting Felicity's brother, then saving him from drowning, only to learn that Jack would be sent to prison. He spoke softly, mindful of the broken windows behind them where Felicity's family might overhear.

"I can't believe it." Savannah's face paled. "Luke suffered from amnesia for months. And then to remember he shot Jack. Felicity spoke of her older brother often in the old days when—"

"When Willie was still alive?" Travis glimpsed her sorrow and then looked away. "Do you miss those days?"

"Oh, yes." She heaved a deep sigh. "I long for the days before the world went mad...when ships in the wharves brought treasures, not mortar." She closed her eyes.

Travis had known her less than two weeks. Yet he somehow believed she didn't often allow such raw glimpses into her heart. "I'm sorry for the nightmare you endured." He had only to walk the broken city streets, step around the rubble to understand a portion of her loss. Yet...if not for this war, how many years would pass before slavery ended? The North must win.

But, in his opinion, there was no reason to cripple the South beyond what it took to win battles.

"I still am enduring the nightmare, as a matter of fact." Her beautiful brown eyes dulled. "What with Papa searching for a job in Tex—"

Thunder rumbled.

"It appears about to storm." She straightened. It was as if a veil once again shuttered her face. "Is there anything more you want to tell me about Felicity and Luke?"

"Not me." The rest was their story to tell. "There may be more Felicity wants to say. I'd ask that you keep it to yourself. I don't believe her family knows anything about it."

Lightning flashed.

"Of course." She stood. "Let's go inside before the rain starts. Will you shelter with us?"

If only he could. "I've tarried too long. Some matters await my attention."

Such as searching for spies.

Filled with regret that the approaching storm interrupted their conversation, he left during a rumble of thunder. It had been the first time Savannah really opened up to him. Sharing her innermost feelings was something he sensed she didn't often do. What had she been about to say about her father? She seemed guarded...or maybe defensive about him. There was something... Perhaps she resented her father leaving.

A raindrop splashed on his face, shaking him from his reflections. Spy catching was his new task. He'd start at the landing. He had a hunch secrets were coming and going on ships—perhaps even the very vessels bringing in food for citizens.

He couldn't unmask traitors by sheltering at Savannah's mansion.

≈

"*J*'ll go to the grocers this morning." On Thursday after breakfast, Savannah set her cup half filled with coffee beside her empty plate. She and Mama dining alone since Papa left the previous week felt all too familiar. This was the day she delivered her first message to Mrs. Lakin. Shopping for food was a good excuse.

"You've never done so before." Staring at her, Mama ate her last dainty bite of corn cake.

Savannah had stopped collecting rations after Mrs. Beltzer assumed that responsibility. Those provisions had since been moved into a city building. "I heard that some ships have brought flour. Perhaps sugar too."

"I haven't eaten a biscuit in months. Or bread." Mama's expression brightened.

"Either one seems like a delicacy these days." Savannah stood. "I'll see you when I get back."

Up in her room, she riffled through her wardrobe until spotting an old brown dress. Her least favorite frock without lace, ribbons, or bows had pockets that hid her prepared message. She extracted the sealed letter with Sam's name, empty of an address. She trusted the letter carrier to know his direction.

On a stroll about the city yesterday, she'd learned that the Union had now put Jackson under siege, and this information had been added to her note. Sam had warned her to burn the cipher, but she didn't trust her memorization enough yet to destroy it.

She patted her looped braids, satisfied that she was growing more proficient at the style. Even Mama had been practicing fixing her own hair. They helped one another with their corsets but didn't tie them as tightly as in the old days because their clothes fit looser from weight loss during the siege.

A half hour later, Savannah strolled the still-wrecked sidewalks. Union soldiers drove wagons on rutted streets. There were easily three or four times the number of black families milling about or lounging on porches than before the siege. She looked for Ellen, Josie, Alvera, and the others among them. What had happened to them? Her hope hadn't died that at least Ellen and Josie would return.

Savannah was growing accustomed to the absence of Southern soldiers. It was easier to walk around the city. One felt able to breathe.

Or she could were she not about to deliver a spy message.

She was outside the apothecary a quarter of an hour early. Mrs. Lakin had said not to arrive before ten. Neither did Savannah believe the woman would wait for her above five minutes. She'd stroll down to the end of Monroe Street perusing window displays at a sedate pace that allowed her to return at the exact time.

Her stomach quaked at the potential danger. No, nothing would stop her.

"Good morning, Savannah." Travis strode away from a vaguely familiar home. "Are you doing some marketing? I can tote your basket home."

Savannah's heart raced. What was she to do now?

~

Colonel Haversham had just given Travis unfortunate news. A band of Rebels had attacked a Union foraging party yesterday. Everyone escaped, but two soldiers had been wounded. The colonel advised him that spies in Vicksburg were well informed of the Union's activities and to keep his ears open for trouble.

Spotting Savannah immediately upon leaving the meeting was like a breath of fresh air.

"Good morning, Travis. Don't trouble yourself. I—I won't be finished for some time." Her hand covered a linen cloth inside the basket.

Why did she seem agitated? "Is something wrong?"

"Nothing." A quick shake of her head. "Thank you for your concern."

"Has Felicity heard from Luke?"

"No. She thinks he'll arrive today or tomorrow."

Perhaps he was wrong about her tension. She answered his questions readily enough. "Does Felicity's family know Jack was in Libby Prison?"

"Yes. She told her aunt first. Mrs. Beltzer advised her to tell her cousin Petunia immediately in hopes she'll be calm when Jack arrives as an exchanged Union prisoner from a Southern prison. Petunia is fiercely proud of her husband fighting for the South. They worry about her anger over Jack's Northern loyalties." Savannah glanced over her shoulder.

"Understandable." Travis peered behind her. Soldiers patrolled the street beyond them. A few women carried large round baskets, likely headed to pick up free rations provided by the army. A mother holding a baby and two youngsters running to catch up to her scurried past them. He didn't see anything out of the normal. "General Grant is relocating sick and wounded Confederates today."

"Oh?" That brought her attention back to him. "Where are they going?"

Her concern for her former patients warmed his heart. "Mobile, Alabama. Some will go to Monroe, Louisiana." He sighed. "No telling where the wounded in your home went."

"I'll tell Felicity. She's quite concerned for them." Her hand remained on the linen cloth inside her basket. "I won't keep you. Good day to you."

"Good day." He watched her walk away at a faster pace than normal. She hadn't seemed pleased to see him, just when he thought they were progressing toward a closer friendship. Perhaps she felt she had been too open with him in their last conversation and had her guard back up. She wasn't weak, nor would she respect weakness. His admiration grew for her with each meeting.

Enough of this woolgathering. He had a job to do.

He strode toward the river. There was a wharf worker he had his eye on. So far, Travis's suspicions were only a hunch since he hadn't witnessed the man saying or doing anything incriminating, but there was something about the man's watchfulness when Union officers were around...

~

A clock nearby struck ten times. Heart thudding, Savannah stopped to look in a display window for men's hats. Glancing from the corner of her eye, she spotted Mrs. Lakin approach the apothecary.

Savannah scanned the street for Travis. Grateful that he was gone, she closed the distance between her and the letter carrier, who sat on a bench.

Sitting on the other end, Savannah put down her basket.

"Keep looking at the shop window."

Surprised at the tense command, Savannah pretended an interest in the signs about Old Indigenous, the new quinine, a substitute for quinine made of dried poplar, dogwood, and willow bark, used to treat fevers and malaria. "What—"

"Next week. Same time. We meet outside the theater."

"All right." That was better. Plays might return in the coming weeks.

"Don't look at me. Edge your basket closer to me."

She complied with the soft-spoken command.

The letter carrier stood, stumbled, and dropped a package

into Savannah's basket. "Pardon me," she said in a normal tone as she extracted her package. "Good day."

"Good day." Savannah stood, about to call Mrs. Lakin back. She hadn't given her the letter. She rummaged for it and then stopped. It was gone along with the money.

Impressive.

CHAPTER 13

riday morning, Travis called at Luke's home to discover if he'd made it home. Drawn by the sound of something heavy being dragged, he went straight to the open door of the saddle shop. The room was almost clear of debris, and Luke hunched over in the middle, pulling a large box of tools. "Good morning, Luke. I see you received the army's letter about the exchange. How did Felicity's family react to her brother's Northern loyalties?"

"Better than expected." Luke released the box to shake Travis's hand, his whole demeanor joyful. "I talked with her and her family until late last evening. The shock of Jack serving as a Union soldier has passed somewhat. They didn't want the apology I pressed upon them. Instead, they were overjoyed that I initiated the exchange." He grinned. "With help."

"You'll meet the officers who had a hand in the exchange once you muster in." Travis leaned against the wall.

"That will be in three to four weeks. Felicity and I discussed our wedding with me future aunt and uncle." He flushed. "I will have family again. 'Tis a blessing."

Travis's thoughts flew to Uncle Dabney, who had never

married. Sharing the farm with his brother's family and his parents must have eased that loneliness. As did hiding fugitives.

"We hope to wed while Jack is here and can give Felicity away. Not knowing the loyalties of her other brother and sister, she's not inviting them."

Tough days, when allegiance to one's country created division in families.

"Savannah gave Felicity one of her silk gowns as a gift. She's modifying it to wear as her wedding gown." Luke's brown eyes softened. "Their friend Julia used to be the one who knit all three together as friends. I'm pleased that Savannah and Felicity are becoming closer on their own now."

"I'm happy for all of you." Would he ever find a woman with whom he could share the kind of happiness Luke and Felicity enjoyed? Maybe Savannah?

Travis frowned. Savannah hadn't been herself yesterday when he'd seen her outside the colonel's headquarters. Later, when he looked for her to carry her purchases, she was gone. Had she been avoiding him, as he'd suspected? Maybe she wasn't over the beau she lost early in the war. Even if she was, she might never consider being courted by a Union officer.

"Whenever Jack comes, we'll be married. You'll be invited along with the Adairs." Luke hesitated. "I'd like to invite the officers who arranged the exchange, if that's a good idea?"

"It's a fine idea." Travis was touched. This man was as thoughtful and compassionate as he was honest. "May I pass along the invitation?"

Luke's face cleared. "Please do."

"Jack may be delayed due to battles in the east. General Sherman's forces are fighting to take back Jackson. We've got the city under siege and are continuing to exchange artillery shots. I've no doubt of Sherman's success. Felicity may have a few days to finish her alterations."

"Good to know." Luke eyed him. "There are more freedman in the city than even when I left. How are they making a living? Where do they live?"

"They've established tent communities. Some live in homes —possibly in houses where the owners are away. I'm not certain what will be done about that or when." It frustrated Travis that these families' first taste of freedom was a struggle to find shelter in the already overpopulated city. "You're right about them needing jobs."

"Even the citizens struggle to find employment." Luke shook his head. "I hope citizens who can afford to hire their former servants do so."

"Me too." But too many former plantation owners were now destitute. Would the Adairs forgive and hire back their former staff?

Within a few minutes, Travis left to continue his so-far-fruitless hunt for solid evidence of spying. This was new territory for him in his army service. Nevertheless, he aimed to excel.

But how?

A tall, husky black man with a touch of gray at his temples sat alone under a mature crepe myrtle tree, his back against the trunk. He'd sat there yesterday. That spot gave an excellent view of the sloped street heading toward downtown. What had he noticed?

Impulsively, Travis sauntered over and introduced himself.

"I'm Clifford Jamison." Rising, the man stepped from under the tree. "What do you want with me?"

A man who cut right to the heart of the matter. Travis appreciated that. "I believe citizens of this city are sneaking our secrets to the Confederate soldiers who left a few days ago."

He grunted.

"I'm wondering if you've seen anyone acting suspiciously,

perhaps stopping to exchange only a couple of whispered words."

Clifford folded his arms. "Didn't see that, but a farmer shook hands with tow-headed gentleman toting a cane yesterday and then just walked away."

Travis scratched his ear. "That's not exactly what I meant. Why did you notice those men?"

"'Cause the farmer left a folded paper on the gentleman's palm. The tow-head dropped the paper in his pocket real sneaky like."

Travis's senses sharpened. "That's more like it. Can you describe what they were wearing?"

"That was the skinniest farmer I ever did see. Stood about so high." He touched a spot below his shoulder. "Ain't seen nobody else wearing red suspenders since the Rebs left." He spat. "The gentleman had a mustache and wore a gray coat and blue vest with swirls on it."

Travis thanked him and left to comb the streets with renewed vigor at his first real lead on two spies.

~

*E*arly-morning rain on Saturday prevented Savannah from walking about the city to overhear soldiers' conversations. The only thing she'd learned from Travis was that Confederate wounded had been sent to either Mobile or Monroe. She'd pass that along but doubted it was the information Sam desired.

She told her mother that she wanted to visit the shops that afternoon and headed toward Washington Street. Many shops, businesses, and the Washington Hotel where she'd often dined with Willie were on that street. She would blend into the activity easily and listen for information vital for Sam.

Dozens of Union soldiers and officers congregated in

groups on the busy thoroughfare. She scanned the blue-coated men for Travis's ruggedly handsome face but didn't see him. Although Travis always seemed to be in town, there wasn't a particular area or location where she always found him.

Where did he attend worship services? They hadn't discussed their beliefs, but she discerned that he shared her faith, which had been strong as a child, deepened by reading the Bible with her housekeeper, Ellen. Savannah had slacked off on her church attendance after Willie died, when her world had crumbled around her and God seemed so very far away. Her prayers might have dwindled to bedtime and blessings on meals, yet she did believe in God.

Felicity had mentioned seeing several Union soldiers at the church on Walnut Street last week. She'd persuade Mama to attend services there tomorrow. They had no cook on Sundays, so they couldn't invite him to lunch.

But what prevented her from inviting him on another day? Men loved to speak about their work. Sam said even seemingly insignificant details might be important. Mama was ever the gracious hostess. Even if dining with a Union officer wasn't to her liking, her guests would never guess.

A group of soldiers smoked cigars outside the hotel. She paused in front of a milliner's display window nearby.

"I knew it was only a matter of time before we took back Jackson." A man in his mid-twenties clapped another soldier on the back. "Don't tell me you doubted it."

"Not me." His companion shook his head emphatically. "I wasn't surprised to hear that General Johnston abandoned the city Thursday night."

Heat flamed in Savannah's face. This was a catastrophe. Mississippi's capital was under Union control for the second time.

Savannah wandered the streets and ended up outside Julia Dodd Mitchell's childhood home. Mrs. Dodd had left a couple in charge of the home in exchange for a place to live. A week before, newly freed men and women from surrounding plantations had lounged on the porch and stairs. Not today. Had Silas and Hester banished them from the home?

It was a good thing she and Mama had stayed in Vicksburg.

A sudden longing to see Julia welled up. How she missed her friend. Julia and Ash had been wise to move to Texas. Vicksburg was in shambles.

She didn't realize that she was staring at the house until the front door opened. Ellen and Josie stepped outside.

They had left her home to live at the Dodd home in their absence? Savannah gaped at them.

"Miss Savannah." Ellen descended the stairs with her daughter a step behind.

"Ellen, how is it that you're both staying in Mrs. Dodd's home?" Savannah tried to temper the shock and anger from her tone. An invitation to stay there should have come from the owner.

"We came here that first day." The short woman with a turban covering her black hair stopped a few paces away. "Hester and Silas said they had plenty of room for everyone from your house." She sighed. "But then others came. Too many. By nightfall, there was nigh on fifty freed folks just like us in there."

"Fifty?" Savannah gasped.

"More came after we all bedded down wherever we could find a spot to lay our heads. Silas finally locked the door and said no more could stay." Ellen clutched the white apron that hid most of her gray dress. "They couldn't be expected to feed so many. We got free rations, or we'd have starved."

"What about Ollie and the others?"

"They got jobs as police guards and with the Union army. Alvera is here." Ellen lifted her chin. "Hester and Silas can't keep putting us up. They said everyone who doesn't have a job has to add a tent to the rows of them outside town."

"I've hired a cook. Felicity has been my part-time house-keeper, and her cousin is my maid. But Felicity is getting married soon and will want some time off until her husband musters into the Union army. And I told her that I'd hire you as my housekeeper if you ever wanted the job." Savannah gazed at the proud woman steadily. "My offer still stands."

"What about Josie?" Ellen glanced back at her sixteen-year-old daughter.

The hope stirring in Savannah's heart was reflected in the girl's eyes. "I want Josie to come back also." She quoted them the same salary that her father had offered Felicity, Mrs. Beltzer, and Petunia. "You can stay in your former rooms, but they need attention." Bedrooms on the third floor hadn't been cleared of dust and broken glass.

"We get one day off a week." A satisfied glint brightened Ellen's dark eyes. "And Sundays until three for church."

It was more than fair. "Which day?"

"Wednesday"—she gave a crisp nod— "so we can go to services midweek."

"Agreed." Having Ellen and Josie back would go a long way to restoring Mama's sense of normalcy.

Papa would be pleased. If he knew.

Had he found a job? Was he coming back, or would Savannah eventually be forced to leave Vicksburg and let the servants go again?

~

On Saturday afternoon, Travis pretended to search his pockets for a cigar as he leaned against a brick wall at the end of a street. A tow-haired Southern gentleman in a gray coat was just around the corner. He'd stopped to speak in low tones to a plainly dressed man with red suspenders, one who fit Clifford's description of the farmer. So far, he hadn't observed enough to arrest them.

Travis's heartbeat escalated when he heard the location and layout of a Union camp past the Eighth Illinois Regiment's location discussed in detail. Rebel bands had attacked a foraging detail earlier in the week. Did they plan to attack an outlying camp?

He pulled out his sidearm and rounded the corner. "You men are under arrest."

Both of them turned to bolt.

"Stop." Travis cocked the gun. "It's loaded, gentlemen."

They stopped. Hands raised, they slowly faced Travis. "We didn't do anything wrong." How quickly the Southern gentleman's shock became bluster.

"I'll let you tell your story to the colonel." Colonel Haversham wanted to interview all suspects. "Head to Monroe Street." He gestured with his gun.

Heads whipped in their direction as Travis trailed his prisoners up the sidewalk, Union soldiers and fellow officers among them.

"Want me to walk with you, Lieutenant?" This offer came from a sergeant unfamiliar to him.

"No. Obliged to you." He regretted the spectacle. His was a secret mission. Folks would wonder why he trailed two citizens at gunpoint.

It couldn't be helped.

He gave short directions until they reached the colonel's headquarters, where he left them temporarily in the care of Lieutenant Christopher Dunn, who also claimed a room as his office, while Travis briefed the colonel. He explained about the lead he'd received from Clifford Jamison and what he'd overheard.

Then he brought them in. Travis didn't invite them to sit,

nor did he sit. He requested their names and occupations, which the colonel recorded.

Although the farmer's hands shook, his companion's bravado continued. When pressed, they both admitted to spying.

"Who are you spying for?" Colonel Haversham folded his hands.

The cocky one grinned.

"I repeat..." The colonel's tone roughened. "Who are you spying for?"

"I can't say." He peered at the bookshelf beyond the colonel's shoulder.

"Can't or won't?" Travis's eyes narrowed.

No answer.

He hadn't expected to learn the name easily. "Is there anything you *want* to tell us?"

The grin disappeared. "There are too many of us. You'll never catch us all."

A surge of energy shot through Travis. "I accept that challenge."

~

On Sunday morning, Savannah asked her mother to attend the church on Walnut Street over corn cakes Mrs. Beltzer had left for them. They dined in the family dining room that was quickly becoming a haven to Savannah. The formal dining room, with its foot-wide holes in the floor and ceiling, only served as a reminder of all they'd lost.

"Why?" Mama's pleasant mood had begun when Savannah brought Ellen and Josie home yesterday. "Our church on Cherry Street has the added advantage of being close to our house."

"The other church appears more popular with Union soldiers. Perhaps Travis goes there."

"Oh?" Mama sat back in her chair. "Are you interested in him as a potential beau?"

"No." She spoke too quickly. Was she? No, she couldn't court a man while spying on him. Mama mustn't know about it. "There are repairs to the city that must be addressed. I want to bring them to an officer's attention."

"Are you certain that's your only consideration?" Mama folded her napkin and set it beside her empty plate.

"Not really." Though it made her uncomfortable, Savannah's goal was to establish a deeper bond with Travis to secure information from him. "Travis has been good to us."

"He did aid in carrying our patients to the hospital."

"Exactly." That small service had begun to build Savannah's trust in the officer. Mama's, too, apparently. "And Luke will invite him to their wedding."

"When is it?"

"We don't know. Jack hasn't arrived yet."

Leaning back, Mama eyed her. "Savannah, we loved Willie dearly and would have welcomed him as part of our family, but he's been gone nearly two years. If a young man of good family has captured your attention, your father and I will be pleased to meet him."

"Thank you, Mama." She'd never spoken of courting another man. Travis's smiling face popped into her thoughts. Mama was right. Willie wouldn't want her to remain unmarried forever, but he'd certainly not want her to wed a Union officer. Her breathing grew ragged. In light of this conversation, it was better to wait on inviting him to supper. "I'm merely saying we must appear to accept Union soldiers in our beloved Vicksburg."

"Your father advised that very thing." She studied the

crumbs on her plate. "All right. Let's go to the church popular with the Yankees."

It was another step toward learning vital information for Sam.

But why the heaviness in her chest?

~

ravis had spotted the Adairs sitting near the front of the church on Sunday while he scooted to the middle of a back pew beside Ben and Enos in a row filled with his comrades. The possibility of talking to Savannah had lifted his spirits, already high from jailing two spies yesterday. He planned to find Clifford tomorrow and thank him.

After the service ended, his brother-in-law turned to Travis. "Enos wants to go fishing today. Want to come?"

"Along the Mississippi River?" Travis wasn't free to discuss the soldiers who'd been attacked outside of camp.

"Thinking about walking to the creek behind our lines." Enos stood to follow Ben from the pew. "We fashioned some poles back at camp. We'd welcome your company."

"The Mississippi has more variety." Rebel attacks weren't well-known yet, but the spies had spoken of details concerning the outlying camp...near the creek. Neither could he tell them about yesterday's spies. "Fish just outside the City Landing on the other side of the ships. I'll join you there."

Enos frowned. "We'll have to fetch our poles and our lunch from camp."

"Is there a reason to stay close to the city?" Ben studied him.

Travis tensed. His brother-in-law knew him better than Enos did. "I have some business in the city. Can you fetch my lunch while you're at camp?"

"We'll do it." Easygoing Enos was the first to agree to the

change in watering holes. "We'll double-quick and see you down on the river in about an hour."

"Thanks." After they left, Travis met Savannah's glance. Her mother was speaking to two well-dressed ladies.

She said something to her mother before approaching him. "Good morning, Travis."

"Good morning." Something in her smile did strange things to his heart. "I didn't see you here last week." Worship services grounded him in his faith, and facing the terror of battles had intensified his prayers. He attended church at every opportunity. Occupying a town provided that blessing.

"We normally attend a church closer to home. Mama and I decided this morning to come here." She tilted her head. "Strangers outnumber city folk, no matter the location."

"Good morning, Travis." Mrs. Adair joined them. The church was nearly empty.

He returned her greeting. "May I escort you ladies home?" As much as he hoped they'd invite him to lunch, he couldn't stay, though it would be pleasant to be asked.

Savannah's smile warmed her eyes. "You may."

Outside in the bright sunlight, he offered an arm to both ladies. They all discussed the sermon from the fourth chapter of Nehemiah about opposition to rebuilding Jerusalem's walls along the way. Though it was obviously a familiar chapter to both ladies, neither seemed inclined for a deep discussion. Nehemiah's courage had made him one of Travis's favorite heroes in the Bible. Perhaps the destroyed buildings in Vicksburg made it a sensitive topic. As he pondered that possibility, the Adairs' mansion loomed over them.

"Is that Felicity and Luke on our portico?" Mrs. Adair shaded her eyes. "And another man."

"It must be Jack. Let's meet him." Savannah tugged on Travis's arm. "I certainly hope she finished altering her dress."

CHAPTER 14

A pang of jealousy struck Savannah at Felicity's wedding on Wednesday evening that had nothing to do with Luke. Looking lovely in the white silk gown that Savannah had given her, Felicity was marrying the man of her dreams in the church where they'd met. True, it didn't look the same, not with the windows missing and a United States flag waving in the breeze from its spire. The radiance on Felicity's face, however, with her hand resting on the arm of the gaunt man beside her, would have lit up the room had the sun not been shining. Tears pricked Savannah's eyes at the happiness on Luke's face when Felicity reached his side.

Her family resemblance to Jack was in the same blond curls and blue eyes. The former prisoner had spent two days in bed. Nourishing meals had gone a long way to restore his strength.

Mrs. Beltzer wept openly on the front row. Petunia's petulant look might have been caused by Felicity choosing Savannah to stand up with her—or, more likely, Petunia was angry her cousin was marrying a man about to enlist in the Union army.

Savannah's attention wandered to Travis, who stood beside

Luke in the absence of Ash...and Willie. Here at this wedding of two of their closest friends, it gave her a pang to think of the man who would have married her. But Julia and Ash's wedding last year had wounded her more. Perhaps she was recovering.

Travis smiled at her.

A chunk of ice seemed to melt from her heart.

"I now pronounce you husband and wife. Luke, you may kiss your bride."

Luke lifted Felicity's veil and kissed her.

Savannah chanced a look over at Travis. He was looking back at her. He held her gaze.

"Ladies and Gentlemen..." The minister turned the radiant couple around to face the congregation. "It's my very great honor to introduce to you for the first time...Mr. and Mrs. Luke Shea."

A tear trickled down Felicity's cheek. Heedless of onlookers, she cupped Luke's face with the hand not holding a bouquet of daisies and kissed his cheek.

Wilma and Little Miles ran over and grabbed Felicity's legs. Family members hurried forward, faces beaming.

Savannah stepped aside to allow them to celebrate. To her surprise, Travis followed.

"It was a beautiful ceremony." He handed her a large white handkerchief.

"It was." She dabbed at her eyes. "I usually don't get emotional at weddings. It's just that they've been through so much, and I..." Mrs. Beltzer's tears were sparking her own, no doubt.

"I understand." He shifted so that he shielded her from the dozen or so guests just now arising from the pews.

She had to change the topic, or she'd be weeping like a child. "There are more military men than I expected to see this evening." A colonel was among them.

"Yes, Luke invited everyone who helped with his exchange."

Travis's face softened. "Will you attend the reception at the Beltzers' home?"

"Oh, yes." Savannah relaxed. "I love parties." The last one she'd attended had been in the spring. "Thank you for shielding me from prying eyes. I rarely cry in public." Not even at Willie's funeral had she cried.

And it was more important not to show weakness now that she lived in an occupied city.

～

*T*ravis and Brian ambled back to camp in the light of the moon after the wedding festivities ended.

"After tonight, I'm doubly grateful we went the extra mile to get Luke exchanged for Jack." Brian kept his gaze on the dirt road. "I talked with Jack for a quarter hour. His experience at Libby Prison makes me hope there are enough exchanges to release all those prisoners."

"Privates aren't as well-fed as officers. It's distressing to learn of the overcrowded conditions and poor medical care." He was glad Luke had found a way to save Jack. "Savannah and I talked with Luke and Felicity on the veranda." The stars had come out while they were outside, and they had all searched for constellations. The children and Petunia joined in the fun.

"Yes, I noticed the looks you gave Savannah during the ceremony." Brian chuckled. "I'd say that you're falling for a Southern belle."

Travis wanted to protest but could not do so. Savannah's beauty in her pink silk dress had captivated him. In truth, it was the glimpses beneath her armor that intrigued him even more. "Her beau died in 1861. I don't believe she's over her grief."

"Maybe not. A friend's wedding would be difficult under those circumstances."

"Her tears were about to spill over at the end." Brian knew more about women than Travis did. Brian had married his childhood sweetheart before the war began. Travis's one courtship had ended when Janet Patton had fallen in love with the banker's son. His heart had mended in a matter of weeks because, as he later realized, what he'd felt for her was infatuation, not love.

"My mother cries at every wedding she attends." Brian chuckled. "That doesn't mean Savannah's heart is still broken."

They passed a farmhouse damaged by artillery that Travis had studied on many long walks to Vicksburg because it symbolized how even outlying areas of the battle suffered. Beyond it were woods in advance of the camps.

"Do you get the feeling we're being watched?" A few feet into the forest's darkness, Brian's gaze darted in every direction.

"I'm uneasy all of the sudden." He felt for his sidearm. Not there because he'd been at church. Pickets guarding Vicksburg were too far away to hear them should they run into an ambush, while those guarding the camps were still ahead.

A twig snapped.

Both men halted. Travis strained to see whether a figure crouched behind the bushes or trees on either side of them.

"Someone's letting us know they're here," Travis whispered. It was about eleven. Long past "Taps."

"Could be a bear." Brian's voice shook.

"Could be." His gut told him differently.

"If they were going to attack, they'd have done it before we noticed them." Brian's whisper was barely audible. "Let's quicken our pace through the woods until we reach our pickets."

A hundred yards never appeared so long. Travis heard no sounds save their footsteps on the packed dirt and his own rapid breathing.

Once out of the woods, they silently maintained their pace until reaching their pickets. Travis gave the code. Brian explained what happened and sent half the pickets to investigate. Brian and Travis kept watch in their wake.

The guards returned around midnight. They hadn't found anyone hiding in the woods. No bears either.

Travis thanked them and reminded them to be vigilant.

"It could have been an animal," said Brian as the two of them continued on to camp, "but all the smaller ones were eaten during the battle."

"We need to lengthen our picket line."

"Agreed. You'll be in town tomorrow. Report the matter to Colonel Haversham in the morning."

Travis's mind flew to what the spies had said last week. There were so many spies that the Union would never catch them all.

Had someone hidden along the path in order to spy on those returning late to camp?

Travis would also voice that concern to the colonel.

~

*O*n Thursday morning, Savannah opened her wardrobe and stilled. Her dresses had been moved to different hooks. The hem of her plain brown dress stuck out where before it had been completely hidden behind a green satin.

Frantic, she skimmed her fingers over the soft fabric for the pocket until she felt the envelope she'd prepared with news of Jackson's fall. Relief was followed by consternation. Who had moved her things?

Josie had nearly finished the laundry piles that somehow had defeated Petunia's meager efforts. Whereas Petunia had left clean clothes draped across the bed for Savannah to put away, Josie always completed the job. Or Ellen might even have been the one to put the clothing away, shifting dresses around to make room for the clean ones.

If Petunia had discovered the letter, the whole household would know by now. The woman could not keep a secret. On the other hand, Josie would have shown it to her mother without delay. Yet neither maid had acted any differently toward Savannah.

Had Ellen found the letter? Her blood ran cold. Ellen was too sharp by far to miss the crinkle of the letter concealed in the pocket. It was already addressed to Sam. If she found it, did she imagine Savannah sent secret correspondence to a beau of whom Mama didn't approve? Ellen had known Savannah since she was a child and would realize such behavior was uncharacteristic of her.

With Josie and Ellen back in the home, Savannah could no longer hide anything in her room. They mustn't find the cipher in between her mattresses. It would be burned today. Instead of writing information as she discovered it, she'd write it on the days of her meetings and not allow the messages to leave her sight.

She stared down at the letter. The seal hadn't been broken —thank goodness.

Perhaps it hadn't been discovered. Perhaps she panicked for nothing.

Savannah tapped the paper against her hand. It had been updated with the Union army's destruction of factories and businesses and even the burning of homes in Jackson, hardly the actions of respectable men. They'd destroyed her capital.

Sam would be equally as incensed as Savannah. Did he have enough men to do something about it?

*T*ravis was in Colonel Haversham's office at eight o'clock on Thursday morning. He explained what happened on their walk back to camp. "I remembered that spy's warning that there were too many of them for us to catch."

"It's concerning enough that we'll extend our picket line." Seated at his desk, Colonel Haversham frowned as he studied Travis. "Were you and Brian talking about your orders or our attacks elsewhere before you felt yourself being watched?"

"No." Heat rushed up his face. "We were speaking of the wedding and how women seem to love to cry at them."

"Not much fodder for a spy there." His shoulders relaxed. "Any leads on other spies?"

It pained him to shake his head. "I've been monitoring the areas by the river." Ship crews could be spy contacts, but so far, whenever he drew close enough to overhear their conversations, the men spoke of their families or their girls. If nothing was happening on the river, he'd check with Clifford Jamison about spies. "I'll stay near the heart of the city today."

"Yesterday afternoon, twenty troops were attacked by about fifty Rebels while fishing in a stream east of our camp. Our men were armed and made a good account of themselves. One was shot in the foot. They left behind their poles and catches. News should be all over camp before you go back for supper." The colonel peered out the window. "We can't ignore this. Tomorrow Brian is taking a company of our men to search for the culprits up to the Big Black River, the direction our troops saw them head. You'll go with them."

The colonel had Travis's full attention. That river was some fifteen miles from Vicksburg.

"Yes, sir." Tomorrow, he'd be more than happy for the chance to take the culprits as prisoners. But today he hoped to arrest another spy.

Five minutes later, Travis passed the headquarters of Major

General James McPherson, who was now in command of the District of Vicksburg, at the corner of Crawford and Cherry Streets. He meandered about the heart of the city, listening to snatches of civilian conversations. Nothing of interest. He stopped to greet Union soldiers filling holes in the streets, a sight certain to please Savannah. As he talked with them, his gaze darted in every direction, on his guard for anyone acting suspiciously. He had discovered it was much easier to survey the area while carrying on a conversation.

Farther down the road, Savannah stopped in front of the theater. She appeared to be waiting for someone or something.

As he about-faced to wish the workers a good day, he scanned the area and blinked.

A woman wearing a silk dress that had seen better days drove a buggy pulled by a donkey toward him. The two-seated vehicle was also occupied by an older woman in all her finery. Based on their similarity in looks, the two gaunt women were mother and daughter. Two trunks, bags, and boxes filled the second seat to the roof.

Travis didn't need to see the misery in their eyes to sense they'd seen difficult days. He glanced back at Savannah. A woman, a large hat shadowing her features, approached her. Who could that be?

"Pardon me, sir."

Travis turned back to the buggy. "May I help you, miss?"

"Am I to understand your army is giving free rations to citizens?" The daughter's voice was scratchy as if from lack of use. A blue hat decorated with white silk flowers sat atop brown ringlets.

"Yes, miss." He gave her directions to the building. "Are you a Vicksburg resident?"

"We are now." Her face hardened. "There's nothing for us to go back to." Picking up the reins, she drove off.

His heart went out to her. There was little Travis could do

for her beyond direct her to the free supplies. Besides, he was more interested in what brought Savannah out today.

~

Savannah studied an old advertisement on the theater building without seeing it. All her senses were focused on her surroundings because the letter carrier she was supposed to be meeting was nowhere in sight.

Union soldiers working one street over made her nervous to tarry longer than necessary.

Mrs. Lakin was ten minutes late. To anyone watching, a quick turn up to the Catholic Church and back might look less suspicious than just standing so long in one place. She set off at a sedate pace.

"Miss Adair, is it?"

Savannah swung around, relief flooding her that Mrs. Lakin chose to speak to her this time. "Yes, good morning." The letter carrier pretended this was a chance meeting for those nearby who might overhear the softly spoken conversation.

"May I walk with you?" Though the words were gracious, the tone suggested a command.

"Of course." Savannah transferred her basket to the arm between them and began to walk. "Shall we meet outside the Washington Hotel next week?" That was near a notion shop where Savannah could watch for her.

"Fine. Tilt your basket toward me."

Savannah did so. The letter carrier fussed with her shawl over the top of the basket. Only by the grasping fingers against the weave did Savannah realize the note and money were gone.

"Sam says that you're doing good work." Mrs. Lakin gave her side glance. "So far." With that implied warning, she crossed the street and disappeared into an alley.

"Savannah."

She cringed at the familiar voice. Travis. Why was he always about when the letter carrier was near?

Booted steps drew closer. "Good morning." Travis's smile warmed his hazel eyes to almost green. "Do you have errands?"

She gaped at him. She hadn't prepared an excuse. "I... that is, I'm picking up my family's rations." She'd explain to Mrs. Beltzer that she'd wanted to save her the trouble of collecting them later. "Ellen and Josie are now employed by us—my former housekeeper and her daughter, who is a maid."

"Say, that's good news." His face brightened. "So many of the former servants taking refuge in Vicksburg struggle to find jobs and shelter. I'm glad. I'll escort you to the warehouse and then carry your provisions home, if I may?"

"Please do." His praise brought a pleasant warmth to her heart.

"Will Felicity continue to work for you?" He matched his steps with hers.

"As a maid." Savannah nodded. "She asked to be excused until August third. They're moving Felicity's possessions to Luke's home in those ten days."

"Do you need that much staff?" They waited for a wagon to pass before crossing the street.

"Maybe not permanently. But they all need jobs, and Papa left enough money to pay their salaries. Besides, they're still cleaning layers of dust and glass from little-used rooms." She sighed. "What I most need is someone to fix the ceilings and floors from the cannonball strike. All our male servants—that is, former servants—work for your army."

"I see." A gleam of approval lit his features. "You and your family are so kind to others that, of course, I want to help. But my only day off is Sunday. I can work on patching the holes beginning this Sunday after church. Will that suit you?"

"Thank you." Giving up his only day off to repair her home was a sacrifice, but she was in such desperate need that she didn't want him to reconsider. "That suits me very well indeed. I may be able to persuade Ellen to cook supper for us." Alvera, who had a knack in the kitchen, hadn't returned. "No promises, though. She's off until midafternoon on Sundays." It was a schedule that had worked last week. Ellen and Josie had been there nearly a week and seemed content. For her part, Savannah was comforted to have their familiar presence again.

"If not, I can fry bacon for sandwiches." He grinned as he opened the door to the warehouse.

Savannah joined the line of women waiting that was thankfully a tenth of what it had been on Independence Day nearly three weeks before. When the woman ahead of Savannah turned toward the door with an overloaded basket, Savannah stepped forward to give her name and the number of people living in her house to the bored clerk.

A sack struck the dusty floor behind her. The woman who just left must have dropped it. Savannah, concentrating on obtaining her own supplies, didn't turn to look.

Travis retrieved it. "May I help you to your buggy, miss?" he asked the woman who had been in front of Savannah in line.

"Thank you kindly."

At the vaguely familiar voice, Savannah glanced over her shoulder. Her jaw slackened. The disheveled woman wearing a stained silk dress and matching hat was indeed familiar. This was her former childhood friend, Mary Grace Jung. They hadn't spoken since the day Papa had interrupted the severe whipping Mr. Jung's overseer was giving Gus.

Once upon a time, Mary Grace would never have permitted herself to be seen in public in a stained garment. Her pride must have taken a beating. Savannah's gaze fell to the rations provided by the Union army. Hunger couldn't afford pride.

Savannah looked up, and the two women stared at one another. "Hello, Mary Grace." Compassion stirred for what must have been difficult days.

"Hello, Savannah." A ghost of a smile touched her lips and as quickly vanished. "I didn't know if you'd speak with me. I prayed you would."

"You prayed I'd speak to you?" Savannah tilted her head. "Why?"

"Not just speak to me." Her face crumpled. "But also to give Mama and me a place to live."

CHAPTER 15

ravis somehow found room for Miss Jung's rations in her overloaded buggy. Savannah had invited the mother and daughter to come to her house for a discussion with her and mother. In Travis's opinion, Savannah had been careful in her choice of words. The whole exchange left him curious about what transpired in the past.

Outside the warehouse, he studied Savannah's shocked stare as the Jungs' donkey's hooves clopped forward on the cobblestone. The poor animal strained against the buggy's weight. He hefted Savannah's basket to his shoulder as they began the walk back to her house. "Do you want to tell me about it?"

"One can't wonder at your curiosity." Her already halting pace slowed as she explained that she and Mary Grace had been childhood friends. Savannah had picked flowers from Mrs. Jung's garden despite her friend's protests and then the gardener had arranged the blooms in a treasured heirloom vase that originally belonged to Mrs. Jung's grandmother. As they drove home, Savannah saw Mr. Jung's overseer whipping his servant and begged her father to do something. He had reluctantly intervened and ended up purchasing the whole family to protect them from Mr. Jung's wrath.

Travis's head reeled that a little girl's innocent desire for a floral bouquet had escalated to such a travesty. He could only imagine how upset she must have been. His opinion of Mr. Adair, which hadn't been very good, improved. He'd stepped in to save a man from a severe beating. That required courage and sacrifice. "Mr. Jung didn't appreciate the interference, I'd imagine."

Savannah gave a bitter laugh. "He'd agreed to use my father as his cotton broker, but after the incident, the Jungs cut all ties with us. The worst part"—she wrung her hands—"was the rift I caused between my parents."

"You didn't—"

"But I did." Regret burned in her brown eyes. "It was my fault. Mama said Papa can't refuse me anything. Since that day, I've been careful not to ask for anything big. It even affected my fai..." She caught herself as they approached her family's mansion where the Jungs waited outside the gate.

"Wait a minute, Savannah." He touched her arm, stopping her at the street corner opposite her home. He settled the over-loaded basket on the sidewalk. "Were you about to say the incident affected your faith? That you fear to ask God for things too?"

"I don't seem to know what's appropriate to ask. I ruined my parent's marriage, and I didn't even help anyone. Gus ended up running away."

A bolt of lightning couldn't have stunned him more. She didn't trust herself—or God. "Savannah, please. Never fear asking God for things you need, things that are bigger than you. He can say 'yes' or 'no'—that's up to Him. We can trust Him to decide. It may take a while to get the answer, and the answer may not be what we want, but we can have faith God will do the right thing. Don't be afraid to pray, Savannah."

Her gaze clung to his. It was as if she wanted to believe him but couldn't.

"You did the right thing all those years ago, Savannah." Holding her gaze, he cupped her cheek with his free hand. "So did your father, though it cost him dearly. I wish your mother could see it."

"Me too." She touched the hand on her cheek and then drew it down to be sandwiched between hers. "That's how Ellen and Josie came to us originally."

"And you said Gus ran away?"

She sighed. "Gus wasn't happy here either. He and his son, Riley, ran away the next summer. I never saw them again."

"I'm sorry." He shook his head. "But Mary Grace was innocent in all of this too. Please remember that when you all talk."

She tilted her head, studying him. "Thanks for toting my heavy load for a few minutes." She released him and picked up the basket, taking a step away. "Mama's not going to be happy about this. It's best you don't come in."

"One moment."

She turned back.

"May I take that poor donkey to your stable and feed and water it?" The exhausted animal might drop on the street otherwise.

"Yes, thank you. I imagine there's plenty of fodder in the stable. Let me speak with them first." She approached the buggy.

He waited on the corner until the soft-spoken, brief conversation ended. Then, with her back ramrod straight, she mounted the steps to her mansion.

Travis hastened to the buggy to assist the women in alighting. The ladies thanked him effusively for his kindness to their animal as Travis took the donkey's bridle and went around the house into the dank stables with the packed buggy.

He crossed to the outdoor pump for fresh water and helped

himself to a long, refreshing drink. Then he placed a full bucket in front of the donkey. It sucked up the water while Travis unhitched it. He filled a feed trough in one of the stalls with oats to coax the animal inside.

"I don't know your name, fellow." Travis began brushing it down. "But I'll call you Dusty." He grinned. "Which you won't be when I get done with you."

Dusty nibbled his lunch, clearly uncaring about his name as long as his belly was getting filled.

Shaking the dust from his uniform, Travis washed his hands at the pump and placed a full water bucket into the stall. Dusty's eyes were closed when he left.

Travis turned toward the river. He had wanted to chat with Clifford, but he'd return later to unload the buggy. He had a feeling the Jungs would be staying because of Savannah's compassionate heart, one that needed healing.

~

Savannah's legs felt as heavy as lead climbing the steps to the portico. How she dreaded the upcoming conversation with Mary Grace and Mrs. Jung. But first, she must prepare Mama.

Ellen opened the door for her. "Miss Savannah, are you ailing?"

"I'm fine." Heartsickness wasn't an ailment one treated with medicine. Ellen had been at the Jungs for years. Her children had been born there. Had Mr. Jung been cruel to her? "You may as well know that Mrs. Jung and Mary Grace have asked to live with us."

Ellen stiffened. "And what of Mr. Jung?"

"I don't know. He's not with them." Savannah set down the basket of supplies. "I'll inquire. If they want him to stay here..."

"I won't stay in the same house with him." Ellen lifted her chin. "I got a say so in that much."

"You do." Would it come to that? That the upright Christian woman who coexisted peacefully with everyone didn't like Mr. Jung was a good reason to turn him away. Savannah knew what *her* choice would be in the matter, but her heart ached for the misery in her old friend's eyes. Her head began to throb. "I know nothing of their circumstances beyond that they've endured difficulties."

"I always figured Mr. Jung as the culprit of cruelty in that house."

Savannah rubbed her temples. "Will you ask Mrs. Beltzer if lunch can stretch to feed two more? And where is Mama?"

"In the upstairs parlor doing needlepoint." Ellen picked up the basket and headed back to the kitchen.

Mama had been too upset for months to settle back into her favorite diversion. Ellen's calming presence had done that for her. Mrs. Jung would probably shatter it.

∽

Striving for a calm demeanor, Savannah awaited their guests with Mama in the upstairs parlor because Felicity hadn't had time to wash blood stains from the formal parlor rug. When she had invited the Jungs in for refreshments —coffee and corn cakes would have to do until lunch was ready —Mary Grace had asked if they could freshen up before joining them. Savannah had no objection. It gave her a few minutes to gather her thoughts because at first Mama had balked at talking to them. Only reminding her of her Christian duty convinced her.

Footsteps on the stairs warned her. Petunia led a timid Mary Grace and her mother into the parlor. Their faces and hands were now clean, but their once-fine silk dresses bore so much dust from the road that Savannah could only guess at the color. Mary Grace's brown ringlets were swept back from her face with combs. Savannah remembered being a year older than Mary Grace, making her twenty. Mrs. Jung's beautiful brown hair had wide iron-gray streaks, and it was fashioned into a bun at her crown.

"Mrs. Jacqueline Jung and Miss Mary Grace Jung are here, Mrs. Adair. Savannah."

"Welcome to our home," Savannah said. Petunia lacked a bit of finesse, but at least she'd left her children with their grandmother today, allowing for a quiet conversation. "Thank you, Petunia. I've requested refreshments. You may bring them now." Their guests looked as if they hadn't eaten in days.

"Yes, Savannah." She scurried from the room.

"Thank you for seeing us, Mrs. Adair. Savannah." Mrs. Jung tugged on her sleeve. "We didn't part on the best of terms all those years ago."

Mama inclined her head.

It was a start. "Please, make yourselves comfortable." Savannah gestured to green cushioned armchairs, and the women were quick to comply. "We'll have coffee and corn cakes as refreshments." Supplies in Vicksburg were more available but not yet enough for the sweet cakes and cookies one expected to serve guests. "And of course, you must stay to lunch." More than that, she was unwilling to commit as yet.

"Thank you." Mary Grace exchanged a worried glance with her mother. "We have nowhere else to go, but we know we are not deserving of such kindness."

Strange to hear her admit that. Mr. Jung had spread the news far and wide that Papa had interrupted him disciplining a slave. Papa had lost a few customers, though most returned after a year or two. For her part, Mrs. Jung never attended a party where Mama and Papa were also invited. The bitter quarrel had been fought in silence between the two families.

There were invitations Mama hadn't received due to the feud. That had stopped as the Adairs gained popularity, but Mama hadn't forgiven it.

"Many have suffered greatly during the recent battle." Savannah's thoughts flew to the Sandersons' destroyed plantation.

Petunia knocked. "Here are your refreshments." She passed out individual servings of the mealy cakes.

"Thank you, Petunia. That will be all." Savannah gave the first two cups to her guests and then served her mother. By the time she was seated again, both Jungs were eating their final bite. She felt immediately better about offering refreshments within an hour of lunch. "Please tell us...what happened with you?"

"The worst that's happened is that I'm a widow." Mrs. Jung's thin lips pressed together as if seeking control. "Marcus died at the Battle of Fredericksburg last December. In Virginia."

"Please accept our condolences." The news shocked Savannah. Mr. Jung had to have been in his mid-forties. Why had he been fighting?

"Mama hasn't been the same since the news came." Mary Grace patted her arm. "She's still in shock."

"Understandably so." Mama's face softened.

"Things were to get worse for us, though we didn't see how at the funeral. This May, hundreds of Union soldiers camped on our cotton fields before the battle. Not only did they trample our crops, but they also told our field hands they were free." Mary Grace's ringlets fell across her shoulder as she studied her nearly empty coffee cup. "All of them grabbed their possessions and ran off that very day to stay at Yankee camps."

Shocking that she now considered Travis's announcement to her servants as a good thing. She was happier with Ellen and Josie being here as paid staff. She topped off their guests' coffee without asking, afraid that they might refuse for politeness's sake.

"The house servants stayed a few weeks longer. I thought that the battle would be the most terrifying thing we had to endure." Her blue eyes hardened. "It wasn't. Yankee soldiers came to our home. Groups of them. Sometimes the same ones on different days. But Yankees came daily, never less than three times. The first thing they took was the musket Papa left for our protection."

"That's what happened to the Sandersons."

"I heard about Willie's death." Mary Grace leaned forward. "I'm sorry, Savannah."

"Thank you." The simple words, so often spoken to her at the funeral, touched Savannah with their sincerity. "My condolences to you both as well. It must be difficult without Mr. Jung."

"It's been a nightmare without him. Marcus was never one to back down from a fight. I'd have felt safer for his presence. I did believe our servants would stand up for us." Mrs. Jung's cup clattered against the saucer. "Instead, they showed soldiers where we'd buried our silver."

"And then shared in the spoils." Mary Grace shook her head. "Yankees would always ask for weapons first. When we told them that we'd already given them to other soldiers, they insisted on searching the house. They took gloves, clocks, hats, chairs, ribbons, lace, dresses—even the combs for my hair, heedless of the damage they caused while looting our home." She patted the ivory comb holding back her corkscrew ringlets. "Papa's clothes and shoes were the only things that made sense since they could readily wear them."

Savannah shivered. What would she have done under those circumstances? Had she and Willie already been married, she would have suffered a similar fate.

"Later I realized that stealing our food was the worst." Mary

Grace sipped the last of her coffee and put the cup on a side table. "First, they took all our horses and chickens. They took the cows one by one. Servants dug up our hoarded sacks of dried fruits and vegetables and shared them with the looters. By the time the cannons stopped roaring, everything of value was gone. Then the rest of the servants deserted us. When our food ran out, I knew we must do something."

Savannah's heart ached for all they'd lost. Somehow, it was even worse than what the Sandersons had suffered because they still had their family. Mary Grace only had her mother—whom she was taking care of and not the other way around.

"So we came to Vicksburg." Mary Grace covered a stain on her dress with her hand. "None of our friends stayed in town. Then I thought of you."

"We brought rations." Mrs. Jung crumpled her handkerchief. "We will share them."

"And I will work for our board." Mary Grace lifted her chin. "Perhaps you need help in the kitchen? I've always wanted to try my hand at cooking."

Savannah turned to Mama, who was wiping her eyes. "Do we need to discuss the matter privately?"

"I think we know our answer." Mama met her gaze steadily. After learning all they'd suffered, she could no more turn them out on the streets than Savannah.

No one had escaped unscathed.

"We're happy to have you stay with us until the hostilities end." She looked at Mary Grace. "I'll accept your help in the kitchen. Mrs. Beltzer is our cook. She's off on Sundays and has hinted she'd like Saturdays with her husband as well."

"I accept." Tears glistened in Mary Grace's eyes. "I'll work hard to learn quickly."

Mrs. Jung wept openly. "God has heard our prayers. God bless you both."

"One more thing." Savannah clasped her hands together.

The past couldn't stay buried. There were too many who'd been wounded. "Ellen and Josie have returned. They are paid employees."

Mary Grace stiffened. "What of Gus and Riley?"

"They both ran off about a year after the whole family came to live here."

"Ellen was always our best worker." Mrs. Jung's mouth pinched. Then she sighed. "I guessed she'd be gone by now."

Petunia knocked on the door. "Lunch is served in the family dining room."

Family? What a misnomer. *Survivors* was a more apt description.

How would Ellen respond to the Jungs staying? Would she leave before living with Mrs. Jung again?

Savannah rubbed her temples, willing her pounding headache to recede.

~

Travis found Clifford under the same crepe myrtle, nearly hidden beneath the pink blooms.

"I ain't seen no more notes changing hands, Lieutenant." Clifford whittled on a limb six inches in diameter that fit easily in his callused hands.

"That's all right. We got lucky with your last tip. Both men were arrested." Travis leaned under a well-laden branch and rested his hands on it.

"No foolin'?" Clifford grinned. "Well, that do beat all. Folks don't notice me, sitting under this tree. 'Cept, you did."

Travis's heart went out to him. He seemed lonely. "Do you have family with you?"

"Not since my boy joined up with your army." The shape of a horse's head grew more pronounced with each wood shaving that fell to join the pile on Clifford's trousers and the surrounding grass. "Wouldn't take me 'cause I'm too old. No other jobs to be found."

"What was your old job?"

"Massa was a saddler. Taught me everything he knew. I got real good at it." His proud shoulders drooped. "I found a saddle shop in town, but the fella ain't never been there when I knocked. Don't know as he'd hire me, anyways."

Luke's shop would lay idle when he mustered in unless... Blood pumped faster through Travis's veins. "I know the man who works there. Luke Shea. He just got married and will enlist in my regiment in a week or so. Want me to ask him if he's hiring?"

Clifford studied him. "No, suh. I'll do my own askin', but I don't mind if you introduce us since he ain't never home."

"I'm on duty now. Can I come for you this evening? Maybe about half-past five?"

Clifford half stood and walked bent over until from under the tree. "I'm obliged to you." He held out his hand.

Stepping away from the tree, Travis shook it. "Luke is the one who will be obliged to *you*—that is, if he's hiring." He turned to go.

"Lieutenant."

Travis turned back.

"You might want to search the wharf. I heard something about a spy on a supply ship."

"Thanks." That had been Travis's hunch last week. He headed toward the City Landing.

~

*T*ravis pulled his hat down on his forehead later that morning. It shielded his eyes from the bright sun and also hid that his focus was really on the ship from Louisville being unloaded at the City Landing. The *Emmaline Grace* had captured Travis's attention when it came through last week. Something about the watchful attitude of one of the crew had made him suspicious because it continued the entire time the man unloaded supplies onto a wagon bed.

Travis spotted the sailor in question on the landing, stacking supplies and looking in a different direction every time he added another crate to the pile. Travis meandered closer, wishing someone he knew was in the area. Blending into the surroundings would be easier were he in conversation. At least the activity of wharf workers and local men at the landing helped mask Travis's presence—as much as an officer could hide in an occupied city.

Something caught the crewman's eye on the road above them. Leaning his elbow against a hitching post, Travis glanced over his shoulder. Within moments, a man dressed in gray trousers and a red shirt hastened toward the Louisiana ship.

A storeowner claiming his order? Perhaps. Travis headed closer to the wharf, giving the man a wide berth and keeping both men in his sights. The red-shirted man walked straight to the watchful crewman.

His gaze fixed on the pair, Travis closed the distance between them. A group of townsmen walked past, blocking his view. That meant the pair couldn't see him either. He increased his pace to approach behind the crewman.

"There's fighting at Manassas Gap where we're trying to protect our passes into the Shenandoah from the Yanks. Good news is that General Morgan's cavalry has been destroying bridges and railroads in Ohio for over a week. Our men have raised quite a ruckus. Apparently, the Ohioans are plenty spooked. Our fellas will do the same here when we retake Vicksburg." The local fellow didn't so much as glance in Travis's direction.

"Gentlemen, you are remarkably well informed." Travis

clamped a hand on the crewman's shoulder, his other resting on his sidearm. "And under arrest for spying on the Union."

"My captain's not going to like this." The crewman glared at him.

"Perhaps he should be more careful whom he hires." Travis felt no sympathy. What else had been said before he was within earshot? It didn't matter. After talking with the colonel, they'd probably be discussing it with their fellow prisoners in jail. "Let's go, gentlemen."

Two more spies caught. One step closer to cleaning up the city. After these men were in jail, he'd return to Savannah's to see if he could help there before meeting Clifford.

CHAPTER 16

Travis knocked on Savannah's door around midafternoon. Two more spies cooled their heels in jail, pleasing Colonel Haversham and allowing Travis some personal time.

A petite black woman in her mid-thirties opened the door. "Good afternoon."

Where was Felicity? Ah, yes, the wedding. "Good afternoon." This must be the new housekeeper Savannah had mentioned. "First Lieutenant Travis Lawson. Am I correct in assuming that your name is Ellen? The new housekeeper?"

"Yes, sir." She inclined her head. "I'm surprised Miss Savannah told you about me."

"She's very glad you and your daughter are here." He liked her calm manner. "I'm here to see Savannah."

"They're just finishing their lunch in the family dining room with...with the new family that will live here." Her lips pinched, and her thick lashes swept down. Unless he missed his guess, there'd be tension between Ellen and the Jungs. She widened the door opening. "You may wait in the parlor."

Voices in the hallway halted him just inside the parlor.

Savannah swept down the hall first, looking over her shoulder. She didn't seem to notice Travis. "Ellen, Mr. Jung was killed in battle." She leaned to whisper. "It's a sad tale. Please trust that we could not turn them away upon hearing it. I will tell you everything later."

Mary Grace, followed by her mother, entered the hall. The two middle-aged mothers stared at one another. The proud tilt of Ellen's head hinted at her strength of character.

"Ellen, I'm glad to see you well." Mrs. Jung tugged at her high collar.

"Yes, Mistr—Mrs. Jung." Ellen gestured to Travis. "Lieutenant Lawson is here to see you, Miss Savannah."

Looking around, she gave a start. "Travis, forgive me for not greeting you immediately. You haven't met everyone formally. Please allow me to introduce you."

Travis nodded as she introduced Mrs. Jacqueline Jung, Miss Mary Grace Jung, and her housekeeper, Ellen. "Ladies, I am happy to meet you all. It seems I've come at an inopportune moment."

Mrs. Jung inclined her head, eyeing him.

"Thank you for your earlier kindness, Lieutenant Lawson." Mary Grace clasped her hands together, her gaze dropping to the marble floor.

"Good afternoon, Travis." Mrs. Adair stepped around the Jungs. "Jacqueline and Mary Grace will be staying with us a while."

"Good." He searched Savannah's anxious face. No matter what she felt, her inability to turn them away bespoke of a compassionate nature that rivaled his sweet mother's. "I left the buggy with Dusty in the stable. At least, that's what I called your donkey. I didn't know his name."

"I don't either." Shrugging, Mary Grace extended her hands, palm up. "The donkey—that is, Dusty—plodded into our yard a few days ago. Mama and I had prayed about how we would get here. I was prepared to pull the buggy myself. It seemed an answer to prayer."

"Indeed." Travis was especially glad he'd tended the exhausted animal's needs.

"Lots of answered prayers today." Mary Grace looked at Savannah.

Flushing, she crossed the hall to Travis. "They will want to get settled. Do you—"

"I can bring in their possession from the stable." He smiled.

"Thank you." Her brow wrinkled. "You may exit and enter from the veranda. Mama, we didn't discuss their rooms."

"Well, I thought the third floor..."

Savannah made a strangled noise.

Mrs. Adair's eyes widened.

Ellen stiffened.

Mrs. Adair must not wish to treat them as honored guests. Or maybe Ellen's bedroom was located on the third floor. Oh, boy. If only he'd delayed his visit a quarter hour.

"I meant to say that with one bedroom damaged, we might consider putting them in the back wing where the Sanderson girls slept." Scarlet color flamed in Savannah's face.

"Yes, dear, but those two rooms are smaller." Mrs. Adair fluttered her hands about her face.

"I'm certain they will be more than adequate. We are not guests—more fugitives from the storm, shall we say?" Mary Grace's eyes shone with unshed tears. "And I will help you carry in our belongings, Lieutenant Lawson."

Her humiliation struck him like the brick he'd saved as a battle souvenir. "No, Miss Jung. I'd hardly be worthy of the rank on my shoulder strap if I allowed you to do that."

"Lieutenant, you have no notion what my mother and I have endured from Union soldiers who had no qualms about looting two defenseless women of all their cherished possessions." Mary Grace's guardedness melted into respect and thankfulness. "I've met too many officers unworthy of their rank. May I say that I'm happy to meet one who is worthy?" Tears spilled over. "Thank you for your kindness."

In those few words, Travis grasped the reason Savannah looked emotionally spent. "Miss Jung, I'm sorry for what happened to you. Please allow me to apologize for my comrades." It was unlikely Miss Jung would ever hear it from them directly. "But know this—I serve with many honorable men."

Mary Grace shuddered. Mrs. Jung's hands clenched.

Their reactions to his assertion made Travis determined to earn their trust, made him desire peace for the North *and* South so this madness found an ending. "I'll just fetch those trunks." He exchanged a chagrined look with Savannah. She could show them to their rooms, and he'd head to the back wing of the second floor, wherever that might be.

Long strides took him to the stable. Afternoon sun slanted through the broken windows. He poured more oats into Dusty's trough, enough for tomorrow. The donkey deserved it for what he'd endured. Travis patted Dusty's neck. "What a day, huh, boy? Started off with a sleepless night for worrying who was watching us from the woods on the way back to camp. Then it got a lot better than expected. I put two spies from the wharf in jail. Can you imagine? Walked right up on them talking about their men retaking Vicksburg. And it got even better. I ran into Savannah before we met you and your owners...and then I had a talk with her where she finally opened up to me..."

Dusty brayed.

"Right. Been waiting for her to let that guard down for some time now." He moved to the buggy in the center of the stable and went to work undoing the knots on the rope holding the Jung women's possessions in the backseat. "I doubt tomorrow will be as fortuitous, though. Got to flush out some Rebels who've been attacking our soldiers who venture too far from camp along the Big Black."

~

Savannah halted at the stable door. Her desire when she followed Travis out was to thank him. But who was he talking to? She peeked through the window. The donkey? Yes, Travis was indeed alone in the stable. She smothered a smile. She could well imagine him talking to animals on his Illinois farm.

What amazed her was how much information he'd just provided for her next communication to Sam. The first thing she'd heard was that he'd been waiting for her to let her guard down. Perhaps he was beginning to care for her. Savannah appreciated his friendship more each day and had to admit, if only to herself, that her heart was becoming engaged.

"Whew." He straightened next to the buggy. "Finally got those sloppy knots out. Sorry to leave you, my friend, but I'd best start toting their belongings inside."

Her eyes widened. He mustn't know she'd heard him. She ran to the veranda and then, when the stable door creaked, turned around, pretending she'd just arrived when he exited with crates in his arms.

"May I help you?" While she made her voice sound innocent, heat rushed to her face. How could she use him this way? Even for the good of her country?

"My question to you is the same." Travis set two crates down in front of her. "I wanted to thank you for not turning the Jungs away. These are difficult days for us all. You're a courageous woman."

"I don't feel courageous just now." Exhaustion swept over her in waves. "*Battered* is a better description."

"I'm certain." He tucked a wispy blond strand that had

escaped her looped braid behind her ear. "But I'm proud of you. And no, I don't require your help with the baggage." He picked up the crates and strode to the door.

She rushed to open the door with an aching heart. His words and tender gestures showed he believed they were growing closer, but if she did as Sam and Mrs. Lakin wanted, she would forever spoil any chance of a real relationship with a man she was beginning to care about.

~

*W*ith Clifford at his side, Travis knocked on Luke's door that evening about six. Hopefully, the couple wouldn't mind an interruption to their honeymoon. His prayer was that they'd hire a good man in need of a job.

Booted steps sounded from inside and then the door opened. Luke, dressed casually in a white shirt and brown trousers, held out his hand. "Lieutenant Lawson, what a pleasant surprise." He shook Travis's hand. "And you brought a friend."

"Good evening, Luke. I hope you don't mind the intrusion." Travis placed his hand on Clifford's shoulder. He performed the introductions while the two men shook hands. "Mr. Jamison would like to speak to you."

"Aye. Please, come inside." Luke swept his arm wide.

"I'd just as soon talk right here, if you don't mind." Clifford met Luke's gaze squarely. "Then I'll be on my way if you don't need me."

Luke's brow wrinkled. "What's on your mind?" He stepped onto the porch, leaving the door open.

Clifford explained that he was an experienced saddler in need of a job, if Mr. Shea was hiring. Luke asked a few questions about saddles, which Clifford answered.

"Will you both come in? You can wait in my parlor while I

discuss this with Felicity—er, Mrs. Shea." His smile when he spoke his new wife's name nudged into life a hope for similar happiness in Travis.

"That will be fine." Clifford's hands shook as he removed his hat and followed Luke inside.

Travis trailed behind, whispering a prayer that Luke was able to figure out a way to please everyone, for he suspected Luke was far from wealthy.

Clifford wasn't inclined to talk, so he and Travis sat quietly on comfortable armchairs in the cozy, inviting parlor. From a bouquet of daisies to needlepoint wall hangings that hadn't been there the only time Travis was in the home, Felicity's presence was already making a difference.

They both rose as footsteps approached. Luke entered with Felicity on his arm and made the introductions.

Clifford nodded to her. He twisted his hat around and around. "Have you decided?"

"Aye. You've got the job." Luke was quick to set the man at ease. "But I'm not a rich man. I had planned to close the shop until the war ends, for I'll be serving as a soldier for the Union army. You've given us a way to keep it open. We'll fix you up a room in the stable for your living quarters. Room and board is included in your pay. Will ye agree to work for ten dollars for every saddle sold?"

Travis held his breath. It was a fair deal for both. The shop would provide for Luke's wife and also give Clifford a good salary.

Clifford stopped crumpling his hat. "I accept."

"Good." Felicity smiled at her new employee. "You must both stay for supper so we can discuss this further. My brother is resting. I regret that he won't join us."

"I can't either." Travis rejected the offer with real regret. "I've got paperwork that will keep me up late as it is." He turned to Clifford. "I'm happy for the way things turned out."

"Me too." Clifford's whole demeanor had changed. "I've got a job."

Travis quickstepped to camp with a lighter heart. He thanked God for providing for Clifford. The regiment was leaving in the morning, and he'd be up past "Taps" finishing paperwork.

∾

By Saturday morning, Travis fought down his frustration. The dense forest shaded the sun and kept him cool. Buzzing bees hovered over flowering bushes in the thick underbrush beside a rutted dirt path. Brian had split them up in four groups of twenty-five yesterday to cover more forest, but as of yet, there was no sign of the enemy. Their orders were to search for the Rebel bands as far as the Big Black River but not to engage superior forces. They were to discover if there were multiple groups, how many men they were comprised of, and their weaponry.

Travis's troop included Ben and Enos. Ben was good enough to be a sharpshooter, but only a few soldiers knew it. He didn't want to sit in a tree or in a bell tower and shoot unsuspecting soldiers. Enos was a good tracker.

In the absence of Brian, Travis took command. His men could rest while he took stock of the situation.

"Halt." About two miles from the river, Travis raised his voice slightly so that only his soldiers heard him and hopefully not the Rebels they'd yet to spot. "Enos."

Enos scrambled over from the edge of the group. "Lieutenant?"

"Did you see anything?" Even Ben called him "Lieutenant" when on official duty.

"Nope. Smelled a campfire over to the right. Just a whiff."

Travis sniffed. Nothing. But he trusted Enos. "Lead the way. Stay low. Be ready, men."

They set off with Enos in the lead.

Twenty paces in, Travis smelled a fire. Adrenaline kicked in.

A shot fired up ahead. Then another.

"Take cover." He ducked behind a maple tree and then peered toward the front where Enos now hunkered with the rest of his men. "Ready. Aim. Fire!"

Sounds of musketry reverberated in the trees. This ought to bring Brian and the other three groups.

Answering shots weren't as deafening. Either there were fewer men in the Rebel band, or they conserved ammunition.

"Reload." Delivered softly, this order was passed through his soldiers.

Running steps sounded from their rear. Travis swung his rifle around and immediately lowered it. "Reinforcements behind us!" He shouted this loud enough to be heard by the enemy.

"You found them, huh, lieutenant?" Brian squatted beside him as troops filled in gaps around them.

"Yes, Captain. Not certain how many."

"Let's give them another round, men." Brian gave the order.

The musketry was louder this time. Only a few shots answered.

Travis peered at movement in the trees ahead. "I think they're in retreat."

"Let's wait." Brian put his field glasses to his eyes. "I don't see anything."

At another flurry of footsteps rustling the underbrush a few minutes later, Travis looked behind them. "The rest of our reinforcements are here."

"I still don't see movement." Brian put his glasses in their case. "Let's see what we can find. Advance with caution, men."

The order went through the ranks.

Approaching slowly, they finally made it to splintered trees their bullets had pierced. Evidence of a large fire in a clearing easily large enough to hold one hundred was all they found.

~

O n Sunday morning, Savannah entered the church Travis had attended with Mama and the Jungs. Never when Mrs. Jung had refused to attend parties where they were also invited guests had Savannah imagined the four of them attending services together.

Their closest neighbors and friends such as the Mitchells and Dodds hadn't returned to Vicksburg, yet others were coming back each week. Fellow citizens sat among the soldiers filling the pews.

Folks poked one another and stared. Everyone in their social circle who had been around before the war knew of the Adair-Jung feud.

Taking her seat, Savannah lifted her chin. Let them stare. She'd leave the explanations to Mary Grace and Mrs. Jung.

Travis wasn't there yet, more's the pity. He would have been a solid presence, a support, even if he didn't sit beside her.

Services seemed to stretch excessively long. All she wanted to do was leave. Yet she sat with her eyes fastened on the preacher though she heard not a word he said.

After church, neighbors flocked to Mrs. Jung and Mary Grace, who seemed both happy and flustered at the attention.

Savannah touched Mary Grace's arm. "Talk as long as you like. We will see you at my house."

"Thank you." Mary Grace gave a nod and turned her attention back to Mrs. McGruder, who also nodded and greeted Savannah.

Anxious to escape, Savannah looked about for an excuse. Thankfully, Travis had finally arrived. She touched her mother's sleeve. "Mama, Travis is waiting near the door. Let's speak with him."

He lifted his hand with a smile. Two men waited with him.

Within a minute, she and her mother had reached his side. "Good morning, Travis." Had he found Sam or another Confederate band? She had composed another note for Sam after Travis left and searched the city for Mrs. Lakin. Thankfully, she had found her and delivered the message before the letter carrier left the city.

He greeted her and Mrs. Adair and turned to his companions. "Savannah, Mrs. Adair, I'd like for you to meet two friends from my hometown of Charleston, Illinois." He clapped the shoulder of a man of medium height with black hair and beard. "Benjamin Woodrum is actually family. He's married to my sister, Mary. They made me an uncle with Benny. He's one."

"Benny will be two in September." He nodded to them. "Pleasure to meet you ladies."

Savannah studied the brother-in-law, fascinated to learn more about Travis. "I didn't know Travis had family at Vicksburg."

"We both serve the Eighth Illinois." Ben held his kepi to his chest.

"This is Enos Keller." Travis drew a thin man nearly as tall as himself into the group. "Enos's family owns a nursery in Charleston near my family's farm."

"Of the type that raises flowers and garden plants." A friendly smile revealed a gap in his front teeth. "How do?"

"Very well, thank you." Mama inclined her head.

Savannah liked them immediately because she could see the affection Travis held for both men. Mama also seemed to accept the Northerners more readily, perhaps because of Travis's kindness to the wounded recently in their home and to them the day the Jungs arrived. He was a good man. Savannah was glad Mama recognized it. For herself, his compassion and gentleness when she'd been hurting had comforted her more than she'd dared believe possible, especially with someone who came from such a different background.

"Did you still want me to work on patching your dining room today?" Travis's glance lingered on Savannah. "I persuaded Ben and Enos to help. You did say something about supper?"

With the turmoil of the last few days, she'd forgotten. And he'd brought help. What a kindness—one she didn't deserve. "Of course." Mary Grace was supposed to prepare omelets for lunch and chicken stew for supper. She'd need to warn her of extra guests as soon as possible. "If you don't mind a simple luncheon of omelets and biscuits, you'd be welcome for that meal also."

"Eggs and biscuits." Enos's brown eyes lit up. "Fellas, this is going to feel like I'm back home."

Savannah cringed inwardly. Had Mary Grace ever prepared either meal? The fare had been Mary Grace's suggestion. Despite her worry, Savannah looked forward to an afternoon with three gentlemen guests—as long as one of them was Travis.

～

*T*ravis's slightly burned omelet was a welcome meal. He hadn't eaten eggs in any form in Mississippi. Nor had he dined in a home since winter. Mary Grace had cooked the meal, served it, and then sat down to eat with them in the family dining room...just like Travis's mother and sisters always did back home. What a treat it was to eat in Savannah's home.

"That omelet was delicious, Miss Jung." Enos stared at the blushing cook. "I'm mighty appreciative of the butter and biscuits too."

"Mrs. Beltzer made the biscuits." Her blue eyes shone at the praise. "I churned the butter."

"Everything is delicious." Travis understood why Enos couldn't take his eyes of the brunette. A clean yellow dress enhanced her brown ringlets. He smiled at Savannah, who had seemed nervous at the beginning of the meal. Mary Grace didn't hold a candle to Savannah's blond beauty in his eyes. "As much as we'd like to linger over our meal, I believe we ought to start on those repairs, men. Thank you, ladies, for a wonderful meal."

"Yes. There's only so many ways to make hardtack edible." Enos grinned.

"You found one?" Travis teased him. The only way he could get the hard cracker down was to soak it in coffee.

Ben and Enos chuckled.

"We're grateful for your company." Mrs. Adair stood and everyone followed suit. "I must say, I'm anxious to have the repairs done." She turned to Travis. "Arthur wrote that he ordered new windows for our house. Will you also put in the new windows when the order arrives?"

Savannah winced.

Travis understood her reaction. It was a huge job—and a lot to ask before repairs to three levels of flooring had even begun.

"I can help you with that, Travis." Enos stepped closer to Mrs. Adair. "I helped my pa put new windows in the nursery three summers ago. We can figure it out."

Mary Grace smiled at him.

"We'll feed you dinner and supper every Sunday that you all work on repairs." Savannah seemed almost embarrassed to offer only meals as payment.

"Hungry soldiers don't often get the opportunity to enjoy home-cooked meals." Travis was well aware that the damage was caused by the Union navy. Making the repairs would ease some of his remorse that Savannah had suffered so much loss.

He glanced at his comrades. "That will do nicely for me. Fellas?"

"I'll be here." Ben grinned.

"Me too." Enos smiled at Mary Grace.

"That will be lovely." Mrs. Adair gave them a gracious nod. "Savannah, will you show them into the formal dining room? That's the best place to get started on the floor."

Travis followed Savannah. He didn't mind the hard work since it provided an excuse to dine with her weekly.

CHAPTER 17

wo days later, after Travis took the daily roll call and oversaw the posting of the pickets on the last Tuesday in July, he went to Brian's tent, knocked on the main post, and after Brian called from his desk for Travis to come inside, entered through the open flap. "Morning. I wanted to report that five of our men were too sick to make roll call." The illness that had begun to strike soldiers and civilians alike troubled him. "They've been moved to the hospital tent."

"The stench of death still hangs over Vicksburg." Brian put down his pen. "We may have missed some carcasses. We certainly don't need pestilence here."

With the Confederate soldiers and wounded gone and the battle at Jackson behind them, some measure of normalcy had been restored. The hospitals were starting to return to their pre-siege capacity. The last thing they needed was a contagious disease decimating the community.

Travis fixed his hands on his hips. "What do you want to do about it?"

Brian tapped his bearded chin in thought. "Two of our companies will scour the streets and immediate surroundings.

Order them to tie a handkerchief over the lower half of their faces to protect themselves as much as possible. The rest will work on filling in the caves, a task which may take weeks even with the other regiments assigned to the same duty."

"Glad to hear we'll have help." Were he a private, he'd prefer to fill in the caves. Having a shovel in his hands again would have increased his nostalgia for his farm, his family.

"Enlisted officers will oversee the tasks. You have oversight for our regiment in town today. I'll be occupied with meetings and paperwork." Brian, his gaze returning to his ledger, picked up his pen. "Monitor our men for illness and get me a list of our sick."

"You'll have it within a quarter hour." Travis left to prepare the report.

Later that morning, Eli Jeffries, the sergeant in charge of the teams driving wagons through Vicksburg streets, jumped from the driver's seat and approached Travis, who monitored their score of wagons from a street corner near the courthouse. "Lieutenant, you're not going to like this."

"Out with it." He braced himself.

"We found the body of a freedman in the tent community on the north side of the city." The balding man put his hands on his hips. "His death happened three days ago, and his companions failed to report it."

Travis's head spun. "Had he been a victim of..."

"No foul play, sir. His wife said it was due to the pestilence."

Travis hardly knew which was worse. "Where is he now?"

"I left two guards at the tent to keep folks away and came to find you."

"Take me there." They set off at a rapid pace, soon leaving the sidewalks for ramshackle homes on cobbled streets. "We'll have to contact the minister at the African Methodist Episcopal Church to request a funeral service today." There were three other black congregations if that one couldn't oblige. "We must do all in our power to prevent the pestilence from spreading." This tragic news struck him in the gut. "Did you search nearby tents for others?"

"I came straight to find you." Lines in Eli's forehead deepened.

"That's our next task, then." Travis prayed there weren't more. "By the way, did you find any animal carcasses?"

"Three." Eli shifted a knotted handkerchief from around his nose to rest at his neck. "Two among the rubble and one in an oak grove. We buried them straightaway."

The sergeant's orders would now shift to searching the tent communities.

Travis quickened his pace. After he learned the man's name and if there were other deaths, he'd report it to Colonel Haversham at his headquarters.

~

"Good morning, Travis." Savannah descended the stairs on Wednesday as Ellen answered his knock. She hadn't seen him since Sunday's supper. He, Ben, and Enos had discovered they needed more supplies than the Adairs had on hand to repair the floors. Materials for patching the ceilings had been stored in the stable, and so far, the dining room ceiling had been the only thing completed. Mama had entered the room several times daily to stare at the patchwork, obviously anxious over what Papa would think. The repairs were solid, the wood painted white to match the ceiling, yet there were hints of the patchwork in the formerly elegant room. It was a great improvement, and Savannah was grateful to them. "Thank you again for your work the other day."

Ellen returned to the parlor where she was scrubbing rusty stains from the wood floor.

"We'll return Sunday." He seemed distracted. "We found two dead men in one of the tent communities yesterday."

Ellen rushed back to the foyer. "Do you know who it was?" She clutched a wet rag.

Travis provided the names. "Did you know them?"

"No." Ellen pressed her palms together in prayerful pose, the cloth sandwiched inside her hands.

At the woman's obvious relief, Savannah cocked her head. "You weren't in the tent community. You stayed at the Dodd home."

"Yes, Josie and me stayed with Silas and Hester." She looked back at Travis. "I had been waiting in case Gus and Riley came. I didn't think you'd hire Gus after he ran away."

Savannah blinked. "We'd love to hire Gus. Our dilapidated orchards require someone with his knowledge to save them."

"He won't come here, even if he's in the city. Not now that Mrs. Jung lives here." Her eyes darkened. "It's hard enough for me because I remember how her husband treated mine."

Savannah's guilt rushed back. "I'm sorry." The apology was far too little for causing a man to be beaten. "If I hadn't asked him to pick me those blooms…"

"Miss Savannah." Ellen's tone was firm. "That wasn't the first time Gus was punished, but it *was* the last. You're not to blame."

She turned to Travis, shaking her head in an effort to release the shadows of the past. "Travis, you didn't tell us the cause of death."

"Pestilence."

Savannah gasped. "Only in the tent communities?"

"No, though that would be bad enough. Citizens and soldiers alike are sick." His Adam's apple bobbed. "Our army is working to find additional dead."

She'd instruct her staff to cover their mouths when out and about.

"I actually stopped by about another matter. Soldiers from the Eighth Illinois—my regiment—should be here this week or next to fill in your cave shelter. We're making our way around the city."

Ellen pressed her lips together.

"What is it?" Savannah asked her.

"Have your soldiers look inside really good before they fill in the caves." Ellen cleared her throat. "Freedmen have been living in some of them."

With a groan, Travis rubbed his temples. "Thanks for the warning."

Savannah peered toward the back of the house. "Travis, may I prevail upon you to peek inside our shelter before you go?"

While he did so, she waited on the veranda, longing to prolong his short visit partially because she missed him but also for the sake of learning more for Sam.

He emerged within seconds. "No one is living inside." He joined her. "Hope that sets your mind at ease."

"It does. Thank you." Looking into his eyes, she rested her hand upon his sleeve. "Is there anything else I should know?" Her implication was about the pestilence or the shelters being filled in. What she really wanted to hear was about his expedition to the Black River.

"I mustn't linger." He covered her hand with his. "I've many tasks awaiting my attention."

Her breath quickened at his touch. "Understood. I will see you on Sunday, then." Stepping back, she freed her hand.

"You will." It sounded like a promise.

After he was gone, she pressed the hand he'd held to her cheek. Her father might not be around, but Savannah was beginning to trust that Travis kept his word.

~

*T*hat night, Travis sat around the fire in the waning twilight with several of his troops, including Enos and Ben. Travis had just finished his supper while half listening to talk about the day's gruesome tasks when Brian emerged from his tent and beckoned him over.

Travis pushed himself to his feet and then gathered his canteen, empty plate, and utensils which he carried over to Brian's side. "You wanted to see me, Captain?"

"The evening's cooling off. Put your dishes away and then join me for a walk."

Travis returned quickly and then fell into step beside Brian.

"I've got a new task for you." Brian shot him a side glance. "I believe it will be to your liking."

"Sir?" He could use a change, as could his men. Locating the dead and burying them had been a priority. His men alone had dug nine fresh graves in the city's cemeteries, not to mention what other regiments had dug. Travis ached to help the freedmen still without jobs.

"You had asked what we might do for the fugitives still streaming into the communities maintained by the freed people." Brian's pace slowed as they left the camp behind them.

"I did." Some lived in shacks. Others lived in tents. "There must be other jobs available for them." They didn't want charity. They wanted paying occupations.

"There's good news." Halting, Brian turned to face him.

Travis stopped, hope stirring. "What is it?"

"We have an abundance of abandoned plantations in the area. Northern citizens have begun arriving in Mississippi to take them over." He poked Travis's shoulder. "The best part is, they will hire the people who once worked there as slaves to plant cotton again."

"Paying positions?" Excitement rushed through his veins. Mississippians had burned thousands of dollars' worth of the white gold before the Union army arrived. Such a tragic waste.

"The Northerners have agreed to this stipulation. It's to their benefit because all the knowledge and experience with the crop is from the workers."

"True." He was glad the leaders recognized the wealth of knowledge the former field workers possessed.

"One of these plantations is a mile from our camp. You're to gather one hundred men and women who want the jobs and move them to the property with our wagons. Take two of our companies. Does that suit you?"

"More than anything the army has ordered me to do." Travis's grin widened in response to Brian's excitement.

"Plans are for these efforts to eventually employ thousands and help restart the agrarian economy."

"I needed this good news. Thanks, Brian." This was something he could do to directly aid the freedmen and women. Uncle Dabney would be proud.

~

Travis dragged himself toward town for church the next Sunday, August second, with Ben and Enos. "The last part of our week was better than the first, huh, fellows?" Unfortunately, his spying had suffered while he fulfilled his other duties. He'd done little after arresting two spies at the river.

Enos's face brightened. "Moving them former plantations workers to jobs on two plantations felt good."

"Right." That had lifted Travis's spirits too. "I hope you have enough energy to work for the Adairs again today."

"As long it involves a meal, I do. Will Miss Jung cook lunch for us again?" Enos rubbed his hands together.

"I believe she is their cook on Sundays." Travis was glad to think about something else besides trouble from the Rebel bands. They had attacked a score of Union soldiers who were enjoying leisure time while Travis's troops were moving the workers from Vicksburg to the plantations. It could easily have been an attack on the Eighth Illinois. Those Rebels weren't letting up.

"Anything I don't have to cook over the campfire is a good meal." Ben grinned as they reached the sidewalks.

"Say, you're not trying to imply Miss Jung isn't a good cook, are you?" Enos frowned.

"Not me." Chuckling, Ben tugged Enos's kepi down over his eyes. "You're not getting sweet on Miss Jung, are you?"

Church bells rang.

"Hurry." Travis lengthened his stride.

Perhaps Miss Jung would someday reciprocate Enos's regard. After what she had suffered, kindness from Northern soldiers might begin to heal her scars.

And Savannah's.

～

"*D*o you mean to tell us that Northerners who know nothing about cotton are taking over our plantations?" Mrs. Jung sneered at Travis and his friends over the table Sunday evening.

Savannah wanted to cheer her on. Her practice had been to keep the peace between Mama and Mrs. Jung when sensitive topics surfaced. Not this evening. Someone had to say it. Who better than a woman who'd been looted so repeatedly as to beggar her?

Mary Grace's face hardened. All day, she'd been nervous but excited to cook for guests. There was not a trace of good will in her face after Travis's news.

Savannah ground her fork into her apple cobbler, smashing the crust. Lunch had gone well because Mrs. Jung had remained nearly silent. Work on the bedroom room ceiling was progressing better. Perhaps last week's practice had lent some experience. However, this discussion was ruining Mama's good feelings about the men—and certainly, Mrs. Jung looked fit to be tied. How was Savannah to know that her innocent question about their regiment's tasks last week would lead to such disharmony? Her main goal had been to dig for tidbits to pass on to Sam.

"Some of the Northerners rent the land." Enos shifted in his chair, his gaze fixed on Mary Grace.

"I've not received a penny of rent." Mrs. Jung's eyes narrowed. "Was my plantation taken over?"

An uncomfortable silence settled over everyone.

"I'm not certain that your land has Northerners on it. I'd like to think this action will save the plantations and provide hundreds of jobs." Travis spoke quietly.

"I'd like to think that, too, Lieutenant." Mrs. Jung tossed her napkin onto the white linen tablecloth. "But I've endured too much to the contrary." She stood. "Pray excuse me." She swept from the room.

Savannah couldn't find fault with a word she'd uttered. Perhaps her scornful tone should have been tempered, but not the substance of her observations.

Red blotched Mary Grace's cheeks. She and Enos stared at one another across the table.

"Gentlemen, I believe we'd best get back to camp." With a searching look at Savannah, Travis folded his napkin. "Thank you for two delicious meals."

"Our pleasure. Thank you for patching the bedroom ceiling." Savannah stood. She strove for a gracious tone. It wasn't Travis's or Enos's fault that the Union allowed this travesty, but they didn't have to seem so pleased about it. "We appreciate your fine work." Everyone followed her down the main hall to the table containing the men's hats.

Enos turned to Mary Grace. "Thank you for the home cooking, Miss Jung. That apple cobbler was the best thing I've put in my mouth since my last leave."

A ghost of a smile touched her lips. "It's the first time I made it on my own. Thank you."

"You've been through more than I can imagine." Enos picked up his hat. "If you'd ever care to tell me about it, I'll listen."

She looked away.

Enos gave a nod and stepped outside.

Ben murmured his thanks for the meals and followed his friend.

"Savannah, may I speak with you on the portico?" Travis gave her a questioning look.

She preceded him out the front door. Ben and Enos waited by the gate.

"I regret that I didn't consider the Jungs' situation when I mentioned the plantations." Sincerity rang in both his tone and in his hazel eyes. He sandwiched her hand between his. "I'm sorry I ruined the meal."

The warmth of his hands was welcome, yet it was impossible to deny the scene that had just unfolded. "Much has been done to us during this war that is difficult to accept." She tugged on her hand.

"I'm certain of it." He released her immediately. "I will always rejoice at the death of slavery. I see it as a monstrous evil."

She couldn't justify slavery, but she'd grown up around it as an accepted thing. The experience with Gus had haunted her. Perhaps it had been paving the way in her heart for emancipation all those years. Both Ellen and Josie had exhibited a new contentment after she'd hired them. Even Mama and Savannah had felt less burdened knowing their employees were free to stay or go...free to make their own decisions about their lives. That had lasted until the Jungs moved in. "Why does it matter so much to you?"

"I'd like to tell you. Someday."

They stared at one another.

"Let me know if you want us to return next Sunday. The wood you ordered may be here then."

They all needed some breathing space. Tonight had been uncomfortable.

"Goodnight." Quick steps took him to his friends. At the gate, he lifted his hand. Then the men walked away.

What did Travis want to tell her? Her curiosity was piqued. He had his reasons for rejoicing at Yankees taking over their plantations. The new paid positions for field workers was a good thing—it had made all the difference to Ellen—but the other part didn't sit well with Savannah. Not at all. The thought of Willie's ruined plantation under a Northern stranger's control scorched her soul.

Sam would hear about this one. If there were any Yankees on Willie's land, she'd ask him to run them off.

CHAPTER 18

*T*ravis added two more names to the sick list after roll call on Monday morning and then started a three-mile walk to the city. His regiment was back to filling up the caves, work that had been delayed last week. Savannah's shelter hadn't been done yet either. Because there might be more families living in the caves, both he and Brian were to monitor the situation. It took precedent over his spy search, but he'd keep a sharp eye out while going from group to group.

It was August third. Luke should muster into the Union army this week. Travis planned to place him in the same company with Ben and Enos. Some of the soldiers would likely mistrust Luke. He'd have to prove his trustworthiness.

As Travis would have to do for Savannah.

His steps slowed. Had her reaction to the occupation of the plantations been in support of the Jungs—

He struck himself across the forehead. No, her deeper ties were to the Sandersons. Had her former beau lived, as his wife, that would have been *her* plantation. *Her* loss. Little wonder she'd been tight-lipped while Mrs. Jung berated him.

Not that he couldn't withstand disagreement. He wasn't a child. But it had been as unexpected as it was unpleasant.

"Travis." Luke hailed him from across a cobblestone street and then crossed it.

Travis looked around to get his bearings. His thoughts had so consumed him that he had arrived on Savannah's street without realizing it.

"I reckon I should refer to you as Lieutenant Lawson after signing the documents." Luke grinned as he joined him. "Which I'm prepared to do."

"I see you're dressed for it." Travis studied the loose cut of Luke's dark blue sack coat and baggy trousers the color of the sky. "Where did you find your uniform?"

"Felicity made it for me." Pride shone in his eyes. "She hopes I'll be camped in Vicksburg a long time."

"I believe so." One of Travis's reasons for wanting to remain in Vicksburg also involved a woman—Savannah. He'd ask Brian if the newlywed could stay in town as long as he was in camp for daily roll calls and to get his orders and such. "However, war is unpredictable."

"That it is."

"To answer your earlier comment, refer to me with my rank when on official army business. When we're alone, call me Travis."

"Understood."

"Are things working with Clifford as saddler?"

"Aye." Luke shook his head as if in wonder. "He's taught me a few things. He and I built a bedroom and a common room for his use in the barn. We kept one side for stalls. Likely won't have horses again until the war ends." He grinned. "I'm ready to enlist—this time for the side I support."

"Let's get to camp and make it official." Luke's excitement was contagious. "As your first duty, you'll employ a shovel rather than a musket."

～

"*L*et's discuss how we'll divide the work." On Monday morning, Savannah sat in the downstairs parlor with Felicity, Ellen, Josie, and Petunia. Wilma and Little Miles were eating cookies in the kitchen with Mrs. Beltzer and Mary Grace. This was Felicity's first day back after her marriage. "Felicity, as was our understanding from the beginning, Ellen is our housekeeper. You and Petunia were hired as part-time staff."

"Unlike Felicity, I've been here five days weekly since I started." Petunia narrowed her eyes at her cousin. "I need my job but won't want so many days."

"Good, because we won't need that to continue." The children spent more time with their grandmother in the kitchen or playing on the veranda than following their mother through the home. Six people weren't required, yet everyone here needed jobs. Papa had left them sufficient money for six months. If that wasn't replenished, Savannah would have to release half of them. She'd decided to also pay Mary Grace a salary because Ellen and Josie received board as part of their pay. It was only fair. "Do you prefer to work two or three days weekly?"

"Two. More of my friends have returned and invited me to visit. Besides, I don't need full-time work while living with my parents. But I want to be paid for all I've already worked."

"Of course." Savannah tamped back her irritation. Why did Petunia grate so on her nerves?

"Why don't you assign laundry room tasks to Petunia?" Sitting on the sofa next to her daughter, Ellen folded her hands. "Washing could be done on one day and ironing the next day."

"Excellent suggestion." That kept Petunia and the children near the kitchen—and their grandmother. "Shall we say Tuesday and Thursday?"

"Fine." Petunia frowned.

"If that's a problem, speak now." Ellen's calm demeanor and sage suggestions had kept the household running smoothly for years. Mama had been content for Savannah to handle the home's management—although her one stipulation was that Ellen retain the housekeeper position.

Petunia spoke quickly. "Those days are acceptable."

"That's settled, then." Thank goodness, one decision made. "Ellen and Josie have been with us for years. Given that fact, they will retain their former positions. Josie is the upstairs maid and assists her mother to clean the downstairs when necessary."

"I'm not certain you need me." Felicity gazed steadily at Savannah. "I had thought to help Aunt Mae cook, but Mary Grace is growing proficient in her skills, particularly baking. She told my aunt she'll have to learn to make her own way now. I won't take that from her."

Savannah nodded toward Ellen, Josie, and Petunia. "The rest of you can get back to your tasks. I'll speak to Felicity."

Ellen arose as the others left. "I'm still working on those rug stains. They've faded under my diluted vinegar treatments but not enough. Miss Lila may still be affected."

"You may work in here while we talk. Thanks, Ellen."

"I'll fetch my supplies." Soft steps took her from the room.

Savannah shifted in her seat to face Felicity, whom she didn't want to lose. Then the perfect idea struck. "What I require most from you is your seamstress skills. Two new comfortable dresses and aprons for the whole staff. And for Mrs. Jung."

"Calico?" Felicity leaned forward, a hand on her knee.

"No." They didn't have to choose the cheapest fabric. "Lawn or muslin. New dresses of mousseline or cambric for Mama and me with smaller crinolines." Full hoops had grown quite tiresome during the war. The extra yardage was an extravagance nearly everyone in Vicksburg had long since discarded. "After that, you'll alter several of our full hoops to use as smaller crinolines."

"I can't believe this." Felicity's hands shook. "Luke and I have prayed for an opportunity to use my seamstress skills."

Savannah hated to admit that she'd only just thought of it. The cost of fabric gave her pause. Perhaps she'd write her father, who was staying at Julia's Texas home while he searched for the right occupation, for additional funds.

Ellen entered quietly with a bucket of water, a jar of vinegar, and rags.

"I accept. That will require months." Felicity clasped her hands together, resting them against her lips. "My dream— beyond being Luke's wife and a mother—is to be a seamstress."

Savannah had never been instrumental in making *anyone's* dream come true. It humbled her. "I'm glad."

"Me too." Leaping to her feet, Felicity hugged Savannah. "I can't wait to tell Luke. I'm not certain when I'll see him again. He's mustering into Travis's regiment today and will stay at the camp."

Savannah arose, happy that everyone seemed content with her decisions. "I often glimpse Travis when I'm out. He'll know where Luke is. Shall we shop for fabric today? We might see Travis."

~

At midmorning, Travis introduced his newest recruit to a digging crew that included Enos and Ben. The men were happy for an extra set of hands. He told them to fill the Adairs' shelter next, thinking it might be easier for Luke to ease into his separation from his new wife.

Satisfied that all was under control there, Travis visited four more caves that were being filled in. No evidence of recent occupation had been found in those, either, easing that worry.

Another reared its head. Sickness was still a problem for everyone. He prayed the recent burials helped minimize its spread. *A good soaking rain might help, too, Lord.*

Guiltily aware that he'd spent little time searching for spies in the past week—for good reason—he decided to take a quick turn on the main roads. Then he'd return to Savannah's home.

Army wagons were everywhere. Soldiers worked in teams to fill ruts in the streets. A mother with young children bustled past him as if he walked at a snail's pace. He quickened his steps toward the downtown area.

Savannah and Felicity emerged from a shop on the opposite corner with baskets of colorful cloth.

Travis took a deep breath. Whispering a prayer that she'd want to talk to him after the fiasco last evening, he crossed the street with other pedestrians. "Savannah. Felicity." He raised his hat to them. "What a pleasant surprise." At least, he hoped so.

"Travis." Savannah pursed her lips. "We've been shopping for fabric, as you see. Felicity has agreed to be our seamstress. The scarcity of fabric sent our last seamstress packing up her shop last April. We're all looking forward to new dresses."

"Yes, I will also fashion dresses for Savannah's staff. It's what Luke and I have prayed for." Felicity's eyes glowed. "Did he muster in yet?"

"Already filling in caves." He grinned, happy that the couple had good news after the turmoil they'd endured. "Is your brother still with you?"

"Jack left on Friday for his Louisiana home. It required two weeks of nourishing meals to recover his strength." Her smile dimmed. "I'll miss him, but I can only imagine the joyous reunion he's having with his family."

"If he decides not to return to the army, no one will think less of him." Travis spoke gently.

"That's what Luke told him. Is...will it be possible for me to tell him my good news today?" Felicity clutched her basket.

"Very possible." He turned to Savannah. "The crew that Luke joined will be at your home later this afternoon to begin filling in your cave shelter."

"I'll be pleased to see it gone. Thank you."

"Enos and Ben are on the same crew. I hope that will not bother Mary Grace." What an idiot. Why hadn't he assigned that home to another crew? Because putting Luke near Felicity had been his priority.

"I will mention it to her." Savannah's glance faltered and then returned to hold his gaze. "She likes to bake. Would your men appreciate apple cider and cobbler?"

"It will be a kindness." One they'd remember. "May I carry your baskets home?"

Maybe they'd also offer cobbler to a hungry lieutenant later.

~

*I*t was late morning when Travis left. Savannah had been glad for Felicity's presence to ease their meeting after the way they parted. The three of them ate cobbler on the veranda.

"Do you mind if I begin with Mrs. Jung's dress?" Felicity asked as she laid out the fabric in the parlor. "Of everyone, she seems the most embittered."

Savannah agreed. "I've only seen her wear two different dresses in the nearly two weeks they've been here."

Felicity covered her mouth. "I had no idea they'd lost so much. Weren't they as wealthy as the Sandersons?"

"Wealthier. Unfortunately, all their possessions now fit on a two-seated buggy pulled by a donkey." When Savannah recalled that sight, her anger against the Jungs eased.

"Then I shall take her measurements now." Felicity scurried up the stairs.

The aroma of chicken soup grew stronger as Savannah entered the kitchen, where Mary Grace set a plate of oatmeal cookies on the table in front five-year-old Wilma and two-year-old Miles while Mrs. Beltzer stood over the stove. "Hello, everyone."

"Lunch will be ready in about an hour, Savannah," Mary Grace told her.

"I can't wait." Crumbs fell onto Wilma's yellow dress. Her blond hair was gathered into a single braid.

"Me too." The towheaded boy propped himself up on his knees to reach the table.

Savannah laughed. "The wealth of supplies at the grocer expands daily."

"Gives us more variety." Mrs. Beltzer stirred a pot. "I hope the children aren't too noisy."

"Not at all." Savannah smiled at the children's suddenly anxious expressions. "Ladies, I wanted to prepare you. Union soldiers are coming to fill our shelter this afternoon. Ben, Luke, and Enos are included in that group."

"How many?" A look of panic crossed the cook's face. "Will we serve them supper?"

Mary Grace poured water into tumblers with a shaky hand.

"No." Savannah shook her head. "You have a supply of that apple cider you made last week?"

"Nearly three gallons chilling in the cellar." Mrs. Beltzer stepped toward the open door. "Do you want some for lunch?"

"Not lunch. I thought a glass for each soldier would be welcome."

"I'm certain of it." Mrs. Beltzer wiped her hands on her apron. "I'll be glad when they reach our yard."

"Mary Grace, will you make another cobbler to serve with it?" Savannah studied her miserable expression. "Apple, peach, or pear—whatever you like."

"I'll have to pick peaches." Mary Grace set water glasses on the table for the children without looking at her.

"I'll help." Savannah wanted to give her a chance to talk. If she wanted it.

"Thanks." The short response wasn't a gracious one. She retrieved a bushel basket from a table and led the way outside.

"I don't like Union soldiers occupying our town any more than you do." Savannah hurried to catch up on the terraced hillside.

"You don't know how I feel, so don't say you do." Mary Grace stopped under a peach tree with low-hanging fruit.

"I know you've suffered." But Savannah wasn't crazy about her tone, especially after she and Mama had offered hospitality to former enemies.

"Hah! A lot you know about suffering. You still have a home."

That bounced on a raw nerve. "*You* lose the man you intended to marry and then you tell me about suffering." Savannah turned away. "You hide in a dank shelter, terrified, with gunboats blasting away at your town almost without cessation for six weeks. You wait all those horrible weeks for your papa to come home and when he does, he leaves again."

"I'm sorry."

Savannah crossed her arms to shield herself from further pain.

Mary Grace took a step closer. "My father will *never* return."

That pulled Savannah from the depths of her misery, a place she strove never to enter. She met Mary Grace's tear-stained gaze.

"You don't know how ashamed I am of my father's actions that day. I'd found a new friend...and he'd ruined it." Mary

Grace swiped at her cheeks with a linen handkerchief. "Does it have to stay ruined?"

Mary Grace didn't know all that day had cost Savannah and her family, how they were still paying the price. But the Jungs had suffered too.

"No." She held out her hands.

Mary Grace hugged her instead and then stepped back. "It will be difficult to bake for soldiers that might have been the ones to destroy our plantation."

"Enos will be here."

"I believe him to be a good man. Travis too." She began picking peaches. "Enos wants to know what happened. I may tell him. When I can talk about it."

"I believe you should."

Travis wanted to tell Savannah why he was set against slavery. She must be as open to what he shared with her as she was encouraging Mary Grace to be with Enos.

CHAPTER 19

Savannah strolled toward the oak grove outside the City Hospital on Thursday morning. This week's note was about disease in the city, the men found dead in the tent communities, the repairs on the roads, and the filling in of caves. The main thing—and this might not be a secret to Sam —was about the Northern planters. Her message included a request to run them off Willie's property.

She hoped those planters paid a price for their arrogance.

It was unfortunate she had run into Travis on a few occasions immediately after delivering messages. His duties must vary widely for him to be in so many locations in the busiest areas. The hospital was well northeast of those. She kept an eye out for him just the same, exchanging a nod with townspeople she knew slightly. More people felt safe to return to the occupied town—and little wonder. The enemy was done attacking.

They were here to stay.

Up ahead was the hospital where Felicity still volunteered a couple of days a week. Not today or Savannah would have insisted Mrs. Lakin select another spot.

The letter carrier wasn't there. Savannah slowed her steps.

There was no bench to sit upon as if to rest a moment from a long stroll.

"Miss Adair."

Savannah peered into the trees where the whisper had originated. Mrs. Lakin beckoned her over from the cover of a spreading bush.

She stepped into the foliage.

"Did you bring it?"

Savannah extracted the letter and money from her sash. "Tell him to open it immediately and bring his answer back to me next week. I'll sit on a bench outside the notions shop on Jackson Street."

Mrs. Lakin stuffed the envelope into her skirt pocket. "Letters back to you cost the same. Bring three dollars next time."

When the woman started to turn away, Savannah touched her sleeve to halt her. "Are we doing any good? Is the risk of getting caught worth what we're accomplishing?"

"I reckon your beau didn't tell you." Mrs. Lakin eyed her. "Our soldiers are making it hot for the Yankees, don't you worry about that. Keep your information coming from that lieutenant." Then she was gone. Only the shaking of the limbs proved she'd been there.

Savannah took a circuitous route home, pondering the meaning of "making it hot." She didn't want anything happening to Travis. Because his duties often kept him in the city, he'd be fine. Wouldn't he?

~

"Remember those Rebel bands?"

Travis lifted an eyebrow at Enos, content to let others talk. It was Saturday after sunset. A group of them sat around the fire at camp, including Brian and Ben. Luke had slept all week at camp but had leave to spend from

Saturday evening through Sunday evening roll call in Vicksburg with his bride. Evening roll call had been taken.

"We went looking for them and engaged with them two weeks ago." Ben yawned. "Of course, we remember."

"Well, they attacked two plantations run by the new Northern planters." Enos shook his head. "I didn't see that coming."

"It's true." Brian rested his wrists on his knees. "Happened yesterday. Shots were fired at the first one. Four horses were stolen from the second."

Travis stared at him. Why hadn't his captain mentioned it earlier?

"The Southerners don't like that they've been run off their land." Enos stared into the dying blaze. "Don't seem fair to me, either, now that I've had time to think. What's wrong with having the Southerners who own the land come back and run it?"

"It's nearly time for 'Taps,' gentlemen." Brian stood. "I suggest you ready yourselves to bed down." He strode down the row toward his tent.

Everyone else left except Ben and Enos.

"Fellas, I've been thinking a lot about Mary Grace." Enos put his hands on his hips. "Her losing her plantation and all because Union soldiers looted them continuously. It sticks in my throat like a chicken bone. It just ain't right."

"Agreed." Ben clapped him on the shoulder. "Not much we can do about it."

The whole situation bothered Travis too. Enos needed some good news. "Savannah invited us back again tomorrow. Let's stay away from this topic because it's a source of pain for everyone."

"Savannah too?" Ben's brow wrinkled.

"Yes. Her dead beau was the son of a plantation owner."

Would Savannah approve of plantation raids? She might.

That reminded him that he needed to share his perspective —and listen to hers so he could understand her background better. However, he preferred a more private setting than Sunday meals where there were always others to listen in.

～

Savannah breathed a sigh of relief when her guests finished their main course at Sunday's supper. Mary Grace had carried both lunch and supper to her mother's room to protect Mrs. Jung's nerves. She needn't have bothered. The men were on their best behavior. Even Mary Grace relaxed as they neared the end of the meal.

"It's a lovely evening. This morning's rain cooled the relentless August heat." Savannah glanced between Mama and Travis. "Why don't we eat our baked pears on the veranda? Will you mind holding your plates while eating?" There were sufficient small round tables for cups, not plates.

"What a lovely suggestion, dear." Mama gave her an approving look.

Enthusiastic praise of the idea brought new life into the men, who had been quiet at both meals while Savannah and Mama brought up a variety of topics for discussion.

Savannah rose with a rustle of her pink taffeta skirt. "Mary Grace, will you carry the desserts outside? Everyone, please bring your coffee cups with you."

"I'll help Mary Grace." Enos gave the brown-haired girl a bashful look.

"Thank you." Savannah spoke up before Mary Grace could refuse. "We'll await you on the veranda."

Travis and Ben arranged the furniture in a semi-circle facing the damaged trees. The shelter had been filled in and leveled off with the hillside. It looked so much better, and the soldiers performing the service had enjoyed the desserts and cider served both days. Ben mentioned the townspeople who had been appreciative of their efforts while they waited for dessert to be served today.

What was keeping Enos and Mary Grace so long? Savannah's coffee was beginning to cool when they brought out two plates apiece.

"I'll get the last two." Enos disappeared back into the house.

Mary Grace lifted an eyebrow at Savannah, who motioned for her to sit.

Had the two of them had a chance to talk while dishing up the servings? Mary Grace certainly seemed less tense.

Savannah met Travis's gaze. She would give him an opportunity to tell his story. A buggy ride might provide the needed privacy, but she had no horse. A stroll along the Sky Parlor?

Curiosity was getting the better of her. She'd suggest that if he didn't offer another plan.

~

*T*ravis looked up from his recordkeeping tasks at the approach of booted steps outside his tent on Monday evening. Twilight had fallen. Travis had been working by candlelight, sweating inside the hot canvas shelter.

"You in there, Travis?" Brian poked his head through the flap of his officer's wall tent.

He stood. "Come in." He gestured to his only chair situated at a small rectangular folding table holding his ledgers, candle, and pen.

"Thanks." The captain sat. "I just came from a meeting with the higher-ranking officers in our regiment. We've got new orders, along with some of the other regiments." His jaw set. "Beginning tomorrow, we're to remove all unemployed freed people from the city."

"What?" Travis's head jerked. He sank onto his cot, the only other furniture in his tent.

"More dead have been found among the living. The conditions in the communities are worse than we imagined." Brian removed his hat and rubbed his hands through his sweaty hair. "After we had those funerals, we thought the pestilence would improve. Folks are still getting sick."

Travis could vouch for that. As quickly as sick soldiers recovered, new ones were added to the list. Thankfully, Savannah and her loved ones remained healthy.

"We can't allow disease to run rampant." Brian heaved a sigh.

"We can help them move to another area, though, right?" Travis leaned forward, hands clasped, elbows resting on his knees.

"If they want help, provide it." Brian blew out his breath. "We also want men and women living together to be married in churches as husband and wife. We want to change their lives for the better."

From what Travis had heard, many couples wanted a church wedding. That was good thing.

After Brian left, Travis sat on his cot unmoving. How he dreaded this task. All he could think about was the night his uncle went missing while assisting two Mississippi fugitives in flight to find freedom.

The bugler began to play "Taps," the mournful tune reminding him of Uncle Dabney's sacrifice.

Freedom might have come to Vicksburg, but they had a long and hard road ahead before the former slaves actually felt free.

*E*arly morning mists and drizzle shadowed the camp on Tuesday. Travis listened as Brian gave careful orders to enlisted officers in charge of companies in his regiment. Companies generally held one hundred men yet that number varied due to deaths of previous soldiers and new recruits. For this task, the men were further divided into groups of twenty. Travis's job was one of oversight.

It heartened him to see that Luke was in the same group as Enos. Neither man looked happy. Few men did, a feeling Travis shared. But they were getting the newly freed men, women, and children away from the pestilence and filth to save their lives.

An hour later, the overnight rain had stopped and they were in the first tent community. Empty bottles, trash, and crates turned upside down scattered around the grassy road separating the tent rows. The stench of death was stronger. It wasn't a healthy environment for anyone.

The men looked at Travis for guidance. He held out his hand for the blank ledger. It was to be used to document names of those to be relocated and their location. The first one was on his shoulders. His men would copy his actions.

He stepped in front of the first tent in the row. No one was outside the tent. "Good morning. Is anyone inside?" A black woman with a turban covering her hair pushed aside the flap, and Travis offered a tentative smile. "I'm First Lieutenant Travis Lawson. May I speak with you?"

Her eyes widened at the score of soldiers gathered in the grassy road. "Morning. Yes, of course."

"Ma'am, there's a pestilence in the city that has claimed some lives. Are you aware of that?"

The petite woman looked behind her, then nodded.

Travis looked over her shoulder at scared children huddled together. "Is there sickness in your tent?"

She tightened her lips.

"We've buried several folks in the last couple of weeks. We're trying to prevent it from happening again. If someone is sick, we want to help. We're here to relocate folks who haven't yet found a job. We'll help you and your family move outside the city away from the pestilence."

"I worry about my children being in here, sure enough." She eyed Travis. "You'll erect my tent in the new spot?"

"My men will."

Her breath shuddered. "You'll discover my husband when you come inside. He died last evening before the rain. Sickness took him."

Travis had hoped she wasn't going to say that. Yet the odor had alerted him to the possibility. "May I extend my sympathy to you?"

"I want a Christian burial for him." Her eyes shone with tears that did not fall. "We've attended the AME Church."

"I'll see to it." He turned to Sergeant Pierce at his side. "Sergeant, please send one of your men to the African Methodist Episcopal Church to request a funeral service today. Mention to the preacher that there are grieving folks in need of prayer."

"Yes, Lieutenant." The clean-shaven officer pulled one of the men aside.

"Ma'am, I'll need your husband's name, your name, and everyone else's living in this tent before we can move you. Their ages too." He opened his ledger and wrote the names of two adults and four children under the age of twelve, all living in a tent twice the size of Travis's. Getting them away from the disease was key. They'd have food because the army planned to continue feeding townspeople and folks in the nearby area for the coming weeks.

"Ask everyone to come out of the tent." Travis spoke gently. This next part was going to be difficult for them.

"What you going to do?" She took a step back.

"We'll take your husband's body to the church or to the

hospital, depending on the preacher's answer." There was no part of this job that was easy. "If there's no room at the AME cemetery, we'll find another one."

She brought the children outside. The two youngest, a boy and a girl, were crying. Travis's heart bled for their grief.

He prayed there were no more fatalities, that the army's actions were in time to save the rest. If Savannah could witness the suffering of the people like he had to, it would surely change her heart.

~

On Thursday morning, Savannah sat on a bench outside the notions shop on Jackson Street. She set her basket beside her with a stack of handkerchiefs hiding the money and a message about freedmen without jobs being moved outside the city. She hadn't seen Travis all week and believed he was involved with moving folks. A long stroll on Wednesday had borne fruit. Soldiers outside a cigar shop were rattled by continued attacks on Union troops that strayed outside of camp—and they were outraged at raids on Northern planters leasing Southern plantations.

Sam must have acted on her request. She'd know in about one minute.

She'd asked Felicity if she needed supplies from the notions store. White thread and blue thread were her excuse today in case Travis saw her afterward, as he so often had done.

"Good morning."

Savannah looked up, surprised at the greeting because most exchanges were done swiftly and nearly without words. "Good morning."

Placing a basket half filled with sacks and jars beside Savannah's, the redhead sat on the bench. "Pleasant day."

"It is." Puffy white clouds in a blue summer sky. If only Savannah was here to enjoy it.

"A mutual friend said to tell you, 'With pleasure.'" Mrs. Lakin glanced at her from the corner of her eye. "Does that suit you?"

"It does, indeed." A wave of gratitude swept over her.

"We feel the same about such things."

That gave Savannah a jolt. Did Mrs. Lakin read her letters?

"We're back at the oak grove next week."

"Understood." That had worked fine.

"May I borrow a handkerchief?" Mrs. Lakin raised her brows.

My. Mrs. Lakin was a quick thinker. "Of course. It's my gift." Savannah didn't look at her basket as the older woman seemed to fumble with the handkerchief on the bottom of the pile. Her fist flashed into her pocket with the hankie, money, and note and came back out again with only the linen. Savannah marveled at the dexterity of the action. Did the woman practice furtive movements, or did she serve many spies?

"Thanks for the handkerchief." She stood. "Good day."

"Good day to you." Savannah fussed with the contents of her basket so she wouldn't leave her seat at the same moment as Mrs. Lakin. Another minute passed before she looked at the clock on the corner as if surprised at the time. Then she entered the notions shop. She wreathed her face with a pleasant expression, but inside, she was anything but calm. Her body shook with reaction to the news.

Sam was making the situation uncomfortable for the Yankees on Willie's property. If they weren't already gone, he'd run them off soon.

That's for you, Willie. The last thing I'll be able to do for you.

CHAPTER 20

By the following Monday, exhaustion was setting in for Travis. After his men left, he'd lagged behind in camp to catch up on recordkeeping. Moving the folks had demanded all of his time for the past week. Not that they didn't deserve his full attention, especially when they'd discovered two more dead, but how was he also to catch spies?

Added to that, Brian kept his tasks loaded to the brim—and this one would fill at least another week. Here it was August seventeenth and he'd caught only four spies. He was glad those men were imprisoned. On the other hand, spies didn't announce their secret missions, so he supposed he wasn't doing too badly on that score.

He closed his ledger and strode toward the city to check on his men and then search for spies.

The first soldier in his regiment he spotted was Luke near the center of town. He toted a bulging blanket bound on both ends from which a skillet handle protruded. "Luke, where are you going?"

"To the growing tent community on the north side of the city." Luke set the edge of the blanket on the sidewalk and swiped his sweaty brow. "Ben is taking down the tent of the family all this belongs to. He'll meet me over there. The family's helping friends pack their belongings."

"You've got a trek before you." Travis drank from his canteen.

"Thank ye kindly." Peering around them, Luke took a long swallow from his own canteen. He sputtered.

"You choking?" Travis clapped him on the back.

Shaking his head, he glanced to his left.

Travis followed his gaze. A woman toted a basket of candles toward the middle of the city. A gentleman wearing a brown coat tapped his cane nonchalantly while crossing the street. Three children under the age of seven followed their mother into the grocer. Two soldiers—

"Don't look." Speaking softly, Luke slowly screwed the cap on the canteen. "That man with the cane just dropped a note in that woman's basket of candles."

"What?" Travis's heartbeat sped. He had been peering down another street. "Are you certain?"

"I used to be a Union spy. Trust me. They're Confederate spies, Travis." Luke glanced after the man. "They're getting away. She's already out of sight."

"I'll get him. You stay with her. I'll find you." Travis followed the cane-toting man down the street.

Luke, a spy for the Union? That man was full of surprises. The two of them were going to have a long talk.

～

On Monday morning, Savannah studied the two exquisite dresses draped over the backs of chairs in the parlor with her mother. The lavender-colored one had a high neck. Lace trimmed the bodice, the hem, and the sleeves. A wide deeper lavender sash would accentuate Mary Grace's trim waist.

"I'm certain Mary Grace will be pleased." Mama fingered the lace. "The muslin fabric lends itself to her baking but will also be pretty should she take a stroll with a certain young man."

"Exactly. Though I believe Mary Grace has a lot of healing to do first."

"I'm glad the two of you are cordial together." Mama tilted her head. "Perhaps even friends?"

"Perhaps soon." Since that day in the orchard, Savannah's and Mary Grace's lost friendship had begun to mend. "What about Mrs. Jung's dress?" Savannah touched the black muslin with cambric cuffs and collar.

"I hope our instincts that Jacqueline will want to wear mourning for a few more months are correct." Mama sighed. "She's more unpredictable than I remember, though I can't say I knew her well."

Mary Grace was also in mourning for her father, but if Savannah guessed right, the girl wanted to push past the difficulties she'd endured. Her second dress would be the color of ripe peaches.

Steps on the stairs hushed the women. They and Felicity had intended this as a surprise for mother and daughter to receive together. Had they guessed correctly? Should they have consulted the women about the gifts?

Savannah turned toward the open parlor door at Mama's side.

"And here we are." Felicity stepped aside to allow Mary Grace and her mother to enter first.

"Savannah, what a beautiful lavender gown." Mary Grace stared at it with yearning in her eyes. "You shall look a dream in it."

"No, I shall never wear it." Savannah smiled. "Felicity made it for you as a gift from Mama and me."

"It's mine?" Her hand flew to her throat. "Truly?"

"Truly."

"Thank you." Mary Grace caressed the lace. "Thank you, Mrs. Adair. And Felicity, you are indeed a gifted seamstress."

"I'm happy you're pleased with it." Felicity turned to Mrs. Jung. "Your gift is a full mourning dress. We thought—"

"They took my mourning dresses and dragged them in the mud—made it look like I didn't care enough to grieve for Marcus." A tear ran down her cheek. "I will finish out the year wearing mourning in public. You could not have pleased me more."

Mama inclined her head. "It was our pleasure."

The reactions of both women warmed Savannah's heart. They'd taken another step toward healing the rift in their friendships. "Mary Grace, please try it on for us. We can't wait to see it."

~

*T*ravis caught up with the gentleman spy. "Halt."

The civilian turned around. His eyes widened and then turned wary. "Good morning. What may I do for you?" He rested a hand lightly on his cane.

The soldier in Travis immediately recognized the walking implement as a potential weapon. "I'm First Lieutenant Travis Lawson." He touched his sidearm in silent threat. He'd use it only if necessary. "What is your name, sir?"

"Gerald Finkler. I sell life insurance." His tone gained bluster. "A benefit indeed to a man in your profession. Stop by my office on Mulberry Street anytime. Good day to you." He turned away.

"One moment." If Travis weren't so tense, he might have chuckled at the fellow's pouncing on an opportunity for a sale.

"Mr. Finkler, a witness saw you exchange a note with a woman on Jackson Street."

"Why, you malign me, sir." His eyes narrowed. "I spoke with no one on Jackson Street."

"Then you won't mind coming with me to prove your innocence."

"I'm expected elsewhere. This is quite inconvenient." His outraged tone belied his darting eyes.

"My apologies." Travis gestured, and Mr. Finkler silently fell into step beside him. As they neared the spot where Luke had dropped his blanket bundle, he spotted Luke walking back toward him. Alone.

It was a blow. The female spy had eluded capture, unfortunately.

"Good work." Luke strode up. "The woman got away."

Mr. Finkler took a step back. "No harm done, Lieutenant. I'll bid you good day."

"Stop. I got close enough to grab the rim of her basket, and this fell out." He held out his other hand, palm outstretched. On it was a page folded into a square.

Mr. Finkler paled.

Travis snatched the paper and read the nonsensical message. It had been written in cipher. His heartbeat quickened. Pocketing the message, Travis gave his newest recruit a slow smile. "Deliver your bundle. I'll find you later." Yes, they needed a long discussion.

First, to take this spy to Colonel Haversham and discover what he knew.

~

*A*n hour after Mary Grace had tried on her new dress and announced it an excellent fit, Mrs. Beltzer, basket in hand, stepped into the main parlor where Savannah and

Mama enjoyed a midmorning cup of coffee, with the news that they needed eggs.

What Savannah needed was war news for Sam. She hadn't overheard Travis, Ben, and Enos talking about anything new yesterday. They'd finished the repairs on her floors and ceilings. It had taken long enough. She suspected them of procrastinating because they enjoyed home-cooked meals and the company.

She liked Travis coming to supper, though, and didn't deny it was easier to get to know him with his friends in attendance. He was more relaxed and comfortable on Sundays, away from official army business. She'd decided to reiterate Mama's request to install her windows. If they arrived before her hair turned gray. Papa had ordered the windows shortly after surrender, and September was two weeks away.

Seizing the opportunity, Savannah offered to go to the grocer for Mrs. Beltzer. Within a quarter hour, she strolled the streets in search of soldiers gathered together. There were plenty about town today but none stopped. Army wagons filled with tents, crates, and boxes headed north.

She continued toward the heart of the city, employing her parasol on the hot mid-August day to mask the direction of her gaze. Travis entered a home on Monroe Street with another gentleman. Her emotions were torn between relief that he was occupied elsewhere and disappointment at missing an opportunity to talk with him.

Four soldiers stood outside the tailor's shop. Once within earshot, she studied a window display of fabrics. The two youngest soldiers turned to look at her. Men had been turning their heads to stare at her since her sixteenth birthday. One man had told her she was the loveliest woman in Vicksburg. Willie had never treated her any differently after she began receiving such compliments, so she'd dismissed the praise, deeming friendship and love more valuable than admiring glances.

The soldiers' conversation picked up when she studied the display and ignored them.

One soldier spoke in a deep bass voice. "General Rosencrans is finally moving the Army of the Cumberland again."

"Last I heard, they were south of Tullahoma," an older soldier with a British accent commented.

Savannah pretended to study a white muslin fabric printed with rows of white daisies. In her head, she memorized each word.

"You're correct." The deep voice again. "They're moving toward Chattanooga. I wanted to be in Tennessee with them this spring—anywhere but Mississippi. It's not so bad since surrender."

They started talking about their battle experiences.

Savannah listened long enough to ascertain it was all old news and then stepped into the shop to purchase the fabric as a gift for Felicity. As a member of her staff, the seamstress also deserved a new dress.

Better still, she had some good information for Sam, in addition to the relocation of freedmen camps and road repairs. With drivers still swerving their horse teams around cannonball pits, and the holes in the sidewalk she avoided so routinely that she barely noticed them, it was good to see repairs happening—and not just by soldiers. Former slaves and citizens were also busy with repairs and cleaning up glass and rubble from walkways.

She never knew what information others were passing along. Taken together, it painted a portrait of what was happening in Vicksburg. It would require concentration to cipher all this into Sam's message, but the effort was worth it.

~

*L*ater the same day, Travis sat across from Colonel Haversham in the office of his Vicksburg headquarters and studied the coded note. He'd taken Mr. Finkler to jail after he and the colonel questioned him. The spy hadn't divulged his co-conspirator's name, the contents of the note, or whom he spied for.

"Doesn't make sense, does it?" Colonel Haversham sat back in his chair, his hand resting on the polished table.

"No." Travis placed the message in front of the officer.

"I'll give this to my aide, Lieutenant Christopher Dunn." The colonel didn't seem concerned about the garbled message. "He has several ciphers in his file. This message may fit one of them. If not, I'm confident he'll decipher it by tomorrow morning."

"Great news." Travis barely knew the man, who also used a room in the home for an office. His stomach began to unknot.

"You couldn't speak freely in front of the spy. Tell me exactly what happened with Luke Shea."

Supplying the details, Travis explained that Luke had spotted the exchange and later shared he had been a Union spy. "I intend to discover how that came into being today."

"Report back to me about it." He drummed his fingers against the desk. "If he spied while in Vicksburg—which seems likely—let's have him work with you one or two days a week."

"I'd like that." His trust in Luke grew weekly. "But I'd not want to pull him aside too often at camp. It would be noticed, especially since he's new."

"Noted. Perhaps I need another aide one day a week. That would keep him in the city. He can spend Sunday night at his home here and serve as my aide on Monday. I'll inform your captain."

"That would be ideal." His head reeled at the swift thinking of his superior officer. "I haven't had as much time as I'd like to search for spies lately. Having Luke work with me will increase my efforts."

"Good. Try to discern his willingness to serve his country in this way without mentioning what we've discussed. Discover his story and report back to me today. If he's willing, we may have him work with you tomorrow. He was the one who saw the female spy." The colonel studied the note. "Send Lieutenant Dunn in on your way out."

"Yes, sir."

As he left headquarters, excitement built in Travis over the potential of working with Luke. This could be just the answer he needed.

~

Travis ate a late lunch at a recently reopened restaurant. Three of the ten tables were occupied at half-past one. He relaxed over a turkey sandwich in near solitude.

That was good because his thoughts were in turmoil. What a blessing that Luke's prior experiences allowed him to recognize an exchange. A spy was in jail but another known spy wasn't. He'd search the area where the spies had been in hopes that the woman lived or worked nearby, check on his men, and then find Luke.

After a fruitless two-hour search, Travis sought out Luke's sergeant in a tented community. "Sergeant Pierce, a word with you."

The clean-shaven man of medium height followed him away from the troops folding tents and packing crates. "Yes, Lieutenant?"

"How are the moves coming?"

"Best day so far, sir." Sergeant Pierce gave him an update.

They might complete their orders by Thursday. "Finish up

the day at five and get a fresh start tomorrow. I'll take Private Shea on an errand with me. If it takes too long, he'll return to camp this evening."

The sergeant's brow furrowed, though he agreed readily. "I'll fetch him for you."

"Thank you, Sergeant." Travis frowned as he left. The fellow's curiosity was reason enough for Luke to work as the colonel's aide so Luke could monitor the streets with Travis. Luke's comrades would be curious too.

A few minutes later, Luke strode up with his canteen and haversack over his shoulder. "Sergeant Pierce said you had an errand for me?"

"That's right." Travis led Luke away from their comrades, who were glancing their way. "First, let's go to your saddle shop. We need to have a private conversation. Is Clifford there?"

"Mondays are his day off. His home is in the stable. That's where he'll be if he's home. The windows are broken—just like everywhere else. We'll have to speak softly." Luke fell into stride with him. "But we can hear if someone walks outside."

"Right." It would not be totally private, but it was better to be out of earshot of Luke's cook who might support the South. Clifford had proven his loyalty to the North by informing Travis of the spy activities. Even so, his and Luke's upcoming conversation must remain confidential. It was fortunate Luke was already trained to think that way.

They talked about the people that had moved that day until reaching the empty saddle shop. Luke checked the stable. Clifford wasn't there.

"How about if we refresh ourselves with a drink before we talk?" Luke asked. When Travis agreed, Luke raised and lowered the pump handle on his well, and water gushed out. He stepped back and gestured toward the flow. "Help yourself."

"Don't mind if a do." Cold water soothed his hot skin and

quenched his thirst. What he wouldn't do for a bath in the cold stream back home right now.

After taking a drink, Luke opened the door and ushered him inside. Hides lay stacked in the corners. "I dug up the skins that Ash, the owner of this property, had hidden from the soldiers."

The smell of leather struck Travis as much as the cleanliness of the room. "Our peacetime occupations are quite different from wartime."

"Aye." Luke gestured the room's single bench and sat at one end. "I figure ye have questions."

"Tell me about your spying." Speaking softly, Travis sat.

"I'll mention very few names, but I'd appreciate them going no further than the colonel."

"I will not pass them along to anyone but Colonel Haversham. However, he may tell General McPherson and possibly General Grant." The general had his own spies, and Colonel Haversham or General McPherson reported significant findings to their commander.

"Then I will mention only two spies. My friend, Ashburn Mitchell, and his wife invited me to stay here while I recuperated from me amnesia. Julia wasn't a spy, but Ash and Felicity were."

Travis sucked in his breath. Luke's wife—Savannah's friend —had been a Union spy. He listened with growing respect to how Ash had trained him. Both he and Ash had spied for a fellow who had multiple spies reporting to him until he was captured. The Union army had been getting closer, and several spies had quit. Felicity's information had come mainly through her work at the hospital. One man reported to Ash and then to Luke after Ash moved. They'd ridden miles to deliver messages to fellow spies who sent them on up the line.

"That's dangerous work." Travis couldn't imagine all he'd endured.

"Aye. Ash was imprisoned for five days. Felicity and I also faced danger. There was a fellow who helped both us and Ash at different points. He wasn't a spy, but he seemed to know everyone in the area."

"What's his name?"

"Michael's all he told me. Likely a farmer. Dressed like one, anyway. Gray hair and whiskers. Eyes the color of the Mississippi River. I trusted him for some reason. Drives a wagon pulled by a mare he calls Old Nell." Luke peered out the window as if not seeing the empty panes. "That horse outran my much younger one."

"Sounds like an interesting character." But he wasn't a spy. Travis couldn't afford to get sidetracked. "Anything else?"

"That was the day a Confederate captain saw me getting off the train with Felicity in Vicksburg. She didn't have a pass. He was more interested in having me fight in his regiment. As desperate as he was, he didn't care that I'd been discharged. That's when me spying ended."

"You seem to excel at it. Would you do something similar again?"

Luke looked at him squarely. "I'll be proud to serve me country in whatever capacity needed."

No doubt about it—the colonel would want Luke's spy expertise.

Luke's help would relieve some of Travis's pressure. He wanted to spend more time with Savannah in hopes that it led to a courtship. He'd invite her to lunch or to take a stroll with him. She needed to hear the reasons for his abolitionist beliefs if their relationship was to become more than a friendship.

CHAPTER 21

Savannah poked her head into the second-floor family parlor on Tuesday morning. Mama wasn't there.

"Looking for something, Savannah?" Mrs. Jung looked up from her knitting. She'd claimed this room. Not that she wouldn't share, but she had selected a favorite green-cushioned chair as her own. She claimed it had the best light for her knitting, her only pastime.

"Mrs. Beltzer brought a letter to Mama from my father. I wondered about the news and was looking for her." It rankled that Mrs. Jung spent her days in this room to avoid Ellen. In Savannah's opinion, Mrs. Jung felt shame over her husband's actions.

"Your mother rarely comes in here now." The older woman didn't look up from her needles and blue yarn. "Have you tried the front parlor?"

She was right. Mama had begun using the front parlor again after Ellen got all but the faintest of stains from the rug. The floor underneath had defeated her, but Ellen and Savannah had agreed that as long as the rug covered that area, blood stains didn't hurt anything...though it did make Savannah's skin crawl to think about it.

"I'll go there next." Biting back her irritation, she headed down the stairs. No doubt Ellen was happier that Mrs. Jung stayed upstairs, but underlying tension always hung in the atmosphere.

Just as it had between Mama and Papa. Would she ever have a peaceful home again?

She found her mother in the parlor, an open letter by her side. "Mama, what's the news from Papa? Is he coming soon?"

"No." Bitterness overshadowed Mama's face. "He's interested in the Longhorn cattle, the kind Ash's uncle owns. He's got a job for one of Ash's neighbors to head up an expedition to deliver a small herd to a fort in Texas. It will take weeks. If all goes well, he hopes other ranchers will also hire him."

"Can't he come back and look for something closer to Vicksburg?"

"It's too late for that. You know I already pleaded with him to stay here and see what jobs become available as the situation settles." Trembling hands folded the letter, blocking it from Savannah's view. "In any case, he's uncertain when he'll return."

Savannah sat on the edge of the sofa. "Did he send the money I requested?"

"Yes, but he asks that you be less generous with the staff until he's certain how lucrative this position will be. We're not as wealthy as before the war."

"He's really not coming." She had tried not to get her hopes up but failed.

"Not yet." Mama sighed. "The Sandersons have purchased land twenty miles from Ash and Julia. They'll have a home built in the next few months. Things are looking up for them."

But not for her and Mama. It was up to them to figure out how to make the best of life in an occupied city.

~

"Thank you, sir." Travis sat beside Luke at Colonel Haversham's headquarters on Tuesday morning. They both had learned Luke would work with Travis one day weekly—normally Mondays but today, Tuesday, was an exception. "Having another person to engage in conversation while monitoring potential spy activities will be of benefit to me. And alerting Brian that we'll both be serving you on Mondays will clear me of new duties."

"Exactly. I see now that you were hindered in many ways. You will still be on the lookout for spies the rest of the week in addition to performing your other duties as ordered by your captain." Colonel Haversham set a page on the table before them. "Christopher was able to decipher Gerald Finkler's message. We've got the proof we need to charge him with spying."

Travis picked up the paper. "'Yankee troops on Morris Island in Charleston Harbor have been firing for days toward Fort Sumter. Naval guns were also employed. Attack considered imminent.'" He tapped the page. "Spies aren't simply interested in what's happening in Mississippi."

"I found the same to be true in me own spying." Luke peered at the message. "Whatever is uncovered is passed up the line until reaching Union officials. They decide whom to inform. With secrets, time is of the essence."

"Just so." The colonel exchanged a satisfied look with Travis.

"I can provide Christopher with the cipher Ash and I used." Luke scooted to the edge of his chair.

"Excellent."

"We'll search for the woman who received the note." Travis gripped the chair arms. He had concentrated on monitoring the male citizens for spy activities. That had been a mistake

Travis wouldn't repeat. His excitement for the mission escalated. He had an entire day to devote to the task and another set of eyes and ears. They'd get rid of the danger from Rebel bands by cutting off their information.

~

*T*he realization that Papa would be gone months instead of weeks came as a shock to Savannah. Papa had deserted them. Just being with Travis calmed her spirits. There were no excuses to see him, though. The windows Papa ordered hadn't come, and that was their next task.

But what prevented her from inviting him and his friends to Sunday lunch? Felicity and Luke too. Felicity's cheerful disposition and Luke's ready sense of humor could be counted upon to ease the atmosphere should Mrs. Jung decide to grace them with her presence at the meal.

The more Savannah thought about it, the more she liked the idea. She needed Travis's solid presence, and Mama needed something to anticipate after Papa's upsetting news. She presented her idea to her mother, who approved the plan. Savannah fetched Mary Grace to the front parlor to discuss it privately with her since Mrs. Beltzer and Petunia weren't on the guest list.

"Please, sit a moment with us." Mama, who had been awaiting them, gestured to the chair on her left side. "Savannah has a plan that involves you."

Mary Grace clutched the frills of her new white apron.

"There's no reason for apprehension." Savannah smiled. "We want to invite Travis, Ben, Enos, Felicity, and Luke to lunch on Sunday."

"And you and your mama, of course." Mama wrinkled her brow at Savannah.

"Of course." She turned back to Mary Grace. "You've

prepared lunches and suppers for our guests before. Does that suit you?"

"Mrs. Beltzer has taught me new dishes. I can make gumbo soup and fried chicken for lunch." She clasped her hands together. "If the men want to fish that afternoon, I'll fry their catches and serve them with potato cakes, with bread pudding for dessert."

"Include a vegetable or fruit dish with both meals," Mama suggested.

"Sounds lovely." Savannah hadn't planned on supper, too, but a whole day of company without the men working on repairs was more like the old days. "Let me present our ideas to Travis. I usually find him near the middle of the city."

She was strolling toward Washington Street within a half hour, frilled yellow parasol shading her from the August sun. The parasol matched her summery dress. Other pedestrians were mostly soldiers in a hurry to some destination. If she learned more information for Sam while searching for Travis, so much the better.

As she scanned the blue-coated men for Travis's curly brown hair and Hardee hat, she hoped he not only accepted her invitation but also sat with her a while. She was ready to learn his story.

Three soldiers smoked cigars outside a cigar shop. No harm in listening to their conversation for a moment.

Wait. Travis was across the street with Luke. How wrong it felt that he now wore blue instead of his former gray. She waved to get their attention. What duty brought the private to town with his lieutenant?

$\sim$

*T*ravis spotted a woman of medium height with her brown hair in a bun at her nape outside a grocery store. "Luke, does that look like her?"

His glance darted at her and back again. "Maybe. A third of the women in Vicksburg fit the description. We must be cautious."

The woman continued past the store, her pace increasing.

"She noticed us looking at her." Travis pretended to read a sign tacked to a building. "Two men staring would make any woman nervous. I don't think it's her."

"Let's trail her for a bit." Luke peered across the street. "Change of plans. There's Savannah."

Travis swung around. Heart sinking that the spy might be getting away, he returned her wave. "Let's talk with Savannah." They crossed the street where she waited near a group of soldiers from another regiment. He gave them a nod and then focused on Savannah, looking as fresh as the daisies on her dress. "Good morning."

"Good morning, gentlemen. I didn't expect to find you together." A suspicious glint was gone almost as soon as it appeared. "But it's a blessing just the same."

"It's not often I'm described as such." That smile did things to his heart.

"I said seeing you *together* was a blessing." Smiling, she tilted her head. "How did that come about?"

Travis blinked. It was an unexpected question coming from her but one for which he had readied an answer. "The colonel has requested we tend to errands for him."

Luke's shoulders relaxed.

"Ah, I see. You're in a hurry, then. I had hoped to talk with you." The light in her brown eyes dimmed.

A jolt shot through him. It was the first true indication of a desire for his company.

"It's nearly noon." Luke wiggled his eyebrows.

Lunch. Should he invite her? They'd been alone often but had never even intentionally taken a stroll or a drive in the country.

"I'll go home for lunch. Meet you at the saddle shop afterward?" Looking at Travis, Luke half turned away.

"One moment, Luke." Savannah tilted her head. "Mama and I wanted to invite you and Felicity to lunch on Sunday. Travis, you, Ben, and Enos are also invited."

"I know Felicity will agree, but a fellow has to check with his wife before accepting an invitation." Luke grinned. "She'll be sewing at your home tomorrow. Can she tell you then?"

"Of course." She laughed. "That's very wise. How about you, Travis?"

"Speaking for only myself, I wouldn't miss it." Without the excuse of home repairs, he hadn't known when he'd see her again. "I'll tell Ben and Enos tonight."

"Thank you. One more thing—if you men want to go fishing that afternoon, Mary Grace said she'd fry the fish you catch." Savannah held Travis's gaze.

Better and better. "I don't even have to ask the fellows about that one. We all used to fish together back home and go whenever possible. Luke, how about it? Want to fish for supper?"

"If Felicity agrees. Thanks for the invitation, Savannah." He touched his kepi. "See you at the shop, Travis." He strode away before anyone could say another word.

Travis took a deep breath. "Will you dine with me, Savannah? I found a small restaurant called Katie's Home Cooking that I enjoy. Or we can go somewhere else..." He wasn't certain how to proceed. The only other woman he'd courted was Janet, and he'd grown up with her. Everything had been casual and easy between them, not at all the way he felt right now.

"I've never been to Katie's Home Cooking." She twirled her parasol. "Let's go there."

"All right." He offered her his arm. She looked enchanting in that yellow dress splashed with tiny white daisies.

Savannah rested her gloved hand on his coat sleeve. "Thank you for the invitation. I needed a distraction today."

"Oh? Did something happen?" He set off at a sedate pace.

"My father has decided to remain in Texas a while longer."

"Looking for a job?"

"He's found one that will require a few weeks on the trail. If he likes it, I don't know how it will affect us."

"I'm sorry." If her father found a job, would he attempt to move his whole family? No...that couldn't be. Not just when he was finally getting to know her...

"It's not your fault." She held his gaze. "I suppose...well, I simply wanted to tell you about it."

Travis's footsteps faltered at another hint of her growing regard. Did this mean her heart had mended from the loss of her beau? And could she look past him being a Yankee officer?

~

*I*n a quaint restaurant with eight of its ten tables occupied by soldiers, Savannah ate a delicious apple tapioca pudding for dessert while listening to Travis talk about his Illinois three-hundred-acre farm, fifty acres of which were for crops of sweet potatoes, corn, string beans, potatoes, and green onions.

"One hundred acres of woodland is where I picked blackberries with my sisters, Eliza, Mary, and Nancy. There's a stream running through it where I fished with my pa and Bill, my brother."

As he continued, her imagination began to paint hazy images of barns, cattle pastures, horse corrals, chickens... How she'd love to see it. "Tell me about your parents."

"My father is James Lawson, but everyone calls him Jay." He

grinned. "Except his children, of course. He loves the land. Farming is the only thing he's ever wanted to do. I look like him. My mother, Charlotte, comes to about here on me." He touched his chest. "She has brown hair and eyes. They both have a great sense of humor. We laughed a lot." His smile vanished. "In the early days."

Savannah could relate to that. Her own childhood was divided in her mind from before the incident with Gus and after it. She waited for him to elaborate.

He gave his head a shake. He consumed two bites of pudding before continuing. "Eliza is twenty now. She was betrothed to a farm boy, Giles Benedict. Her heart broke when he died at Shiloh."

Savannah empathized with that grief, except she hadn't been betrothed to Willie. "That sorrow gets less sharp with time. At least, mine did."

Travis's fork stopped midway to his mouth. "You don't know how happy I am to hear that." Hazel eyes searched hers.

Her gaze dropped to her empty dish. Her stomach danced with joy that he reciprocated her regard.

"Mary is married to Ben, whom you know. She's nineteen. They married before he left for war, in 1861. Mary and their son, Benny, will live on the farm until Ben musters out."

"I've heard Ben mention his son. You have another sister?"

"Nancy. She's seventeen now, and I never saw a girl who wanted to be married more." He chuckled. "She's professed to love at least three boys and is now courting one of our farmhands."

She laughed. "You'll likely have another brother-in-law before long."

"I don't doubt it. That leaves my brother. Bill is the youngest at sixteen." He shook his head. "I hope this war ends soon, or he'll muster in too."

"You think it will?" Savannah wanted the South to claim the

victory tomorrow. That wasn't Travis's wish, obviously. She was drawn to him, but they were so different. Was there a chance for a courtship to flourish?

"I hoped it would end at Vicksburg and at Gettysburg." He sighed. "The victory for both battles was decided the same day."

How well she knew. Their country's Independence Day would never be the same for her.

"But as you know, it didn't happen. So many more battles have been fought since." Travis put down his fork. "I fear more will happen in the future."

This opened the door for him to tell her what he'd clearly wanted to explain over two weeks ago when Mrs. Jung reacted so violently to news that Northerners were leasing plantations. "You said you wanted to tell me something. What is it?"

He glanced at the crowded restaurant and then consulted his pocket watch. "I still do, but that will have to wait. Perhaps we can take a drive in the country?"

Savannah froze. Was this the beginning of a courtship? Sudden realization struck of how much she wanted that to be so. "I would enjoy that very much. We have a buggy, but no horses."

He held her gaze. "My mount was killed during a skirmish this spring, and I haven't yet been furnished a replacement. I will ask my friend, Captain Brian Eaton, if I can borrow his horse for our outing. I will stop by later this week and inform you if he's agreeable."

"That will be wonderful." Savannah's breath fluttered in her throat. It had been over two years since she went driving with a beau. Surprisingly, she was beginning to think of Travis in that light.

CHAPTER 22

*A*fter a wonderful meal with Savannah that left him with cautious dreams for the future, Travis and Luke spent a fruitless afternoon searching for Mr. Finkler's accomplice.

At camp that Tuesday evening, Brian pulled Travis aside after supper. "Attacks on small numbers of troops by these Rebel bands have increased...not to mention the harassment of the Northerners leasing plantations." They began walking toward the edge of camp. "One of those mansions is less than two miles from us."

"Too close for comfort." Travis peered into the forest ahead, searching for the guerrillas and finding only the Union pickets guarding them.

"Yes, I'm taking half our regiment out on patrol at dawn. If we don't find these Rebels, we'll at least run them from the area. We'll be back on Thursday. Then our regiment will be leaving for an expedition to Louisiana."

Travis sucked in his breath. Leaving just when his courtship with Savannah was beginning. "Not leaving Vicksburg for good?"

Brian shook his head. "I don't believe so. We'll pack up camp early Friday. I expect we'll be gone over a week."

He'd have to tell Savannah they'd all be gone because it affected the Sunday luncheon. Ben and especially Enos had been excited about the invitation—and Travis, most of all.

Brian halted just outside the tree line. "Our part in the relocation of the freedman camps will end before we leave. You'll oversee the task."

"I had no idea there were so many freedmen taking refuge in Vicksburg." His regiment alone had moved over one thousand people away from the filth.

"Hopefully, former slaves coming into the city now will find a place in these communities or start new ones." Brian peered in every direction. "By now, our noncommissioned officers are well versed in what to do. You'll also oversee tasks here at camp."

"I'll see to it." The next two days just got much busier. It limited his time to find that female spy.

"Let's get back and prepare the troops." Brian took off at a rapid pace.

Travis matched his stride, fighting a sinking sensation in his stomach. His plans with Savannah must wait. Orders changed quickly, as she'd learn. Borrowing a horse for an evening buggy ride was out of the question. He'd be in Louisiana for a week or two.

Travis would stop by Savannah's home to tell her of their plan's delay at the first opportunity. Would she be as disappointed as himself? Did she have feelings for him, or was he just a friend?

≈

*O*n Thursday morning, Savannah strolled under cloudy skies to the oak grove for her delivery for Sam. Her letter today included news that Fort Sumter was still under Confederate control and the Yankee bombardment against it had been unsuccessful thus far. This was information she'd gleaned from soldiers talking near her orchard yesterday.

Guards on patrol headed down Locust Street. There'd been some trouble between the black men policing the town and citizens this month. Savannah never glanced their direction, hoping not to see Leland, Robert, and Fred among them. But there were plenty of folks passing on the opposite sidewalk, soldiers and officers in nearly equal numbers to townsfolk.

No one at home seemed to notice her weekly Thursday outings. Most often, she purchased cooking ingredients for Mrs. Beltzer, sewing notions for Felicity, who sewed in Papa's study as it had the best lighting and widest table, or she fetched the mail.

Today she'd walk to the post office for Mama. Because she went for solitary walks nearly daily, no one seemed suspicious. Savannah worried more about Ellen than anyone else, for little escaped her housekeeper's scrutiny.

Her lunch with Travis hadn't gone unnoticed.

Because they lived in an occupied city, Mama seemed resigned that a Union officer would want to court her. She liked Travis personally yet...

Savannah understood. She shared the same reservations about courting him. But he didn't *feel* like the enemy. How she'd longed to see him and had even walked for an hour in the hot sun yesterday to catch a glimpse of him, without success.

Butterflies fluttered in her stomach at the thought of their upcoming drive. She'd been alone a long time.

Best not think of that right now. Delivering her message was her priority.

The oak grove seemed deserted, but Mrs. Lakin had hidden in wait the last time they met here. Savannah stepped off the road and entered the canopy of trees, darker due to rain threatening.

Mrs. Lakin wasn't there.

Travis approached the city from the camp. Savannah panicked. He mustn't see her. In this instance, he wasn't a man who wanted to court her, but a Union officer to her Confederate spy. If he caught her in the grove, how would she explain it?

She crept backward into the shadows, grateful that she wore a green dress. He mustn't see Mrs. Lakin either. It was good the spy was late.

Travis paused a moment on the lane outside the hospital, then his swift, booted steps brought him closer. He peered in every direction. What was he looking for?

She slipped behind a massive trunk, her skirt sticking out a foot on either side. If she had the courage to ask God for big things, she'd ask Him to shield her from Travis's probing gaze.

Ten seconds. Twenty seconds. Patience wasn't her virtue.

Savannah peeked through the foliage and nearly gasped. Mrs. Lakin climbed the hill toward their meeting place.

No! Go back. Her whole body screamed the warning silently.

The letter carrier glanced Travis's way. Mrs. Lakin ducked her head as if studying the ground for broken glass.

Savannah tensed. Travis glanced toward the spy and then peered ahead of him.

Mrs. Lakin disappeared down Poplar Street.

Travis looked toward the grove where Savannah hid. Her legs trembled. Beyond that, she didn't dare move lest she capture his gaze.

He ambled on, continuing to scan his surroundings.

Were all soldiers so aware of their surroundings, especially when alone? It likely had something to do with his battlefield experience, yet it troubled her just how close she had just come to being caught.

Travis disappeared around a bend.

She waited five minutes, hardly daring to breathe. Mrs. Lakin did not return.

Rain began to fall. After checking once again that Travis was out of sight, Savannah stepped into the clearing. She raised her ivory parasol. It wasn't much protection. Quick steps put the oak grove behind her. She'd be wet well before reaching the post office, her supposed destination.

But at least a Union officer hadn't caught her or the letter carrier with a message she'd burn at her first opportunity.

~

*B*ig splashes of rain drove Travis under an awning near the post office. The whole day had been frustrating. Assigning pickets for the next twenty-four hours and updating the list of sick—which, thankfully, had shrunk by a third—along with attending Brian's duties had kept him from town until late morning. They'd leave tomorrow for an expedition.

His first goal was to check with his enlisted officers about the relocation. If there were no problems, he'd try to find the woman spy who'd eluded him and Luke earlier. Unfortunately, he didn't have much of a description to go on—a brunette who wore her hair in a bun at her nape.

Travis scanned the faces of people running along the sidewalks to escape the rain. He prayed that God would lead him to the spy. Colonel Haversham wasn't the only one who wanted this woman caught.

A woman in a green dress, an ivory parasol covering her hair and face and little else, ran toward the awning. The parasol shifted.

"Savannah?" He reached for her hand and guided her out of the steady rainfall. "What brings you out in this weather?" The touch of her wet fingers dwarfed against his large hand. Reluctantly, he released her.

"Travis, I—I didn't expect to see you." Her frock was wet from the waist down. "It wasn't raining when I set out for the post office."

"Ah." Soldiers quickly grew accustomed to dealing with bad weather when on the march and in battles—not the type of weather a Southern belle usually endured. That accounted for her tense expression. "You've made it to your destination. I will accompany you home once the rain slackens."

"I appreciate that." Her gaze held his and then she smiled. "Parasols aren't much protection. I should have carried my umbrella."

"I will purchase one for us while you gather your mail." He probably sounded like the bumbling idiot he felt like. Purchase an umbrella just to shelter with her in seclusion? Who was he kidding? He was a farmer and a soldier—not a gallant gentleman like her former beau.

~

"*T*hat will be lovely." What a thoughtful gesture. Savannah's relief that Travis hadn't spotted her in the oak grove made her knees weak. Nor did he know about the spy message tucked securely in her sash. She glanced down. Good. That part of her dress had remained protected. The envelope was barely discernable.

"I'll be back." He sprinted across the street as she entered the post office. She'd written one letter to Julia after the post office reopened and was anxious to learn how her friend fared in her final weeks of pregnancy.

To her delight, a letter from Julia was waiting for her. She returned to the awning she'd shared with Travis. A few soldiers dashed up the street, but otherwise, the rain had chased everyone indoors.

Savannah didn't mind the rain because it meant she'd walk close to Travis on the way home.

Unable to wait until she got home to read the letter with Mama, she broke the seal. As she scanned the lines, her heart began to race. Julia was a mother at last.

"It must be good news." Travis joined her under the awning carrying a blue umbrella.

"It's wonderful." Joy coursed through her. "My friend Julia has written. She and her husband Ash became parents on"— she consulted the letter— "Monday, August tenth."

"Ten days ago." Hazel eyes sparkled back at her. "Is the child healthy?"

"A boy. And yes, the midwife says he's a fine, strapping boy." She giggled at the description. "Ashburn Harrison Mitchell has his father's first name and his grandfather's—Julia's father's—as his middle name."

"Good news, indeed." He studied her face.

"Yes, she says she'll write more later." Savannah folded the note. Shadows under the awning lent an intimacy to their seclusion that both excited and unnerved her.

"When you answer her, please mention my happiness over their news. Of course, you will have to introduce me in your letter first." He chuckled.

"Which I will be pleased to do." She laughed.

"I have a bit of bad news. None of us can accept your lunch invitation."

"Oh?" The depth of her disappointment gave her a sign that Travis was becoming important to her happiness. Mary Grace would be disappointed not to see Enos, whether she admitted it or not.

"Nor will I be able to borrow a horse this weekend or next."

He took a deep breath. "My captain is out on patrol. We've been troubled by Rebel bands of late. Half of our regiment is out searching for them."

Her smile wavered. Sam's troops? Nothing she could do to warn him now, but she'd mention it next week—if she was able to deliver a message. "I hope everyone returns safely."

"Thank you. There's always danger, especially since we don't know how many of them are out there. We may have a better idea once this patrol is back."

Savannah feared the number of Union troops in Vicksburg still exceeded Sam's troops.

"After they return, we'll all leave on an expedition."

"An expedition? Where are you going? For how long?"

"That I can't say. Look." Travis gestured toward the road. "The rain has slowed considerably. Shall we see if this umbrella is waterproof?"

"Let's." Why didn't he tell her where he was going? With the umbrella in place, she tucked her hand around his arm, and they set off at a leisurely pace. His nearness made her worries dim. The warmth of his side against her arm made her yearn for a long walk.

Unfortunately, ten minutes later, she was thanking him for his escort from her portico. He left almost immediately in the drizzle, leaving the umbrella with her.

When he turned at the gate, Savannah waved. She was beginning to care for him very much. His upcoming military expedition reminded her of the wedge between them. What future was there for a Union officer and a Confederate spy?

CHAPTER 23

"*I* wonder why I didn't think of it before."

"Think of what?" Travis stood beside Luke on the City Landing on Monday afternoon, September seventh. They'd returned from Louisiana nearly a week ago and still hadn't seen the female spy with brown hair worn in a bun, but they'd followed a fellow who looked over his shoulder every few paces. The tall man with a mustache shaped into a curl on each side had led them to the bustling wharf. Crates and sacks were being unloaded from five ships. Travis kept the man in his peripheral vision.

"I have a friend who may want to help us." Luke's whispered words barely reached Travis.

A former spy contact? He couldn't ask right now, even in a whisper. A burly man toting a small barrel on his shoulder passed them two feet from Travis. Trying to overhear what they were discussing? Too much risk. "Don't do anything until we talk."

Their suspect, who had exchanged greetings with three men in passing, stopped to talk with a muscular wharf worker wearing a green shirt, brown trousers, and brown suspenders.

"Let's get closer to our mustached friend," Travis whispered. Then, as they began to move toward him, Travis raised his voice to carry on a cover conversation. "Yes, when I asked the captain to borrow his horse on Saturday, he said he can now replace mine that was killed months ago." Savannah's luncheon finally happened yesterday, expanded to include the Beltzers, Petunia, and her children. A successful fishing expedition had provided everyone's supper. Travis had been in a hurry to return to Savannah. How he had missed her while away.

"Aye, that's good." Luke's gaze settled on their suspect ten feet from them. "You'll be able to take Savannah on the promised buggy ride Felicity mentioned to me."

A chuckle rumbled in Travis's chest that Savannah had been excited enough to mention it to her friend, but he'd best attend the matter at hand. They were close enough to hear the man's conversation. Travis slowed his pace and veered slightly to the left, giving the appearance of going around them.

"Right, there are Yankee troops in Tracy City up in Tennessee. Rosecrans's army is still marching to—"

The wharf worker's eyes widened as he glanced at Travis. He shook his head. "I don't care about that."

"What do you mean? You said troop movements—"

The wharf worker shoved him into Luke, and both men tumbled to the muddy bank. The green-shirted man bolted.

"Take this one to the colonel." Travis spoke over his shoulder to Luke and then sped in pursuit. The man weaved through the crowd that closed up after him. "Let me pass, or you'll be arrested too."

A break opened. Travis raced through it toward the green-shirted runner who headed away from the river. He closed the gap between them when they reached the hillside.

"Halt!"

Breathing heavily, the man stopped on a grassy yard. Red-faced, he bent over, hands resting on his knees.

"You're under arrest for spying." Travis's hand hovered over his sidearm.

The burly man closed his eyes and shook his head sadly.

It was a sorrow Travis didn't share. They deserved whatever sentence they got. Two less spies roamed Vicksburg's streets. It was a job well done.

～

Savannah left her home a quarter hour early on Thursday morning. Army wagons on nearly every street were now as common of a sight as the blue-coated soldiers, any of whom would despise her if they knew of the envelope and payment tucked into the folds of her sash. Her hands shook at the thought of possible discovery. No, she mustn't think of that. She looked around for a distraction.

Black couples stood in lines down the steps of the AME Church. The preacher inside would be performing weddings all morning judging by the numbers waiting. She'd seen just as many the last couple of weeks whenever passing this way—a change she liked. She'd never felt it was right to deny anyone a church wedding.

No sign of Travis this morning. This was the only time she didn't want to see him—that, and when she was spying on soldiers. She hadn't told Sam that Travis's regiment would be gone a week or two last month because she didn't know where they were going. However, she had warned Sam that Union soldiers searched for him. Her only news this week was about the city and a clash between a black guard and a citizen that had turned violent. She wrote that most of these confrontations were minor but concerning, nonetheless.

She hastened her pace as she approached the grove.

Five Union soldiers sat in the shade of a mighty oak, mere

feet from the place where she was to meet Mrs. Lakin. What was she to do now?

Torn by indecision, she continued on as if the hospital was her intended destination, peering in every direction as she went. She spotted Mrs. Lakin on First North Street and turned to walk toward her.

Mrs. Lakin plopped onto a bench and began rummaging through her basket.

Pretending to adjust her sash, Savannah covered the letter with her hand as she dropped it in the basket when passing. "The bench outside the dress shop on Jackson Street next time," she whispered.

"Agreed."

Heart racing, Savannah reached the next corner before daring to look back. The letter carrier was gone. The grove was blocked from her sight. So were the soldiers. They'd been out of eyesight of the bench too.

Unless they'd left the grove.

The danger was real. She didn't want to end up in jail. Not to mention, some spies had been hanged in Richmond. Julia and Ash had told her that other spies had gone missing altogether, and no one knew what happened to them.

And then there was the fact that spying on Travis didn't feel right any more. If it ever had.

Should she quit? No. If her city was to be free, she must not be silent.

~

On Saturday, Savannah reveled in the admiration in Travis's expressive eyes. Their conversation had floated from teasing to serious and back again. Such a common thing as candlelight reflecting across his features created a sense of awareness that their time together mattered very much, indeed.

Evening sunrays entered the broken windowpanes in the dining room of the Washington Hotel, dispelling the shadows and warming the room. Platters covered a serving table at the end of the room. Two couples sat at the adjacent table. Three matrons quieted school-aged children dining with them. Soldiers filled two long tables, their loud conversation something Savannah would normally monitor for secrets...but not tonight. This evening, her focus was on her ruggedly handsome officer escort.

"Have I told you how lovely you look in that pink dress?" Travis pushed his half-empty bowl of green corn soup to the side.

"Twice." Savannah was pleased with the compliment. She'd been told her favorite satin dress with lace overlay on the bodice and wide ribbon sash of deeper pink added a delicate blush to her cheeks. That was why she chose it. She'd wanted to look her best for their first outing. "But I don't mind."

A waiter wearing a brown coat and trousers picked up their soup bowls. "I'll be right along with your baked chicken."

"Thank you." Travis gave him a smiling nod and then turned back to Savannah. "It's such a beautiful night. I'd enjoy seeing the countryside on our drive, but I agree with your mother that we'd best confine our ramble to the city."

The waiter delivered their supper of baked chicken, summer squash, and fried tomatoes.

"We can ask Mama, Josie, or Ellen to accompany us if you want to go for evening rides into the country—when it's safe to do so." Part of Savannah regretted society's rules because she'd enjoy the solitude with him. "Or Mama won't mind an unchaperoned afternoon ride—as long as we don't go far."

"We'll do that next time, but only if it's safe." He reached for her hand across the table. "Shall I ask the blessing?"

Her eyebrows shot up. She and Willie had never blessed their meals when at restaurants. She placed her hand on his, loving the sensation of his fingers curling around hers.

Travis bowed his hand. He thanked God for the food and for Savannah sharing it with him. He asked for protection and blessings for her in these dangerous and trying times. He also asked God's blessing on their evening.

He released her hand and began slicing his chicken.

She sat unmoving.

"Is something wrong?"

"No." She gave a slow shake of her head at how touching it had been to have him pray for her. "It's just...well, the only time someone prayed for me aloud was when Willie died."

"Surely, that's not the only time..." He rested his fork on his plate. "When your parents prayed with you at bedtime, didn't they pray for you then?"

Savannah's brows drew together. "Mama listened to my nightly prayers when I was a young child, but that ended when I started school. Did your parents pray for you?" She ate a bite of squash. Delicious.

He nodded. "My father added prayers for Mama and each of us children at supper every night. Mama was the one who listened to our prayers. My faith has always been important to me."

"We attend church most weeks." She sliced into her chicken to avoid his probing gaze. "Remember that I don't pray about important matters, though."

"I remember." His brows lowered as he ate another forkful of meat. "You don't trust yourself to ask wisely."

"Exactly. I learned my lesson." Sadness washed over her. How she wished for greater wisdom.

"To my mind, you asked for *exactly* the right thing that day." Putting down his fork, he leaned forward. "Both your actions and your father's actions were heroic. You were asking the only person you knew who could help Gus to save him from cruel punishment. Your father tried to ignore the cruelty. You made him face it. And your actions also saved Gus's family from retribution."

Savannah toyed with her fried tomatoes. She hadn't thought of her actions as heroic.

"Please, Savannah, hear me."

She raised her gaze to his earnest expression.

"Your Heavenly Father loves you so much. He hears every prayer, even the ones only our hearts whisper." He held her gaze. "One day, you'll need to pray a big prayer. Please don't be afraid to ask. He'll decide whether to say 'no' or 'yes' or 'wait a while.' Pray and leave it up to God."

Could she do that? Was it really that simple? "Is that what you do?"

"It is."

"What was the catalyst for your deep faith?"

"I'll tell you about it." His face shuttered. "How about during our ride?"

"Perfect." She loved the deeper glimpses into his Christian beliefs. Ellen had been the one to remind her to trust in God as a child, and she'd taught Ellen to read the Bible. Maybe she'd been wrong to stop praying...

~

"That's Millie." Travis grimaced at his mare's name. Savannah had complimented the chestnut Quarter Horse after they set off on their buggy ride. "She was already named when I got her. I'm told she's got good heart. Sixteen hands. Muscular build."

"Spoken like a man who knows farm animals." Smiling, she lifted her brows.

"Guilty." He chuckled. "I'm lucky to get her."

"Indeed. Papa left money for us to buy a team whenever horses are available again."

Travis guided Millie onto Walnut Street. "I'll ask the sergeant in charge of our horses who found Millie." Now that was a man who knew horses. "If he knows of a team for sale, I'll tell you. Don't get your hopes up for something soon. I waited six months for Millie."

"Whenever they are available, Mama and I will appreciate purchasing them." She folded her hands in her lap and looked at him expectantly. "Won't you tell me your story?"

"I will." He sighed. "It's about my Uncle Dabney. I was twelve the last time I saw him." He explained about finding two fugitives from a Mississippi cotton plantation at his bachelor uncle's cabin, and Uncle Dabney preparing to take them to the next home on the Underground Railroad on their flight to freedom. "He made me promise not to tell *anyone* I'd seen them. That especially meant my ma, who loves to gossip."

"Why keep it a secret in Illinois?"

Travis turned onto Monroe Street, taking one parallel street at a time in a gradual climb up the hill. The sun sank over the tree line. A breeze gave a slight reprieve from the heat. "Someone was on their trail. Besides, the Fugitive Slave Act of 1850 made it illegal to give food or shelter to a fugitive. The penalty was up to six months in jail and a fine as high as one thousand dollars."

Her face paled.

"When Uncle Dabney went missing, Pa looked for him. No one had seen him. Finally, I told my pa and asked him not to tell Ma." Travis passed Cherry Street and headed toward Adams, the next one up the bluff. He wasn't ready to take Savannah home. "It took two weeks to find the wagon twenty miles north. Empty. Three bullet holes and blood stains on the seat and bed made us fear the worst. Pa and I scoured the woods near the wagon."

"You never found him." A soft hand closed over his right hand gripping the reins.

"No," he whispered.

"I'm sorry."

He looked into her compassionate brown eyes. "I still regret not going with him."

"You'd have met the same fate."

"Which was?" Driving past folks sitting on their porches in the cool of the day, he shook his head. "That's the worst part. We still don't know if he died that night. Maybe he escaped with the men he was trying to help."

"I hope you one day discover the truth." Her hand tightened around his. "But had you gone, do you think you'd be a Union officer now?"

His head jerked around. He searched the sweet face so close to his in the dim light of a streetlamp. Had God worked through Uncle Dabney to protect him for his future? "I never considered that." His hand shifted to clasp hers. Millie's plodding gait slowed.

"It seems to me that serving the Union army means a great deal to you." She sandwiched his hand between hers. "And you're a good officer. I observed you with your men when they filled our cave. They respect you."

"I believe they do." It felt good to hear her praise something that meant so much to him.

"I am sorry those men fled from a Mississippi plantation. It makes me think of Gus."

"Yes, me too. My experience made me an abolitionist." Travis was out of words. Emotionally spent.

After a moment, she drew her hand away with seeming reluctance. "This helps me understand your Northern loyalties better. Is it hard for you to talk about?"

Travis's throat tightened. "I've never told anyone but Pa. Not even my brother knows the whole story."

Her eyes widened. "Thank you for trusting me with the truth."

"It felt important that you know." A sigh came from the depths of his soul. "I still wish I knew what happened."

"I know. You would have changed the outcome if you were able. I would, too, even after all these years." She gave him a tremulous smile. "It's getting dark. Mama will be waiting to visit with us. I hope you have room for apple cobbler after eating blackberry pie for dessert."

"Two desserts?" Travis pretended to groan. "Now I see why you refused the pie."

"And only ate one bite of yours." She giggled.

"A wise woman." He grinned. "I'd like that." Both Savannah and Mrs. Adair embodied gracious Southern hospitality. He'd already written his parents about them, especially Savannah. A longer letter was in order now that they were courting.

His parents would like them. Uncle Dabney would like them if he were...

Was he alive?

Savannah had learned why he must fight for the Union tonight...the reason he'd fight until the war's end. They'd both suffered from their inability to change an outcome during a pivotal life moment. But did she truly understand why his beliefs were so important to him?

CHAPTER 24

The next two weeks flew by for Savannah. She and Mama had returned to services at their own church while Travis was away, and the Jungs went with them. When Travis returned from his expedition, he sat with them. Then he ate both lunch and supper with them. By now, Savannah felt comfortable in including both Enos and Ben for Sunday meals, a fact which pleased Mary Grace. In fact, she consented to a stroll with Enos on the second Sunday in September.

The windows arrived two days later. Mama invited Travis, Enos, Ben, Luke, and Felicity for lunch after church. While the men worked, Mary Grace and Ellen prepared a fried chicken supper. Except for the nearly floor-to-ceiling windows opening onto the portico that were coming on another ship, all the first-floor windows were installed before they left that evening.

Travis escorted Savannah on Saturday evening strolls to the Sky Parlor, where the serene view made negotiating a long flight of wooden stairs worth the effort. It was a great place for couples as there usually dozens of folks around. Savannah introduced him to acquaintances from the city, and she met some of his comrades courting Vicksburg ladies. Some citizens ignored Savannah when Travis was at her side, but that only served to nudge her closer to him. The best part was hooking her arm around Travis's as they strolled.

Travis hadn't let any more military secrets slip into their conversation, so she didn't have to feel guilty. But for some reason, she did feel increasingly uncomfortable about her undercover assignment.

On Monday, September twenty-first, she stopped to listen to two soldiers outside the apothecary talking about the number of Rebel spies caught in the city—maybe a dozen in the past month. Her heart leaped to her throat, but she wasn't able to hear the details because Travis and Luke hailed her from across the street. She'd walked with them to the dry goods store, which was her supposed reason for being out that day. The men were performing errands for the colonel again. Travis had asked to take her for a late-afternoon buggy ride on Saturday and then to supper. Savannah had been thrilled to accept. But by the time the men left her and she made her purchases, the soldiers were also gone.

Three days later, Savannah put her coded letter about the spies who'd been captured in an egg basket. Mrs. Beltzer needed at least eighteen eggs from the grocers, preferably two dozen, and Savannah had offered to fetch them.

She strolled toward the dress shop on Jackson Street where she'd been meeting Wanda Lakin since the two close calls at the oak grove. Black police guards approached from the other direction. Were they the ones who were capturing all the spies? Best not take the chance.

Savannah turned at the next road and entered the flower shop. The dozen or so guards lingered at the corner, peering in every direction. One looked her way. Savannah purchased a small bouquet of black-eyed Susans with part of her egg money. The shop owner tied a yellow ribbon around the bouquet. By the time she finished, it was three minutes before ten, and the guards were gone.

Savannah left and managed to make it to the dress shop at precisely ten, but Mrs. Lakin wasn't there.

Perching on the bench, Savannah pretended to fumble with the ribbon's ties around the yellow blooms protruding from her basket.

"Good morning." Mrs. Lakin sat beside her. "Is it under the bouquet?" she whispered.

"Yes." Savannah answered just as quietly, then spoke more loudly. "Good morning." She raised the flowers to allow the letter carrier room to reach under them. "I love the sweet aroma of these yellow flowers, don't you?"

"Indeed." The redhead reached into the basket while bending near as if to sniff them. "Watch yourself. There are spy catchers on the streets."

Savannah's smile froze. She peered in every direction.

"Don't look." A scornful whisper. "Next time—inside the dress shop."

Then the spy was gone.

Pretending to sniff the flowers, she looked again. Soldiers on horseback and driving supply wagons toward camps were nothing new. Neither were the officers and privates striding by. Women hurried along the sidewalk with children tagging after them. Gray-haired businessmen tapped their canes with every other step.

This was getting too dangerous. She might not come next week.

❧

"I'm glad we finally get the opportunity to drive into the country." Travis smiled at Savannah in the buggy beside him on the last Saturday in September. They'd been courting over a month. He could feel himself falling in love with this Southern belle—so fetching in her white dress with blue cornflowers.

"Me too." She shifted her blue parasol to block out sunshine from the side of the open vehicle. "I thought we'd travel toward Union camps. Why are we headed north of the city?"

"I mentioned the Rebel bands that have harassed our troops..."

They had reached the outskirts of the city. Tall trees shaded the wooded lane they were entering, the temperature blessedly cooler. Birds chirped in the branches.

"Yes, I believe so." Peering ahead, she straightened.

"They've also been harassing plantations near our camp."

"This is still happening? Have there been more patrols sent out looking for them?"

"Yes, I've been on a couple, but mostly, Brian—my captain —has taken charge of our patrol duty." They'd gone earlier that week and engaged with Confederate soldiers of greater number. It had been a quick skirmish with only one man wounded slightly in the wrist. Other regiments had also searched for the Rebel bands in the area, sometimes finding them. Yet none could claim victory.

"Was it dangerous?"

She was as tense as a bow. Was she afraid?

"Don't worry. You're in no danger here. There haven't been any problems in this area, but just in case, I have my sidearm." He touched her shoulder, hoping to reassure her.

"Good." She sank back in her seat.

"You know I would never put you at risk, Savannah..." He gave her a concerned glance. "I won't let anyone harm you. I'd die first."

She gasped. Her brown eyes clung to his. "I believe you."

"Good." My, but she was beautiful. And her temperament

toward him had become sweeter, giving him hope that their differences didn't stand in the way of a future together. "It's a beautiful day."

"It is." Smiling up at him, she twirled her parasol. "I'm enjoying our ride."

The escalation of his heartbeat had nothing to do with the threat of raiders. "Savannah, I..." He wanted to kiss those pink lips that were almost puckered in invitation.

"Yes?" Brown eyes huge, she leaned closer a fraction.

He allowed Millie to slow to a stop and loosened his right hand from the reins. Shifting, he skimmed her smooth cheek with his fingertips.

As she stared up at him, her fingers curled around his hand caressing her face. Could she...did she want him to kiss her?

Hardly daring to breathe, he lowered his head. Slowly, to give her the opportunity to end the moment if she chose. Her gaze fastened on his mouth. Travis touched her lips with his in a light kiss.

She didn't move away.

He kissed her again, reveling in the sweet sensation of her kissing him back. He lingered over their third kiss, keeping his passion for his Southern belle in check. She was a lady and he was a gentleman. He lifted his head, staring at her in wonder. Was it possible she returned his love?

"Oh, Travis." She nestled against his shoulder. "How do you feel about me?"

It was time to express his feelings. He cradled her head to his chest. "I love you, Savannah." Her spirit, her graciousness. Even the fact that she refused to show weakness except the small glimpses she gave him. "I hope you feel the same."

"I do." She pulled away. "I never thought there'd be any man for me except Willie, but..." Her brown eyes searched his. "I love you, Travis."

"That makes me very happy." His fingertips caressed her

lips and she kissed them. "Shall we continue our drive?" As much as he wanted to linger, it wasn't a good idea.

"Let's." Her smile radiated in her eyes. "Then let's dine at the same restaurant where you first took me to lunch."

The romance of the suggestion struck him as being just right. "Katie's Home Cooking it is." His heart sang as the buggy took off again behind Millie's easy walking gait. Life couldn't be any more perfect than it was right now.

~

Savannah's euphoria over Travis's declaration of love lasted through their simple supper at her now-favorite restaurant and later, the two of them sipping lemonade on the veranda with Mama, Mary Grace, and Mrs. Jung. It lasted as she walked Travis to the door at sunset because he had to have Millie back at camp before dark. He kissed her on her portico. She remained at the same spot, waving as he rode away.

Later, doubts set in as she sat beside her broken bedroom window in the darkness. He was a Union officer heading to his Union camp for the night. He'd return in the morning to escort her and the others to her Southern church in her Union-occupied Southern city.

Worse, she was a Confederate spy, a secret she must keep from him. Should she quit? No, she had to warn Sam of the continuing danger from Union troops looking for him and his comrades.

Savannah looked out over her city. Multiple ships now anchored at the City Landing. Shop shelves were filled with a variety of goods not seen in months. Soldiers and freedmen continued street repairs. Some business owners and home-owners had replaced their windows and went about property repairs. Poorer citizens were receiving rations from the Union.

Federal soldiers, including the recently mustered-in black troops, policed the city.

Savannah secretly appreciated the Union army's peace-keeping and cleanup. She was beginning to doubt Confederate bands could retake Vicksburg, so entrenched did the Union army appear to be.

But she had given her word to keep Sam informed. Her love for Travis didn't alter her desire for the war to end with a Southern victory.

Tomorrow, Travis and the others were spending the day installing new windows on the second floor. The front parlor windows had arrived, but those would take all day next Sunday. In addition to the meals, Mama planned to pay the men when the job was finished.

She touched the lips Travis had kissed so thoroughly. She marveled at the way her heart reacted to his kisses.

The Confederacy didn't hold all the good men in this conflict. Travis was a good man and he loved her. Their differing loyalties must not come between them.

~

*I*t was after six on Monday, and Travis walked back to camp with Luke after another successful day. The female spy still eluded them, but he'd caught thirteen men—four on his own, the rest with Luke—in the five weeks they'd worked together. "We've done well, so I haven't pursued your suggestion about reaching out to your former associate. The colonel left the decision up to me. Do we need your contact?"

"Aye." Luke's long stride matched Travis's. "In me humble opinion, townsfolk are the first to notice anything amiss. Me friend is like a dog with a bone when it comes to spies. He'll give us leads to find them."

"Will he keep our identities a secret?" Although they tried

not to use weapons or make a scene when arresting spies, it hadn't always been possible. Travis wanted to keep his job as spy catcher a secret as long as possible. He enjoyed the intrigue.

"The man knows how to keep his mouth shut."

So did Luke. "I've learned a lot from you." Travis rubbed his jaw. He trusted Luke as a comrade and a friend. "Should we meet this man together?"

"Nay." Luke rubbed the back of his neck. "We ended our spying together before the battle. He's a good man but hardened from years spent around rough characters. I'll speak with him privately first to discover if he's interested."

"Do you trust him?"

"Aye. With my life."

Impressive. Still, Travis hesitated to make himself vulnerable with a townsperson. Yet trusting Clifford had been the right choice...

"We're having trouble finding female spies." Luke grumbled as they approached the forest in advance of camp. "No doubt there're more of them than the one we nearly caught. My friend may be able to help. Or Felicity—"

"Not Felicity." Travis didn't want to involve Luke's wife. "All right. Talk to your friend."

"Good." Luke's face relaxed. "I will search for him on Saturday."

"What's his name?"

Luke shook his head. "Let me speak with him first."

The fellow seemed a mite prickly. Travis nearly regretted his decision, but they were within earshot of the pickets. He would trust his gut—and Luke.

The following afternoon, Travis was on his way to check on a crew repairing Clay Street when he spotted the drably dressed woman Luke had seen accepting a coded message last month. She had slipped through their fingers twice before. It wouldn't happen again.

When the woman entered a notions shop, basket in tow, Travis crossed the street. He blocked the door. The shop was empty except for his spy and the owner. When the spy turned, a look of recognition shot across her plain features, followed by fear.

She'd recognized him, proving that he'd found the right woman. "Will you kindly come with me, ma'am?" Travis reached for her basket.

"Why?" She swept outside with lifted chin. "I'm not doing anything wrong."

Travis met the curious gaze of the shopkeeper. He leaned to whisper. "A known spy dropped a ciphered message into your basket last month."

Her forehead wrinkled. Then she glanced at the shop-keeper. "Where are you taking me?"

Travis took the basket from her unresisting grip. "To my superior. This way." He gestured with his free hand.

The spy stalked from the building and set off down the hill.

"I'm First Lieutenant Travis Lawson." He maintained a quick pace to match hers. "May I ask your name?"

"Mrs. Nellie Cameron."

Was that her real name? "Take Monroe Street."

She didn't speak again, and within five minutes, they were inside Colonel Haversham's headquarters, with her seated in front of the officer's desk. Taking the colonel aside, Travis explained his suspicions that Mrs. Cameron was Gerald Finkler's co-conspirator.

"Mrs. Cameron, my lieutenant tells me that you were caught spying." Colonel Haversham seated himself at his desk. "What have you to say for yourself?"

"'Tisn't a word of truth in it." The brown-haired woman shot Travis a hard look. "I was out to buy thread, is all."

"We're not speaking of today. You accepted a coded message from a Mr. Gerald Finkler on"—the colonel flipped a page and found the notation— "Monday, August seventeenth, around half-past eight in the morning. It fell from your basket when one of our spy catchers lunged for it."

Her eyes widened.

"Do you know Mr. Finkler?" The colonel studied her.

She pursed her lips.

"Are you a spy for the Confederacy?" Travis crossed his arms.

"I am." Mrs. Cameron's tone sharpened. "No use in denying it, since you caught me."

Travis blinked. He hadn't expected such a quick confession. "Why?"

"Why?" She tapped her foot. "Your army waltzes in here like you own the city after starving us near to death and you wonder why I want to aid the Confederacy? I'm proud to serve my country."

This spy was proud of her treachery. Were she a man, he'd be escorting her to jail, which was already filled with men. What were they to do with her? Travis's temples began to throb.

❧

Four hours later, Mrs. Cameron was under arrest, a prisoner in her home with two guards outside the front door and two posted behind her two-story home. Travis would schedule six-hour shifts that evening. He was back at the colonel's headquarters at seven that evening. Was it still Tuesday? The day had stretched too long already.

Travis knocked on the open door and stepped inside when bid to enter. "We've got four guards posted outside the home that will change every six hours. We've erected a tent for sleeping quarters for our men this evening. I'll make up a schedule for a three-day rotation."

"Any weapons in the house?"

"One." Travis reached into his pocket for a Colt 1849 pocket revolver and laid the short-barreled weapon on the table in front of Colonel Haversham.

"Ah." The colonel picked up the pistol. "The perfect size for a basket or even a skirt pocket."

"Agreed." He rubbed his temples. "If there's nothing else…"

"Good work, Lieutenant." The colonel sat back in his chair. "There's just one more thing."

Travis's stomach rumbled. "Pardon me, sir. I missed my supper."

"I won't keep you long. I'm hosting a dance here on Saturday evening. I thought you, Miss Adair, and Mrs. Adair might like to attend."

"Savannah loves to dance." It was as if a weight tumbled from his shoulders. Some of the officers had been hosting dances, but this was his first invitation. "I will tell her of the party this evening so she can plan for her dress and everything that goes with it."

Colonel Haversham chuckled. "My wife used to do the same." His smile died.

Recalling that the colonel had been a widower before the war, Travis waited.

"Invite Luke and his new bride as well. We're short on women. Do you know of others?"

"Mrs. Jacqueline Jung and her daughter, Miss Mary Grace Jung, are living with Savannah now. Felicity's aunt and uncle, Charles and Mae Beltzer, likely support the Confederacy but have been gracious to myself, Ben Woodrum, and Enos Keller. Mae's daughter, Petunia Farmer, is married to a Confederate soldier. She'd appreciate an invitation, but I don't know if she'll accept."

"We live in an occupied city, my boy. We must try to get along with one another." The officer's expression brightened.

"Invite them all to the dance beginning at eight. Include Ben and Enos since the women in your party already know them."

Upon leaving, Travis headed straight for Savannah's home. She had told him how much she enjoyed parties. This would be his first opportunity to dance with her.

~

*O*n Tuesday evening, Savannah was eating dessert with her mother and the Jungs when Ellen came into the family dining room with the news that Travis waited to speak to her in the front parlor. She looked at Mama, who didn't like interruptions during meals.

"Invite him to join us for dessert." Mama smiled at her. The longer Travis courted Savannah, the more Mama seemed to like the Union officer.

"Thanks, Mama." Savannah flew to the parlor. "Travis, what a lovely surprise." She held out her hands to him and was thrilled at the tingle that traveled up her arms when he clasped them.

"I won't keep you long." Hazel eyes twinkled at her. "I've just had an invitation for all of us for Saturday."

"I'm certain we shall love it." Her heart lit up at the excitement in his face. "Come back and have dessert. You can tell us all at the same time." Turning, she tugged on his hand. She retained her hold of his work-roughened hand until they were in the dining room. "See there? Ellen has already set you a place." Next to Savannah's. How lovely to have a beau again, to belong by Travis's side.

Everyone greeted him, even Mrs. Jung, whose mood had mellowed toward the regular guests of the home.

Once he was seated in front of a generous portion of plum pudding, Savannah could contain her curiosity no longer.

"Travis has an invitation for us all on Saturday. Travis, don't keep us in suspense."

Mary Grace's gaze fastened on Travis.

"I've just come from Colonel Haversham's headquarters." He put down his spoon. "He is hosting a dance on Saturday at eight. He's invited all of us."

Savannah gasped. "A dance?" How she longed to dance with Travis. She'd even approached Mama with the idea of hosting a ball, but they didn't have the money to host a big event until Papa returned.

"That's right. In addition, he has invited Luke, Felicity, the Beltzers, and Petunia Farmer. Will you pass on the invitation to Felicity and Mrs. Beltzer?"

"Of course." Savannah's excitement was building. Irises had been budding when she last danced.

"Thank you." He glanced at Mary Grace. "Oh, and I'm to invite Ben and Enos as well."

Mary Grace's face turned the shade of rose petals. "I haven't danced for two years."

"I shall enjoy the music, but I'll wear my widow's weeds." Mrs. Jung looked at her daughter. "And nine months isn't enough time for you to set aside mourning your father."

"Oh, but..." Savannah crossed her arms at the crestfallen look on Mary Grace's face. "*Everyone* is mourning someone in these war times. I believe it perfectly acceptable for Mary Grace to dance when asked for this special occasion."

"No one will think the worst of her under the circumstances." Mama nodded as if that settled the matter. Savannah silently applauded her. She was acting more like her old self. "We've no horses to pull our carriage. Where is the colonel's headquarters?"

"On Monroe Street, opposite the apothecary shop." Travis shoveled in a forkful of pudding as if starved.

Savannah nearly choked on a plum. She'd seen him there

weeks before when she'd met with Mrs. Lakin. They'd never meet at the apothecary's again.

"Oh, that's the Wagner house. Savannah, you recall Mrs. Wagner and her daughter Bethanne. They didn't return to the city after the battle."

Like so many others. "That's right." They'd taken tea there twice in the days of endless rounds of social gatherings. "I hope they are doing well."

"I haven't been out to hear the latest news. Regardless, that's not too far to walk." Mama pushed away her empty plate. "Not on the first Saturday in October, anyway."

"I must go, ladies." Travis stood. "Enos, Ben, and I will be proud to escort you to the dance."

"I'll see you to the door." Savannah set a slow pace in the hall. "Thank you for delivering the news tonight so we can decide on our gowns." Her mind was already racing over her wardrobe. The setting sun shone in her eyes as she stepped onto the portico with him.

He gave her a gentle smile. "This has been a rough day. I'm glad it ended like this." He leaned down and kissed her cheek.

The gesture felt so completely right that her heart fluttered in response. But his day had been difficult? "What happened?"

"Army business can challenge a man's patience." He squeezed her hand. "Nothing to fret about, but it will be a busy week. I may not see you until Saturday."

"I will see you then." She tilted her head. "Remember to compliment my dress."

He chuckled. "I already know you will be a vision of loveliness."

Her heart melted. "Then tell me so." The sun sank over the horizon, relieving her of the need to shade her eyes.

"I shall." He kissed her hand and then ran down the steps. "Thanks for the pudding. My compliments to the baker."

"It was Mary Grace. I'll tell her." Why was it so hard to end conversations with him? There always seemed to be more to say.

"Sleep well, my love." He spoke softly.

"And you, my dearest."

Hazel eyes fastened on hers.

Time seemed to stop.

"I must go." He strode to the gate, and as always, waved to her before hurrying away.

Savannah loved him more every time she saw him.

CHAPTER 25

O n Friday morning, the guards outside Mrs. Cameron's home told Travis she wanted to see him. Yesterday her demand had been for groceries. She had given him a list of foods she required. The colonel had told him to oblige her, so Travis did her shopping. Leaving the door open for propriety's sake, he entered the parlor containing one sofa, two wooden chairs, and an oval table. The home was clean if sparsely furnished, as he'd discovered when searching for weapons and ciphers on Tuesday. The colonel had stored her only gun in his drawer.

"Good morning, Mrs. Cameron." He nodded to the woman clad in a dark green dress. "Did you wish to tell me who the coded messages are being sent to?" That's what he and the colonel really wanted to know. The satisfaction he'd imagined he'd experience upon arresting her hadn't come to fruition— quite the opposite, in fact. He took no joy in arresting a woman.

"If I tell you, will you let me go free?" Gone was the belligerence of yesterday. Her tone was quiet, her demeanor tense.

This was a change. Travis perched on a chair opposite the

sofa, where she sat twisting her embroidered cotton handkerchief. Her distress twisted his gut in a similar fashion to the crumpled cloth. "You'll have to agree to stop spying *and* take the oath of allegiance."

She heaved a sigh. For a moment, he thought she'd refuse. "I will as long as you remove my name from your spy records."

She was thinking ahead to the future. None of them knew what it held. "Agreed."

"Then I'll help you." Her shoulders slumped. "Coded letters have been sent to Sergeant Sam Epley."

That name struck a bell. Where had he heard it? Then he recalled the arrogant sergeant who had hid gunpowder in his canteen. "Where is he?"

"Don't know that. He leads troops somewhere around here."

A leader of one of the Rebel bands. Important information.

She rubbed her arms as if chilled on the mild autumn day. "I kept my end of the bargain. You keep yours."

"I'll send someone to take your oath today." He stood. "Thank you, Mrs. Cameron."

He stopped to give his guards instructions and then hastened toward Monroe Street to report to Colonel Haversham. Travis thought back to the day he'd met the sergeant. Whether that Rebel led just one band or had organized the attacks that had caused the Union army so much trouble, he'd done an excellent job eluding them. Perhaps now that they knew his name, they could find him.

~

Savannah descended the stairs in her favorite pink silk ball gown with its lace-covered bodice, her gaze fastened to the tall, curly-haired officer waiting in the foyer in his dress uniform, complete with one gold bar on his epaulettes. Holding his black Hardee hat under his arm, Travis stared up at her with his heart in his eyes. Desiring to make an entrance in hopes to see that very look he was giving her, Savannah had waited two full minutes after Ellen came to her bedroom to announce the men's arrival. Savannah had a vague impression of murmurs in the crowded foyer—Mary Grace in an old yellow silk that Ellen had labored over to revive its former glory, Mama wearing her green satin, Mrs. Jung in black taffeta, and three other men in blue uniforms. Felicity, Luke, Charles and Mae Beltzer, and Petunia were meeting them at the colonel's headquarters. But Travis's love-struck gaze was all she clearly recognized as she reached the bottom.

"Savannah, you take my breath away." Travis held out his gloved hand. "I—you look beautiful."

Her fingers inside her kid gloves closed around his. "And you are quite handsome." Her beau's reaction pleased her.

"Savannah, I'd like you to meet our captain, Brian Eaton." Travis gestured to a man of medium height with straight blond hair and a full beard.

Although she hadn't known he was coming with them, she responded graciously.

"It's a pleasure to meet you, Miss Adair." The officer's dress uniform accentuated his broad shoulders. "I wasn't certain I'd be able to attend this evening's festivities."

Out on patrol again? There wasn't time to ponder this possibility as she greeted Ben and Enos, who couldn't keep his gaze from Mary Grace's blushing face. Savannah had already complimented Mama's dress when they helped one another with final touches but deemed it more compassionate not to draw attention to Mrs. Jung's mourning dress. "Mary Grace, you look radiant."

The brunette's blue eyes sparkled at the compliment. "No one can hold a candle to you, Savannah."

Obviously, Enos didn't agree, for he scarcely looked Savannah's direction when returning her greeting. Perhaps Mary Grace would agree to court him soon.

"Ladies, if you are ready, a stroll of about ten minutes will take us to Colonel Haversham's quarters." Travis raised his brows.

The women gathered their shawls and fans from the foyer's long table.

"Allow me." Taking the pale pink shawl from Savannah, Travis draped it over her shoulders. Then he extended his arm. "Shall we?"

"We shall." She smiled up at him. With her hand hooked around his arm, they stepped out onto the portico into the rays of a pleasantly warm sunset.

Her first dance with Travis awaited.

~

*T*ravis had introduced the ladies in his party to Colonel Wilbur Haversham upon arrival. Mrs. Mary McCarter, Major Levi's McCarter's wife, acted as his hostess for the evening. The petite woman had come south on a steamship, an easy trip for her since she lived near the Mississippi River. Travis also introduced them to Colonel Henry Lieb. Brian had stopped to talk with Major McCarter.

Luke was already there with Felicity's family, in the large parlor with the furniture pushed to the sides. They had saved seats for the women, who complimented one another's dresses. Luke and Mr. Beltzer immediately joined Ben and Enos, both of whom looked uncomfortable as the only privates in their party until Luke joined them. There were some thirty men, mostly officers with a few civilian businessmen, and over twenty women wearing vibrantly colored gowns.

Brian, Ben, and Enos fetched glasses of lemonade.

Cigar smoke hung in the dining room where men gathered around the refreshments—ham sandwiches, pickled oysters, lobster salad, chicken croquettes, grapes, orange slices, lemon cookies, and plum cobbler served with tea, coffee, or lemonade. Travis didn't often partake of such a spread, and he intended to escort Savannah there later in the evening.

Within minutes, the band—a piano, violin, flute, clarinet, French horn, and trumpet—began the strains of a waltz. He turned to Savannah. "Would you like to dance?"

"It will be a pleasure." Her brown eyes sparkled up at him. They walked arm in arm to the center of the room.

Mary Grace looked up at Enos, who offered her his arm. Mrs. Adair accepted Brian's invitation, and Ben led Petunia to the dance floor. Charles held his wife's hand as they waited for the dance to start.

Luke and Felicity had eyes only for one another a few feet away. How Travis had envied their happiness. Now he was the happiest man in Vicksburg to court Savannah.

This was his first dance with his girl.

Travis's heart skipped a beat to clasp her gloved hand, touch the silk fabric at her waist, and waltz with her to the rhythm of the music. He guided her in a slow circle around the perimeter of the room. "I haven't danced since the war began. I'm a little rusty."

"I didn't notice." Her looped braid skimmed her shoulder when she tilted her head up at him. "But I won't mind making certain you get plenty of practice this evening."

"I'd like that." He chuckled at her teasing. "There are too many men without partners for me to dance with you as much as I'd prefer."

"True." She peered around the room. "Mrs. Jung is the only woman sitting. Colonel Haversham is talking with her, though."

"He's been a widower for years." He was having a hard time

focusing on anyone but the beautiful woman looking up at him.

Her eyes widened. "You don't think..."

"They could be a match?" He shrugged. "I don't think she likes Northerners."

"I suppose you're right."

Her tone was so disappointed that he laughed. "I'm glad you do."

"Some of them." Her tiny frown disappeared so quickly, he must have imagined it.

She'd given an honest, fair answer. However, he wanted to focus her attention on their courtship and what they shared in common. "Have I told you how radiantly beautiful you are tonight?"

"You have." She giggled. "Just as instructed."

Her sweet smile melted his heart. If only this waltz could last all evening. Unfortunately, the music ended, and hopeful dance partners flocked around Savannah before they'd even reached her chair. How was he ever going to do the polite thing and surrender her to the arms of other men, even for a few minutes?

~

Savannah danced with strangers more often than she did with Travis for the next hour. She hadn't needed his untimely reminder that she was at a party with conquerors of her city to bring her back down to earth, for every blue-coated officer who partnered her made her long for the not-so-distant past when she'd danced with her heroes in gray.

Travis danced with Mama and Mary Grace and Felicity. He even sat with Colonel Haversham and Mrs. Jung for two songs. Mostly, he stood around talking with his comrades and watching for an opportunity to dance with Savannah, which she allowed as much as possible.

Her trodden-on slippered feet were happy when the band took a break. She scanned the room for her beau, and he was instantly at her side.

"Are you hungry? There are a variety of refreshments."

"Just a cold drink." She was too hot to think of eating. "Can we take our lemonade outside?"

"Agreed. I'll fetch our drinks."

As soon as he disappeared into the dining room, Mama walked over with the rest of their party, including Felicity's family. "I can't remember when I've danced so much." She waved her ivory-handled fan over her red face.

"You enjoy it as much as I do." What a shame her father was still in Texas, for Mama loved dancing with him, though she'd hardly mention it now and ruin her mother's evening. They'd both written to him when Savannah and Travis started courting. "Travis is fetching drinks. He and I will sip our lemonade in the fresh air. You all should join us."

"Oh, yes. That will be lovely." Mary Grace hadn't sat out for a single dance, and only three of those had been with Enos.

"I'm ready for a rest." Felicity also fanned herself with vigor.

The others agreed. The ladies followed Savannah to the walk outside, where the men joined them with cold drinks moments later. Travis stood beside her. A nearby lamppost illuminated a circle around them.

"Such a pleasant evening." Savannah lifted her face to the breeze.

"I didn't believe I'd ever attend another party such as this." Mary Grace looked at Travis. "I'm grateful to you for mentioning our names to our host."

"It's my pleasure." His gaze darted from her to Enos.

"Such a nice man." Mrs. Jung cupped both hands around

her glass. "I talked with Wilbur for quite three-quarters of an hour. He's a widower. We have much in common—more than I could have imagined."

Wilbur? They were already on a first-name basis. Savannah blinked. The colonel was a Union officer. After the cold shoulder Mrs. Jung had given Travis for a month, her change in attitude was rather shocking. That chilly treatment of Savannah's beau and the woman taking over the family parlor as her own were just two of the reasons she avoided their uninvited guest whenever possible.

"I'm glad, Jacqueline." Mama patted her hand. "Perhaps we can invite Colonel Haversham to supper one evening and repay his hospitality."

"An excellent idea." Mrs. Jung gave a crisp nod.

"And the rest of you as well." Savannah hastened to add Brian Eaton and Felicity's family to the invitation. The captain had been quiet all evening. Perhaps that was his nature, or perhaps he missed dancing with his wife.

"I will be happy to accept if I'm able." Captain Eaton gave Savannah and her mother a smiling nod.

"You'll find the home cooking second to none, Brian." Travis grinned at his superior officer.

"I'm certain of it."

Their guests were replacing the parlor window tomorrow. Savannah didn't like to suggest the captain come for that job.

The night grew darker. Pedestrians across the street caught Savannah's eye. Her heart thudded as she met the shocked gaze of Mrs. Lakin. The spy increased her pace, avoiding the next pool of lamplight.

"What is it?" Travis followed her gaze.

Both Felicity and Luke craned their necks to peruse the area.

"Nothing. I just thought I heard something." She had—footsteps. Travis must not see the spy. He couldn't discover

Savannah's secret. "I believe the music has started again. Travis, will you dance the first one with me?"

"I was going to request it. Sounds like a polka."

"I pity your poor feet, Savannah." Ben grinned.

Savannah joined the laughter at Travis's expense, relieved that no one but herself had spotted Mrs. Lakin.

CHAPTER 26

On Monday morning, Travis's shoulders and back ached from installing Savannah's windows the day before. He walked toward the city in the drizzle with Luke. Once they were beyond the pickets, Travis quickly explained what had happened with Mrs. Cameron.

"She'll face no other punishment for spying beyond three days of imprisonment?" Luke kicked a pebble ahead of them on the muddy road.

Travis hadn't thought of anything more befitting the crime since releasing the spy. "She gave us the name of the spy who received her messages. She'll be banished from Vicksburg until the end of the war if she spies again."

"That would be punishment, indeed." Luke cleared his throat. "What's the recipient's name?"

"Sergeant Sam Epley. He's in the area."

"A leader of a Rebel band?"

"That's my hunch. I met him the day he left on parole. My impression was that he might not wait for the exchange to rejoin the fighting. We'll use his name to try to convince spies we catch that we know more than we do." Which helped sweeten his side of the deal he'd struck with Mrs. Cameron.

"Good idea."

"Did you locate your spy friend?"

Luke shook his head. "Not with the dance and helping with the parlor windows. I was glad Uncle Charles helped us."

"Me too." Travis rotated his shoulders. "We might still be there, otherwise."

"Will ye mind if we work apart until this afternoon? I will search for me friend this morning."

"Fair enough. Perhaps he knows something about the sergeant who's receiving ciphered messages. Let's meet at your saddle shop after lunch. One o'clock."

They parted upon reaching the city. Most of the male spies they'd caught had been transported to Washington to await trial. Two had accepted banishment as punishment and were set to leave sometime this week. Travis would interview the spies held in jail to ascertain what they knew about Sergeant Epley. Then he'd see if there were any Vicksburg women acting suspiciously…

～

Savannah waited for the drizzle to stop on Monday morning. When it ended at eleven, she was out to ferret out more information for Sam. One of the countless soldiers she'd danced with on Saturday had mourned the loss of a big Georgia battle in mid-September at a place called Chickamauga. She'd never heard of it but was pleased that the Confederates claimed the victory. Unfortunately, Rosecrans's army of perhaps fifteen or twenty thousand was now at Chattanooga, which the soldier had stated was a major railroad hub. This information about General Rosecrans seemed important. Tennessee bordered Mississippi.

Troop information such as numbers were vital, so she planned to place herself near soldiers talking on the streets to see if she could discover a more accurate number.

Standing close enough to Travis to brush against his arm on Saturday when spotting Mrs. Lakin had frightened her. Her heart was too much engaged to continue her spying indefinitely. He was her beau, the man she loved. As much as she hated to disappoint brave soldiers fighting for the South, it was becoming too dangerous to continue. Not to mention the expense. Papa hadn't sent them money for weeks.

Her service to the Confederacy must end. This week and maybe one more, if she discovered something important after delivering Thursday's message.

That decision made, she ambled down Washington Street. One soldier leaned against a building while the other rested his hand on it. She slowed her pace.

"General Sherman has been ordered to take command of our forces in Chattanooga. Left last week."

With his troops? Savannah paused in front of a tailor shop displaying a man's brown sack jacket, a cotton brocade waistcoat, and striped trousers.

"I heard he had a good camp between the Big Black River and the Yazoo."

"Savannah?" Travis touched her arm. "Why are studying that sack jacket with such concentration?"

Her basket fell from suddenly shaky fingers. How had she not heard his footsteps? And how was she to answer?

He retrieved the basket and then looked at the nearby soldiers, who spun on their heels and strode away.

"My father's birthday is next month." Bless Papa for having a fall birthday. "I'm uncertain what to purchase for him. Do you like this coat?"

Glancing at it, he tugged on his ear. "It's a fine coat but too small for him."

"You're right. How fortunate that you happened along at just this moment to save me from buying the wrong thing." Her conscious smote her. This was a terrible predicament. Implying that she'd considered buying the coat for Papa was a lie.

"Are you feeling well, Savannah?" Hazel eyes probed her face. "You're flushed. There has been a possible instance of yellow fever in an outlying camp."

He worried she was ill when she was heartsick only. "No, I'm fine. Perhaps I'm still tired from dancing."

"Understandable. I will accompany you home."

"Thank you." She expected no less of him, always acting out of concern for her. She had allowed herself to become so focused on the soldiers' conversation that she neglected her surroundings.

And therefore, her safety.

~

Travis left Savannah's home, anguished thoughts swirling. The two spies in jail had denied knowing Sam. Travis had caught them doing an exchange of notes within a handshake, and one of them insisted the other was his only connection. The second spy, while refusing to reveal his contact, had been believable in his assertions that he'd never heard Sam's name before Travis mentioned him. Later, when he had noticed a woman standing close enough to overhear the soldiers' conversation about General Sherman, he'd thought he caught a spy. He'd approached without making a sound only to discover Savannah.

Staring at a tailor's display of a jacket too small to fit her father.

There was no way her story rang true. Even in their short acquaintance, Mr. Adair had struck him as a man who made his own decisions. He'd consult with a tailor directly on his clothes...or possibly his wife, though Travis doubted it.

It was unlikely Savannah had ever purchased so much as a cravat or even a handkerchief for her once-wealthy father.

For the first time, he suspected Savannah had fabricated something she said. Lied to him. Why?

His stride hastened with no destination.

Her face had been first the shade of ripe strawberries and then as pale as milk, alarming him. His initial reaction had been that she was stricken with illness. Her faltering steps, her silence on the walk to her home lent credence to that concern.

Except for his hunch that she'd lied to him.

It was unfathomable that the woman he loved, his sweet and feisty Southern belle, could be spying for the Confederacy.

Wasn't it?

She had been standing close enough to overhear Union soldiers speaking of General Sherman's orders, something he'd learned of last week. That the soldiers had been wrong to speak of it around civilians scarcely alleviated Savannah's guilt—*if* she had been spying.

Travis had been careful not to discuss battles with her. Wait. He had mentioned the harassment by the Rebel bands and that he and Brian had patrolled the area in search of them to explain the delay in his buggy ride with Savannah.

In fact, he'd let his guard down with her as he'd grown to trust her.

If she was a spy, she *might* have passed on information he told her first as a friend and later as his girl. If so, it was betrayal of their love.

No, he would not believe it of her. She loved him.

She also loved the South. Did she love her country more? Neither she nor Mrs. Adair had taken the oath of allegiance. He respected her Southern loyalties—how could he not when he was prepared at any moment to die for his?—but he couldn't condone her using her courtship with him to pass on secrets.

If she had betrayed him.

Travis didn't recall walking to the river north of the City Landing where he now found himself. The solitude of the Mississippi River suited his mood. A splintered log nearly hidden among the weeds paralleled the shoreline. He ran his hands along chinks in the thick trunk, finding an affinity with the fallen tree. They'd both been scarred by battle.

He sank onto the log facing the river. He must think about this logically.

The first day he and Luke had worked together to catch spies, Savannah had been standing near a group of soldiers. A coincidence?

On that rainy day that drove pedestrians inside, Savannah had walked to the post office carrying a parasol, not an umbrella. Rain had begun a quarter hour before, and it had been a ten-minute, leisurely walk to her home. She'd left before the rain threatened. Where had she gone?

Come to think of it, he'd encountered her on solitary walks on numerous occasions. Usually, she was on some errand for her staff. After their courtship started, he'd flattered himself that she was out in hopes of casually meeting him. He'd taken her to impromptu lunches at their favorite restaurant twice earlier this month.

Now he wondered if she'd actually been in search of information.

A church bell rang once. He groaned. His meeting with Luke.

Duty called. He arose, answering the call just like the good soldier he prided himself to be.

If he quickstepped, he'd only be a quarter hour late for his meeting with Luke. Should he share his suspicions about Savannah with his fellow spy catcher?

~

a knock on Savannah's bedroom door after lunch had her scurrying from the window where she'd watched for glimpses of Travis, back to lounge on the thin-cushioned chaise in her room. She'd decided that Travis's initial worry that she was ill held merit. She'd pretend an illness for a day. In case he returned, someone would inform him of her indisposition, giving her the time she needed to sort through their encounter on the street. She called in a weak voice, "Come in."

Mama entered, studying her with concern. "You're still resting. Are you feeling better?"

"Not really."

"Dr. Bennett has returned to the city. Shall I call for him?" Mama laid her palm on Savannah's forehead. "No fever, thank goodness."

"He can come tomorrow if I'm worse." Which Savannah had no intention of professing.

"You barely touched your lunch." Mama examined the bowl of vegetable soup and plate of crackers and applesauce.

"Two crackers were all I could manage." In this day of lies, that much was true. Her stomach was in knots over what Travis had so nearly discovered. She'd not hurt him for the world.

"Ellen is hovering near in case you need anything."

"That's not necessary. A day of rest is all I require to restore me." Dear Ellen. She'd been the one to care for Savannah through every childhood illness. Truly, Mama had never been good in the sick room.

"Shall I bring in my needlepoint and sit with you?"

Savannah needed to think. "I'm rather tired. I may take a nap." Another lie. She hated the woman she was becoming. She didn't deserve Travis's love.

"Well, then. I'll leave you in peace." Mama kissed her forehead. "Just have a nice rest. I'll bring you a cup of tea later in the afternoon."

"Thanks, Mama." Her heart swelled with love for her mother. She had been the one taking care of Mama since before the attack. This was a nice change. For a day.

Her mother gathered the nearly untouched dishes. "Sleep well, dearest." She slipped out of the room and closed the door behind her.

Savannah hurried back to the window to scour the streets. No Travis. How frighteningly close he'd come to discovering her secret. He had known something was wrong. An illness was the best explanation...because he must never discover she'd been spying for the Confederacy for months. It had begun before their courtship, but he'd be hurt, regardless.

Especially considering she had passed on secrets learned from him repeatedly. That hadn't stopped when her feelings had become very much engaged.

She loved him. Somewhere deep inside, she had realized it when he comforted her about her childhood incident with Gus. It had taken root at his compassion for the plight of Mary Grace and Mrs. Jung. He'd even spurred her faith. She'd been praying more than just at mealtimes of late.

She didn't pray now. The outcome was too important.

So was the information she'd learned—too valuable not to pass on to Sam.

But this was the last time.

She'd not risk hurting Travis again.

~

"Sorry I'm late." Travis entered the open saddle shop door and stopped at the sight of a rugged man of about forty standing back from the window with Luke. Had Luke's friend decided to help them? Travis's heart was in such turmoil that it didn't seem only two hours had passed since he'd seemingly caught Savannah spying. He must calm himself enough to attend the matter at hand.

"Travis, I'd like you to meet Nate Miller. He already knows who you are." Luke spoke softly, no doubt mindful of sound carrying through the broken windows. "He's a wharf worker."

"A pleasure to meet you. I reckon this means you'll work with us." Travis extended his hand to the man with a short-cropped beard. "I'm glad of it."

"I keep my mouth shut so I can listen." Nate gave his hand a firm shake.

"He knows nothing about the sergeant. Then I asked if there were any female spies in the city." Luke folded his arms.

Please, God, don't have him tell me about Savannah. Travis steeled himself.

"Oh, there are plenty." The broad-shouldered laborer propped one shoulder against the wall. "Wanda Lakin is the widow of a saloon owner. She's a spy for the South and a letter carrier. Charges one-and-a-half dollars to deliver secret messages from at least a dozen women around Vicksburg."

Travis sucked in his breath. Savannah might be one of them. "What does she look like?"

"Mid-thirties. Red curly hair. On the plump side. Dresses in plain, dark colors when on spy missions."

"Impressive." Such details proved the man a worthy spy. "Why didn't you come to us with this information?"

"Didn't know who to tell." Nate shrugged. "I've seen you watching folks. Making arrests. I was trying to figure if you were trustworthy. I saw Luke with you a time or two. A man's got to be careful."

"You can trust me." The more the man talked, the more Travis regretted ignoring Luke's earlier requests to contact him. "Do you want to walk with us to point out the guilty ones?"

Nate gave his head an emphatic shake. "Don't want my face

or name connected to arrests. I figure on living here a long while after the war ends."

"Understood." Travis applauded the man's farsighted thinking.

"In my opinion, lots of spying will end when you arrest Mrs. Lakin. The others might be just as guilty, but they're humble folks with children for the most part."

Travis stiffened. *Don't mention Savannah. Please, don't mention her as a spy.* His very spirit cried out silently.

"Follow Mrs. Lakin. You'll spot the spy activity, same as I did." He strode to the door. "I missed lunch to tell you this. If you want to talk to me before next Monday, come to the last ship on the north side of the City Landing. Stay ten minutes and then leave. I'll find you. Otherwise, I'll meet you at the old place on Mondays at two." His tread on the stone path made little sound as he left.

Travis stared at Luke, impressed despite his heartache. "I'm glad he's on our side."

"Aye." Luke chuckled. "That's the most I've ever heard him say. He probably used up all his daily words in the last quarter hour."

Travis was too upset about Savannah to see the humorous side.

Luke sat on the room's only bench, his head bent. "Travis, once we catch Mrs. Lakin, I'd be comfortable to stop looking for her accomplices for a week or two and see if the harassment from those Rebel bands eases. Felicity was just like them... barely a penny to her name but doing all she could to serve her country."

A jolt shot through his whole body. Maybe he wouldn't have to continue investigating Savannah. Yet...she'd betrayed him. *Please, Lord. Show me the way.*

"Let's take Nate's advice and concentrate on Mrs. Lakin." That gave Travis a reprieve. "We'll tell the colonel what we've discovered about the letter carrier."

"Don't mention Nate's name." Luke's eyes turned smoky as he held Travis's gaze.

"I gave my word."

Might he be able to save Savannah from arrest, after all? If the colonel agreed with Luke and Savannah stopped spying in the meantime, perhaps Travis wouldn't have to pursue evidence against her.

But was that the right course for one tasked as a spy catcher?

CHAPTER 27

On Wednesday morning, Savannah donned a light-orange dress decorated with a peach pattern shortly after sunrise in hopes that the cheerful colors would convince Mama she felt well again. Remorse over potentially hurting Travis caused a nearly sleepless Monday night that left her listless for Tuesday's breakfast. Both Mama and Mrs. Jung had insisted one more day in bed was what she needed—along with a doctor visit. Savannah had difficulty convincing Mama not to fetch Dr. Bennett and agreed to another day in her room to appease her.

But she wasn't staying inside this room one more hour. The need to talk with Travis had escalated steadily until she was nearly mad from the inactivity. She'd read half the Gospel of John in one sitting yesterday, achieving her only modicum of peace since Travis found her outside the tailor's.

The last pin went into her looped braids as someone knocked on her door. Breakfast wasn't for another quarter hour according to the cherub clock on her dressing table. "Enter."

Ellen came in wearing her new blue dress and closed the

door behind her. "Miss Savannah, I have news. First of all, do you still feel poorly?"

"I'm well. What is it?" Bracing herself, she stood.

"Gus is back."

Savannah gasped.

"Came back last night without Riley. My son didn't want to come." Ellen's usually calm demeanor was tense. "Gus says he's sorry he took Riley without talking to me first."

He'd been gone a dozen years. That must have wounded Ellen deeply. "And now he came back without him. Are you angry?"

"I've been angry with him for twelve years. He said that's long enough." She sighed. "I reckon he's right. But forgiveness is not an easy thing."

"No." Savannah was the one whose actions could hurt the man she loved. She had prayed last night that he never learned her secret. "Does he want a job?"

A hopeful glint sparked in her eyes. She nodded. "Gardening's what he does best."

"I'll need a driver when we buy horses."

"He can do both."

That was a relief, especially with money growing tighter. "Good." Savannah drummed her fingers against her dressing table. "He can start tomorrow, if Mama agrees. The quarter ended last week, and I'm certain Mama paid you then."

"She did." Ellen patted her apron pocket with a satisfied smile. "The first money I've earned will pay my minister to marry us. Today is Wednesday, my day off with Josie, so it won't be no trouble to anyone."

"It's no trouble but—*a wedding*?" They had come while Savannah was yet a child. She'd thought they were already married.

"The Union army says a man and woman have to marry in a church to live together. Gus slept in the stable last night. I told him if you hire him, he'll have to marry me before we can live as man and wife again."

"It's no more than he should." Savannah was proud of her.

"That's what I think. I wanted to wed him at the church from the first, but the Jungs only allowed us to jump the broom."

"I'm glad that changed." Surprising how hiring Ellen and Josie had eased some inner stress she hadn't been aware existed until it was gone. Unfortunately, spying had multiplied her turmoil a hundredfold lately.

"I'm surprised to hear it. Have you forgiven us for leaving you on Surrender Day?" Ellen gazed at her steadily.

"Too much changed in an instant. It hurt but I understand why you left." Savannah thought back to that day over three months before. She had indeed changed in that time. Her love for Travis accounted for a big part of that alteration.

"I ain't certain you understand all the reasons, but I'm glad you understand some of them." Ellen folded her hands. "Gus will want to talk to you soon as he can. He's nervous." She smiled. "I am too. It's my wedding day."

Her joy touched Savannah's heart. "I'm very happy for you." Someday soon, perhaps she could experience that same sort of joy. Her decision to stop spying should ensure Travis's proposal one day. Without that secret between them, she was as secure in his love for her as in hers for him.

"Thank you, Miss Savannah."

"Oh, no." She clutched her head. "Does he know Mrs. Jung lives here?"

Ellen's brown eyes clouded. "Yep. I told him about her plantation being destroyed and everyone deserting them. He said she got her just desserts."

No one deserved that much misfortune to Savannah's way of thinking. "If he stays, he must be respectful to her and Mary Grace. To all of us."

"He will, but it won't be easy on him. Bitterness runs deep in him. I'm praying for him something fierce. It'd be best to keep them apart as much as we can."

Savannah saw the wisdom of that. "We've got to figure a plan."

"I hardly got any sleep praying about it." Ellen clasped her hands in a prayerful pose. "I got an idea about time for the sun to rise. The stable has two bedrooms. How about if we use one of them for a sitting room and dining room and the one in the loft as a bedroom?"

"We'll have horses again, and the donkey is already there. The smells..." She didn't want to lose Ellen. Savannah had leaned on the woman's wisdom throughout her childhood.

And how wonderful if her flower gardens returned to their former glory.

"There's too much better about it to mind the smell."

Ellen really wanted her husband to find a job with them. They'd make this work.

"Let me talk to Mama." Savannah was glad for the good news. It had the added benefit of distracting her nervousness about tomorrow when she'd inform Mrs. Lakin of her intention to quit.

～

Tuesday had been a fruitless search for the elusive letter carrier. No telling how long before Travis caught her. He'd gone to the wharf around five yesterday, and Nate caught up with him on Jackson Street, as promised. If Nate spotted her on the docks, he'd come to find Travis on Washington or Monroe Street today because Travis planned to make an endless loop.

Before that meandering walk, Travis strode to Savannah's home with a bouquet of heath asters he'd purchased for her.

The white flowers with yellow centers looked like daisies to him. He hoped she liked them. If she was ill, they might cheer her.

If she'd not been ill, his suspicions had merit.

He knocked on the Adairs' door at nine o'clock. "Good morning, Ellen. That's a pretty dress."

"Good morning, and thank you, Lieutenant." The house-keeper caressed the blue fabric. "It's my wedding dress, as it turns out."

"My heartiest felicitations." He hadn't expected that news. "Is your husband..."

"Gus returned from up north last night without our son. He ran away with Riley twelve years ago, and I haven't seen hide nor hair of them since."

Just like those two Mississippi runaways that Uncle Dabney had helped. Travis was doubly glad that Gus and Riley had made it to safety.

She ushered him inside. "He's talking to Miss Savannah and Miss Lila about a job right now. We'll leave for the church as soon as he's done."

"I'm very happy for you. Does this mean Savannah is feeling better?"

"My, yes." Ellen smiled. "She was two days in her room. She ate a hearty breakfast, we were all glad to see."

"That's good." So she had been ill on Monday. That accounted for her pallor and agitation, if not her proximity to soldiers discussing military business. "Will you give her this bouquet and tell her how pleased I am that she's feeling herself again?"

"I will." Accepting the asters, she glanced at the closed parlor door. "She'll want to see you. Can I give you a cup of coffee in the dining room while you wait?"

He set his hat on the hall table. "That will be most welcome." He wanted to see her. Desperately.

Footsteps approached down the hall. Mrs. Jung greeted him as Ellen set the bouquet beside his hat.

"Good morning, Mrs. Jung. I trust you are well?"

"Quite tolerable, Lieutenant." Mrs. Jung glanced at Ellen's rigid back. "If you'll pardon me, I'll return to my knitting."

The parlor door opened. Savannah exited first, followed by Mrs. Adair and a tall, husky black man that must be Gus.

The man stopped midstride upon spotting Mrs. Jung. The animosity on his face was quickly masked.

Travis took a step forward, hands outstretched. "Good morning, Savannah."

"Good morning, Travis." She gripped them. "I regret that I kept you waiting. I didn't know you were here."

"I was happy to wait." His thumbs caressed the back of her hand, trying to convey love and support in the suddenly tense atmosphere.

"Mrs. Jung, Gus has returned, as you see." Savannah retained her hold on Travis as she shifted her focus to the ashen woman. "He will be our gardener and driver. He and Ellen are to be married today. Is that not wonderful?"

"My felicitations." Mrs. Jung clutched the folds of her lavender dress.

"Ellen and Gus will have the privacy of living quarters in the stable." Mrs. Adair spoke gently. "All else will remain the same."

"Gus, my...my husband has fallen in battle." Tears pooled in Mrs. Jung's eyes. "I apologize for...his actions to you."

Travis held his breath.

Gus widened his eyes, clearly surprised by her apology. Then his gaze dropped.

"Thank you, Mrs. Jung." Ellen crossed to her husband's side. "We only want peace."

"That's also my desire." Mrs. Jung clung to the handrail as she climbed the stairs.

No one moved until she was gone.

"Ellen, as you heard, Gus now works for us." Savannah smiled at her housekeeper. "And I believe you have somewhere to go."

"Yes, Miss Savannah." Ellen removed her apron. "Gus, let's fetch Josie and be on our way."

After they left, Savannah turned to Travis. "I'm sorry that you witnessed—"

"No need to apologize." Not for that scene, anyway. "I came to see if you were recovering and bring you flowers to cheer you."

"Asters." Her face relaxed into a smile. Releasing him, she held them to her face. "They're lovely. Thank you. They have cheered me, indeed. Would you like refreshments? Mrs. Beltzer prepared sausage, biscuits, and gravy for breakfast. Come to the dining room. I'll have another biscuit with you while you eat."

"Yes, please stay, Travis." Mrs. Adair rubbed the back of her wrist. "We are much in need of your calming influence this morning."

"I'm sorry. I wish I could stay." It was difficult to leave after the emotional scene that had drained them all. "Duty calls."

"Oh? What are you tasked with today?" She averted her gaze.

She'd never asked him that question. Why did he have to notice it? "The colonel keeps me busy. Will you be all right?"

"Yes. Thank you. We have a plan to keep Gus away from Mrs. Jung." Savannah spoke bluntly. "He will seldom be in the house."

"I believe it will work." Mrs. Adair sighed. "I do wish Arthur was here. We had to talk about duties and such."

"Will he tend to Dusty? Give him exercise?" Travis had shown Josie how to feed the donkey and muck out his stall. Travis also took Dusty out for walks in the yard twice weekly.

Savannah nodded. "He's also a gifted gardener. I look

forward to the restoration of our flower gardens more than anything else."

"Good." He had lingered too long. "I must go. You can always come to me with any problem. I will do all I can to aid you."

"I believe you." Savannah stepped closer and kissed his cheek.

"Have a good day, Travis." Mrs. Adair entered the parlor and closed the door.

Savannah tilted her face up, looking into his eyes.

Groaning, he put his arms around her and gave her a lingering kiss.

"I love you." Her brown eyes pleaded for reassurance.

He gave her one more kiss. Grabbing his hat, he opened the door. "I will always love you, Savannah."

He closed the door behind him. After donning his hat, he ran down the stairs.

It was true. He'd always figured that once he gave his heart, it would be for life.

Even if she had betrayed him.

This heartache wasn't leaving until he discovered the truth.

*L*ater that afternoon, after Travis had made a score of loops between Monroe, Walnut, and Washington streets, Nate caught up with him at five o'clock.

"Mrs. Lakin is in the apothecary shop. Don't know if anyone is making a delivery to her, but you'll know what she looks like."

"Good." His first lead since Monday. Travis was already on Monroe Street, two squares from the shop. He lengthened his stride toward the apothecary. "Anything else?"

Nate fell into step beside him. "She has a brief encounter

with a well-dressed young woman with looped blond braids every Thursday morning."

Travis's blood ran cold. Savannah?

"My source didn't recognize the society lady, but I have a guess."

Travis steeled himself.

"Could be Miss Adair. All the locals recognize her."

His heart plummeted. "Might not be her." Travis rubbed his hands over his face. "But I'll be out in the morning to discover the truth."

"You'll need help to get them both. I'll follow Mrs. Lakin but can't be seen at the arrest. Can you ask Luke to assist?"

"I will." They were approaching the apothecary.

"She's coming out the door now. Good luck tomorrow." Nate entered a hat shop.

Travis adjusted the brim of his own hat while studying the plump woman wearing a straw hat over red curls and then strode back to camp, his heart in turmoil.

Nate had provided the lead he'd dreaded. Now to talk to Luke. He pulled him aside after a supper of bacon and hardtack that might as well have been sawdust for all the enjoyment he took from it. Together, they walked toward the tree line on the fringe of camp.

"I need you in the city tomorrow." Travis summarized what had happened that afternoon.

After he mentioned Savannah's name, the only sounds were from their footsteps in the tall grass, men in the camp behind, and crickets.

"'Tis sorry I am to hear Savannah is a suspect, though 'tis much harder for ye." Luke darted a glance at him and then away. "Will ye be able—"

"I'll do what duty demands." He'd done that since entering the army. This duty tore the very heart out of him.

Luke shoved his hands into his pocket. "Felicity mentioned

on Sunday that Savannah offers to run errands for the staff every Thursday morning without fail."

Travis looked away. The evidence against her mounted.

"She goes out at half past nine."

His heart shuttered. They had a suspect, a day, and a time.

"I might have seen Mrs. Lakin on the street during Saturday's dance." Luke's shoulders slumped.

"Savannah gave a start that made me notice the woman that caught her eye, but she was out of the lamplight." Had the spy been monitoring who attended the party?

"We'll catch the letter carrier tomorrow." Luke clapped him on the shoulder. "I'm praying the woman she meets isn't Savannah."

Travis was too. Fervently.

But if it was, he'd do what had to be done.

CHAPTER 28

*S*avannah left her home carrying an ivory parasol that enhanced the cream-colored sash around her brown dress. It was half-past nine on Thursday morning, an hour she had dreaded. The final message to Sam had taken until past midnight to compose. It was now tucked into her sash. She'd written about Chattanooga and General Sherman's orders and then told him this was her last communication, ending with her thanks to him for serving the South.

Her love for Travis had changed her. After today, she'd never contact Sam or Mrs. Lakin again. Long after the sting of war ended, she'd confess her spying to Travis. Even with the passage of years, it would come as a blow but not as life-shattering as in the midst of war.

Overcast skies fit her mood. Dropping off her letter and money inside the dress shop on Jackson Street would be the easiest location so far because she planned to look at frocks afterward. Not that she'd buy any. Felicity was cutting out the last dress for Josie today. Thinking of that...she should consult Ellen about new clothing for Gus. The man likely had no notion of such things.

She nodded to townspeople passing her and avoided looking at two police guards lounging against a lamppost. A supply wagon driven by a soldier meandered past her. Nothing of note happening this morning.

An uneasiness overtook her, possibly because it was her last delivery. Shielding her face with her parasol, she looked over her shoulder. Businessmen, women, and two boys rolling a hoop down the sidewalk were all she saw in a quick glance.

Her uneasiness persisted. There was a quarter hour before her meeting. She took a side street to extend her walk.

Something clapped into her arm. She jumped. A trundling hoop fell into the street.

"My apologies." A boy of about eight snatched up the toy. He ran off in the other direction with his friend.

Savannah almost laughed at herself for jumping when the hoop got away from the boys. She must relax or someone might grow suspicious.

A woman beat a rug in her yard, raising dust clouds. Savannah coughed and then crossed the street. Was someone watching her? The woman beating her rug was intent on her task. Savannah turned around.

An officer entered a business. The height and build reminded her of Travis. She chided herself. Every man in uniform reminded her of her beau.

At the corner, she began climbing Jackson Street. It didn't matter that she was five minutes early. Upon reflection, for ease of delivery, it was better to be shopping when Mrs. Lakin came. There was no need to expect anything out of the ordinary. And after today, she could put this part of her life behind her. A blessing, indeed.

~

*T*ravis, heart as heavy as a cannonball, stepped behind a maple tree, crushing brown leaves under his feet when Savannah entered a storefront. He applauded her wise choice of a dress shop for the meeting even as he steeled himself for the possible ordeal ahead.

"Where is she?" Luke, who had followed Travis at a discreet distance, stepped under the fall foliage.

"That shop displaying the blue gown." He scanned the road for the letter carrier or Nate.

"Haven't seen Nate yet?"

"I pray we don't." Savannah *might* shop in advance of running staffs' errands.

"There he is."

Travis followed Luke's gaze and spotted Nate...several yards behind the letter carrier.

What a nightmare.

Luke gave him a concerned, assessing glance. "Are you—"

"No. I'm not." Travis wasn't okay. He would rather face an oncoming charge than arrest Savannah. How could he have known the colonel's assignment would lead to a broken heart? "Just trust me to do my job."

They waited until Mrs. Lakin entered the dress shop and then stepped away from the tree.

Nate crossed the street toward them. "Catch her in the act." He strode by them without glancing their way.

Just what Travis intended, no matter how it ripped at his heart. "Let's get inside."

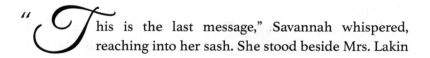

"*T*his is the last message," Savannah whispered, reaching into her sash. She stood beside Mrs. Lakin in front of a pink dress hanging in the back as if in admiration of the cotton frock.

Mrs. Lakin's fingers closed around the envelope as the shop door opened.

Both women scurried to opposite corners of the room.

"I'll take that." A man's voice. He snatched the envelope from Mrs. Lakin.

Travis? Savannah spun around. A silent Luke stood at his side.

"How dare you?" Mrs. Lakin snarled at him. "Return my property."

"You're under arrest for receiving Union secrets."

Travis was a spy catcher? The room spun.

"I'll not stand for this." Eyes blazing, the letter carrier drew herself to her full height.

Travis turned to Savannah, hazel eyes the color of smoke. "I imagine this letter is written in code."

Heat rushed up her throat.

"You are under arrest for sending Union secrets." Sweat ran down his forehead despite the mild temperature.

Her legs threatened to buckle. The years she'd imagined to have before he discovered her betrayal disintegrated like ashes. "Where are we going?" *Please don't send me to jail. Mama will never recover from that indignity.* Thankfully, her proud father wouldn't witness it.

"First, to Colonel Haversham's headquarters."

Oh, no. Not the gentleman who had hosted the dance, extended such kindness to all of them, especially Mrs. Jung. Savannah's humiliation intensified.

Travis gestured the door. Luke stuck close to Mrs. Lakin as she stepped outside.

Savannah peeked up at Travis's tormented face and then followed them. She tried not to notice that the man who had held her in his arms yesterday avoided touching her.

He knew her secret. Could their love survive her betrayal?

~

*I*nside the colonel's headquarters, Travis told Colonel Haversham everything that had transpired in the past two days. An initial assessment of the note showed it was an unfamiliar cipher. The older man's shock that his party guest was a spy quickly turned into angry disappointment. Travis's emotions catapulted past anger to anguish. How could she betray him?

"This is worse for you." The colonel swiped at his forehead. "What a bitter disappointment...to arrest your girl. Young Shea and I can conduct the interview if you need a few minutes."

"No, sir. I will see this through." His face must show his heartache—unacceptable in front of his colonel. He straightened his shoulders. "I'll not shirk my duty."

"Very well. Ask Luke to bring in the prisoners."

Prisoners...

As the ladies entered the room, the difference in their attitudes struck Travis. Mrs. Lakin marched in, boldly unrepentant. Savannah didn't meet his gaze as she seated herself beside her fellow spy.

"Miss Adair, I'm certain I don't need to tell you how disappointed I am to discover a guest at my ball has been spying on the Union army." Colonel Haversham swiped a handkerchief across his brow.

"Don't answer him, Miss Adair." Mrs. Lakin's red curls bounced as her head swiveled toward Savannah.

"Colonel Haversham, I did not attend the party to discover military secrets." Savannah folded her hands.

"Then why did you attend?" Travis drew her attention with his question. He would have sworn her love for him was true.

Now he wasn't so certain. Had she courted him to obtain military secrets?

She shifted to face him. "To dance with the man I love."

How could he believe her when she'd passed on secrets learned from him?

"Your letter"—Colonel Haversham held up Savannah's envelope— "is addressed to Sergeant Sam Epley. How do you know him?"

Biting her lip, Savannah glanced at the spy, who shook her head.

"What does your letter say?" the colonel prompted.

"Don't answer," Mrs. Lakin hissed.

"You don't make my decisions." Savannah glared at her.

In spite of the situation's gravity, Travis was glad to see a return of Savannah's feisty spirit. He turned to Colonel Haversham. "Perhaps it's best to interview them separately."

"Agreed. Private Shea, please escort Mrs. Lakin into the hall. And tell Christopher to bring me the deciphered message as soon as he finishes."

"Aye, sir." Luke crossed to Mrs. Lakin, who rose when he extended his arm. "After you, ma'am."

Lifting her chin, the letter carrier preceded him into the hall.

"Miss Adair?' Colonel Haversham eyed her. "Have you anything to say for yourself?"

"Yes, sir." She raised her eyes to Travis, who stood to the side of the colonel's desk. "Surrender Day came after weeks of siege. Want, terror, and starvation etched themselves into the hearts of every citizen enduring it. Further insult was that it came on the anniversary of our independence from England."

Travis stiffened. Union troops had experienced want and terror, though it was unlikely she'd believe that.

"Our bedraggled, starving soldiers plodded into our city, grateful beyond words for dippers of cold water. Then your army marched in as if on parade, the conquering heroes." Her tone was more sorrowful than bitter. "You took over the city, making decisions and passing laws we must follow. General McPherson currently has command of Vicksburg, not our elected mayor."

It was all true. Major General James McPherson commanded the District of Vicksburg—leading compassion-ately from what Travis had observed. Colonel Haversham kept the general apprised of their arrests. Travis tried to see her side, but bitterness over how cruelly she'd betrayed him prevented it.

"That's *why* I began."

"When did you start spying?" Colonel Haversham pressed his fingertips together.

"I agreed to spy before the Southern soldiers left the city." She gripped her chair. "Sergeant Sam Epley approached me. He had witnessed our initial meeting, Travis."

Months. He remembered her feisty spirit, how she chal-lenged him in front of interested bystanders. His fists clenched at learning one of them had lured her into her crimes.

"He was interested in everything going on in Vicksburg."

Her honesty tightened the chains around her. There was one thing he had to know. "Did you agree to court me to learn military secrets?"

"No. I agreed because I fell in love with you." She met his gaze squarely. "I did pass on details you told me about moving the freedmen, the pestilence, city repairs, and the like. And other things." Her knuckles turned white as she clutched the chair arms. "You explained that a horse wasn't available to you for our buggy ride. Your captain was out searching for Rebel bands that had troubled your soldiers, and you weren't coming into the city that weekend and likely the next."

The colonel frowned.

"That was my lapse. You were so disappointed that our ride

must be delayed." Disappointment tasted like bile. "And our soldiers are still being ambushed and harassed because spies like you keep them informed of our actions."

"I'm sorry. I never meant to hurt you." Her brown eyes were huge in her pale face. "I didn't plan to fall in love with you."

Colonel Haversham cleared his throat. "Be that as it may, this is a serious matter that I must bring to the general's attention. Is there anything you can give us to help yourself in the charges against you?"

She looked at Travis. "Will it help if I give you the cipher?"

~

"*W*hat did you tell them?"

"I answered their questions." Sitting beside Mrs. Lakin in the eight-foot square hall, Savannah tried to avoid the letter carrier's suspicious gaze. Luke stood, arms folded over a rifle, in front of the main door. She had written the cipher while Travis and the colonel conducted an interview with Mrs. Lakin. She doubted it had gone well because a grim-faced Travis had escorted the spy back into the hall within ten minutes.

Strange to think that description fit her too. How she wished she hadn't learned significant military secrets this week.

"You betrayed your country." Mrs. Lakin spat the accusation.

True. But only after she had betrayed the man she loved. At this moment, it was difficult to discern which was worse. Her uppermost concern was that she'd hurt Travis. How humiliated he must feel over courting a spy. How could she blame him for believing their courtship had been about obtaining secrets? Her very actions screamed it. That Travis believed it slashed her heart.

It wasn't true. Yet she had listened for secrets to benefit the South and shared them with Sam, no matter the source.

Even when that source was Travis.

How could she have sunk so low? He might never forgive her.

The colonel said it was serious. She'd confessed her guilt. What would happen to her now? Spies had been imprisoned, banished, or hung. Would they hang a woman?

Jail, though a revolting prospect, might be the best punishment she could hope for.

Mrs. Lakin's belligerent pronouncements certainly weren't doing Savannah any good, although the letter carrier was guilty of greater misdeeds. Perhaps that would go in Savannah's favor.

Mama would be publicly stoic and privately crushed if her daughter went to jail. She'd lament that her husband was in Texas, too far away to aid them. Savannah lamented her father's absence too. Were he in the city, he'd have been at the colonel's headquarters now, demanding his daughter's release.

Travis had arrested her, so she couldn't depend on help from him.

Who, then?

Travis had encouraged her to pray big prayers. He had told her that one day, she'd have to make an important request and trust God to do what was right.

Could she trust herself to pray for the right thing?

Perhaps not. But she could trust God as Ellen had taught her to do.

Clasping her hands together, she bowed her head to pray silently. *God, I've never trusted myself to ask for big things, but I'm asking You today to save me from hanging. I don't want to go to jail, either, if You don't mind. And help Travis to understand my reasons for spying and forgive me.*

The office door creaked open. Savannah opened her eyes.

CHAPTER 29

*T*ravis followed Colonel Haversham into the hall where Luke was guarding Savannah and Mrs. Lakin. With a loaded rifle. It was as if a bayonet pierced his own heart. He steeled himself.

There was more to come.

The colonel stopped in front of the women. "Ladies, instead of incarcerating you both in jail with the men, we've decided to place you under house arrest in your home, Miss Adair."

"That's outrageous." Mrs. Lakin rose, her color high. "If I'm under arrest, I'll stay in my own home."

"It's not your decision." The colonel widened his stance. "Keeping you at the same residence requires less guards. Miss Adair has a bigger home."

"For how long?" Mrs. Lakin's eyes narrowed.

"That has yet to be determined." The colonel looked at Savannah. "Is there an available bedroom for her?"

Savannah's hands shook. She rose. "Yes, sir."

"I'll speak with General McPherson straight away about each of you." The colonel's jaw clenched. "You've both confessed your guilt. Further punishment and its duration will be communicated to you."

A brown-haired officer of medium height joined them.

"This is my aide, Lieutenant Christopher Dunn." Colonel Haversham swept a hand toward him. "He will accompany all of you to the Adair home."

Mrs. Lakin gave him a haughty stare.

Savannah focused on the colonel. "This will be a shock to my mother. Might I be allowed to go ahead and prepare her and the others?"

"I'm sorry, Miss Adair. Travis will explain the matter to her."

Savannah covered her face with her hands.

Despite her betrayal, his heart went out to her. All of this would indeed be a shock to Mrs. Adair, unless she already knew of her daughter's spying missions. But he could not argue with his superior officer.

"Ladies, after you." Travis looked over at Luke, whose wife was a close friend of Savannah's. He hoped she was working today. Savannah would require support and friendship if the former Union spy wasn't too angry to offer it.

Savannah led the way on the silent walk over with Travis at her side. Christopher stayed with Mrs. Lakin. Luke followed with his rifle resting against his shoulder.

There was so much to talk about but nothing he wanted to say in front of the others. Perhaps she felt the same.

Savannah's pace slowed as she climbed the steps to her portico. Ellen opened the door before Savannah reached it.

"Miss Savannah, we're keeping lunch hot for you." Accepting Savannah's parasol, Ellen peered beyond her at Travis and the others as they entered the home. "Your mama and the Jungs are already in the dining room. Shall I set more places at the table?"

"No." Savannah seemed to choke on the implied invitation. "Please fetch Mama."

After closing the door, Ellen hurried down the hall.

"Fancy." Mrs. Lakin studied the curved staircase, the marble floor. "Sam said you could afford the cost."

Savannah shot her an outraged look.

Travis regretted not fighting the colonel harder to keep the two ladies in separate residences.

Mrs. Adair came straight to her daughter. "Dearest, I was getting worried about you. It doesn't require three hours to walk to the post office and back. Travis, I'm glad you are with her. With all the guards and soldiers in the city, one never knows."

"Mama, I never made it to the post office." She covered her mouth with her hand.

Travis stepped forward and kept his voice low. "Mrs. Adair, may the three of us talk in the parlor?"

"Of course, Travis." Holding her daughter's free hand, she led the way. "My dear, you're trembling."

Travis cringed. He'd almost rather face a firing squad than be the bearer of such news to Savannah's mother.

~

"I'm sorry, Mama." Savannah stared at her mother's ashen face. Travis had provided all pertinent details of her and Mrs. Lakin's arrest. In addition, he'd told her that both Savannah and Mrs. Lakin were under arrest within her home.

"Savannah...why did you continue spying after your courtship with Travis began?" Mama sandwiched her hands between her own trembling ones. "This makes no sense."

Savannah was asking herself the same thing. "I will tell you all later."

"I wish Arthur was here." Tears shone in Mama's eyes.

"I do too." She needed someone to lean on. Not Travis.

There had been compassion in his expressive eyes when telling Mama the bad news, but he'd spared her nothing. Seeing her proud mother struggle again after so recently regaining her footing added to Savannah's humiliation.

"I will send him a telegram." Releasing Savannah's hands, Mama rose quickly.

Travis stood.

"Yes, please do, but there are things we must prepare first." Savannah pushed herself to her feet.

"Lunch. No one has eaten." Mama reached to open the door.

"Please wait." Travis held out his hand. "I suspect Mrs. Lakin will be uncooperative. At least four armed guards will be here at all times, one on each end of the house to start with. Perhaps another outside Mrs. Lakin's bedroom door if it proves necessary."

At least he hadn't called Savannah uncooperative.

"Everyone will know." Mama's eyes closed.

"Your staff and guests will certainly know, as will officers and guards. Perhaps Ben and Enos." Travis spoke gently. "Beyond that, I will not speak of it."

"You won't need to." Bitterness shot through Savannah. "The armed guards on our property will tell the tale."

"Savannah, they could have placed you in jail. Or worse," Mama chided her.

True. Her punishment hadn't been completely decided. *That* was something Travis hadn't told Mama. Savannah was grateful for that much.

Mama lifted her chin. "We must ask Ellen and Josie to prepare a bedroom."

Following her to the door, Savannah steeled herself for the rest of the household to learn her crime.

Mama twisted the knob.

Shocked faces gaped at her. Felicity stood next to Lieutenant Dunn and her husband, who must have told the news to her, Mrs. Jung, Mary Grace, Mrs. Beltzer, and Josie.

Along with another one whose eyes showed a look similar to the one on Travis's face—betrayal.

Ellen.

~

*T*ravis told Brian that evening that he and Luke had caught two spies...and that one of them was Savannah. He could barely force out the words. They were in his captain's tent an hour before "Taps" would play. Travis could think of little else.

"That must have ripped your heart out." Brian eyed him. "You and Luke, huh?"

Travis nodded. The colonel had sent him to inform Brian of the events but hadn't given him leave to talk about his spy-catching responsibilities. His captain was a smart leader. He likely had a hunch what Travis's extra duties had been.

Brian stood. "Let's take a walk."

They didn't speak until out of camp.

"Want to talk about it?" Brian spoke softly.

"I'm to check on the prisoners several times a day and be there when the shift changes for the guards." He'd sent Mrs. Adair's telegram that afternoon. At least Savannah's mother was talking to him, seemed to understand the difficult situation her daughter's actions had thrust upon them all. "They're using provost guards for this duty." It didn't affect Travis's regiment beyond the need for him to monitor the men.

"Do you want to sleep in the city a couple of days?"

"That will help me. There's a shift change coming up at ten o'clock and another at six on Friday morning. I must be on my way within half an hour. I'll ride Millie to save time." Travis would stable his mare in the city. "Colonel Haversham offered me a room at his headquarters but didn't say for how long."

"How is Savannah?" Brian's brow wrinkled.

Travis was grateful for his captain's concern. "I've never seen Savannah so forlorn, so spiritless, but she is cooperating. The other spy isn't. It's not certain what the punishment will be if that attitude continues. Colonel Haversham will discuss the matter with General McPherson."

"I can't do without you indefinitely. It's good you caught a couple of the spies, but the Rebel bands continue to trouble us. Our patrols haven't kept them at bay, and they seem well-informed of our movements."

"That will likely decrease with today's arrests—of the letter carrier, in particular." Travis was grateful that defiant woman had finally been caught.

"That's good to hear." Brian put his hands on his hips. "Word is, our whole corps will go on another expedition."

"When?" The Eighth Illinois was part of General McPherson's Seventeenth Corps.

"Not certain yet. Three or four days."

"What direction?" His anger burned against the sergeant who had played upon Savannah's Southern loyalty. Mrs. Lakin had implied they wouldn't have asked her to spy had she not been wealthy enough to pay the cost of mail delivery.

"East, I believe. We'll know more soon."

Even though Travis would rather stay close to Savannah to protect her from prying eyes, at least he'd get the opportunity to undo the damage she'd done.

~

Savannah sat at her bedroom window, open to allow a crisp fall breeze into the room—and to listen to Travis giving orders to the new guards outside. Her lantern was snuffed out. The room was dark. He couldn't see her, but she saw his muscular outline. His words were indistinguishable, but the deep voice was one she'd recognize anywhere. Upon leaving the parlor, she had gone to her room to avoid the questions Mrs. Jung flung at her. Felicity had brought her lunch and supper, inviting her to talk, but Savannah had no words. For anyone.

Certainly not for the man that she'd deceived. She couldn't stand to see the pain in his eyes. She'd caused it.

Mama's agitation and worry increased Savannah's guilt. Once the initial shock passed, she'd been outwardly strong, as Savannah had expected.

Both of them locked their wounds inside. Years of practice had taught them well.

Mama would likely forgive her first—if Travis ever did.

"I'll be by at six when your shift ends." Travis's voice reached her. Perhaps he suspected her window was the one open on the second floor.

He strode to the gate where his horse was tethered. The clip-clop of the horse riding toward the city's center at half past ten echoed until he turned onto another street.

He was gone.

How she regretted her decision to deliver this one last note. And her prayer? She'd prayed Travis wouldn't discover her spying—and then *he'd* been the one to arrest her.

At least God had heard the part about not sending her to jail. The rest was still unknown.

Savannah closed the window against the night's chill and crawled into bed.

This was the first night of her arrest. How many more?

～

*B*y Saturday morning, Travis's patience with Wanda Lakin's demands was wearing thin. He'd had only glimpses of Savannah in her room since the house arrests began but had talked with Mrs. Lakin at least twice daily. She'd demanded he fetch a particular blue dress hanging in her wardrobe when he came to change the guards at eight.

Frustration sped his pace to her now-familiar clapboard home near the river. As he collected the garment from the wardrobe, the weight of the fabric warned him. As always, he checked the clothing for items stashed in pockets, hems, or hidden panels. The outline of coins followed a line of ribbons along the hem, accounting for the weight.

What need did Mrs. Lakin have of money in a home where her every need was met?

He and Luke had already searched her home for weapons, letters from spies, and ciphers. They'd only found a Colt pistol, now in the colonel's safekeeping.

Travis performed a careful search of the remaining clothing without result and then carried the dress to the colonel's headquarters.

"You say she asked most particularly for this dress?" Seated at his desk, Colonel Haversham fingered the outline of the coins still inside the fabric.

"Yes, sir. She described the wide-ribboned pale-blue sash. From the size and weight, I believe those to be gold coins."

"Agreed." He set the fabric aside. "Does she merely want her money close to her?"

"Or to finance her escape?"

"How? There are four armed guards on the property at all times."

"No guards who have spoken to her have any love for her." Travis raised his palms. "She seems determined to be disagreeable."

"Interesting. Perhaps so she can be confined to her own home instead?" The colonel tapped his fingertips together. "The general is in favor of banishment from the city if she can't be trusted to stop spying."

"I've no doubt she'll continue to spy if given the opportunity."

"Give her a different dress. I will speak with General McPherson again. He's busy planning the next expedition for the corps. We leave Monday."

Savannah and Mrs. Lakin would still be under house arrest. He hated leaving his responsibilities to someone else. This was...Savannah. Even after she betrayed him, he still wanted to be the one to watch over her. "Who will oversee the guards?"

"I'm staying to monitor the situation with Christopher. He will take over your duties while you're gone."

He trusted Christopher. Then a new fear struck Travis. "Savannah won't be banished as well?"

"I don't know." He sighed. "It's unlikely because she's provided the cipher and hasn't given us trouble since her arrest. But can we trust her not to spy again?"

"Her note to the Rebel sergeant stated that this was her last communication with him." Her decision to quit before she knew of her arrest was of some comfort.

"And yet she showed great temerity in that she spied while courting a Union officer." Colonel Haversham studied him. "Do *you* trust her?"

Clearly, the officer was not ready to. Travis's chest constricted. He didn't know when he himself would trust her again. If ever. "I thought I could." Savannah was avoiding him, perhaps too ashamed to look at him. He wasn't ready to talk to her either.

He'd written three letters home about her. His mama was excited to meet her. But he hadn't written his parents of her spying, her betrayal. Hope died hard.

"Exactly. She'll remain under house arrest for now." The colonel tapped the desk. "Let's deal with Mrs. Lakin. She wants to leave the Adair residence. She may get her wish if she continues her defiance."

Travis was reminded of the general's desire to banish the letter carrier if she couldn't be trusted. Indeed, she deserved her punishment, but he didn't want to see that happen to Savannah.

Colonel Haversham picked up the dress. "You and Christopher extricate one of the coins to verify our hunch, then leave him to finish the task while you deliver a different frock to Mrs. Lakin."

Within ten minutes, Travis and Christopher had freed the first gold coin. She must have delivered many secret letters to have obtained such wealth.

Travis headed to Mrs. Lakin's residence to pick up another dress for her. He'd allow the woman to wonder if they'd found the money.

It was doubtful he'd see Savannah. As hurt as he was, he still longed for a glimpse of her lovely face to let him know how she fared.

The sorrow in Colonel Haversham's eyes suggested he'd also been wounded by her actions. Unfortunately, the colonel seemed to be relying on him for reassurance of Savannah's trustworthiness.

At this moment, he could not give it.

CHAPTER 30

*T*ravis went to Savannah's church alone on Sunday. Neither Mrs. Adair nor the Jungs came. Savannah was barred from leaving her home. Ben and Enos had duties at camp in preparation for leaving tomorrow.

Savannah had been in her room for Travis's visits. Every one.

On the other hand, Mrs. Lakin had numerous complaints each time—from the temperature of her coffee that she preferred burning hot to the numerous items she demanded he fetch from her home. On one occasion, she couldn't do without her toothbrush another minute. The one provided by the Adairs wasn't good enough. On another occasion, he had fetched an extra pair of slippers after he'd already retrieved the shoes she'd described. On Friday, she'd demanded her pink dress with tiny red roses. He had exchanged the dress with hidden coins for another yesterday, which she received without raising a big fuss. This morning, the guards told him she needed her tortoise shell comb.

Well, she could wait until after services on that one. Travis suspected that Mrs. Lakin enjoyed treating him as her assistant.

Colonel Haversham hadn't spoken to the general last night. The decision about whether to banish Mrs. Lakin might come before he headed to camp this evening to ready his troops for the expedition. Hopefully, whatever decision was made relieved Savannah of Wanda Lakin's company, for he suspected she wasn't a pleasant guest.

He needed to ground himself in a good sermon after the difficult week he'd endured. Unfortunately, he could not focus on the preacher's teaching. His gaze strayed to the empty pew he'd shared with the Adairs for weeks.

He sneaked out during the last hymn to avoid questions about Savannah's absence. He had arrested her because it was his duty. He shied away from telling her neighbors that was the reason she missed church.

~

Savannah had awoken that Sunday morning in a melancholy mood that she'd miss sitting by Travis at church and then spending the entire day with him.

Another regret in an ever-expanding list was her association with Wanda, as Mrs. Lakin had insisted on being called. The spy had run Mrs. Jung out of the second-floor parlor with her incessant complaining, something not even Mama's hints had accomplished during the summer.

Why, the woman was more unpleasant than Mrs. Jung in one of her moods. In fact, Wanda's entry to a room often cleared it within minutes—with the exception of the dining room. Mama didn't like to send meal trays to anyone's bedroom unless they were ill. She really ought to make an exception in this case.

That Wanda had worn her robe at lunch yesterday because Travis hadn't yet brought the dress she desired from her home rankled. If the woman had set out to be a disagreeable guest—prisoner—she could scarcely have been more successful.

Savannah had been too ashamed to talk to her beau while Wanda made demands of him every time he arrived to check on his prisoners.

His prisoner. That's what she'd become to him.

Savannah was the last one to the dining room for lunch. Mary Grace had already set a bowl of stew at each place and seated herself. Mama asked the blessing and then they began to eat.

"I don't care for chicken stew." Wanda put down her spoon. "Bring me something else."

Mary Grace flushed.

"This is what we're serving." Savannah's irritation reached new heights. How long must they endure this woman? Four days already seemed an eternity. "You may eat it or wait for dessert."

Wanda pushed it aside. "I doubt it's worth the wait."

Mary Grace's eyes shimmered with tears.

"That's enough." Mama gave Wanda a piercing look. "Suit yourself about the main course. But you will refrain from complaining about meals you didn't buy or prepare, or you'll be eating in your room."

"The lieutenant will hear of your impertinence." Wanda tossed her napkin to the side and flounced from the room.

"Thank you, Mama." Savannah let out a soft breath, and the atmosphere lightened.

"I'm sorry the meal isn't as good as usual, Mrs. Adair." A tear ran down Mary Grace's cheek. "I'm so upset and worried for Savannah that it's hard to think."

Mama lifted her chin. "We don't know what will come of all this, but we shall weather the storm as we always do."

"I apologize to you all that my actions caused us to endure four days of Wanda's company." Not to mention possible censure from their friends. Savannah kept her tears locked firmly inside. She felt too broken to allow any weakness to show, or she'd lose control completely.

"If you ask me, it's a deliberate act." Mrs. Jung ate her last bite before continuing. "No one with any breeding can be *that* disagreeable."

Savannah had never considered that possibility. "To what purpose?"

"That I cannot say." Mrs. Jung folded her hands. "But she's caused me to consider my own actions since Mary Grace and I accepted your hospitality. I owe you all an apology for the unpleasantness about Northerners taking over the plantations. It struck a raw nerve that may never mend, but that wasn't the fault of your young man, Savannah."

"Thank you, Mrs. Jung." If only he still *was* her young man.

"That's another thing. I've no objection to you referring to me as 'Miss Jacqueline' since we share the same home."

Such a small gesture. Yet it was a sign of healing in Miss Jacqueline.

Something they all needed. Was it true what the Scripture said, that God could work what was intended as evil for good?

~

That afternoon, Travis mounted the Adairs' portico steps with Christopher, three armed soldiers, and Mrs. Mary McCarter. The major's wife had agreed to help Mrs. Lakin pack in readiness for her banishment from the city. If Mrs. Lakin refused to stop spying, that was her punishment.

He had overseen changing the guards with Christopher an hour before without visiting the prisoner while decisions were finalized among his superior officers. He didn't envy Mrs. McCarter's unpleasant task. The brunette in her mid-twenties had been warned of Wanda Lakin's surly disposition. Hopefully, she was up to the task.

Outside the door, Travis spoke in low tones to Christopher and Mrs. McCarter. "Are you ready for this?" Travis intended to speak with Mrs. Lakin first and then Savannah.

"I am." A determined glint lit Mrs. McCarter's eyes.

Ellen answered his knock, widening the opening for them all to enter. "Good afternoon. Shall I fetch Mrs. Lakin?"

Travis nodded. "And Mrs. Adair. Savannah is welcome to come now, or I will speak with her later privately."

She glanced at the soldiers' rifles resting on their shoulders. "Please seat yourselves in the parlor."

Agitation kept him on the edge of his seat. The soldiers took a stance near the door as previously instructed.

He and Christopher arose at footsteps on the stairs. As the ladies entered, Mrs. Adair looked frightened and Mrs. Lakin defiant as she seated herself on a cushioned chair. Savannah's apprehensive gaze clung to Travis's and then she sat beside her mother on the sofa.

"Good afternoon, ladies." He introduced Mrs. McCarter as Major Levi McCarter's wife.

Mrs. Adair and Savannah murmured greetings to the officer's wife.

"Mrs. Lakin, I've come to ask you to sign a document to stop spying and stop acting as letter carrier." Travis extracted a folded page from his pocket. "Your punishment will be greatly eased by this promise."

"I've no intention of signing it." The redhead lifted her chin. "I'm proud to serve my country."

"Mrs. Lakin, I must ask you to reconsider. The charges against you are serious." He extended the document to her.

She slapped it away. "I absolutely refuse."

Travis kept his anger in check. "Your punishment is banishment from Vicksburg."

"Outrageous!" She leaped to her feet. "You cannot keep me from my home."

"Your own actions will keep you from your home. Unless you will reconsider..." He tapped the document.

"Never."

Despite his frustration with her, he admired her fierce loyalty. "That's unfortunate."

"I cannot see it that way." She pressed her lips together.

"Then you will be banished from this city for the war's duration." He extracted another document from his pocket. "This explains your punishment."

"Do not read it aloud." She barely glanced at it. "I do not care to hear more from you than I must."

"Then I will oblige you." He turned to his hostess. "Mrs. Adair and Savannah, Mrs. Lakin is leaving your home today. Mrs. McCarter will assist her in packing."

"I require no help from a Yankee."

"Nevertheless, you shall have it." Mrs. McCarter arose with dignity. "Additionally, you will treat me with respect as we work together."

Wanda Lakin turned to Travis. "I never received my blue dress."

"The one with twenty gold coins hidden along the ribbon?"

Her jaw slackened.

"Lieutenant Dunn freed and counted each one. Why did you hide them?"

"That money is mine. I earned every penny of it. You've no right to my property."

"Your dress will be returned to you. Your money will be returned at war's end." The colonel feared she'd pass it to the Rebel bands if the coins were given back into the woman's possession now.

Color ebbed from her face. "You cannot do this."

"Sign the document." Travis took no enjoyment from this

task. Savannah's face was as pale as Mrs. Lakin's. "Your imprisonment in your own home will extend through December if you sign it, and your actions will be monitored, but you won't be banished." The thought of guarding her until the new year was a daunting one.

"I will leave. My sister lives in Bolton."

"Very well." If he recalled correctly, that was some twenty miles from Vicksburg. "You will be escorted there by armed guards."

"Let's get you packed." Mrs. McCarter accompanied her from the room.

The mood in the parlor changed. With any luck, that was his final conversation with her. He turned to Savannah. "May I beg a moment alone?"

~

*H*ardly daring to breathe, Savannah stared at him as everyone but Mama left. Was he about to banish her as well? Fearing for her own fate, she'd listened to the strict terms of Wanda's punishment. Surely, her own crimes were not at the same level.

"Travis..." Mama's voice quaked. "You do not mean to banish my daughter from her beloved home?"

"No." Understanding lit his hazel eyes. "Savannah, the duration and severity of your punishment has yet to be decided, but rest easy that banishment has not been a consideration for you."

"That much is a blessing, although this confinement isn't easy on any of us." Mama crossed to the door. "Savannah, please talk to him." The door closed and they were alone.

Travis sat on the chair next to her. "I understand that your turmoil over the loss of Vicksburg instigated your acceptance of Sergeant Epley's mission, but—"

"Do you?" She clutched the skirt of her brown mousseline dress. "How can you possibly understand my deep love of my city, my state, the South? It crushed me when your army captured my city."

He shifted to the edge of his seat. "'*Your*' army? '*My*' city? Have we not grown past those obstacles?"

After watching him mete out Wanda's punishment, she didn't know the answer. "Do you respect my abiding love for the South?"

"Absolutely. I understand it only because my love for the North is equally as strong." He ran his hands through his hair. "We must win this conflict. I see no other way for slavery to come to an abrupt halt."

"I don't want to see the South destroyed in the process, as my city and others have been."

"Neither is that my desire." He walked to the fireplace and stared at an unlit log among the ashes on the mild autumn afternoon. "Let me ask you something."

She braced herself.

Resting an elbow against the mantel, he turned to her. "Why did you continue to spy after we started courting?"

"It was a mistake." Wringing her hands, she crossed to him. "I didn't want to hurt you. If you read my letter to Sam, you know it was to be my last."

"And I wonder that it took so long after you professed your love." His shoulders hunched.

"I agonized over the decision." She touched his arm, feather soft.

"I'm grateful for that much." He stepped back.

Her hand fell. There was no way to mend what she'd done.

"Duties will keep me from Vicksburg for a week or two. Christopher will oversee the guards while I'm otherwise occupied."

A mission? She gave her head a little shake. No need to listen for military secrets. She was done.

He read her like an unciphered letter. "You're wondering if an expedition will take me from the city." His face shuttered. "You're done with spying, remember?"

With that, he strode from the room, leaving her with a broken heart that would never mend.

CHAPTER 31

*T*ravis pulled on Millie's reins to keep her from munching the grass alongside his marching men on Thursday, October fifteenth. The expedition provided a welcome distraction to keep his thoughts from Savannah. Nights were a different story. With nothing but the familiar song of the crickets, heartache caught up with him then. Kept him awake deep into the night and greeted him with the dawn.

When he'd told her that duties would keep him from the city for a week, a look of calculation had crossed her features. As if she wondered at his mission and whether to tell Sam. That brief lapse proved her guilt. It had splintered his heart.

She had indeed betrayed him.

He gave his head a shake to clear it. Best focus on his troops. General McPherson led the Seventeenth Corps toward Canton, Mississippi.

The columns had slowed almost to a stop.

Brian rode back to him. "The Big Black River is just ahead. Our men, caissons, and wagons will cross on the bridge. Officers will let our horses swim us over while our men are on the bridge."

"Fine by me." Travis patted Millie's neck. "We'll see how this girl likes the river."

Travis passed the order to the other officers and then got down and walked to give his mare a rest. Their regiment was almost to the river when the unmistakable sound of musketry alerted him to trouble ahead.

Rifle shots were too few for it to be a large engagement, but it was enough to shift his focus away from his heartache and back to the task at hand.

~

$\mathcal{U}$nable to relax, Savannah stared up at the starry heavens on Thursday night. Lieutenant Dunn had escorted in the new guards an hour before and, as foolish as it was, she wished Travis had been there instead.

Where was he tonight? She had daily spent hours at this very window hoping for a glimpse of him.

Creeping back to bed, she pulled a quilt over her cotton nightgown, lonelier than she'd ever been.

She had dreamed of marrying Travis...foolish dream. She should have guarded her heart against him.

He was a Northern lieutenant, an Illinois farmer.

She was a Southern belle. What did they have in common?

The next morning, a restless night drove her from bed before dawn. She donned an old gray dress and fixed her hair. The forced inactivity of her arrest grated on her nerves. How she longed for a simple walk to the Sky Parlor or to attend church services.

Someone was singing downstairs. The horizon was just beginning to lighten. Rain masked the sunrise due in about an hour. Who was singing?

Once Savannah made it to the first floor in the otherwise silent home, Ellen's voice reverberated down the hall.

In the morning when I rise,
in the morning when I rise,
in the morning when I rise,
give me Jesus.
Give me Jesus, give me Jesus.
You may have all this world, give me Jesus.

Savannah was struck by the faith and trust of the simple words, by the beauty of Ellen's rich alto tones. Down the dark hall to the kitchen, then Savannah crept inside so as not to disturb the singer kneeling before the window, face raised toward the heavens.

Oh, when I come to die,
oh, when I come to die,
oh, when I come to die,
give me Jesus.
Give me Jesus, give me Jesus.
You may have all this world, give me Jesus.

Ellen's abiding faith sustained her. How had Savannah missed the source of this woman's strength and wisdom all these years?

"Ellen, that was lovely." Savannah joined her at the window as she pushed herself to her feet. "Yet mournful. Are you unhappy?"

"I reckon someone I love hurt me." Ellen adjusted her white apron over her gray dress.

"Gus?" The man had worked until nearly sundown every day on the orchard, picking apples and plums that the women had been drying and canning.

"No, Miss Savannah." She looked her straight in the eye. "You."

Savannah's hand crept to her throat. "Me?" The words

struck her as a blow. Another person that she'd hurt. It was too much. Worse, Savannah couldn't recall any conflict between them. "What did I do?"

Raindrops pounded the windowpane.

"You ripped the lieutenant's heart out. You betrayed him. Do you think your spying only hurt your beau?" A clap of thunder rumbled.

Savannah stared at her. "You?"

"And Josie and Gus." She rubbed her palms together. "You spied to help the Confederacy. Do you want to return to slavery?"

"No." The question shocked her. "I simply want my country to win. Is that wrong?"

"You said you understood why we all left on Surrender Day, but you don't." Ellen turned to the rainy view outside the window. "Once my family came to live here when you was a child, I didn't have any complaints about our treatment."

Savannah at least could take comfort in that much. And yet clearly, that had not been enough.

"But I've never been free to go about my own business, or choose where I work." Ellen gripped the windowsill. "I might have stayed for my own sake on Surrender Day because I'm comfortable here. But I had to leave for Josie's sake and for her children's sake."

"I don't understand." Josie wasn't even married.

Lightning flashed in the dark room.

"It wasn't right that my children became slaves instantly at birth just because I was one. And Josie's children would have been the same if the Union army hadn't come." A tear trickled down her smooth cheek. "It's wrong. It's just plain wrong."

"I'm sorry, Ellen. It's not an excuse, but I guess I never looked past the way things had always been." Society had accepted the cruel fact that a large portion of the Southern population was enslaved, so Savannah had ignored it too.

Nothing about the system was fair. In fact, it had been evil from its inception. It was going to be difficult to forgive herself.

"You ain't alone in that, Miss Savannah. Not too many Southern folks have."

"I don't feel that way now. I'm glad you're free."

"I could tell you had changed. Maybe the lieutenant's influence?" Ellen tilted her head, studying her.

"And yours." Savannah squeezed her eyes shut to hold back the tears. "And, most of all, Gus. That day left an indelible mark on my soul."

"I figured." Soft fingers touched her arm. "Too bad that experience didn't do what the Good Lord intended."

Savannah opened her eyes. "What do you mean?"

"I think God allowed you to see what you saw to save Gus, me, Josie, and Riley."

She gasped. "There was a bigger purpose?"

"What greater purpose is there than to save a person's life... unless it's to share the Savior's love and save their soul?" Ellen gave her arm a little shake. "Or open their eyes to Scripture like you did when you taught me to read the Bible?"

Savannah slumped against the windowpane. "I did all that?"

"You did. But you lost yourself along the way."

"You're right. And I've hurt the people I love most." Tears that must not fall clogged her throat. "Please forgive me."

"Oh, child." Ellen folded her into her arms. "You're like one of my own children."

"When I was a child, I always ran to you first for comfort." She returned the fierce hug that was beginning to heal something broken in her.

"That's what I know." Ellen pulled away far enough to look at her. "And you're the reason me and Josie came back. You and Miss Lila." Another rumble of thunder, this one farther east.

"Please don't make me cry." Savannah squeezed her eyes

shut to keep the tears from falling. "If I start, I don't believe I'll stop."

"What's the harm in that?" Ellen led her to the table where the two of them sat side by side. "You have plenty enough to cry over."

Her comforting words unleashed the dam. Sobs wracked Savannah's body. She cried for her broken relationship with Travis and how her betrayal of his trust had pierced his soul. She cried over unwittingly hurting Ellen and Josie and Gus. She cried for Willie, who would never grow old. She cried for the rift she had caused between her parents so many years ago. She cried for her ruined city, for her father's absence.

Ellen pressed a cotton handkerchief in her hand, patting her back now and then until the storm passed. "Feel better?"

"I feel..." Savannah searched for the word. "Cleansed. As if God healed something broken in me." It was as if all the pieces of a large puzzle were coming together.

"I'd say that was a good cry." Ellen fetched a stack of handkerchiefs from a drawer, kept one, and gave the rest to Savannah. "I might have joined you for a bit." She swiped her wet cheeks.

"Thank you, Ellen." Savannah blew her nose. Once she had recovered a bit of composure, she reached for her housekeeper's hand. "I never meant to hurt the people I love. You and Josie are among them."

"You never said that before." She smiled. "But I knew it, anyway."

Savannah laughed and clutched her head. "That hurts."

"Yep, you've got a headache." Ellen scurried to the stove. "I'll make you a nice cup of tea."

"That sounds lovely." Emotionally spent, Savannah watched rain drip down the window pane.

Travis, I was wrong. I'm sorry. Please come back so I can tell you.

≈

*T*he day's skirmish near Brownsville had left Travis exhausted rather than energized. It had gone well with only two wounded. Evening's roll call was done and it was nearly dark. Ben, Luke, and Enos sat around a campfire with several others, telling stories that Travis was too melancholy to hear. His tent was set up. All was in readiness for much-needed rest, but a strange restlessness overtook him.

He strode into the woods. He wouldn't go far. Their pickets stood guard in case Rebel bands sneaked up on them.

Savannah was heavy on his mind tonight. Despite his hurt, Travis was still trying to figure a way to protect her good name. She loved her city. He'd once hoped she'd grow to love his Illinois farm.

That wouldn't happen now, for how could he trust her? Nor did she understand his abolitionist beliefs, so fundamental to his character. Slavery was the evil Uncle Dabney had fought and possibly gave his life to eradicate. Travis could do no less. Any woman who professed to love him must realize it. Accept it.

Head down, intent on his predicament, Travis continued deeper into the forest. What could he do to help? The colonel didn't trust her. Likely, her attendance at his party made this more personal for him as well.

Unlike Mrs. Cameron, the first letter carrier he'd arrested, Savannah had willingly given the cipher code that matched her note. That counted in her favor. If Travis convinced her to take the oath of allegiance and promise not to spy, that might turn the tide of Colonel Haversham's bad opinion.

What his colonel held against her most was that she'd been courted by a Union officer while spying and used information revealed in innocent conversation. Savannah swore that wasn't the reason she courted him. Travis wanted to believe that most of all.

Rain that had threatened all day began to drip on him through the fall leaves. He'd best turn back.

There was no trail in the thick underbrush. Where was he? Where were the pickets or his camp's fires? Shivering, he peered to the north, the south. Nothing. It was too dangerous to spend the night in this thicket. He might be close to Southern lines. He chose a direction and followed it.

A quarter hour later, it was still raining. He was soaked to the skin. Night had fallen in the woods, yet he couldn't see his camp. *Lord, help me find my way.*

Thunder rumbled. The rain picked up. Fearing that he headed toward Rebel camps, Travis hunkered under a tree.

Lightning briefly lit the area. Travis looked at the tops of fifty- and sixty-foot trees.

This wasn't a good situation.

Help me, Lord.

Clopping hooves heading in his direction alerted his senses. One horse. No one knew he was here. His comrades believed he was already snug in his tent for the night.

"Someone there?" A strange man's voice. "Nothing to be afraid of. Name's Michael. My horse is Old Nell." Lightning flashed long enough to reveal a gray-haired farmer wearing a wide-brimmed hat, red wool shirt, and gray trousers.

"Over here." Travis stood, cautious of the man with piercing eyes who had seen him in the lightning's flash. How did the man find him in the dark with no trail? "First Lieutenant Travis Lawson."

"Union?"

"Yes, sir."

The rain slackened.

"You're a long way from your camp."

Travis tensed. How did he know that?

"Nothing to worry about. I know everything that happens in these woods."

"Then you know I'm lost in the rain." This chance meeting felt significant. Wait. Luke had said something about a gray-haired farmer named Michael helping him and Felicity. That man had an old mare named Old Nell that had the endurance and speed of a younger horse. There had been something special about the man's eyes—

"Figured as much. But the rain is about to end." He struck a match and then lit a lantern. "You look familiar. Any relation to a Dabney Lawson?"

Heart thundering, Travis stared into eyes the color of the Mississippi. "He's my uncle."

CHAPTER 32

"*M*ama, I'll retire early this evening." They had spent a quiet Saturday night in the parlor, and Savannah hadn't caught up on a week of nearly sleepless nights. She'd last seen Travis on Sunday. He must indeed be on an expedition. She had prayed for his safety.

"Of course, dear." Mama lifted her cheek for Savannah's cheek. "I believe I'll stitch a little longer."

"Pretty." Savannah admired the needlepoint picture of ships sailing on the Mississippi River.

The front door opened. Savannah's heart beat escalated. No one had knocked.

"Who's there?" Mama turned to face the clean-shaven Southern gentleman with surprising calm.

"Papa!" Savannah ran into his outstretched arms. "I didn't know you were coming home."

"I left as soon as I answered your mother's telegram. I couldn't allow you to face this battle alone." Releasing her, he crossed the room to Mama. After kissing her, he cradled her in his arms. "My dear, I can only imagine how terrible this ordeal has been for you."

Savannah's jaw slackened at the most affectionate home-coming embrace Papa had given Mama in years.

"Oh, Arthur." Her voice was muffled against his shoulder. "I'm so glad you came."

"Let's all sit." Keeping one arm around his wife, he beck-oned to Savannah. "Tell me everything that's been happening."

Two hours later, Savannah climbed the stairs to her room, leaving her parents in the parlor.

For the first time in a long time, Papa had put his family's crisis in front of his job. Could it be that God would use this terrible ordeal to unite her parents?

It gave Savannah hope for the future, the first she'd felt since causing the pain in Travis's eyes.

$\sim$

*H*ead reeling, Travis made it back to camp on his uncle's borrowed horse just after reveille the next morning with Michael following behind on Old Nell. The first thing Travis did was find his brother-in-law, Ben.

He grabbed him by the shoulders. "Uncle Dabney is alive."

"What?" Ben rubbed his eyes. "Did you have a dream about him?"

"I haven't slept a wink." Travis laughed. "I took a walk last night and got lost—"

Ben sucked in his breath. "With Rebels so close? What were you thinking?"

"Not what. *Who* was I thinking about." All his closest comrades knew about Savannah's arrest. "Anyway, I met a fellow in the woods who recognized my name. He took me to Uncle Dabney's home *five miles* to the south."

"How'd he end up living in Mississippi?" Ben was now fully alert.

Travis explained that Uncle Dabney had successfully driven

two Mississippi fugitives to the next station, but he was later shot by a ruthless and angry slave catcher who took him back to a Mississippi jail. "Uncle Dabney didn't give them his real name to protect our family. Lies told at the trial earned him a six-month sentence. Afterward, he figured he could smuggle more people north from here than on our farm. He bought a house outside Brownsville far from the trial's location and lived under his real name." Travis couldn't keep a smile from his face. "He's going back home because the slaves have been freed in the area. He's got a hankering to farm again. He'll write home first so he doesn't scare them by simply knocking on the door."

"I'll write too." Ben clapped him on the shoulder. "Mary will be happy. And your pa."

A great weight had fallen from Travis's shoulders. He hadn't been responsible for Uncle Dabney's death, after all. Had it not been for a chance meeting with Michael—

Where was the man? And the horse Travis had borrowed from his uncle?

Travis peered in every direction. Michael must have ridden away to return Uncle Dabney's horse. Michael had talked with him about Savannah and forgiveness on the ride back into camp. There truly was *something* about the farmer that made Travis want to talk longer, drink in more wisdom.

But the big news was finding Uncle Dabney.

Travis could hardly wait to write his family and tell Savannah. She was the only one outside of family who knew the whole story.

Besides Michael, it seemed. *Thank You, God, for sending help in the form of Michael. Please bless him.*

～

Savannah awoke with a sense of hope on Monday. Her parents had attended church together yesterday. Papa had left after lunch to speak with Colonel Haversham directly. When he came back, he walked the orchards with Gus until supper.

Though Papa reported that her imprisonment was to continue, Savannah had a plan.

Whenever Travis returned, she'd ask him to allow her to sign the oath. If that didn't convince him of the sincerity of her promise not to spy again, nothing would.

She was just finishing breakfast with her parents and the Jungs when Ellen brought the news that Travis awaited her in the parlor.

Savannah's stomach fluttered. He was back.

"A little early for callers." Papa raised his eyebrows.

"Oh, but Travis has been calling at this time to check on... things." Mama gave him a look.

Savannah stood. "I want to talk with him, Papa." Her protective father hadn't forgiven Travis for arresting her.

Studying her, he leaned back in his chair. "Very well. We're here if you need us."

Pinching her cheeks to give them some color, she paused at the hall mirror. She bit her lips and then patted her looped braids. She was ready.

Travis turned when she entered. "Good morning, Savannah." His smile lit up his eyes. He started to extend his arms and then lowered them.

"Good morning, Travis. Please, let's sit." She chose the sofa and was relieved when he sat beside her. "I'm glad your duties bring you back with us." Her eyes clung to his.

"It's good to see you." He took a deep breath. "Much happened in the past week."

"For me also." Savannah leaned closer. "Papa is back. He and Mama are happy to be together again."

"That's good news." He tilted his head as if his complete attention was arrested. "Actually, I know Mr. Adair is here. I had a meeting with Colonel Haversham this morning."

"Before you go any further..."—Savannah touched his sleeve—"allow me to speak."

"I'd like to hear whatever you want to say." His hand covered hers.

Her skin tingled at his touch. "I'm sorry for continuing to spy after my heart became engaged with yours."

Hazel eyes searched hers.

"And after a conversation with Ellen, I very much regret spying at all."

His body stilled. "That must have been some conversation."

"It was. I now understand why you're an abolitionist."

"You do?" He sucked in his breath.

"Because I want slavery to end too."

"You don't know how happy that makes me." Looking into her eyes, he sandwiched her hands between his.

She could barely think with him looking at her with so much hope, but there was more to say. "I want to sign the oath. Today."

Closing his eyes, he lowered his head for a moment. When he looked up, there was such joy on his face that Savannah's last fear melted.

"Whatever happens, I want to weather the storm with you." She brought his hands to her face.

"That's not fair. I wanted to say that to you"—he moved closer—"when I proposed." Sweeping her into his arms, he kissed her.

Joy burst into her soul. His kiss brought the forgiveness and love she craved and so much more. This was a love to last a lifetime. But...what had he just said? She pulled away from him a fraction to stare up into those compassionate eyes that always so captivated her. "Travis, did you just propose?"

Sitting back, he released her to clasp her hands. A pained expression crossed his features. "We have a bit of business to attend to before that can happen."

She drew a deep breath. "You are speaking of my arrest?"

"Yes, I planned to ask you to swear that you'll not spy for the Confederacy again—"

"I promise. Never again. Next request?"

"And that you'll take the oath."

"As I told you, I'm ready this minute to do that very thing." Tilting her head, she smiled up at him. "Will that be enough to satisfy the colonel?"

"In order to release you, he awaits only my assurance that I trust you to keep your word." He leaned in to kiss her. "I can now reassure him. Your sentence has been served."

"I'm free?" A weight lifted from her chest. "Papa and Mama will be happy." She started to stand, eager to reassure them.

"There's more I need to share, if I may."

The proposal. She settled back down, her hands tucked in his.

"I'm bursting to tell you my news."

She frowned. She was ready for her proposal.

"Uncle Dabney is alive."

"What?" How could that be?

He told her the amazing story of seeing his uncle again— living in Mississippi, of all things.

"That's the most incredible thing I've heard to date. I know the burden you've carried about your uncle all these years. It must feel like a huge weight has been lifted. In fact, I can see in your demeanor that it has."

"Exactly so." A deep laugh rolled from Travis's chest. "After all my prayers for all those years...I meet a man who recognized my features as looking like my uncle."

"When you were lost on a stormy night?" Savannah blinked. "Wait a minute. You prayed for years—and God answered your prayers. He sent Michael."

"I believe he did." He kissed her. "You wouldn't have seen God's hand working in this situation three months ago."

"No." She'd been too focused on what she'd suffered. "I felt abandoned by Him back then. But that was never the case, was it?"

"Never." He brushed his fingertips over the curve of her cheek. "We've both grown. Do you think we're good for each other?"

"Without a doubt." Was he ready to propose? She could barely breathe.

He went down on one knee and then clasped both of her hands in his warm grasp. "Miss Savannah Adair, will you do me the very great honor of marrying me?"

"Yes, I believe I will." Belying her sedate agreement, she threw her arms around his neck and kissed him.

Someone cleared his throat.

They broke apart and turned to the door where Papa and Mama stood with Miss Jacqueline and Mary Grace just behind.

"Did you forget to ask me a question, young man?"

Red-faced, Travis stood. "I did, sir. You see, I hadn't planned on proposing this morning—though it's been my intention— but with all—"

"Arthur, put the young man out of his misery." Mama giggled. "You know we discussed this very thing last night."

"Ahem." Papa tugged on his coat. Eyes on Savannah, he crossed to them. "Will you have this man as your husband?"

"I will, indeed." She looked up at her future spouse, allowing all her love to shine in her eyes.

The room erupted in joyful shouts as Papa shook Travis's hand. That brought the rest of the household running into the parlor.

Mama cried as she kissed Savannah's cheek. Mary Grace hugged her.

"He's the perfect man for you." Felicity embraced Savannah next. "I can't wait to write Julia. She'll be overjoyed for you."

Josie offered her shy felicitations, but Ellen simply held out her arms. "Looks like mine won't be the only wedding in this family."

"Thanks for showing me the way." Savannah gave her a fierce hug.

As she returned to her fiancé's side, tears ran down Savannah's cheeks at all the love poured over her and Travis.

When Travis gave the news of Savannah's freedom, Mama cried on Papa's shoulder.

Was that a tear in her proud father's eyes? He loved her and Mama. He'd proven it.

She turned to Travis. "Shall I take the oath of allegiance this morning?"

"Let's go now."

Did you enjoy this book? We hope so!
Would you take a quick minute to leave a review where you purchased the book?
It doesn't have to be long. Just a sentence or two telling what you liked about the story!

Receive a FREE ebook and get updates when new Wild Heart books release: https://wildheartbooks.org/newsletter

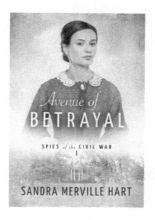

Book 1: *Avenue of Betrayal*

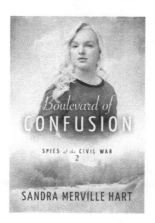

Book 2: *Boulevard of Confusion*

Book 3: Byway to Danger

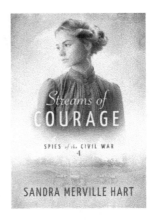

Book 4: Streams of Courage

Book 5: River of Peril

Book 6: Tides of Healing

ABOUT THE AUTHOR

Sandra Merville Hart, award-winning and Amazon bestselling author of inspirational historical romances, loves to discover little-known yet fascinating facts from American history to include in her stories. Her desire is to transport her readers back in time. She is also a blogger, speaker, and conference teacher. Connect with Sandra on her blog, https://sandramervillehart.wordpress.com/.

ACKNOWLEDGMENTS

I've learned much from Denise Weimer, who is a gifted author and encouraging editor. Misty Beller is such an inspiration. The whole team at Wild Heart Books has been a blessing.

Months of research go into my Civil War novels to add authenticity. Research continues as I write the book. The Vicksburg battlefield has been beautifully preserved to mimic conditions, as much as possible, during the 1863 battle and siege of Vicksburg. Walking the battlefield sparked my imagination as it catapulted me back in time the way I hope my stories do for my readers.

My husband and I toured Vicksburg Military Battlefield with Michael Logue, author and licensed battlefield guide. I appreciate that Michael tailored the tour to my needs. Michael's family history is entrenched in the area—his ancestors owned land on the battlefield! Michael also sent me an original map of the city. What beautiful details it provided for the story, as readers may notice throughout the novel. Thank you, Michael.

My thanks to the rangers and staff at Vicksburg Military Battlefield for taking time to answer my questions. I knew little of the battle and what the citizens endured at the time of my first visit. My fact-finding mission bore much fruit.

The two questions I intended to ask George Bolm, curator/director at the Old Court House Museum in Vicksburg, turned into an enjoyable half hour filled with artifacts from 1863. Thank you, George.

Thanks to family and friends for their continued support, especially my husband for taking this never-a-dull-moment journey with me.

Thank You, Lord, for giving me the story.

AUTHOR'S NOTE

Learning that Vicksburg didn't celebrate our country's Independence Day for one hundred years is what inspired me to dig into the city's Civil War history. A desire to learn what happened is what sparked Books 4 – 6 in my Spies of the Civil War Series. The characters and stories in *Streams of Courage,* Book 4, *River of Peril,* Book 5, and *Tides of Healing,* Book 6 are interwoven and best read in order.

In fact, as I wrote *Tides of Healing,* I had a sense that the whole series culminated in Savannah and Travis's story. While writing, I truly felt that I had written all the previous five novels in the series to write Book 6. It's the first time I've experienced that.

This book begins on July 4, 1863, the day Confederate General Pemberton surrendered his army and Vicksburg, the city he'd fought so hard to protect. What many may not realize is that the Union navy gunboats attacked the city while the Confederate army was attacked by General Grant's Union army. Attacks on both citizens and soldiers continued while the 47-day siege starved them. It was a nightmare.

The conquering army marched into the city to occupy it on

Independence Day. Union officers freed the enslaved. President Lincoln's Emancipation Proclamation freeing slaves in seceded states had passed on January 1, 1863.

Freedmen were offered jobs as soldiers and police guards to patrol Vicksburg. Besides those jobs, the military hired many freed people as cooks, drivers, laundresses, and woodcutters.

Plantation owners had a myriad of problems before, during, and after the Battle of Vicksburg. I read many accounts of looting from Union troops and freedmen so repeatedly that they eventually took all the livestock, weapons, personal possessions of value, and food. Looters often damaged the homes and property while looking for valuables. It must have been terrifying. Many plantations were abandoned.

Northern citizens arrived in Mississippi to take over the plantations. They were to plant cotton and hire freed people who had once worked there as employees. It worked in some cases but not others. The Northern planters often had no idea how to grow cotton.

There were plenty of Confederate spies in Vicksburg after the surrender. There were also Confederate soldiers who thought they'd take back the city. This plan gave some citizens who didn't like living in an occupied city hope that they'd be successful.

The Rebel bands outside of Vicksburg created problems for Union troops and for the Northerners leasing the plantations. This was something the Union army was never able to resolve.

The Union army came in and took control of the city. They fed everyone in the city for a while. Freedmen, Confederates, and Union soldiers buried the dead. A new cemetery was established as a burial place for those lost in battle.

Taking the Oath of Allegiance to the Union became increasingly important in the months following the surrender. There were privileges that weren't available to citizens until they signed the oath. For instance, folks who wanted to do business in the city were only given permits if they had signed the oath.

It was fun to include Savannah's unsuccessful attempt to make coffee and the ever-resourceful Tex saving the day. It's easy to imagine many similar scenes in the early days after surrender.

The soldiers that interact with Travis in the Eighth Illinois Infantry—our fictional hero's regiment—are fictional. I included the details I could find about their specific duties and expeditions while camped in Vicksburg. Some of the daily tasks in the city are representative of what Union troops were doing in the city, such as cleanup efforts.

Some generals on both sides of the conflict maintained their own spy network, which Travis's work demonstrates.

I was greatly inspired by my visits to Vicksburg museums and the battlefield. I had such fun talking with George Bolm, Curator/Director at the Old Court House Museum in Vicksburg. He showed me the room used by the Union's provost marshal beginning July 4, 1863, the ledger he used, and even where the officer had etched his name on the courthouse window! It was an enjoyable visit that left me excited to be telling this part of the city's history through story.

After all my research, I'm convinced that most of the spying never made it into the history books. Spies kept their activities hidden to protect themselves and their loved ones. Of course, Northern spies received praise after the war ended. Southern spies received scorn.

I hope you enjoyed this Spies of the Civil War Series as much as I enjoyed writing them. Thank you for coming along on the journey.

Sandra Merville Hart

Want more?

If you love historical romance, check out the other Wild Heart books!

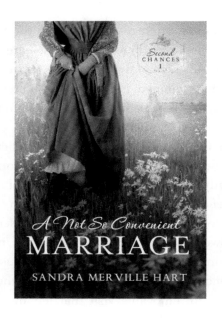

A Not So Convenient Marriage by Sandra Merville Hart

A spinster teacher...a grieving widower...a marriage of convenience and a second chance with the man she's always loved.

When Samuel Walker proposes a marriage of convenience to Rose Hatfield so soon after the death of his wife, she knows he doesn't love her. *She's* loved *him* since their school days. Those long-suppressed feelings spring to life as she marries him. She must sell her childhood home, quit her teaching job, and move to a new city.

Marrying Rose is harder than Samuel expected, especially with the shadow of his deceased wife everywhere in his life. And he has two young children to consider. Peter and Emma need a mother's love, but they also need to hold close the memories of their real mother as they grieve her loss.

Life as Samuel's wife is nothing like Rose hoped, and even the townspeople, who loved his first wife, make Rose feel like an outsider. The work of the farm draws the two of them closer, giving hope that they might one day become a happy family. Until the dream shatters, and the life Rose craves tumbles down around them. Only God can put these pieces back together, but the outcome may not look anything like she planned.

~

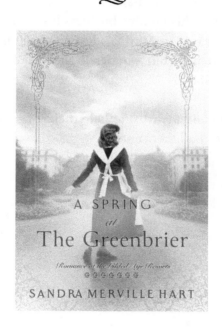

A Spring at the Greenbrier by Sandra Merville Hart

They have so much in common...yet love is not allowed between the wealthy and the staff.

Marilla will sacrifice anything for her family, so when her sister's doctor suggests daily sulphur spring baths, an amenity her family could never afford, Marilla takes a job at The Greenbrier resort bathhouse in order to give her sister the care she needs. When her sister befriends another girl staying at the resort with a similar health condition, Marilla finds herself crossing paths with the girl's handsome, charming, older brother. And despite their growing attraction to each other, anything more than friendship with Wes must remain a dream. After all, resort staff cannot court guests and Marilla will not risk her sister's health for her own happiness.

Wealthy resort guest, Wes Bakersfield, has dreams for a future and plans to make his family's business his own. And while he finds himself drawn to Marilla, despite their differing social classes, he can't help but wonder if she's really interested in him—or in his wealth.

Can the couple find the trust to help their love succeed, or will their differences pull them apart?

∼

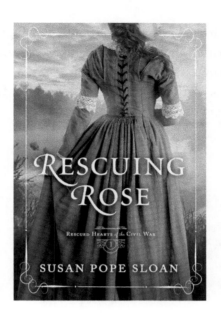

Rescuing Rose by Susan Pope Sloan

His army destroyed her livelihood. She represents the people he scorns. How can they reconcile their differences when the whole country is at war?

When the Union Army marches into Roswell, Georgia, and burns down the cotton mill where Rose Carrigan worked, not only is her livelihood destroyed but she's also taken prisoner and shipped northward with the other workers. Only the unlikely kindness of one of her guards makes the trip bearable.

Union Captain Noah Griffin hates the part of his job that requires him to destroy the lives of innocent civilians, but at least he's able to protect these women he's been ordered to transport to Louisville, Kentucky. Especially the one whose quick wit and kindness draw him.

While they're forced to wait in Marietta, two fugitives arrive to complicate matters between Rose and Noah. As Rose heads north and Noah returns to the battlefront, they each face fears and prejudices. With survival so tenuous, only faith can help them find love in the midst of so much tragedy.